SOMETHING BETTER

SOMETHING BETTER

GAIL R. DELANEY

PRAISE FOR GAIL R. DELANEY

This book was so good. I am not a casual five star reviewer. this was worth it...I really ran through the emotions... at times I laughed out loud, got teary eyed, got angry, and even had to walk away a couple of times since I couldn't physically slap the crap out of Lawrence. This story had everything and I loved it.

- 5 STAR READER REVIEW

Brava to Ms. Delaney for proving, yet again, what a truly brilliant wordsmith she is, capable of pulling every last nuance from characters so alive they jump off the pages and drag you into their story, from the hero and heroine, right down to the random people with whom they cross paths. I couldn't put the book down!

- ESTHER MITCHELL, AUTHOR OF THE LEGENDS OF TIRUM SERIES

GAIL DELANEY did it again. Her book, SOMETHING BETTER, is a five star best read. Her writing is not only vivid, the dialogue and narrative is picture perfect.

- JACLYN DI BONA, AUTHOR OF THE RING

#SupportArtistsNotAI
www.GailDelaney.com

To Jenifer—My own personal "Mags". She found great joy in laughing at me when I finally admitted I was writing a 'Hollywood' romance.

To Patrick—My husband—who is the absolute antithesis of Lawrence. I have never met a writer with a husband who supports them with the same conviction as mine.

To Bill—My peer, my sounding board, and my friend. More than once, you helped me understand the mindset of a man facing the possibility of being a stepfather—and just how wonderful that can be. Thank you.

To Jamie—Thanks for your oh-so-subtle demands. And your help. You provided insight I didn't possess.

To Stacy—Thank you for your last minute help, and for answering my FB emails with a chuckle and a smile when I said, "I know this is going to sound weird, but my hero just informed me he's Jewish..."

To the 'David' in my mind—I'm going to leave you nameless, because if I actually dared put it in print I'm sure it would come back to bite me later. But hey, if this ever gets made into a movie, you're the name at the top of the list...a short list. Just you. Cuz you're the only one who could properly pull off David.

BOOK CONTENT EXPECTATIONS

I do my best to provide a disclaimer for any of my readers who might not wish to read about certain storylines or story elements, or would at least like to be aware of the inclusion before they read.

Andrea Parker, the heroine of this book, has an absolute jerk of an ex-husband who unfortunately still tries to be a part of her life. As mentioned, he's a jerk. He regularly participates in the following: emotional and verbal abuse, gaslighting, cheating (when they were married), and makes both antisemitic and anti-LGBTQ comments in the course of the book. He attempts physical abuse but is stopped with extreme prejudice.

Like I said, he's an ass. But I don't want anyone unnecessarily upset by his words or actions.

There are also discussions of alcoholism recovery in the book.

SOMETHING BETTER SPOTIFY PLAYLIST

Do you like having a soundtrack to the books you read? I've created a playlist for "Something Better" on Spotify.

This playlist is forever evolving, so be sure to check it from time to time.

I hope you enjoy.

Six Years Ago
Chicago, Illinois

"This is your own damn fault, Andrea."

Andi drew in a slow, carefully metered breath and laid her hand on Jake's short hair. Soft curls brushed her fingers, and the contact forced her to carefully temper her anger. She crouched down to bring her to her son's eye level and put on the best smile she could manage.

"Jake, could you please go into the backyard and play? I'll call you when dinner is ready."

Five-year-old Jake nodded silently, his blue eyes shifting briefly toward Lawrence before he turned and ran from the kitchen. When Andi heard the back door slam shut, she set her hands on her knees and straightened. Lawrence stood in the doorway between the kitchen and dining room, his fists set at his waist with his white shirtsleeves rolled to his elbows. His tie was crooked and loose as if he'd yanked it free.

"What do you mean this is my fault?" Disappointment sat in the back of her throat in a bitter ball, and she wished more than anything she could swallow it even if it just made her sick. She'd been sick to her stomach for three days and a violent migraine threatened to explode at the base of her skull.

Ever since she'd learned her husband had been having an affair for three years. Correction…having *affairs*…

"What the hell did you expect?"

"I expected you to honor your vows to me." She wished her voice came out stronger, but she was worn and tired. But, this time, she wouldn't remain silent. This was too much. "I did nothing to make you unfaithful."

"That's the problem, isn't it, Andrea?" he ground out, crossing the space to stand two feet away from her, his face she had once found so attractive twisted into an angry grimace. "You did nothing. Maybe if you'd spent more time paying attention to what I needed, instead of sitting at that damned computer. Maybe if you didn't spend so much time on the phone with that bitch Margaret. Maybe if you left the boy alone for ten minutes to see to your *husband's* needs—"

Andi's mouth fell open and she nearly choked. "*The boy* is your *son*, Lawrence. *Your son.* And he's only five years old, for heaven's sake!"

He continued off as if she'd said nothing of importance at all. "Everything else is more important. Hell, you don't even bother to look decent for me anymore!"

The insult was as harsh as a slap to the face. Instinctively, she raised her hand and touched the smooth braid of red hair she'd woven against her scalp that morning and felt the whisper of small curls that often escaped to frame her face. The braid hung nearly to her waist and had taken twenty minutes to plait, and she'd done it wet so her hair would hold the smell of the shampoo he'd once commented—so long ago now it seemed—he liked. Perhaps the jeans and white sweater she wore weren't pearls and high heels, but jeans were easier when chasing a preschooler.

His words bombarded her, the worst making her suck in her breath. He gave a litany of physical flaws she had allowed herself to fall into to displease him.

"Hell, when I *can* convince you to have sex it's like screwing a rag doll."

Andi closed her eyes, hot tears squeezing free, and clenched her hands at her side. "You're just being cruel now, Lawrence," she managed to whisper.

"Things are going to change around here."

She blinked open her eyes, the haze of tears blurring her view, and her body shook with the effort of not flying apart. He pointed a finger in her face, jabbing at the air so it shifted across her cheeks without ever touching her.

"You're going to give up this bull about writing books. If any of my partners found out you wrote smut—"

"I don't write smut," she interjected, but she took a step back at his look of rage. He'd never hit her, never so much as pushed her, but sometimes she saw the potential in his eyes.

"You're going to stop." There was no room for misunderstanding in the sharp edge of his voice. "You're going to stop talking to Margaret Connelly. She's been a bad influence on you. And you're going to be here for *me*, Andrea. *Me*."

"Will that keep you out of another woman's bed, Lawrence?" she asked, the words forcing their way out of her. Anger collided hard with the pain and sadness in her chest.

"Excuse me?" His expression twisted in angry shock she would question him. It wasn't something she did. Ever.

"Will that keep you out of another woman's bed?" she asked again.

He actually laughed.

His answer didn't matter anyway.

Andi stared into the space he left behind, waiting for the sound of the front door slamming shut and the loud rev of his BMW engine. The tires squealed slightly in the street as he drove away. She held her breath, taking in the air only when her lungs burned for oxygen and she felt the room tip.

Within thirty minutes, the chicken in the oven had baked to a dry brick, her suitcase was packed, and a box of belongings sat by the front door. She didn't want much from this house, and certainly not any mementos of their marriage. Jake's baby books, a photo album from her parents' house, and some framed photos. Her laptop was bagged up and all her files were sorted.

She stood in Jake's room, packing his clothes and all his favorite toys in the largest of her suitcases, when the telephone rang. Jake sat on his racecar track rug, running a plastic fire truck over the streets as he made siren noises. He didn't look up when she slipped from the room, but she knew it wouldn't take long for him to notice she was gone and come looking for her.

He didn't stray far from her, especially after he knew she and Lawrence had fought. For a five-year-old, he understood and saw more than she thought any kid his age should.

But that was okay…it was going to stop.

She picked up the phone before the machine answered, and swallowed hard before speaking. "Hello?"

"Oh, good! You're home! I've got amazing news!" Maggie shouted enthusiastically through the phone before Andi could finish speaking. "Are you sitting down?"

Andi closed her eyes and gripped the phone hard, trying to keep everything reined in tight before she spoke again. She knew right away her pause was too long, and within a heartbeat, Maggie knew something was wrong.

"Oh, crap. What did the bastard do now?"

Instead of answering the question, Andi asked, "Mags, can Jake and I stay with you for a while?"

"Of course. You know that. Tell me when you're landing and I'll be there." Maggie paused. "What'd he do?"

"He had an affair," Andi choked out. "He had several affairs."

"Who the hell would *want* to sleep with *that?*"

Despite the tension that had her tied in knots, Andi laughed. She wiped tears from her eyes and shook her head. "Damned if I know. Maybe that's why he had so many. None could stand him long enough." She huffed a breath and focused on her determination. There were far more reasons to leave Chicago, and for the life of her, she couldn't find a single—even if weak—reason to stay.

She couldn't even say it was because she loved him.

"What does that say about me?"

"That you should be damn proud of yourself!" Maggie declared loudly, her enthusiasm finally chipping away at Andi's buffer. "And hell, you're a self-made woman now. Who needs him, anyway?"

"What do you mean?"

"That's why I called. The publisher loved the series, and they've offered you a contract on all four books. I'm talking about a five-digit advance. These books are goin' *big time*, honey. I told you New York would eat them up. You've done it. You've made it. Screw him."

Andi tipped her head back and looked to the ceiling. God had given her *two* gifts that day…the book contract every writer dreamed of…and the strength to restart her life. Her stomach twisted in a tight knot of nerves, but not because she was afraid.

Not anymore.

She was excited!

"I don't suppose you know of a babysitter in L.A., do you?" she asked, a smile spreading her lips.

Maggie laughed. "Haven't a clue, but I can find one. Why?"

"I think today deserves a drink." She drew in a deep breath, easing the tension out of her shoulders as she let it go again. "To celebrate."

CHAPTER ONE

"**I**'m sorry," David said softly, roughening his voice to give it weight and sincerity. He laid his palm against Taylor's cheek and leaned forward until their foreheads touched.

Too quickly, she pulled away and tipped her head back to look at him. She shook her head, her forehead creasing. "For what?"

He tried again to make contact, touching her cheek. "For not coming home when I promised you I would. For not being here when you needed me. For not being here when—"

"Stop," she snapped, cutting off any explanation he could offer.

He brought both hands up to touch her face, brushing over her lipstick-slick lower lip with his thumb.

"I'm sorry—" The rest went unfinished when Taylor arched up on her toes and threw her arms around his neck. He managed a quick mumble against her lips before she kissed him, her fingers pushing impatiently into his hair.

A low-but-definitely-feminine groan, laced with "Oh, for pity's sake," echoed through the soundstage just before the Director's loud voice drowned it out.

"Cut!"

David detangled himself from Taylor and took a step back, running the side of his finger over his lips to remove any lipstick she'd left behind. The air in the studio was hot, and he'd been under the lights too long because irritation licked at a spot between his shoulder blades, making him even more tense and aggravated. Like he wasn't frustrated enough with Taylor, although he'd never say it.

"What?" Taylor huffed, stepping back from her mark. "What was wrong this time, Benton?"

Benton stepped into the circle of light, his features crinkled and pulled tight with tension. David understood Benton, as director, felt the pinch as much as anyone. Maybe more, because time was money and no one knew better than the man in charge on set. The more times they had to reshoot the further behind they got. "Taylor-Sweetheart-Darling...we've gone over this. We all know just how kissable David is—"

David fought the urge to roll his eyes and took a bottle of cold water offered to him by one of the PAs, snapping the cap open before draining half the bottle.

"But, you need to listen to me on this one, honey. This scene is about..." Benton trailed off, holding his hands out as if silently pleading for Taylor to understand. "It's about..."

"It's about coming home," Andi Parker said from the shadows.

David watched her step into the light, and not for the first time since he met her, he enjoyed the flash of heat skimming just below the surface of his skin. Andrea Parker was not only gifted—he hadn't been able to put her books down once he'd been cast for the movie adaptation—but she was one of the most beautiful women he had ever seen. No...correct that. She was *the* most beautiful woman he'd ever seen.

No more than five-foot-three, she was fair-skinned with sun-touched red hair and a row of freckles across the bridge of her nose just begging to be caressed. She had the curve and shape of a woman—not like stick-figure Barbie imitators he saw in Hollywood most of the time —and a dry wit that kept him laughing most of the time when they had the chance to talk. Her jokes were always subtle and delivered in a single shot, and if you weren't paying attention it was lost on you all together.

That was her nature...if you weren't looking, she could slip into a room unnoticed. Just as easily, she could be the only person in a studio full of people.

Today she wore a simple, yellow sundress with tiny flowers scattered on it that buttoned down the front from the 'v' of her neckline to the hemline falling just a couple of inches above her knees. The fabric looked soft and warm and draped down her in a way that made him want to lay his hands at her waist, just to see what she felt like. Her short hair flipped and curled around her face, and he wondered sometimes if it just *happened* that way, or if she worked at it. Small, oval glasses perched on her nose, the dark frames making her red hair seem even richer. But, today she wasn't smiling…and David had a good idea why.

They'd been working on this single scene all morning. Benton had tried to tell Taylor what he wanted from nearly every direction: left, right, over, and under. Regardless, Taylor had done the same thing with each take—well, with some variation to show she was at least trying. Taylor seemed to have her mind set on this scene happening a certain way and didn't want to give it up. She'd impressed David with her performance in other scenes; nailing them with such emotion and skill it often only took a shot or two to get every angle and delivery they needed.

But this one scene seemed to have her stumped.

Until this last shot, Andi had stayed quiet and left the directing to Benton. The two of them—Writer and Director—were almost always on the same page when it came to the interpretation of a scene. It surprised David now that she would be so vocal.

Not that he minded…he liked her voice. She was soft-spoken with a lilt to her voice and a delicate accent he hadn't ever been able to place. He hid his smile behind the mouth of his water bottle.

"It's about forgiveness, and it's about realizing what you've got… and being *thankful* for second chances." She stopped a few feet from them, crossing her arms. "It's *not* about sex."

"It's about intimacy," Benton tag-teamed.

"Exactly," Andi declared loudly. "It's about intimacy. You can't—" Andi waved her hands in the air, her cheeks flushing. She motioned toward David, her bright eyes settling on him for only a brief moment.

"—latch onto him like he's some kind of life preserver or the air tube to your oxygen tank. Let *him* come to *you*. You're in shock. You're exhausted. You're thankful he's alive, but you have to be tentative."

"Yeah, but wouldn't it be hotter if we're all…you know…excited?"

Without answering, Andi crossed the short space and took Taylor's spot at the mark. Her small hand settled on David's arm, and he immediately felt the heat as the touch snapped his attention to her.

"You're frightening me, Jason."

Without looking to his right, David handed off the half-empty bottle of water and took his spot. He laid his hand over hers and curled his fingers slightly. Her skin was warm and her hand was delicate in his hold.

"Don't be. I'm okay. Now." He smiled, just slightly. "I wasn't, but I am now."

Andi stared at their hands and drew in a shaky breath. When she looked up again, David shifted his stance to face her straight. "I'm sorry," he said softly. Just as he had before, he leaned forward until their foreheads touched. Taylor was taller and he had to bend his knees slightly to bring himself more level with Andi, but he liked the way it aligned their bodies. Her eyes fluttered closed and she raised her chin, bringing their lips closer together without touching.

"For what?" Andi asked, speaking naturally as Anna, his character's wife. Her fingers curled around his wrist and her breath skimmed across his chin, but she didn't pull back or open her eyes.

"For not coming home when I promised you I would. For not being here when you needed me. For not being here when—"

"Stop," she said in barely a whisper. Only then did she open her eyes and tip her head back enough to look at him.

He brought both hands up to touch her face, brushing her lower lip with his thumb. It was slick and smooth, like she may have just applied lip balm, and the idea tugged at something somewhere between his chest and his gut. He bit down for a moment. *Jason would love the feel of his wife's lips after so long…*

"I'm sorry I forgot," he forced out, finishing the line this time. He paused and swallowed, leaning closer to her until their lips almost touched. Her breath was quick and shallow. "How could I forget you?"

The scene said THEY KISSED SOFTLY, but David hesitated. She wasn't an actress, and he doubted she'd initiate the scene with the intent of carrying it this far. Then Andi leaned into him, her body tilting to press against his chest and he took one hand from her cheek to lace it into her hair, soft curls wrapping around his fingers like ribbons of silk.

She gasped softly before he pressed their lips together. He couldn't force himself to take a breath as they held that position, and he swore he could hear the pounding of her heart. Andi played the part just as he imagined, her body shaking slightly in his embrace. Her lips parted as he pulled back a degree, and he kissed her again, letting his tongue skim along the edge of her lips.

Her fingers curled into the front of his shirt, and her head tilted slightly to the side to effectively deepen the kiss. David loosened his fingers from her hair, sliding his hand back to her cheek as he broke contact. Despite himself, he returned for one final, brief kiss before withdrawing. Andi's body swayed with his, but she righted herself on her feet and her eyes fluttered open. Bright color stained her cheeks, and she blinked rapidly.

Andi looked up at him, her face flushed and warm beneath his touch, and she blinked several times. Swallowing, David pulled his attention away from her face to look at Benton.

"That what you want?"

At first, he was met by silence. Benton stood at the edge of the light, his hands hanging limp at his side and his mouth open. Taylor stood beside him, mimicking his look of shock as she fanned herself with one hand. Even the PA who now held David's half-empty bottle of water stared wide-eyed.

Benton nodded. That was the only answer David got. He looked back down at Andi and realized he had begun stroking her cheek with his thumb.

She blinked again and licked her lips, turning away. Then with just as much skill as any actor David had ever seen, Andi took in a long, steadying breath and closed her eyes. When she opened them again, her voice was steady and the flush had lightened in her cheeks.

"Perfect," she said with a lopsided grin and made a thumbs-up.

"You nailed it." She turned to Benton and Taylor, stepping away from him. "I'll be back in a few minutes."

When she brushed past him, David couldn't fight the urge to turn his hand so their fingertips brushed across each other. Her attention never wavered, but David thought maybe her hand angled back to him before the contact broke and she stepped over the mangle of cables and wires to disappear into the darkness of the soundstage.

Benton cleared his throat. "Yeah. Let's do that again."

Taylor stepped to him with a wide smile, looking up at him through her mascara-thickened lashes. She said something, but David's attention had followed Andi in the darkness and he didn't bring himself back to the moment until he no longer heard the soft pad of her sandals on the concrete.

With a performance like that, she belongs in front of the camera, not behind a computer.

Andi tripped taking the two little steps into her trailer. "Ow!" She winced at the sharp pain in her left knee. "That's gonna leave a mark," she mumbled as she opened the door and escaped to the dark interior of the small space she called her own when she visited the set.

Her heart pounded so hard in her chest that each beat thrummed at her temples. She was hot everywhere. Most people flushed in their cheeks, but she swore the heat beneath her skin spread from her red hair to her red-painted toenails. She thanked God for the small refrigerator in her trailer stocked with cold Diet Coke. As soon as she curled her fingers around the cold can, she pressed the metal to the base of her throat, gasping at the near-burn against her flushed skin. She shifted the can to her cheek and forehead before sitting at the tiny, Formica-covered table nestled into the front of the trailer.

Andi set her elbow on the tabletop and leaned her burning forehead into her hand, expelling a shaky breath. "Get a grip, Andrea," she scolded herself in the silent trailer.

But the only thought that would register in her brain was *Wow!*

Right alongside *Holy Cannoli!* It had been a long time, longer than Andi would admit to anyone except maybe Maggie, since something as simple as a kiss had melted her insides into a bucket of girly goo. Years probably...*how pathetic is that?*

"He's an actor," she mumbled, finally popping open the Diet Coke. "It's his *job* to sell the kiss, right? Right. So...that's why he got the job. He's good." Andi rolled her eyes. "Good doesn't even begin to cover it."

Her cell phone rang and she picked it up from the table where she'd left it that morning—always afraid it would go off during filming— and smiled when she saw the name on the screen.

Andi was quite proud her voice didn't quiver when she answered. "Hey, Mags."

"Hey..." Maggie, Andi's literary agent and dearest friend on the planet paused on the other end. "What's wrong?"

Typical of Maggie, all she had to hear was Andi's voice to know something was wrong...okay, so not wrong...just...*No, definitely wrong!* "What makes you think anything is wrong?"

"Oh, please. Spill."

"*Nothing* is *wrong*...really."

"Do I *have* to come hurt you?"

Andi laughed, feeling some of the tension David's kiss had created releasing enough she could drop her shoulders and take a sip of her soda. The cold, crispness eased her throat and spread out in her chest, relieving some of the flush. She drew in a long, metered breath through her nose in an attempt to calm herself further, but realized quickly *that* was a mistake.

The scent of David Bishop clung to her clothes and filled her senses. Just like that—*BAM*—the flush was back. *You're insane, Andrea Parker! Certifiable!*

"I swear, Andi...I'm catching the next plane..."

"Okay, okay. Relax." Andi took a deep breath. "Something just happened on set that has me...um...frazzled." *And hot...and bothered... and apparently insane.*

Maggie huffed on the other end of the line. "I told you, Andi...you can't agonize over every little nuance of every scene. Let Benton direct. The two of you usually see things the same, and—"

"No, it's nothing like that," Andi said, gently cutting Mags off before she went on a rant. Andi quickly explained which scene they had been filming, and the ongoing trouble with Taylor wanting to attach herself to David like some freaky succubus. She took another long drink before finishing the story with, "So, I showed her what I wanted."

There was a silent pause on the other end of the line, and Andi could almost hear Maggie's wheels churning. "You..."

"Yep," Andi answered before Maggie finished the question, popping the 'p' loudly through her recently-David-kissed lips. *Oh, Mama...*

"Aaaand..."

"And I'm hiding in my trailer, sucking down a cold Diet Coke, and wondering just how small that upright coffin they call a shower is in my tiny bathroom—because I could use a cold dousing right about now."

Andi sat and drank her soda in silence for the next two minutes while Maggie first laughed herself breathless, then tried to speak again. When it sounded like Maggie might have herself under control, Andi sighed. "Are you done now?"

There was another loud snort. "Nope, don't think so."

A soft knock at the trailer door stopped Andi from saying something back. "Someone is here, hang on."

"Maybe it's David. He wants to rehearse."

"Not funny. Come on in," she called toward the door. Then anything else she might have said to Maggie froze in her throat when the door opened and David stuck his head inside. Her hand holding the phone slid away from her face, and Maggie's voice grew distant.

"If the trailer's rockin'..." she heard faintly.

David smiled as he took the steps—much more gracefully than she had managed just minutes before—into her trailer. "Hi," he said simply.

"Hi..." Andi managed, already feeling the heat blooming in her cheeks like a California wildfire. Then she heard Maggie calling out her name, and she put the phone back to her ear. "I'll call you later, 'kay?"

"Who is it?"

"I'll call you."

"It's him."

David's mouth tipped into a quick, sexy grin and with it, an all-new flash of heat spreading from her throat to her cheeks, Andi realized her penchant for keeping her phone volume high had let him hear at least the tail end of her conversation.

"I'll call you later, Mags."

"Don't you hang up on me, Andrea Parker," Maggie shouted just before Andi snapped the phone shut and set it down on the table beside her now painfully empty Diet Coke.

"Problem?" David asked with a slight lilt to his voice.

Andi shook her head. "Nope. What's up?"

"Benton called lunch," David said, closing the door behind him as he took the last step into the trailer. Suddenly, the trailer seemed not just small, but microscopic.

The idea of food made Andi's stomach flip. She yanked her hands back from the tabletop and stuck them underneath, clenching them together in her lap. "Okay." One thing Andi had always managed to do, no matter how intimidated or nervous she was, was to meet someone's eyes when she spoke to them. Her father had taught her no matter what was going on in her head if she could look someone in the eye, they'd respect her.

Right now, she could barely manage to glance up from the speckled tabletop to make polite conversation. Any second now, she knew she was going to burst into flame and leave behind nothing more than a pile of ash and a pair of glasses.

"We finished the scene. Benton said you should see it before he calls it."

Andi shook her head. "I'm sure it's fine this time."

"I think it's what you want…" His voice trailed off.

She cleared her throat and nodded, flipping a bit of hair behind her ear so it didn't touch her cheek. "I'll check it after lunch."

"You'll like it."

Andi snapped her gaze to him, and her heart jumped straight into her throat. Where had the weeks of comfortable camaraderie gone? Of sitting at the picnic tables outside during lunch and talking? Him laughing politely at her lame attempts at humor? It wasn't like she didn't *know* he was sex-on-legs, she wasn't blind or stupid. And although her social life in the last few years resembled the life of a nun, she wasn't *actually* celibate. Not by choice, anyway. David Bishop was six-plus feet of hotness with thick brown hair with just enough natural wave for running her fingers through, and eyes that crinkled just right at the corners to show he laughed a lot.

Why was it thirty-year-old men could have laugh lines and it was sexy, but thirty-*ahem*-something women couldn't have a single line without looking haggard? The cosmos wasn't fair.

Andi blinked away the random thought and nervously took one hand from under the table to pick up her empty can, tapping it with a hollow thud against the table. "Good," she managed to say.

David shifted his stance, pushing his hands into the front pockets of his jeans. In an attempt to calm her nerves, Andi drew in a slow breath—which usually worked—except now it wasn't just her clothes that smelled of him, but the entire space. It wasn't an overpowering smell like someone bathed in aftershave, but a subtle mingling of sandalwood and fresh air.

There you go, Andi…waxing poetic again. How exactly does one 'smell' like fresh air?

"Did you ever consider acting?" David asked, his voice in the silence making her jump.

Andi chuckled and shook her head. "No. I can't act."

"Really…" he said slowly, pulling the word out with a slight quirk at the corner of his mouth. His voice was rough and heavy, practically sitting in the air between them. Andi managed to force herself to meet his gaze. He swallowed and she watched the slow bob of his Adam's apple.

Her heart pounded so hard in her chest, she felt each pulse thunder in her ears, and each breath she took echoed like she had her head in a barrel. That little quirk of his mouth turned into a slow grin.

Stop it!

"No," she reiterated. She turned her attention again to the speckled Formica, digging her nail into a nick. "No acting, just..." Despite her resolve to memorize the pattern, she looked up again and found him staring at her. Her throat was suddenly as dry as the Mojave, and she wished more than anything there was one final swallow of Diet Coke left. "I just…I know how it's supposed to be."

He took a step toward her, and suddenly Andi couldn't sit at the tiny table anymore—or share the tiny space—or apparently use her feet properly. She stumbled sideways, attempting to grip the table edge to keep herself from falling, but it was David's hands that caught her. His long fingers curled around her bare arm, and Andi stared down at the contact, unable to look away as his other hand settled at her waist. The shift of her cotton dress over her skin almost made her shiver. As she watched, his fingers relaxed and slid over her skin up her arm to her shoulder. She had to close her eyes, and chant silently in her head.

You're insane, Andrea! Insane and aroused! But mostly insane! Stop it! Just stop it already!

"Andi—"

"I sh-should go check the shot," she rambled, trying to move past him before she made a total and complete fool of herself. *Yeah, like you haven't already.* "I don't want to hold up Benton."

"Andi…" he said again. His hand left her waist to block her escape. Just like he had with the first, he let his fingers brush her skin at the elbow then slide slowly up her bare arm.

A shiver danced up her spine, and she bit back a groan. His hand continued along her shoulder to her throat, his fingertip pausing at her pulse point. Now there was no doubt he knew how hard her heart pounded with him this close. David nudged her chin with his thumb, urging her to tip her head slightly away from him, elongating the side of her neck. He stepped closer and leaned in until the rough bristle of his whiskers brushed her cheek and his breath warmed her skin.

"When you said those lines, and you shook when I touched you, you made me believe you were Anna and I was Jason." His voice was so low she wouldn't have been able to hear him if he hadn't been so close. The timbre vibrated against the side of her throat, and she had to force her eyes from fluttering closed. "And when I kissed you, I felt it. I really *felt* it."

Andi had to close her eyes to keep herself from getting dizzy. *This is one of those vivid dreams of yours, Andrea. That's all. Just a vivid dream. Any second now, your alarm is going to go off and you're going to have to drag yourself out of bed.*

Yep…any second now.

David slid his cheek along hers, tilting his head so their lips hovered against each other. Andi tried not to breathe, but it only made her head swim more. She sucked in oxygen, and her senses filled with David Bishop. His thumb stroked along her jaw and down her throat to the hollow of her collarbone, and even with her eyes closed, she knew he watched her for every reaction. Andi tried to take a step back, but the table was too close and she bumped her bottom against it, her fingers instinctively curling around the edge.

"I want to know something…" David said, his words trailing off unfinished.

"Wh-what?" she managed to ask, and when she spoke, her lips brushed against his and her breath hitched. She wanted to lick her lips, but she was afraid—*no, more like terrified*—her tongue would wet more than her own lips. He was so close.

"I wonder…" His pause finally piqued her curiosity so much she opened her eyes, and gasped. David's face wasn't an inch from hers and his gray-blue eyes watched her intently. "I wonder if I kissed you now—not as Jason and Anna, but David and Andi—would it feel the same?"

Andi shook her head slightly, the first action to come to her muddled brain. His thumbs rubbed across her throat and she swallowed hard.

"Or would it be better?"

"No," she managed to say.

He tipped his chin so it nudged hers. "You don't think so. Are you sure?"

"No," she parroted.

David smiled, and took his hands from her throat to lay his palms against her cheeks. His mouth hovered over hers, his breath warm. When the tip of his tongue touched her lower lip, Andi gasped as a bolt of awareness struck her, shooting down her spine to her stomach like an electrified lightning rod. Before she could finish drawing her breath, his mouth covered hers.

And then he was kissing her without restraint or temperance, and everything inside her liquefied. Andi had to grab hold of his shirt, curling her fingers into the soft cotton behind his shoulders just to hold her feet, and his hands shifted to her back, pulling her closer to him. She whimpered, and mentally groaned because it had to be the unsexiest sound ever heard. But his hold tightened on her, pressing her so close to him it was hard to draw breath into her lungs.

Not that she could because breathing required some level of brain function.

Even though his lips never left hers, Andi groaned low in her throat when he moved his body away from hers. In a fluid motion, David's hands slid over her hips to the back of her thighs and he lifted her the few inches needed to set her bottom on the table, his hands branding her bare skin when the hem of her dress shifted beneath his touch. With a gentle, but insistent, jerk he brought her body flush against him so she balanced near the edge and his denim-clad hips pushed between her thighs. Andi gasped, her head tipping back as reality flashed like a neon sign in her head.

Wake up! This is a dream! This is not going to happen!

David's tongue dipped into her mouth as he tipped her back slightly. Everything tingled, and her ankles hooked behind his legs before any intelligent and sensible brainwave could find a functioning synapse long enough to warn her she was losing control. Her body hummed with vibrations, and as his mouth shifted its attention from her lips to her throat…he stopped.

Vibration shifted through her again, and through the pounding in her ears, she heard him whisper hoarsely, "Do you need to get that?"

Andi blinked and slowly uncurled her fingers from his shirt, leaning back to look at his face. Every inch of her skin was flushed, and even the simple sundress felt restrictive and smothering, especially when his large hand rested on her thigh, and the pad of his thumb brushed the inside of her knee. It took everything she had to focus on his face to realize he'd asked her a question. His eyes were dark, his irises large and intense, and his rapid breath warmed her already-fevered cheeks.

Vibration again…Andi blinked again…*Work, brain! Work!*

"Your phone…do you need to answer it?"

Reality clicked back into place, and Andi looked slightly behind her to the small folded phone on the table now bounced and slid on the Formica as it vibrated again. David's hand left her thigh—the spot suddenly feeling cold and abandoned—and picked it up, holding it up so she could see the screen.

MAGS

"Do you need to answer it?" he asked again.

Andi shook her head. "No."

He set the phone down, but by then she had been given the two whole seconds needed for her brain to work again, her heart to slow just a few beats so it wasn't going to break free of her chest, and her breathing to catch up with the severe lack of oxygen in her lungs. She watched him set the phone down as if that single action were the most important thing in the world and clenched her hands in her lap. David shifted his weight so he could rest his hands on the edge of the table on either side of her legs and lean down so their faces were level.

"Andi—"

Before he could complete whatever he wanted to say, someone rapped on the trailer door and Andi jumped with a short yelp. David's hands slid to her hips as she hopped off the table, steadying her. Which was good since her knees seemed to no longer have functioning ligaments.

"Yeah?" she called out, her voice croaking. She cleared her throat and tried again. "Yeah?"

"It's April, I'm looking for David. Benton needs him. Do you know where he is?"

"I'm in here," David answered, and Andi shot him a shocked look.

Why not tell the whole crew we were just making out like hormonal teenagers, whydontcha?

He grinned, almost as if he knew the reality of her horror. "I'll be right there."

"'Kay," April called back, her voice already distant as she walked away from the trailer.

"Y-you should go," Andi stuttered out, the heat of embarrassment quickly smothering the heat of arousal. Her cheeks burned hot, and she had the almost uncontrollable desire to cross her arms over her body and scurry into the far corner of the table banquette.

"Yeah." He touched her cheek, stroking her skin before nudging her chin up so she had to look at him or close her eyes in denial. Since she couldn't stand there all day with her eyes closed, Andi met his gaze. And the smile on his face made her breath catch all over again. "Probably not the best place for this, huh?"

"Ya think?" she said with a wry chuckle.

He curled a bit of hair behind her ear, the smile never leaving his face. "I believe you, by the way." Andi frowned and his grin widened as he shook his head. "You can't act."

Before she could come back with some buffering, sarcastic one-shot, he kissed her again. Simply this time—just a pressing of their lips together but he hummed softly and the contact ricocheted through her. His hand slid down her spine to rest on the curve of her backside and Andi couldn't breathe.

"I'm glad," he said against her mouth.

He stepped back, and the air around her was suddenly cold and gooseflesh popped up on her bare arms. Andi wanted to say something—*anything*—but nothing would form enough in her head to make it to her throat.

He made it as far as the door, stopping when his fingers curled around the handle. David looked back at her, his eyes skimming from her face to her sandals and back, and Andi held her breath. With a small sound in the back of his throat, he tilted his head to the side with a small jerk and pivoted back to her. "Not yet," he mumbled before coming back to her.

He raised his hands and enveloped her face as he reached her, and Andi only had a split second to take a breath before his open mouth covered hers. Energy and electricity rolled through her, curling in her stomach and she moaned against his mouth. She gasped when he pulled his lips free of hers, only to plant a trail of forceful, almost rough kisses down the side of her throat to her shoulder. He pressed his face into the hollow where her neck and shoulder met, his teeth gently abrading her skin, his fingers pulling aside her dress collar to expose more skin.

Andi whispered his name, not even realizing she wanted to until it passed her lips. One arm tightened around her, pulling her hard against him. Then he let her go, yanked the door open with a hard jerk, and bounded out of the trailer. The small structure shook in the wake of his departure.

Or, maybe that was just Andi's legs finally giving out. She slouched against the edge of the table and pressed a trembling hand against her hot forehead.

The phone vibrated again, and Andi looked down to see Maggie's name on the screen. *That* conversation would have to wait.

Besides, what would she say?

Sorry I didn't answer, Mags. You see…David Bishop…yeah, that's right David Bishop…yep, the guy voted Number Seven on the Hollywood Top Ten Hottest Men of the Year last year…yeah, him. Well, I'm pretty sure we were about to either have sex or something similar right here on my little trailer table. Yep, you heard me right. No, I wasn't asleep. At least, I don't think I was asleep. Stop laughing, Mags, I mean it.

Andi sighed and covered her face with her hands. *Holy Crap!*

CHAPTER TWO

*A*ndi groaned low in her throat when he moved his body away from hers. *In a fluid motion, David's hands slid over her hips to the back of her thighs and he lifted her the few inches needed to set her bottom on the table, his hands branding her bare skin when the hem of her dress shifted beneath his touch. With a gentle, but insistent, jerk he brought her body flush against him so she balanced near the edge and his denim-clad jeans pushed between her thighs. Andi gasped, her head tipping back as reality flashed like a neon sign in her head.*

Wake up! This is a dream! This is not going to happen!

"Just how much coffee do you intend to make?"

Maggie's voice behind her made Andi jump, and she nearly dropped the coffee carafe she was filling. Her heart thudded harder in her chest and an embarrassed flush crept up her neck, blooming hot in her cheeks for being caught in her daydream. *Okay, reliving a fantasy, but that's just nitpicking.* She glanced over her shoulder as Maggie took a seat at the small table near the patio doors, and looked away when her best friend and housemate set her inquiring gaze on her. Andi poured out most of the water in the carafe and finished making their coffee, keeping her back to Mags as much as possible. But, pouring the water in the maker and setting the filter in place only took so long.

All the while, Mags sat silent, watching her with a smile that would have made the Cheshire Cat jealous. It was unnerving! Man, was this what Jake felt like when she gave him the 'stare down' until he confessed? Andi wasn't sure she'd be able to pull it off anymore…now that she'd been on the receiving end. She'd seen hardened businessmen and unwitting waiters crumple into whimpering, spineless piles of nothing under Maggie's scrutiny.

"So…"

Andi set down her empty coffee cup with a loud *clack* and spun around, her nerves snapping. "Fine! Yes! It was him, okay? He came to my trailer and…and…" She stuttered to a stop, pressing her lips together to keep from saying too much.

Maggie just sat silent, grinning.

"What?" Andi snapped.

Maggie chuckled, her shoulders bouncing. "Nothing. I was just going to comment on how much I like your new haircut."

Andi huffed and spun around, busying herself with making Jake's toaster waffles. For two days, she'd managed to avoid answering any questions Maggie asked over the phone, either claiming she had to go or just outright refusing to offer up any information. But, Maggie was home, and she was a powerful inquisitor when she was face to face with her target.

Just when she thought maybe she might avoid the Great Inquisition, Maggie slid in, "I'm guessing David likes it, too."

Andi groaned and slammed her elbows down on the counter, holding her head in her hands. This time, Maggie didn't even try to be subtle. She laughed out loud, her cackle echoing off the high ceilings of their shared home.

"Stop it," Andi begged, her voice too low to be heard over Maggie's laughing. "This is bad. Very bad."

Maggie pushed her chair back, her legs scraping the tile, and came to her side, draping an arm across Andi's shoulders to give her a quick squeeze. "Aw, come on. What's so bad about making out with one of the hottest leading men in Hollywood? Doesn't sound all bad to me."

Andi groaned again.

"So you *did* make out with him!"

Andi whimpered.

"Was it good?"

From her toes to her cheeks, Andi flushed hot and tingly. Except this time it wasn't embarrassment. She remembered every moment of their kiss, every touch and every squeeze. How he tasted and how his lips had felt...how could she not? She'd been reliving the kiss all night, every night, for the last three days. What use did it do to deny anything? Maggie would hound her and poke at her until she 'fessed up, and then would probably offer her a shot of amaretto in her coffee.

"It was better than good," she finally admitted, and straightened to face Maggie, leaning her hip against the counter edge. Maggie was smiling again, her arms crossed, her eyebrows arched waiting for details. "I don't think I've ever been that—"

"Hot? Horny? Turned on?"

Andi chuckled. "I was going to say aroused, but I guess you covered it."

"Tell me *everything*." Before Andi could protest, Maggie whined and gripped Andi's arm. *She actually whined!* "Oh, come on, Andrea. Let me live vicariously through you."

"Oh, please." Andi shrugged her arm free of Maggie's grip and shook of her head, pouring the coffee that was finally done. She inhaled deeply of the fragrant steam before dumping in three calorie-free sweetener packets. "You're the one going out three nights a week with your hot Italian lover. What's his name? Nicco?"

Maggie sighed and looked off toward the ceiling, a wide grin—one that spoke of deep, and probably frequent, satisfaction—bowing her lips. "Ah, yes. Nicco. My Italian Stallion."

Andi groaned and took her coffee to the table, hoping she'd sufficiently distracted Mags with memories of her latest lover. Her reprieve lasted for about 10.2 seconds before Maggie followed her to the table and into the seat beside her, leaning in conspiratorially.

"Oh, come on. You haven't done anything more than go to dinner with *anyone* since coming out here. Honey, that's one hell of a dry spell. And the first guy you decide to make out with is *David Bishop?*"

"Shhhhh!" Andi hissed through her teeth, glancing toward the stairs that emptied into the kitchen. Jake was due downstairs any second. "And for your information, I didn't *decide* anything. It just…"

"Happened? Andi, that is the oldest and most worn-out excuse that has ever been used. Usually, it's by cheating husbands—" Andi shot Maggie a sharp look, and Maggie had the good grace to wince. "Sorry. But, honey, things like that don't just *happen*. Okay, so maybe the kiss on the stage just 'happened'." Maggie made quote marks in the air with her bent fingers. "But, him coming to your trailer for make-out session number two—"

"Do you have to call it that?"

"What? Making out? Okay, fine…was it more like foreplay?"

Andi immediately remembered—with almost painful clarity—the tumbling heat in her stomach when David groaned against her mouth and lifted her onto the table. The way his tongue slipped past her lips, and the way he moved his hips against hers, rhythmically imitating an even more intimate action. She'd wrapped her legs around him and wished he'd do more than just slide his hand along her thigh. She'd wanted—

"I'll take that as a *hell yeah*."

Andi blinked and brought Maggie into focus again, knowing full well she was bright red all the way down her throat from the burning throb just beneath her skin. She laid her hand against her heated fore-head but didn't try to suppress the smile that almost made her cheeks hurt. "Okay, fine. Call it whatever you want, it was…intense. More intense than…" Andi shrugged and shook her head. "More intense than anything I can recall *ever*."

"Not even Eric your junior year of college?" Mags asked with a bob of her eyebrows.

"I knew telling you that story would come back to haunt me."

"Too late to take it back now," Maggie said smugly. "So, better?" Andi just nodded, but couldn't quite drop the grin on her face. "Question is what are you going to do about it."

That killed the smile and gooseflesh broke out over her skin. She looked down at her now-lukewarm coffee. "Nothing."

"You can't just do *nothing*. What are you going to do the next time you see him?"

Andi stared into her coffee, swirling it with her spoon. "Nothing. I'm going to do nothing, and hope he's forgotten about the whole thing. Or, that he wants to forget it as much as I do."

"Why would you want to forget it? And more importantly, why do you think *he* would want to forget it?" Maggie's voice had lost its teasing lilt, and when Andi looked up, Maggie stared at her hard, her mouth turned down in a frown.

Be real was her first thought. *Hello?* He was David Bishop...David Bishop! A week didn't go by he wasn't on the front of *some* gossip rag, usually with the headlines reporting his most recent affair or naming him one of Hollywood's Top Ten Whatevers. He was young and good-looking—scratch that—gorgeous—no, wait...*beautiful*. That's what David Bishop was. Beautiful.

"Tell me something," Mags ordered, leaning in close again. "When he kissed you—not on the set, but in your trailer—when he kissed you, was it just one kiss? Did he kiss you and step back? Let you go? Head for the door?"

Andi swallowed hard, her throat suddenly as dry as the desert. "No," she managed to croak.

"Did he hold you against him like he couldn't get close enough?"

Andi sucked in a shaky breath and closed her eyes against the flash of awakening just beneath her skin. *Mags was trying to kill her...set her on fire, it'd be quicker.*

"Did he make any of those sexy 'I could eat you alive and still not be satisfied' little hums in the back of his throat you're always writing about in your books?"

Andi huffed and dropped her head back. "You're not playing fair, Mags."

"I'm your best friend, I don't have to play fair. I just have to make sure you're happy," Mags said with a wink and a smirk.

Before Andi could sum up her arguments, she was saved by Jake's loud descent into the kitchen. He made a beeline for Andi, nearly knocking her off her chair when he threw his arms around her, planting a loud kiss on her cheek. Not to be discriminatory, he turned and did the same to Maggie before shouting, "Good morning," on his way to his toaster waffles.

"What are you doing today, honey?" Andi asked, sipping her cooling coffee. *Good…that's what they needed, a new line of conversation. And a cold shower. She definitely needed a cold shower. In Antarctica.*

He shrugged as he tore his waffle into bite-sized pieces and drowned them in copious amounts of syrup. "Aunt Maggie brought me some new books. I might read them. Are you gonna be here, Mom?" he asked over his shoulder.

"I sure am. I don't have anywhere else to be."

Maggie squinted her eyes at her. "I thought today they were shooting—"

Andi shook her head, not taking her attention off Jake. "I don't need to be there." Maggie leaned back in her chair, crossing her arms over her chest. Andi refused to look at her, but felt her friend's eyes staring at her. Might as well have had hot pokers jabbing at her head. She cleared her throat and scooted closer to her son. "What books did—"

"You're a chicken."

Both Andi and Jake turned to look at Maggie, but Maggie still glared straight at her, not looking away.

"Excuse me?"

"You. Are. A. Chicken."

"Why is Mom a chicken?" Jake demanded, and Andi already recognized the bristle in his tone. It didn't take much.

"Nothing, honey. Aunt Maggie is just teasing me."

She barely got the words out before Maggie started with "Bock-bock-bock…" She even mimicked a chicken, waving her bent arms like wings and letting her cheeks puff out with each 'bock'.

"Maggie, stop it."

Maggie huffed. "You're scared spitless a man wants you."

"He doesn't want me," Andi snapped, shoving her chair back from the table.

"Who?" Jake asked around a mouthful of waffles.

"Why wouldn't he want you? You *just* admitted—"

"Who wants what?" Jake asked again. "Mom?"

"A man your mom knows thinks she's pretty, and your mom doesn't agree."

"You're pretty, Mom. You're really pretty."

The conversation came at Andi rapid-fire, making her head spin. And her son's final words were enough to push her over the edge. Tears prickled behind her eyelids and she pressed her eyes shut, gripping the edge of the counter. "Can we *please* not talk about this right now?"

The phone rang, and Andi lunged for it, hoping to God and Heaven above whoever it was would rescue her from this disaster of a conversation.

David pushed his sunglasses up so he could pinch the bridge of his nose, rubbing the inner corners of his tired eyes as he climbed out of his car. When the bright sunlight nearly burned through his tired retinas, he let the glasses fall back into place before slamming his car door shut. His head pounded like he had one heck of a hangover, without the night of drinking. Never had he been so thankful his call time wasn't until ten that morning. He'd had a rough, sleepless night. Again.

The past three nights had been fitful and restless, leaving him dragging all day long and pushing himself just to get through the filming. If he didn't get a decent night's sleep soon, he figured Benton—or someone else—would have something to say. It hadn't affected his work yet, but David didn't know how many more nights of no rest he could handle.

When he did sleep, his dreams relived the same thing over and over again. He always woke with his heart pounding and his skin clammy. And his frustration levels at what could very well be an all time high.

All over one kiss.

Okay, so not one kiss. Two kisses. One on the set and one—no, two —three, he forgot the last kiss he went back for—in Andi's trailer.

David stifled his involuntary groan behind the plastic lid of his coffee and entered the darker interior of the expansive set building. He had forty minutes before he had to be in make-up, which gave him enough time to maybe catch a catnap in his trailer. Or refill his coffee for a caffeine push.

"David!" His name echoed through the cavernous space, and he turned toward April, Benton's PA, as she jogged toward him. "I've got rewrites for you."

"For today's stuff?" he asked, shifting the hold on his coffee to take the pages.

"Tomorrow." April pulled her lips back and hissed slightly through her teeth. "Wait 'til you see. Benton has already flipped."

David squinted in the semi-darkness, trying to make out the print. He slid a glance at April. "Why? What'd they do?"

"Just wait until you read it."

She took off again, forever on the run for Benton, and David continued to his trailer, flipping through the pages as he went. It wasn't until he reached for the knob on his door that he read over page four, and his hand stopped mid-air.

"No," he said aloud and scanned the pages again. "Damn."

He read further and shook his head. This couldn't be right. Granted, he was 'just the actor', and he was only supposed to interpret the script...but this, *this* he knew wasn't right. He'd devoured Andi's books when he was given the role, and she never *ever* would have written something like this. Her books—and the subsequent movies— fell under the broad description of science fiction, but her underlying character stories were seeded in romance and life.

This was sensationalism.

David read further and groaned.

Did she know yet?

David set his half-empty paper coffee cup on the steps into his trailer and turned back in the direction he'd come. What he intended to do, he didn't know yet. He didn't have the power to do anything at all, but he could at least voice an opinion. Being the talent didn't make him voiceless.

Benton's office was on the partial second level of the set building, accessible by a steel, somewhat wobbly set of stairs leading up from the set ground level. As he neared the wide-open doors leading into the parking lot, a silver Lexus RX Hybrid turned, taking up two parking spots, and jerked sharply to a stop, the sound of a slamming door immediately carrying across the parking lot. Before the passenger door could open, Andi Parker rounded the back of the Lexus, her sundress flipping around her legs as she practically marched toward the door.

The passenger front and back doors opened, and a petite woman with dark hair cut short and angled around her face jumped from the front of the Lexus, taking the hand of a young boy who climbed out of the back.

"Andi, you need to take a breath," the woman called after her. She took hold of the boy's hand and jogged after Andi. "Don't take anyone's head off until you think this through."

Yep…she knew.

And yet, despite her angry stride and the tight line of her lips, she was beautiful.

"Don't worry, Mags," she said back over her shoulder, her stride never slowing. "I won't kill anyone until I see how bad they butchered my—" Her voice faltered when she turned back and made eye contact with him. Her step slowed for half a second, then she marched again. "Is that the rewrite?" she demanded of him, already reaching for the script pages in his hand.

Before he had a chance to answer, she snatched the script from his fingers and flipped through the pages. She stepped further into the building and out of the sun, effectively bringing herself so close to him that her shoulder brushed his chest, and when she tipped her head to read the script, the scent of her shampoo drifted up to him. David indulged in a deep breath before tilting his head and angling his body so he could read over her shoulder. Her head turned slightly side-to-side as she scanned the pages, and he knew the exact moment she'd hit the offending scene change. Her entire body tensed and her breath hitched.

The woman who had arrived with Andi reached them. She wasn't quite as tall as Andi, with brown eyes and straight, dark brown hair that didn't clear the bottom of her ears. The boy wasn't more than ten or eleven years old but stood eye-to-eye with the woman. His hair was reddish-brown and too long so it waved and hung around his face, almost covering his eyes. He was all elbows and knees like his height had stretched him out before the rest of him had time to catch up. His face was tense, his eyes squinted, as he stepped closer to Andi.

"Mom?"

Andi shushed him softly, and David shifted his attention between Andi and the boy. Before he could process the information—the fact Andi was a mother, and what that could mean—her hand shot up and pressed against his chest.

"Oh, no…" she whispered. "Nononononono…."

David shifted closer to her and covered her hand with his, holding it in place. He knew the contact was probably reactive, but that didn't mean he wouldn't take full advantage of it. He looked over her shoulder again to see what she'd read. Before he could, her fingers curled into his shirt and she groaned. With the tension emanating from her body, and the focus she held on the pages, he doubted she even realized what she was doing.

"I just got them," he offered.

She sucked in a shuddered breath, and a small whimper caught in her throat. Her fingers curled tighter, pulling tight at his shirt, bringing him closer to her. For just a moment, his gaze shifted over the top of her head and caught the eyes of the smaller woman. He thought just for a moment, her mouth ticked up in a quick smile, but it quickly disappeared.

"Andi, let me see," the woman asked and reached for the paper.

Andi twisted away from her—and into him—keeping the script between him and her like a kid protecting their candy. *Forget the rewrites, did this woman have any clue what she was doing to him?* She shook her head and flipped the page.

"They can't…they can't be serious…"

"Andrea Parker, I'm serious. Let. Me. See," the woman demanded.

"Where is Benton?" Andi asked, finally raising her head to look at him. Her eyes glistened bright, and he knew she had been close to weeping just moments before. But her expression was set and determined, her lips tight when she spoke.

"In his office."

Then she was gone, brushing past him as she reached back to pass off the script to the other woman. She followed Andi, scanning the pages, and David took up the rear with the boy.

"Before you ask," the woman said, never looking up from the pages as she started up the stairs. "Yes, she's always like this when someone's gotten her Irish up. So, I wouldn't recommend getting on her bad side."

"Good to know," David mumbled as they followed in Andi's wake. The stairs, which were never meant to be a permanent structure in any of the set buildings, clattered and shook as the four of them ascended.

Andi reached the top before them and used the railing as a pivot point to propel herself down the catwalk to Benton's door. David never would have thought a woman so graceful and lithe as Andi could walk with such heavy-footed determination her footsteps would echo off the metal grating. Taking the stairs two at a time, David watched her legs as she marched toward Benton's door.

The three of them hit the landing together, the woman one step ahead, and she twisted enough to extend her hand to him.

"We haven't met. I'm Maggie Connelly, Andi's agent."

"David—"

"I know who you are, David," she said with a smirk and a wink, giving his hand a firm shake. She tipped her head toward the boy. "This is Jake, Andi's son."

David held out his hand to the boy, but he didn't take it, staring wide-eyed past both of them to where his mother stopped. Andi pounded on the door twice before opening it and barging inside. David, Maggie, and Jake reached the door in time to hear Benton countering whatever Andi had declared upon entry.

"I just got them this morning myself!" he shouted back. "Why do you think I called you, Andi? And let's remember…I called *you*."

"I accepted a *long* time ago this movie wasn't going to exactly be the novel I wrote, but you can't expect me to just *let* something like this go without fighting it," she shouted. "This is supposed to be a torture scene. Jason is fighting to keep secrets he *knows* could be the life of everyone he cares about if he lets anything slip." To emphasize her point, she motioned back toward David. "How does him having sex with his *captor* show his loyalty to his *wife* and his *cause*?"

"Sex sells," Benton said with an apologetic shrug.

"No!" Andi pounded her small fist on the desk. "No! I will not allow this!"

"Andi honey," Maggie Connelly said, moving around David to enter the battlefield. "You need to take a deep breath and step back. Let me make a few phone calls. We'll get this straightened out."

"Damn straight we will," Andi snapped, swinging back to them. She pointed a finger at Maggie, then seemed to think twice about it and dropped her hands to tight fists at her side. "I have a say in this. You made sure of it in the contract. They can't just do this without me."

"I'll fix it," Maggie reiterated, keeping her voice calm and level in comparison to Andi. "Leave it to me."

Andi closed her eyes and turned her face away from all of them, her hands clenched tight at her side as she drew in several deep breaths that shook her small frame. David fought the urge to touch her cheek or lay his hand on her arm. He wanted to, but he had to silently admit to himself he didn't know her well enough to know if she would accept the contact or if it would just make her angrier.

And not knowing her well enough was a problem he fully intended to fix.

She opened her eyes and moved away from them, further down the catwalk to the corner of the two-story temporary structure tucked in the corner of the massive sound stage. A single railing ran the length of the walkway, tall enough for an adult to rest their hands, but also tall enough that a toddler could probably run right under it without ducking. This time her steps were silent as she reached the corner and curled her hands around the metal, her head dropping forward.

The boy took a step toward her, but Maggie Connelly stopped him, her hand on his shoulder. "Let's give your mom some breathing room, Jake." She looked straight at David, that tiny smile tipping her mouth again. "We'll go down to her trailer and get you a soda while I unleash the Dogs of Hell."

The boy let out a sigh tinged with frustration and frowned, turning away to head back to the stairs. Maggie followed, but David shifted his attention back to Andi. With the gracefulness of a dancer, Andi crouched down, the hem of her sundress pooling on the grating for a moment before she swung her legs over the edge and sat down.

David rested his hand on the cool steel piping and walked to her, looking over the railing to the people below as they moved around preparing for the day's shots. A green screen hung along a section of the back wall. He was only a couple of feet away when she curled her fingers around the edge of the catwalk and leaned forward, her sandaled feet swinging.

"Hey," he said, touching her shoulder with his fingertips.

She looked up, and her eyes still shined just a little too bright. It tugged at his chest and made him swallow. David moved behind her, and using the single railing to keep him from shifting too far, he sat behind her and draped his legs on either side of her slim hips. A tiny, soft sound caught in her throat and she looked at him with wide, blue eyes.

"You make me nervous sitting on the edge," he offered in what was probably the weakest explanation ever given for wanting to sit so close to a woman. "This okay?"

He didn't wait for her answer before he shifted forward enough her back brushed his chest and his legs hung over the edge on either side of hers. He wanted to rest his hands on her hips, settle her back against him, and press his face into the curve of her throat. He wanted to…but he didn't.

As much as he'd thought about the kisses they'd shared in her trailer, he also thought about how sudden the whole thing had been. Yes, he'd certainly taken notice of how sexy she was…how she captured his attention. How her smile made him smile, and how he enjoyed being the one to make her laugh. He thought about how much he wanted to be this close to her…but wondered if she thought the same thing.

Andi folded her hands in her lap and drew in a long breath, looking out across the open warehouse soundstage. When she finally spoke, her voice was soft and restrained and he had to sit forward to hear her, his cheek brushing her hair as he leaned over her shoulder.

"Ten years ago, I was a new mom spending my days at home alone with an infant…" She trailed off, then laughed softly. A humorless, wry sound. She shook her head. "And a bunch of *people* in my head screaming for attention. They wouldn't leave me alone. Whenever I sat still, for even a minute, I heard dialogue running through my head. I saw scenes play out like on a movie screen. I couldn't take it anymore." She looked down at her hands, worrying the tips of her fingers together. "Two in the morning, I turned on my computer and started writing. And for the next five years, I was reminded what a waste of time the whole thing was."

Whoever he was…husband, or otherwise…he was an idiot. David didn't need to know another fact about him.

"They're amazing books," he said, and she jumped, tipping sideways slightly to look into his face. This time he *did* set his hands on her hips, but only to keep her from losing her balance on the edge of the catwalk. *Wouldn't want her to lose her balance…*"When they offered me the role, I picked up the first in the series." He grinned when her eyebrows arched and her lips fell open…she was surprised. "I read the whole series in six days."

Color bloomed in her cheeks, and made him remember the way she'd flushed in her trailer. The way her breath had hitched. The way her ankles had curled behind his thighs. His attention shifted to her lips, and she ran the tip of her tongue over them before abruptly turning away. David tamped down the need to curl his fingers into the soft cotton of her dress, and swallowed the groan in his throat. She tensed for a moment, straightening her spine to put more distance between them, then to his sweet surprise, she released a long breath and relaxed, easing back into him until her shoulders rested against his chest and her head tipped back to his shoulder.

"I should be ecstatic someone thought my midnight drabbles were worth putting in print, let alone making a movie from them," she said after a few moments of quiet. "If I were smart I'd just—"

"Let your agent do her job and fix the script," he said gently.

Andi turned her face toward him but didn't lift it from his shoulder. Her breath brushed his cheek, and it would take nothing at all to lean in and kiss her. He conceded by sliding his hands from her hips to press gently against her stomach, letting the cotton shift beneath his palms. The sensation was familiar, and his gut tightened with the memory. "It deserves to be done right."

Her small hand moved over his, pressing his palm just a little firmer against her. "Thank you," she said so softly, he might not have known what she said if he hadn't been watching her lips.

Before he could say, "You're welcome," or finally give in to temptation, two voices echoed through the soundstage. From below, the set costume director called to David he needed to change. From behind, Benton stepped out of his office snapping Andi's name. Holding her gaze, David planted a foot on the edge of the catwalk and pushed himself up. He offered his hand, and she took it, letting him pull her to her feet.

Her fingertips skimmed over his palm as her hand dropped away, and she finally shifted her gaze from him to Benton, stepping away to meet him at his office door. The costumer called David's name again, and as he walked past Benton's door he heard the man tell Andi the script doctor had backed down, and she could call off Mags. The scene would be filmed as originally scripted…and originally approved by her.

David smiled and pushed his hands into his pockets as he went down the stairs, knowing the stance was a lame attempt at hiding the effect one Andi Parker had on him.

CHAPTER THREE

"See? I told you I'd fix it."

Andi jumped at Maggie's sudden appearance behind her and twisted in her chair to look at her friend. "I'm sorry I ever doubted you," she said with a grin.

"Damn straight. And don't do it again," Maggie scolded, wagging a less than threatening finger at Andi.

Maggie smiled and came around the chairs, which were positioned at the edge of the sound stage, and boosted herself up into the empty wood-and-canvas chair beside Andi. She hefted herself into the tall seat and mumbled something under her breath about Amazons, and Andi chuckled.

"What's happening here?" Maggie asked with a motion of her hand toward the set.

"Just setting up for the next shot."

They were between takes on a scene and the swing gang was working on resetting some of the props that had been moved during the last take. After taking a few deep breaths and apologizing to Benton for biting his head off, Andi had come down to the set to watch the filming.

"Jake is in your trailer," Maggie provided, shifting again in the tall chair. If she pointed her toes, she could rest them on the crossbar, but she gave up and drew her legs into the wide seat of the chair, sitting Indian style. "So, is this a one, two, or three? I figure it couldn't be a dreaded four, since I *know* you had thought about coming in today for the filming."

Andi laughed, glancing around surreptitiously to see if any of the crew heard Maggie's question. She didn't think anyone would be offended she considered some scenes not worth taking the time to watch—at least in *her* opinion, and *she* wrote them—but she didn't want to explain her scale if she didn't have to.

"No, not a four," she said, clearing her throat slightly. "They're filming some of the fight scenes next week." Fight scenes were mostly choreography and 'faking it' so CGI effects could be added later. Seeing the scenes only half done ruined her delusion, and since writing action scenes hadn't been her favorite, to begin with, she didn't bother coming in to watch the filming.

"Well, not a one. Undomesticated equines couldn't have kept you away."

No, not a one. The designation of 'One' was saved for the special scenes, the scenes near and dear to her heart. In the midst of her action-packed science fiction story arc was a beautiful romance. "One" scenes were those scenes vitally important to part of the story. Like kisses…

Heat spread over her skin, radiating out from a deliciously warm spot in the center of her body. Andi curled some hair behind her ear that had been annoyingly touching her cheek and bounced her crossed leg to help expend some nervous energy.

"Which is it? Two or three?"

"Two," she tried to answer, but her voice caught and she had to clear her throat. "It's a two."

"And you weren't going to come? Dang, maybe you're more chicken than—" Andi's sideways glare made Maggie stop, but her friend still grinned wide with satisfaction she'd once again gotten her 'loving' jab in over David Bishop.

"Oh, shut up." Andi pushed Maggie's shoulder. The tall chair tipped precariously, and both women chuckled as it settled again.

"Death traps," Maggie mumbled. Once settled again, she rested her arms on her knees and gave Andi one of her best 'You're-gonna-tell-me-anyway-so-spill' inquisitive looks. "So…spent some time up on the catwalk with David, huh?"

Andi shook her head, looking away so she didn't have to attempt to face down Maggie's stare. She was like Wonder Woman with a Golden Lasso. It was probably a good thing Maggie had no children, they wouldn't have stood a chance. Ever. She focused instead on the swing gang moving around the set.

The space was set up as a hospital rehabilitation area, where 'Jason' would begin his physical rehabilitation after being held as a prisoner of war by the enemy. His memories were blocked, and he didn't even know the doctor working on his rehabilitation was his wife. In another couple of weeks, they would film the scene in which 'Jason' regained his memories and knew she was his wife. Just as Maggie said, *undomesticated equines* wouldn't keep her from the set day. Today's scene ranked as a two because the chemistry and attraction between 'Jason' and 'Anna' were evident and played on, but until he knew, the scene didn't hold quite enough intensity to rank as a 'one' for her.

"Did he kiss you again?"

"Stop."

"Is a yes or a no?"

"Mags, seriously—"

"If you don't tell me, I'm just going to assume the two of you had hot, sweaty—"

"No," Andi snapped, immediately clamping her jaw shut when several heads turned to look at her. Maggie chuckled in her throat, arching her eyebrows at Andi. With a slow release of breath, Andi pressed her lips together before turning her attention fully to her best friend. *Though, if she kept up this badgering she might lose the ranking of 'best', and quick!* "No, he did not kiss me," she said just barely above a whisper. "He just sat there with me."

Maggie snorted. "Liar. I saw you."

"You didn't *see* anything."

"I saw him practically wrapped around you." Andi started to protest again, but before she could, Maggie lifted her hand. "You know what, stay in your little delusional world where a man couldn't *possibly* want you because *Larry* didn't, and we *all* know Larry Boner was a man all men should be judged against."

Andi shook her head, not even able to let herself grin at Maggie's deliberate mocking of her married name of Bonherre. She uncrossed and crossed her legs in the other direction, bouncing her foot in aggravation. Her sandal dangled off her toes, flapping against the sole of her foot with each bounce.

Mags just didn't understand. Lawrence hadn't warped Andi's self-confidence so much she didn't think *any* man would ever want her. Despite what Maggie said, she had dated a few times since divorcing Lawrence. And she'd had a good time. The men she'd spent time with had been considerate and pleasant, and each one of them had said in one way or another that she was attractive. She didn't flinch when she looked in the mirror. She hadn't predestined herself to a life of chastity, although sometimes it felt like it.

She was just being realistic.

There were men, and then there was *David Bishop*.

David was sexy, and his voice could melt butter. His touch, when he'd touched her the way he had, could bring that same butter to a boil. He'd been voted 'Most Eligible,' 'Hottest,' 'Best Dressed,' and a few other unofficial rankings more times than he probably ever kept track of. He'd been an actor since his early teens and had been considered attached to some of the most beautiful women in Hollywood.

Beautiful young women who weren't divorced, single mothers. Women who didn't argue with unseen characters and curse at the voices in the middle of the night when a scene wouldn't come together. Women who didn't share a house with their agent and best friend, and constantly had to fend off the questions and implications perhaps they were more than just 'friends.'

Andi also wasn't so delusional to believe everything she read in the gossip rags. Just a few weeks earlier, before trailer kisses and heart palpitations, David had been photographed standing outside a Hollywood club with a rail-thin starlet who had recently left a private rehabilitation clinic for alcohol and prescription drug addiction. The magazine implied they were a couple, and postulated whether David was helping her through her addiction…or feeding it.

He had laughed off the article, saying he'd seen her hovering beneath an awning smoking a cigarette, and had stopped to say hello. Years before, they'd done a movie together. Even though he'd joked about it, Andi had seen his easy smile slip away when no one was looking.

The point was he was a man people watched, and things were said about him—true or not. He was a man who could be with anyone.

He didn't want to be with Andrea Parker formerly married to Lawrence Bonherre, Attorney at Law and resident ass.

The extra lights shut off, and all quiet was called on set. Which was fine, because Andi didn't feel like defending herself anymore. She knew Maggie cared, and it was nice to know someone did, but sometimes…

"And *action!*" Benton shouted.

Positioned so he faced them, David sat in a wheelchair staring out into a lush hillside that would be added later. His head was tipped forward as if he'd dozed off in the chair. Just as described in the script, 'Jason' would be taunted with flashes of memory from his captivity. Bits and pieces he couldn't put together.

David jerked, his head coming up to face the artificial sunshine, his features tense. Later, they would film the flashes of torture to be spliced into the scene, but for now, he was acting purely on imagination. His eyes pinched and he tilted his head to the side, a small groan whispering over the soundstage. Andi leaned forward, realizing she was holding her breath as she watched the scene play. He was amazing. It was like he had seen into her mind and knew exactly what she needed, what she'd intended each moment to be.

With a sharper jerk, 'Jason' opened his eye. His fingers curled around the armrests of the wheelchair, his knuckles white, and he swallowed. Raising a shaking hand, he scrubbed at his face and snuffed his nose, wiping away a single tear that had formed on his cheek.

Andi swallowed hard.

If this scene tore at her this badly, what would she do when they grew more intense? When he filmed the scenes that had torn at her chest just to write, let alone play out in three-dimensional reality?

Taylor entered the scene from behind him and played her part perfectly. She saw his tension and moved toward him, the subtle tensing of her features expressing both the love and concern 'Anna' felt for 'Jason'. As much as Andi found Taylor frustrating at times, she was a very good actress. In this type of scene, she did well. It was when the scene was too sexually charged she pushed forward too fast, losing her finesse.

They ran the scene nearly flawlessly, and by the time Benton called "Cut!" Andi's chest hurt from holding her breath so many times and her head swam. They immediately shifted the camera angles and shot the scene again. Although some moments held far more impact the first time they were shot, Andi already saw the way the nuances would be woven together.

It was days like today she felt like a proud mother. She finally sat back and realized nearly an hour and a half had passed during the filming. She sniffed and wiped at the tears dampening her cheeks. Yep, come the big scenes she'd probably be a blubbering mess.

Maggie cleared her throat and hopped down from her chair. "I'm going to check on Jake," she said, her voice rough.

Andi smiled, and despite her friend's constant teasing, she decided to let Maggie's rare show of emotion go without teasing *her*. Instead, she just ran her fingertips over her cheeks.

"Everything okay?"

Andi jumped and squeaked, turning toward David's voice. He stood beside her chair, only proving how high the wood-and-canvas contraptions were because he was at eye level with her. She blushed hot, embarrassed at her scaredy-cat response and the tears on her cheeks.

"Yes," she managed to say, motioning toward the stage that was now dark as they broke for lunch. "You just—it was very good."

He raised his hand and brushed his thumb across her skin, his eyes watching the action, and Andi drew in a slow, metered breath. She fought the urge to close her eyes and turn into his touch. *You're turning into one of your own characters, Andrea! No one does that!*

She laughed nervously instead and leaned back to break the contact, brushing her fingers over her cheeks to dry them. Her cheeks felt hot, even to her, and she wondered just how bright she had to be glowing. "I cry at long-distance phone service commercials, too."

David smiled, a slow turning up of the corners of his mouth. She'd noticed when they sat on the catwalk his whiskers had grown out a little bit, just enough to give 'Jason' a rougher, unkempt look. She liked it. With yet another flash to her cheeks, Andi realized she was staring like a dolt and looked away, clearing her throat. *Any second now…Poof! I'm going up in a puff of smoke.*

David drew in a slow breath through his nostrils and released it again as he folded his arms on the chair. The new position brought him slightly lower than eye level so he had to look up at her. Andi had the urge to hunker down in the seat. She wasn't used to looking down into eyes like those…

"It occurs to me we've done things in the wrong order."

"What things?" she asked. That darn wayward curl brushed her cheek again, and she flipped it back. His gaze shifted to her hand until she lowered it to her lap. When his steel blue eyes came back up, meeting her stare, it took everything she had not to look away. *No matter how nervous you are, look 'em in the eye.* Andi was pretty sure her father meant people who wanted to intimidate her, not men like David who looked at women with the intent of melting their insides.

"Well, when two people meet who are attracted to each other…" He said the words slowly, and Andi's heart thumped at the base of her throat. His smile spread a fraction of an inch, dimpling his cheeks, and she wished she could breathe. "They usually get to know each other before they move on to the…" Those inside-melting eyes slid down to stare at her mouth. "Kissing."

He leaned forward, the chair creaking under the shift of weight, bringing his face closer and more level with hers. But his hands remained tucked under his chest as he leaned over his folded arms.

"I would like to get to know you," he said so low his voice sounded like it came from the bottom of his chest. No lower. More like his pelvis.

Andi barely managed to stifle her groan, and attempted to cover it by clearing her throat as she shifted in the chair. "It's not like we're strangers," she managed to say. "I've been coming here for weeks, and you've been here on the set nearly every time. We've had lunch together—"

"With twenty other people," he interrupted.

"We've talked about the script. We've..." Her brain stalled when he laid one hand over her two where they were clenched tightly in her lap.

"Let me take you to dinner.

Andi bounded out of the chair so quickly he thought it was going to topple over and he made a quick grab to balance her. But she landed gracefully on her feet, grabbed his wrist, and practically marched across the soundstage.

"Where are we going?"

"Just come on."

After a few steps, when she assumed he would follow, Andi dropped his wrist and crossed her arms over her body, walking just a step ahead of him. She walked so fast he had to lengthen his stride just to keep up. The way she held her body tense, her shoulders back and her spine straight, screamed tension.

"Andi..." he called after her, but her pace didn't slow.

She navigated the cables and wires splayed across the floor, hopping over an especially thick bundle, and headed straight for the front corner of the sound stage where the various individual trailers had been settled. Because the soundstage was designed to break down and clean out easily when shooting was over, very little was permanent, including the spaces provided for the talent.

They garnered a couple wayward glances from some of the grips and other stage crew, Andrea Parker marching through the stage like a woman on a mission with David following behind. He just smiled as if nothing odd was going on, but wondered in his head what part of his dinner invitation had caused this kind of reaction. Especially since he wasn't quite sure what 'this kind of reaction' actually was.

Andi reached her trailer, yanked the door open, and immediately the sound of a television or movie met them. She stood on the top step, just short of stepping over the threshold inside. David waited at the bottom of the steps, his hands pushed into his pockets until Andi told him otherwise.

If his mother taught him anything, it was to not question—or interrupt—a woman when she wanted something.

"Hey," he heard Maggie Connelly say from inside. "I just told Jake—"

"Could we have a few minutes?" Andi cut her off. "Across the lot is the full commissary. Maybe you could take Jake to get lunch." It wasn't a suggestion, even David knew that much.

"Um, sure." Maggie looked past Andi and grinned when she saw David. "Sure thing, my dear. Come on, Jake."

Only then did Andi step into the trailer so her agent and son could pass. Maggie grinned like the cat that ate the canary and winked at him as she hopped off the bottom step. Jake didn't do much but give him a quick look before following behind Maggie. A few feet away, he stopped and looked back—his eyes shifting from David to the open trailer door and back to David—before catching up with Maggie.

"Come in, David."

He reached up to grip the inside doorknob, and skipped the first step, using the second to leverage himself into the trailer. As soon as he stepped inside the dim interior, he looked toward the table nestled into the front of the small space. He remembered with taunting clarity the way she'd felt when he kissed her, the way she'd leaned into him, and the way she'd made small sounds against his mouth that drove him insane.

But Andi wasn't at the table this time. Instead, she stood at the other end of what could only loosely be called the 'kitchenette' with her hip leaning against the counter edge and her arms crossed over her body. She wasn't looking at him, or at the floor, but at some undefined point in the corner of the trailer, and her foot bounced nervously making her entire body shift slightly.

David pulled the door shut, and the only source of light inside the trailer was the image playing out on the small television on the counter. It faced the table so anyone sitting there could watch, and right now it played a ten-year-old action movie that seemed to be on television every time he turned it on.

He took a step toward Andi and she immediately leaned backward. It wasn't an actual step away from him, but it was enough to make him stop. There was no confusion in *that* body language. He let his hands drop to his side and looked away, disappointment pushing his shoulders down. "I'm sorry, Andi," he said in a low voice. "If I came on too strong, or misread things—"

She shook her head and snapped her attention to him, cutting him off. "No, see, this isn't a bad romance novel."

He tilted his head and squinted his eyes. "What?"

Then she started talking so fast, it took all his focus to keep up with her. "If this *were* a bad romance novel, then you'd assume I stepped away from you because I didn't want you to touch me. Which would be wrong. I just stepped back because I need to think, and I don't do very well when you're touching me. But, if this were a bad romance novel, you wouldn't know so you'd assume I didn't want anything to do with you, and you'd back off—or leave—or get angry because I 'sent you mixed signals'. And then I'd get upset because that's not what I intended at all, but being TSTL I wouldn't *say* anything, I'd just let you go because I figured that was what you really wanted all along."

He followed most of what she said, but his focus kept lingering on the part where she couldn't think when he touched her. And since all *he* thought about when she touched him was how much more they could touch, he figured in the grand scheme of things whatever point she was getting at was in his favor.

"What's TSTL?" he managed to slide in.

She stuttered, and her eyes locked with his for a moment while fresh color bloomed in her cheeks. "Too stupid to love. It's a heroine who just keeps making mistakes and doing stupid things to drive the hero away, so she's so stupid she shouldn't be loved anyway."

David nodded and took a step toward her. "But, you're not too stupid to love. Because you're not going to let me assume anything."

"Right," she said with a decisive nod, laying her hand against her chest. "And *I'm* not going to assume anything, either. I'm going to ask you what I need to know and that way there won't be any confusion. And I don't have to sit around wondering what's *really* going on, or try to convince myself you're thinking one thing but you're not."

He grinned at the way she could go on for three sentences without seeming to take a breath and wondered if her thoughts always moved so quickly. If so, he was going to have to get some of those brainpower video games just to train his brain to keep up. He tested the waters by taking another small step toward her. She didn't move away, just tilted her chin up so she still looked at him.

"What do you *think* I'm thinking, Andi?"

She shook her head, tiny frown lines appearing between her eyes. "I don't know. That's what I need to find out. Maybe you're not thinking. Maybe you haven't thought about this enough. Because if you *had* been thinking, then you'd realize…" Her voice trailed off, and she drew in a deep, sharp breath that shuddered as she released it.

"That's a lot of thinking."

She nodded, her eyes shifting back and forth in tiny degrees as she looked up at him. "It's driving me crazy."

You're driving me crazy. He smiled at the random thought and took the last step needed to bring them as close as possible without touching. David kept one hand at his side, not wanting to make her shy off again by touching her the way he wanted to, or too soon. The other hand he set on the counter edge near hers, and watching her face for any reaction, he curled a single finger over hers. She didn't pull away.

"What would I realize?" he asked, keeping his voice low and just between them. Behind him, a car chase screeched and crashed on the television.

"What?" she asked this time. After all that talking, *she* was the one who lost track of the conversation.

David smiled again, something he found himself doing often when Andrea Parker was anywhere near him. "You said if I just thought about things, I'd realize…I want to know what it is I'd realize."

"Oh."

The word slipped from her lips at the same moment she must have realized how close he stood because she looked away, the single finger he held slipped from beneath hers so she could cross her arms, and she took a step back. She couldn't go far before hitting a small partition that divided the kitchenette area from the other half of the trailer housing only a small bedroom and an even smaller bathroom.

David stayed put, curling his fingers into his palms. She hadn't moved far, but it was far enough to frustrate him. For all the women he'd dated and the few he'd had long-term relationships with, he'd never felt the *need* to touch them like he did with Andi. He couldn't help it. If she was within reach, he wanted his hands on her. It made his hands itch not to reach for her now.

"I'm a divorced, single mother with an ass of an ex-husband," she finally said, the words practically running together she said them so fast. "I'm older than you."

"By what? A couple of years?" he managed to get in edgewise.

"I'm just a…a…*novelist*," she continued, not missing a beat. "I listen to voices in my head. I don't fit here, I don't—" Andi shook her head. "I'm just—"

David couldn't take it anymore and stopped her with a kiss. He laid his hands against her cheeks and held her still, pressing his lips to hers until she released her breath through her nostrils and it skimmed across his cheeks as the tension eased from her body. Then he lifted his mouth away only far enough and long enough to cover her parted lips again with an open-mouth kiss.

She leaned into him, and the small purring sound that vibrated in her throat shot a bolt of arousal through him. When her tongue met his first, and her delicate hands settled at his waist, just her fingertips slipping beneath his shirt to touch his skin, all pre-conception he would keep this kiss simple, evaporated. He groaned, not caring the sound echoed in the small kitchen alcove, and wrapped one arm around her to haul her against him. He pushed his fingers into her short curls, cupping the back of her head in his hand. The kiss took on a fevered pitch, and he couldn't hold her close enough, couldn't kiss her deep or long enough, couldn't touch enough of Andi to satisfy him.

Her soft gasp snapped him back to reality, and he stopped short, realizing with almost a feeling of dread he'd turned them so her back was to the hallway wall leading to the bedroom, and he pressed her there, trapping her with his body. He eased away enough to let her take a breath, and set his forearms on the wall on either side of her head, still bracketing her to keep her close. David rested his forehead against hers, their heavy pants mingling hot breath between them.

Andi raised a trembling hand to touch his cheek and he turned his mouth into it, kissing her palm as he held it against his lips. Her lips were slick from their kiss, and her pale cheeks were pink from his unshaven whiskers.

"I wasn't going to kiss you," he said between deep breaths, "until we had a real date." She smiled, her eyes focusing on his mouth as he spoke, and he liked the spike of heat her look shot through him. "I think we need to be in public."

The lines between her eyes appeared again and she frowned slightly. David kissed her forehead, holding his lips there until he felt the furrows ease. "Why?" she asked.

"You ask that question a lot," he said against her skin. "Why do we need to be in public?" She nodded against his lips. David shifted his weight so he could look into her eyes as he pressed his hips slightly against her. Her eyes fluttered closed. "Do you need to ask why?"

She raised her chin, looking him straight in the eyes as she took a deep breath. "You really want this? You want to be seen in public with me, where people will take pictures and assume things and write stories and—"

He laid his thumb against her lips, not trusting himself to stop her again with a kiss. Her kisses were gasoline on fire for him. "You're amazing, and I want to know just how amazing. And you're ten kinds of sexy," he said, dropping his voice so low it made her smile; a smile that lit up her face and made her eyes shine, a smile that instantly made him do the same. "I think the better question is why *wouldn't* I want to be with you."

She stared at him for several moments, her eyes shifting again back and forth in tiny movements, and he wished he knew what she was thinking. What she was working out in her mind that went twice as fast as anyone he'd ever known. Finally, she let out a long breath—

something she seemed to do when she'd made a decision—and nodded her head.

"Okay."

He grinned. "Okay. Okay, what?"

"Okay, I'll have dinner with you. But I can't until Thursday night."

"Thursday night. I can wait two days…I think."

He'd be taking a lot of cold showers in the next two days.

CHAPTER FOUR

Andi woke the next morning with the sun spread across her bed, warming her all the way through. She smiled and stretched like a cat, humming as each muscle tingled and then relaxed. Through her open shades, the mountains behind the house stretched out to touch the perfectly blue sky, and not a single cloud broke up the blue.

She'd been up until nearly two in the morning finishing chapter twelve of her current novel, but the words had come fast and furious and the scene had unfolded so clearly and easily that she had drank an entire pot of coffee to keep up with her muse. For weeks she'd struggled with the last two or three chapters. As the love between her characters unfolded, she'd felt the scenes were stiff and forced. None of the zing or chemistry she'd felt when writing her other books seemed to be happening for these two. But, then when she sat down after returning from the studio, she'd figured out what was missing. Once she started, she couldn't stop.

Andi knew she could attempt to delude herself with the idea she was just that good of a writer, but she knew better.

It was because of David.

When he asked her to have dinner with him, her first gut reaction was to say no. Every argument she'd convinced herself of since the first kiss ran through her mind, and with a virtual slap upside the head, she realized she was no better than every annoying, whiney TSTL romance novel heroine she'd ever read about—and tried to avoid writing. She was assuming things…doubting things…without just doing the one thing every reader screamed at their books when they read women like this…"Just *ask* him, for cryin' out loud!"

And hey-howdy-boy, was she glad she did. The man knew how to use his lips. Andi sighed and settled into the warm bed again.

Then she bolted upright, flipping to her knees to crawl across the bed to the side table where her glasses sat beside the alarm clock. She squinted at the time, trying to make it up before actually putting the glasses on, and groaned. With the glasses on, she groaned again.

How did she sleep until ten?

"Crap," she growled, practically tumbling to the floor in her attempt to free herself of the twisted blankets. She was halfway to the bathroom still kicking her foot free of the sheet, pulling her pajama top off over her head.

Shooting was scheduled to begin at eight that morning, and she'd wanted to be there before cameras rolled—just so she could lay her eyes on the script again. Andi may have thrown a fit, and Maggie may have 'worked her magic', but that didn't mean the script doctors wouldn't try to change things again last minute. Even if it were a simple change, something they thought meant nothing in the grand scheme of things, would mean everything to her.

Andi threw the water on in the shower as she finished stripping, and stepped under the spray before she adjusted the temperature, gasping loudly as the too-cold water hit her back. She washed her hair in record time, skipping the 'two to three minutes' instruction on the conditioner as she practically rubbed in and rinsed simultaneously, and was pulling one of her many sundresses over her head by twenty past ten. By 10:25, she'd fluffed her hair as dry as it would go and pushed it off her forehead with a headband, managing only a dusting of mineral powder on her face. She ran down the stairs with her sandals in hand, waved quickly to Jake as he played video games with a shouted promise she'd be home by lunch, and hopped on one foot to get the shoes on before hitting the front door.

Then she came to a dead stop on the 101 thirty minutes later.

By the time she pulled up to the studio security gate, she had a headache and was ready to eat off her left arm. But, she was considerably calmer and resigned to the fact if they *had* filmed the scene wrong —short of throwing a hissy fit in the middle of the soundstage—there was nothing she could do about it. She hadn't ruled the hissy fit out, but she decided to keep it in reserve until she knew.

Today, when she parked her hybrid she kept it to one space, in a straight line, and left it calmly. She checked the time and knew she'd have to call Jake soon since there was no way she'd make it home by noon. Even with lightning speed, she wasn't getting back to the valley in fifteen minutes. *Stupid traffic.* Since when was there heavy traffic at eleven in the morning?

The interior of the studio was fairly quiet, which either meant they were filming or they'd broken for lunch.

She took a right past the 'hospital' stage, heading to the back of the studio where the alien ship stages had been built. They were more formidable and permanent structures than some of the other stages, and the schedule had some of the torture scenes shot today. Just the thought of seeing those particular images live and in full, human color made her stomach twist. It had been bad enough writing the scenes with them playing in her mind. She wasn't sure she could even watch when the film was done.

Andi reached the alien ship, and except for a handful of set guys moving a few things around, it was quiet. *Lunch.* In the same moment, she was again annoyed with herself for sleeping too late, she was relieved she hadn't had to watch any of the filming.

She stepped over some cables and crouched down to pick up a rolled and creased copy of several script pages from the floor. That someone left the script lying around surprised her. Benton guarded copies of the script like a mama bear with her cubs. After David signed on for the film production, a lot of buzz had stirred up interest in the screenplay, and sales of the book had skyrocketed. Andi's royalties hadn't been anything to sneeze at before, but after the announcement of the main cast, Maggie had taken great pleasure in telling her how sales had increased. With the media rush, copies of the daily scripts were like chunks of gold.

So to have one left behind made the back of her neck tingle.

Andi unfurled the curled paper and scanned the stage directions and lines. She read through page six before some of the tension in her shoulders eased. The script—at least *this* copy—was the right script. The right scene—not the sexed-up, gratuitous scene the script doctors thought would 'sell' better.

She released a long breath, letting the tightness go along with the knot in her stomach she'd had since yesterday morning. Even though Benton had promised, and Maggie had assured her, she didn't believe it until she saw the proof.

Andi rolled the script again and tucked it in her purse with the intent of giving it to Benton on her way out. "Hey, Jimmy," she called to one of the familiar faces working on the set. He was mopping at the concrete floor around the 'chair' that would have held Jason while he was tortured.

He looked up, hearing her over the buds in his ears, and smiled, pulling the buds free as he leaned on the mop handle. "Hey, Ms. Parker. I didn't see you. Sorry," he said with just the slightest of Puerto Rican accents. He grinned wide, his white teeth a sharp contrast against his black mustache.

"It's okay. Do you know where Benton is?"

"Probably still at the first aid center."

"First aid center?" Her attention dropped to the floor as Jimmy lifted his mop into the yellow bucket tucked behind the chair. The cotton strands had a slight pink hue, and then she noticed Jimmy wore latex gloves…a common practice when dealing with…*blood*?

"Is Benton hurt?" Andi stepped over more cables and wires to move closer to Jimmy but stopped short where the darker cement told her the floor was wet. "What happened?"

"Nah, not Benton. It was Mr. Bishop," he said with a jerk of his chin toward the chair. "They took him to first aid about forty minutes ago, or so."

"What happened?" she asked again, her heart pounding so hard in her chest she had to press her hand to her breastbone. "Jimmy, what happened?"

"I didn't see, just got sent to clean it up. But Eddie told me it was real nasty."

"Oh, god…" she whispered, covering her mouth. "Is he still at first aid?"

Jimmy shrugged. "Dunno."

Before he finished answering, Andi spun around and nearly tripped over the pile of cables in her rush. The thump/slap of her sandals echoed through the sound stage as she ran for the door. The first aid office was on the other side of the lot, too close to drive but a good run. By the time she reached the wooden steps leading into the small trailer that served as first aid, she was out of breath. She stumbled inside, the cool air-conditioned air hitting her in the face.

"Are you hurt, ma'am?" a young man dressed in the recognizable light blue shirt of the medical staff asked as he rose from his chair behind a metal desk just inside the door.

"I'm looking for David Bishop," she huffed, quickly regaining her breath in the cooler air. "I was told he was brought here."

"Your name, ma'am?"

"Andi Parker."

The man's eyebrows rose and he grinned. "Of course," he said, nodding his head. "Yes, ma'am. He's in the back."

"How badly is he hurt?" She knew it couldn't be too awful, or they would have taken him to the nearest hospital especially since David was the lead. They'd take no chances if there were any risks.

"He'll be fine, ma'am," he said, taking an almost military stance with his hands tucked behind his back. He smiled a lopsided grin that made him look even younger. He smiled wider. "Just through those doors, ma'am. He's in the last room on your left. Mr. Benton is there with him."

The hallway was quiet, and Andi spared a glance at the young man before she continued. He smiled and raised a hand in an abbreviated wave before sitting down again. Andi pressed her lips together and reached the last door. She leaned toward it for a few seconds, listening to whatever sound might be coming from inside. When she heard nothing, she slowly turned the knob and eased the door open.

First, she saw Benton slouched down in one of the plastic and metal chairs provided in every medical center she'd ever been in with his forehead supported in his hand. His eyes were closed and his face shaded by his ever-present baseball cap with his too-long hair curling out from the rim. As she pushed the door open, he looked up. When he saw her, he sat up and held his finger to his lips.

Andi nodded, pushing the door further open until she saw the narrow bed squeezed into the small room and David's prone form. The bed was too short so his feet hung off the bottom, but his head was inclined slightly and his face was hidden by an ice pack covering his eyes and the bridge of his nose. His shirt was dirty and torn, and dark spots of blood covered the front. Andi winced and tried to console herself with the idea that not *all* the blood was *his*. After all, they'd been filming a torture scene so for the sake of make-up, he would have had fake blood applied to his clothes and his face.

His hands rested loosely in his lap, and each breath rasped through him like a muffled snore, probably from the swelling the ice pack attempted to decrease.

"Is he all right?" she mouthed, barely whispering.

Benton eased from his chair, wincing when the plastic squeaked beneath his movement, and stepped lightly to the door. He motioned her into the hall, and she followed but left the door open so she could see David.

"He'll be fine. Nothing serious," Benton whispered, taking his cap off to run fingers through his flattened hair. "It was a stupid accident."

"What happened?"

Benton huffed and shook his head. "We had him strapped in the chair and had already done several shots and angle retakes. Ellen was mid-scene, crossing the stage to her mark and she tripped on a cable. She fell forward and her elbow went right into David's face. He couldn't do a damn thing to stop it."

Andi felt sick, the image playing out in her mind with vivid clarity. She pressed her hands against her stomach, the hunger of minutes before now replaced with a tight knot. "Did she break his nose?"

Benton shook his head. "No. It just bled. A lot. And hurt like hell. Damn it, Andi, it's a good thing you weren't here. He was yelling and bleeding, and we couldn't get the damn straps off him." He set his hands at his waist and looked down, huffing a sharp breath.

She laid a hand on Benton's arm, rubbing it in a meager attempt at making him feel better for something he had no control over, but felt badly about all the same. Even offering Benton her support, her attention was on David lying still on the cot. It took Benton's voice a few seconds to break through her focus, and she blinked turning to him.

"—managed to get him to sleep. He was…" Benton chuckled. "I don't even know how to explain what he was."

"What?" she asked, trying again to catch up on the conversation.

"The medics said it wasn't broken, so they didn't want to give him more than Tylenol, but I guess one of the guys thought they'd 'help him out' and gave him some super pain killer they *had from before*, so they said. He just swallowed what was handed to him, and probably didn't even realize it wasn't a medic giving it to him. They confessed to it when he started acting…off." Benton grinned. "He was a very happy guy, and he just kept asking for one thing."

"What?"

"You."

Andi stared at Benton, wide-eyed. She blinked several times and her cheeks flushed with heat, the capacity to deny or even act surprised completely lost to her. He didn't push, just kept smiling as he looked into the room.

"Anyway, it took a while but he fell asleep a bit ago. They said he might sleep for a while, and when he wakes up he can go home."

"Why didn't you take him to the hospital?"

"He didn't want to go. When he was calm enough to understand what the medics said—it wasn't broken—he said no. Said he didn't want to dump blood in the shark tank, or something like that. He was getting…weird…by that point."

"He didn't want the paparazzi to find out," Andi offered.

Benton huffed, the seriousness returning to his face. "We're going to have to revamp the filming schedule. He may not have broken it, but he's going to look like hell for a week or so. Probably too much to cover with make-up *even* for the torture stuff."

"What does this mean for the wrap-up?"

"I don't think we'll be far off the mark for the final cut. We're just shuffling around, and he gets a vacation."

Andi nodded, taking a step back into the room. Since the creation of this movie was a dream come true, and every author she'd ever known would have given their eyeteeth for the chance to see their novels on the big screen, she knew she probably should feel some sort of panic or concern for the final outcome. But, right then, she didn't care. It would happen, Benton would see to it.

David was more important.

"Hey, you mind if I go get a coffee or something?" Benton asked behind her. "You okay here with him?"

"Go ahead," she said absently.

"You want anything?"

"Um, yeah." She glanced back at him briefly. "Whatever is left. Muffin. Sandwich. I haven't eaten yet."

He nodded and left down the hall, his heavier boots echoing in the small space. As soon as he passed the young man at the desk, Andi slipped into the room and closed the door behind her. She moved to the head of the bed and sat in another one of the uncomfortable plastic chairs provided in the room so she was level with David's head. From beneath the edge of the ice pack, she saw the traces of dried blood on his cheeks and mottled swelling below his eye.

"Oh, you poor thing," she said softly and gingerly touched the hair falling over his forehead. It was stiff and disheveled and she frowned. How was she supposed to tell what was from makeup and what was real?

His body jerked slightly and he moaned, and she winced because she knew she'd wakened him. He turned his head toward her and groaned again, this time louder and clearly in discomfort. David raised his hand to catch the ice pack as it slid off his face, and Andi reached at the same time. His fingers covered hers and with her hand held by his, he lowered the ice pack and blinked slowly.

Dark shadows had already formed beneath his eyes and his face was swollen from the outer edge of each eye across the bridge of his nose. Flaking blood still sprinkled his upper lip and cheek, and his eyelids looked heavy as he focused on her.

"Hey..." He drew the word out, sounding like his own tongue didn't want to cooperate and he had a stuffy nose. His eyelids blinked slowly. "Hey, sweetheart."

Andi smiled and touched his hair, a warm glow spreading through her chest at his half-sleeping endearment. He probably wouldn't even remember later. "Hey, yourself." He tried to roll toward her but she pushed her palm to his chest. "No. Just lay there."

"I missed you," he said with all seriousness, frowning.

"You just saw me yesterday."

His hand curled over hers, the ice pack forgotten as it fell to the floor, and he settled back onto the pillow facing her. "Do you like being called Andi?" he asked, his words slightly slurred. "Because Andrea is a f-f-f-erry pretty name."

"Let's not worry about my name right now, David. Okay? You need to rest for a little bit."

"I broke my face," he said with a chuckle and a grin, pointing at his face.

She grinned wider, doing her best to suppress the chuckle threatening to escape her chest. Andi pressed her lips together and swallowed before attempting to talk. "You didn't break it, but I think it's going to hurt for a while."

"You're beautiful."

She couldn't keep up with his jumps and wondered if his brain was on high speed while his mouth was in slow motion. "Thank you."

"No, I mean it," he said adamantly, nodding his head. She knew it had to hurt, but perhaps he had enough painkiller in him that he didn't care. "You're beautiful, Andi. Really really beautiful."

He tried to sit up, but she pushed on his chest again. "I know you mean it. Thank you."

He smiled wide and dropped back onto the pillow again. "Okay."

The door opened and Benton stepped back inside, a coffee in each hand with a sandwich balanced on the top of one and a muffin balanced on the other.

"Benton!" David shouted enthusiastically, curling up off the bed. "Aaaaaouwww," he groaned and fell back again, squeezing his eyes shut. "Andi's here, Benton."

Benton arched his eyebrows, handing the coffee and muffin to Andi. "Awake, I see."

"My fault," she admitted softly, taking a sip of the coffee.

"Isn't she beautiful, Benton?" David snagged her hand as she set the muffin aside, bringing it to his lips. He kissed the back of her hand and set it on his chest, closing his eyes with a smile. "And sexy. Ten kinds of sexy…"

His voice trailed off, and Andi hoped he might slip back into sleep before anything else came out of his unhindered lips. She glanced at Benton, who just watched her with curious eyes. Andi smiled small and shrugged. "Loopy. I think that's a good word for it."

Benton hummed an unconvinced "Um hum," and took up his original seat.

"Andi…" David's voice was almost gone now, lost to sleep.

She leaned closer and touched his cheek with the back of her fingers, then caught Benton watching her and rested her hand on David's shoulder instead. "Get some more sleep, David."

"I like kissing you."

He drew in a long, deep breath and slipped back into sleep. Andi didn't look at Benton, just eased back into her chair and finished unwrapping the muffin. After a few minutes, Benton cleared his throat and set his coffee cup down on the floor by his feet.

"Interesting…"

"Not a word," she said sharply, not looking up.

David had woken with enough hangover headaches to know *this* was not a hangover headache.

His face hurt. Not just hurt. It throbbed in rhythm with his heartbeat. His eyes felt like hard marbles that had been dropped into his eye sockets, and his head was a bowling ball. Everything felt heavy, yet disconnected.

He tried to blink his eyes open and realized something cold and heavy sat on his face. With a painful flash of memory that shot a spike through the back of his eyes, he remembered.

He'd been strapped to that damn chair, and they'd run the same scene what felt like a dozen times to change angles and line delivery. He was ready to eat, and fought the urge to give Andi a call. He knew he would see her the next night, and had her number to confirm her address and when he'd pick her up, but he wanted to talk to her. And they had to do the scene 'one more time.'

Ellen Rothschild—playing the part of the psychotic alien enemy who took a sadistic pleasure in torturing 'Jason'—crossed the set toward him, delivering her lines with a perfect mix of sexy-sick and evil. Then she'd stumbled, and he'd instinctively tried to raise his arms and catch her, but the damn wrist straps held him in place.

Then the pain. Black and red blinding pain.

From there, things were fuzzy and the details he *did* remember, he hoped he would eventually forget, especially the pain and the drowning effect of being trapped in the damn chair.

"No, our plans haven't changed, honey."

The soft voice he recognized immediately as Andi pushed through the throbbing pain, and David pulled the ice pack from his eyes. As he looked around the small room where he was lying, he remembered more details. Of the medic giving him something for the pain, and then someone else handing him more, and of drifting into sleep…and waking with Andi sitting beside him.

"A friend of mine got hurt today and I'm staying here until I know he's okay."

David blinked and tried to focus on her form standing just through the door into the hallway. The room was dark, with a small light over a sink in the corner the only source of light. It illuminated her silhouette, accentuating every curve as she stood sideways. She wore another one of her simple sundresses that tapered around her curves and hung beautifully over her hips, always ending just shy of her knees. This one was a dark color with a small white design and the straps met behind her head leaving her shoulders and upper back exposed. Focusing on her too long made his head pound worse. He groaned and let his head fall back on the pillow.

Beneath the shade of his hand over his eyes, he saw her look at him, her features pulled tight with concern. When their gazes met, she smiled and raised her hand in a small wave. Something pleasant stirred in his gut, temporarily negating the pounding behind his eyes.

"Do you remember when Kevin accidently hit you in the face with the basketball?" She paused, nodding. "Well, it was something like that." She smiled. "I'll be home in time to pick you up. We won't be late. I promise."

Andi came back into the room, closing the door until only a sliver of light shined through the space, giving her enough light to cross to the bed. Andi laid her free hand on his shoulder and smiled down at him, still talking into the phone.

"Okay, honey. I love you." She smiled. "Okay, I'll tell him."

She folded the phone closed and set it down on something he couldn't quite see, and didn't want to move enough to try. Gentle fingers brushed over his forehead and a fuzzy memory of that same touch filtered through the drug haze. Whatever it was they gave him had messed with his head. He wanted to find out to make sure *no one* ever gave it to him again.

"Hey." Her voice was softer than when she'd been on the phone. She smiled. "I wondered when you were going to wake up."

David stared up at her, blinking slowly. Fragments fell together a little more, and he remembered asking for her. That was some time after the painkillers kicked in. Then he remembered seeing her, and the bloom of color in her cheeks when he told her she was beautiful.

"If I'd known how much my head would hurt, I wouldn't have."

She took the ice pack from where he'd set it on his chest and tossed it into a nearby chair. "They say you can take some ibuprofen, but probably not any more of whatever someone gave you. Your nose isn't broken, but you're going to be sore for a couple of days."

He watched her lips while she talked, but something still wasn't firing right because it was like watching an old movie where the soundtrack was off just half a second. The sound and action didn't line up right.

"Jake said, and I quote 'Oh, man! Sucks to be him!'" She pulled a face and lowered her voice, imitating a kid. It took David's brain a second to register and remember Jake was her son. "Oh, and he hopes you feel better soon because his face hurt for three days when he got hit in the nose."

"Great."

She smiled again, her fingertips smoothing along his forehead and temple. He felt himself slipping into sleep again and forced his eyes open. "What time is it?"

"Um…" She looked around the room, and not seeing a clock, picked up her cell phone again. "Almost three."

David groaned and rolled forward slowly until he could sit with his legs on either side of the narrow cot. "We lost nearly the whole day."

Her hand skimmed along the back of his shoulders, just touching the back of his neck. He knew it was meant as a touch of comfort, but it still made his nerves tingle. "Don't worry about it. Benton is rearranging the shooting schedule for the next few days until you can come back."

"Is it that bad?"

She arched a single eyebrow and did a terrible job of disguising the truth in her expression. David laughed and tried to smile, but the throbbing took up most of his face and killed his chuckle, turning it into another groan.

"Oh, don't laugh," Andi said with a slight laugh in her voice. "Come on. I'll take you home."

He started to argue he could get himself home, but as soon as he tried to stand, he knew better. The room tilted just enough to have him reaching for the wall, and silently accepting Andi's support when she moved to his side. He wrapped his arm across her shoulders, closing his eyes against the tilting floor. Okay, so he probably *couldn't* get himself home.

She helped him to her SUV, but they couldn't avoid being stopped along the way by several crewmembers wanting to wish him well. The sun hurt his head, and he wished for his sunglasses. Just as they reached her vehicle, Benton's voice carried across the lot, calling their names.

Andi gave Benton a cursory look over her shoulder but didn't pause as she opened the passenger door. Her hands touched his side and his back as she helped him inside. David didn't know what was worse, the way the pounding shifted when he moved different ways or the lethargic, lead-weights-on-his-limbs feeling he couldn't seem to shake.

Benton jogged up to them, stopping when he reached the open car door. David rested his head on the back of the seat, closing his eyes. When Andi's hand touched his thigh, he wrapped his fingers around hers and held her there.

"I was just heading back over to see if you were awake," Benton said, slightly out of breath from the short run.

"Kinda wish I weren't," David mumbled.

"Ellen wanted me to tell you she's sorry. She's pretty damn embarrassed by the whole thing. Frankly, I think she's afraid you'll sue or something."

David shook his head. "Tell her I'm fine. It was an accident."

"Okay." Benton patted David's shoulder. "Take it easy. Don't worry about us here." He took his hand away, and David heard the scratch of his shoe soles as he turned away. "Oh, watch it leaving. Word has already gotten around. The paparazzi smell blood…literally."

David groaned and felt the slight tensing of Andi's hand beneath his.

"I'll slouch, and her windows are tinted. They'll think I'm still inside."

Her hand relaxed and she slipped it free to step away. The door closed and he managed to slide his seatbelt across his chest before she got in. He felt like he'd run a marathon, and yawned…until his facial muscles pulled and he groaned. Andi opened one of the storage bins in the console and took out a pair of dark sunglasses, holding them out to him.

"Thank you," he said, taking them. He slipped them on and the pain eased slightly.

They made it off the lot with barely a glance from the dozen or so photographers camped outside the gate. David slouched down a little and kept his face turned away, but no one gave the SUV a second look. Andi released a slow breath when they cleared the crowd.

The actual drive to his house was more blur than clarity as the remaining grip of the painkiller pulled him back into sleep while they sat on the 101. He vaguely caught Andi mumbling something about the absurdity of traffic this time of the day as he rested his eyes behind his sunglasses, but his brain couldn't engage enough to let him be involved in any kind of conversation yet.

If it weren't for the blood on his shirt, the throbbing in his face, and the muddled state of his brain, he might be thrilled at the idea of having Andrea Parker in his home.

Her laughter pulled him from his meandering thoughts and he opened a single eye. She shook her head and glanced at him, focusing on the road again.

"I think whatever they gave you must be some kind of truth serum for you."

David chuckled and groaned simultaneously and shifted in the deep seat of her SUV so he could see her. "Did I say something funny?"

"When? Now or earlier?" She smiled, and he focused on the dimple in her left cheek and the way the frames of her glasses accentuated her cheekbones. He meant to answer, but the words didn't make it to his mouth. *Great. When I don't want to talk, I do…and when I want to, I can't get things to line up.* "Just now you said something about throbbing and being alone with me."

"Well, I can see how that might be…misinterpreted."

She laughed, and he smiled at the sound of it even though it hurt. He hoped the ibuprofen he took before they left the lot would kick in soon because it was damn hard not to smile with Andi around.

"What else did I say? Earlier…" He shifted again and cleared his throat. "I think I remember asking for you. Did they call you or something?"

"No," she said, keeping her eyes on the car in front of them as she shook her head. "I went to the set to make sure no one had futzed with the script again. Someone told me you were hurt…"

Her features tightened and her lips turned down in a small frown.

David reached out to take her right hand off the steering wheel and kissed her knuckles before settling their hands on the console between them.

She took a deep breath, releasing it with a small shutter. The smile returned, along with a slight bloom of color in her cheeks as she glanced at him. "I don't know if I should be angry with you."

David raised his eyebrows. "Oh? This should be good."

"You told Benton you like kissing me."

Then David laughed, unable to hold back even for the pain.

"I don't think I should leave you alone."

By the time they reached David's home on Mulholland, he seemed to be more aware and moving better, but the discomfort was as clear on his face as the dark bruises beneath his eyes. He gave her the gate code for his property without looking like it befuddled his mind too much, and she drove up the curved driveway to the house. He climbed out of the SUV on his own, and as she came around to him, he took her hand leading her to the front door of the mid-century refurbished home overlooking Los Angeles. At first, she was confused by the house because when she drove up, she only saw one level like an ordinary ranch. He briefly explained the house extended *downward* instead of up, built into the side of the hill. It was very modern looking with multiple levels and lots of glass, but for an actor of David's caliber, it seemed modest.

"Didn't I hear you say to your son you wouldn't be late?"

Andi nodded. "His birthday is next week, and I promised him a trip to a local fun park to get information on having a party there. They have go-carts and miniature golf and bowling. We're going tonight to check it out."

They reached his front door and he took keys from his pocket, wincing as he bent over to unlock the door. Andi took them from him and slid into the space between him and the door to unlock it. David leaned against the wall, his head bending forward so his lips brushed her bare shoulder.

"I'll be fine," he said, and when he spoke his voice hummed against her skin. "You can't break a promise to your kid."

She turned her head to look at him, but his eyes were closed and his mouth hovered just over her skin. The lock clicked and she pushed open the door. Taking her hand, he led her inside and stopped just inside the door to disarm his alarm. The interior of the house was just as she imagined it would be from the outside with a mid-century modern flare. Lots of windows let the late afternoon sun come in and reflect off the pale bamboo floors. Wood accents were light, and across the open floor plan, she could see through multiple patio doors on the far side of the room looking out over the hills. It was clean, modern, and breathtaking.

"Can I make you something before I go? Something to eat? A drink?"

He shook his head and turned to face her, raising his hands to lay his palms on her cheeks. "No, I'm fine. I'm going to take some more Tylenol, take a shower now that I can stand without tipping sideways..." He grinned, but only a little. "And then probably go to bed."

"Can I call you in the morning to check on you?"

He touched a gentle kiss to the end of her nose. "I'd like that."

Then he wrapped his arms around her and held her close, his fingers lingering on the exposed skin above her dress back. His lips brushed her shoulder, and as he raised his head, he touched his mouth to her neck and cheek the same way. He chuckled softly, his breath warm on her skin.

"I've thought about you being here," he said, his voice rough and gravelly, sending a shiver up her spine. "And the first time I get you in my home, my face hurts too much to kiss you."

Andi pulled back and looked up at him, gently touching his swollen cheek, barely enough to make contact to make sure she didn't hurt him. Then she toed up and carefully kissed his lips. "Next time." His hands curled into the fabric of her dress where they rested at her waist. "But, I think we should put off dinner tomorrow night." He started to protest but she touched his lips. "Why don't we see about Friday?"

"Friday. I can wait until Friday."

She smiled and touched his lips again with the softest kiss she could manage.

CHAPTER FIVE

"What are you wearing?"

Andi laughed and shook her head. "Have you been taking something stronger than Tylenol again?"

His chuckle carried through the speakers on her phone, filling her office. Her fingers paused over the keys of her computer, waiting for his answer. She tilted her head toward the phone, a habitual action after talking to him like this for the last fifteen minutes.

"I'm serious. I bet you a hundred dollars you're wearing a sundress."

"No bet," she said, shaking her head as she looked down at the dress she wore. "Apparently I need to change my wardrobe."

"No, no, no," he said quickly, the sound of fabric on fabric whispering behind his adamancy. "You drive me crazy in those dresses. So, is it one I've seen?"

Andi stared down at the yellow cotton fabric, at the tiny flowers scattered over it and the row of buttons from neckline to hem, and smiled at the flash of warmth that started in her cheeks and moved to her toes. "Yes, you've seen it."

There was a pause, and she heard the small sound of a thoughtful hum carry through the speaker. "When did I see it?"

Andi pulled her lower lip through her teeth, smiling as she wondered just how bold she dared be. She turned in her chair, the well-used mechanisms squeaking slightly, and laid her arms on the desk by the phone, resting her chin on her folded hands. "About a week ago."

He groaned softly before asking, "Is it the yellow one you wore when I came to your trailer?"

Andi pulled her lower lip through her teeth. "Yes."

"Damn..." he huffed, and she smiled until her cheeks hurt.

She pushed back from the phone again and returned to her keyboard. Until they hung up, Andi knew *writing* anything was pointless, her attention drifted to him far too easily. But, she opened her email with a few taps of the keys.

"Hey..." he said, and she again heard the rustle of fabric. Early in their conversation, when she'd asked him if he was resting, he'd told her he was resting so well he was still in bed. "Are you on your computer now?

"Yes, I'm in my office."

"Do you have video chat?"

Andi gasped, attempting to sound shocked. "David Bishop. What kind of woman do you think I am?" She paused just for a moment. "Of course, I have video chat." She smiled when she heard his laugh. Andi had smiled and laughed more in the last week than she probably did in the last six months. "I'm on a Mac."

"Once you go Mac—" he started.

"—You never go back," she finished, and he laughed again.

"Hang on a second." She heard more rustling and the familiar twittering music of a Mac system being turned on.

She already knew where he was going, confirmed the program she had, and gave him her screen ID as she opened the program. For a few moments, all she heard was the tap of keys through the speakers, matching her own. "Okay, I see you. I'm hanging up."

He hung up the phone and she reached over to disconnect. Before shifting back in front of the computer, Andi smoothed a suddenly trembling hand over her hair—which was, as usual, curled around her cheeks whichever way it pleased—and ran her hand down the front of her dress. Seconds later, the video call program chimed indicating someone wanted to talk, and Andi engaged the program.

"Hang on," she said, moving her mouse. "I'm turning on the camera."

When his image came on screen, Andi had all she could do not to gasp and knew her face had to have suddenly burst into flames. A pleasant tumbling tickled her stomach. David was reclined on a bed, which he had told her he hadn't strayed far from his bedroom since she dropped him off the night before, with a pile of white pillows stacked behind him to lean back on. If she had to guess, she thought the laptop he used probably sat on some kind of tray on the bed because the angle was wrong for it to be on the duvet.

David took her breath away. She only saw him from the waist up, but what she saw was bare. His body curled slightly because of the angle he reclined, but it only managed to accentuate the definition of his abdomen and chest. He leaned on one arm, the position making his upper arm muscles tense to his shoulders. A shadow of whiskers sprinkled his jaw and cheeks, and his hair was ruffled in a sexy, lying-in-bed-with-you-all-day kind of way.

"Hey, sweetheart," he said with a wide smile. As he leaned a little closer to the screen, she saw the dark bruising under his eyes but the swelling had gone away and he looked much better than when she dropped him off the night before. He ran a hand over his haphazard hair. "Sorry. Wasn't expecting company."

"Neither was I."

Andi hoped the fan in her iMac worked well enough to keep it cool because she was pretty positive her face alone threw off enough heat to melt its processors.

"I love that dress," he said with a slow tilt of his lips. His eyes shifted down as he looked her over, and he drew in a long breath. "Damn, Woman, you're beautiful."

Andi smiled and looked down, noting the slight tremble in her hands. She knew he couldn't see them, but she dropped them into her lap anyway.

"You look good." She cleared her throat and pointed toward the screen. "I mean, your…you don't look like it hurts quite so much."

He touched the dark spot beneath his left eye, wincing only slightly. "It doesn't hurt to smile anymore." David winked at the screen and leaned closer. "Probably wouldn't hurt to kiss you now."

The office door opened behind Andi. "So, what're we doing for dinner tonight?" Maggie was already saying before she entered the room but stopped one step in with her hand on the knob. "Well, well. This is a new twist on Internet porn."

"Maggie!" Andi gasped.

David just laughed and fell back on his pillows. But he made no move to cover himself and didn't look the least bit apologetic. In fact, he raised a hand and wagged his fingers at Maggie in hello.

"So, you wanna hang up from your webcam boyfriend here and help me figure out what's for dinner? Since you're not going out…" she led, arching her eyebrows.

"No, not tonight." Andi looked to David. "Are you sure you'll be up to it by tomorrow night?"

David rolled forward again, bringing his face close to the screen again, and he smiled his most devastating, stomach-flipping grin. "Sweetheart, *trust* me. I'm up for it."

Maggie snorted and turned to leave, saying over her shoulder. "I'll be downstairs when you're…" She cleared her throat. "*Done.*"

"I'm sorry," Andi said softly.

"For what? She's a riot. Do you have to go?"

"Soon, yeah. Maggie doesn't know it but I already have dinner in the oven. She'll smell it when she gets downstairs."

David's brows pulled down over his eyes, his smile relaxing, and she could almost see the wheels turning. She could wait and see if he asked the inevitable question, or she could let him off the hook. Not being one to let someone dangle, she smiled and leaned slightly closer to the screen.

"Yes, we live together. She's my best friend. Maggie was my agent first, over seven years ago, and then she was my friend."

"I didn't think—"

"Maybe not, but given enough time, you would have. It's okay. We're used to it by now. Two women and a kid sharing a mortgage in California, it's a fairly easy assumption."

David chuckled, but it lacked any real humor. He settled back on the pillows so she saw his profile, and the tight pull around his eyes reminded her of the day the tabloids had reported on his tryst with the skinny, drug-abusing starlet. Andi pushed her keyboard forward so it tucked beneath the twenty-seven-inch screen and rested her arms on the desk so she could lean in closer, staying mindful of the location of the camera so he saw *her*, and not the top of her head.

"What is it?"

David shook his head, faking a smile. "Nothing." He flipped onto his side, making the laptop bounce wherever it rested so he looked like he was in some faked, cheap television earthquake. He set his arm on the bed and rested his temple against his fist. "How early can I pick you up? Dawn?"

Andi tilted her head and pressed her lips together. "David…what is it?"

He looked away for a moment, to the sliding doors and balcony she could see in the background. When his eyes returned to the screen, he didn't look as tense but his eyes didn't spark quite like they had minutes before. "People and their assumptions. I guess no one is immune."

She hadn't said anything, because she knew he'd probably seen everything already, but he was right. The local news had reported that morning David Bishop had been seriously injured on the set of his new movie, and the speculation as to how the injury had incurred ranged from studio error to getting into a fistfight with a jilted lover. They'd implied questions about his sexuality when 'a studio insider' reported he'd been asking for someone named 'Andy' while being treated.

"You mean the tabloids?"

"Yeah, and on entertainment news and anywhere else someone can make up a story and throw it out for public consumption."

"I'm sorry," she said softly.

His steel blue eyes focused on the screen. It was hard communicating like this because even when you were looking into the eyes of the person on the screen, you weren't necessarily actually 'meeting' their eyes. But, David managed to do it. Andi held her breath.

"Don't," he said with a sharp shake of his head. "It comes with the territory."

"People making up things about you? I don't care what you do, no one should have the right to do that."

Andi swallowed and tried to keep her thoughts from slipping into her expression. It wasn't the first time the thought had crossed her mind about the ramifications if the two of them were connected. She waged a war in her head every time—going between worries of what might be said about a celebrity like David Bishop being associated with a Hollywood Nobody like her, and then firmly telling herself to get over it. It wasn't like she had leprosy or something. She wasn't going to say no to spending time with him because of what might or might not be said, but she didn't know if she had thick enough skin to listen to it all.

He shrugged the shoulder he wasn't leaning on. "It happens. Next week, it'll be something else. Most of the time, I just laugh it off."

Maggie's voice carried up through the house, shouting the "oven was dinging." Andi smiled, and shouted back "I'll be right down!" She sighed as she looked at him again. "I really do have to go now."

"You didn't answer my question."

"What question was that?"

"How early can I pick you up?"

She pressed her lips together as she thought about her itinerary for the next day. With the filming schedule shuffled, she wouldn't need to be at the studio until after David returned to filming. All the 'one' and 'two' scenes involved him. Regardless, Jake's birthday was approaching along with the start of school, and tomorrow was to be a shopping day for them.

"I'm taking Jake shopping. We probably won't leave the house until ten, or so, and I don't know when we'll be home." She forced a frown. "I don't think I can guarantee being ready until at least five."

"Then I'll be there at five."

"You got someplace to be?" she asked, arching her eyebrows.

"Just with you," he winked. "The more time I have, the better." He leaned a little closer to the computer, giving her the classic David

Bishop Melt-Your-Insides-Like-Butter grin. "I made myself a promise, remember?"

"What promise?"

His gaze tipped down slightly, and she had the intense sensation he was staring at her lips, wherever they appeared on his screen. "That I wouldn't kiss you again until we had a real date."

Maggie shouted again from downstairs.

Andi pressed her left hand against her lower stomach, intensely aware of the warm fluttering his promise—and that look—created, and knew her cheeks had to be flushed. "I've got to go. Promise me you'll get some rest," she said as she pushed back from her desk.

He rolled onto his back again, supported by the pile of pillows. "Trust me, sweetheart. I'm not doing anything that risks tomorrow night."

She saw him reach out his hand toward his computer as she disconnected the call.

It was well after nine before Andi made it back into her office. She wanted to finish the next chapter to get back on track to meet her deadline. The writing spurt of two nights before had been thrown off by her inability to write last night, her worry for David too strong.

He seemed to infiltrate all sides of her writing now, both inspiring and hindering it. And she wondered what he would think of that.

She turned on her office light and scooted to the desk, clearing away her mail program. There were only a half-dozen and none of the names jumped out as anything she needed to deal with tonight. Andi shut down all the extraneous programs she had floating in the background and brought up her current Word file, and her favorite app so she could listen to music from one of her favorite sites. The soft, smooth voice of Michael Bublé played low as she stared at the document, her hands still over the keys.

And nothing came.

She scrolled back several pages and read through what she'd

written in the last couple of days. It was all great stuff, and she loved it. The chemistry was finally coming through and she loved the flow. But tonight…nothing more wanted to be written. Andi sighed and decided to just let it go for the night.

She opened a new browser window, figuring maybe she could do some research and the news feed site she used as her homepage opened to fill the screen. Amongst the news reports about the economy and the housing market, and stories about activities around the world were headlines that immediately drew her eye.

DAVID BISHOP INJURED ON SET OF NEW FILM.

She'd seen most of the early reports, but it seemed it was still 'news' and more renditions of the events appeared every hour. Despite the voice of conscience in her head telling her to just leave it alone—since she knew what happened—she clicked on the hyperlink and pulled up the story.

There was a picture of David, something from their archives, dressed in a finely cut dark suit and white shirt open at the collar. He was looking in the direction of, but not directly at, the paparazzi who snapped the specific shot, with a wide and natural smile on his face. Behind him was a black-and-white wall proclaiming the name of a charity organization.

HOLLYWOOD, CALIFORNIA ~ MIXED REPORTS CAME OUT OF THE HOLLYWOOD STUDIO TODAY WHERE DAVID BISHOP IS FILMING HIS NEXT PROJECT, RISE OF DAWN, REGARDING POSSIBLE INJURIES SUFFERED BY THE ACTOR; EVERYTHING FROM MILD TO LIFE-THREATENING. A LATE-DAY NEWS RELEASE FROM STUDIO REPRESENTATIVES CONFIRMED WHILE HIS INJURY—A HARD SLAM TO HIS FACE THAT CAUSED SEVERE BRUISING AND SWELLING BUT CAUSED NO FRACTURES—WAS SIGNIFICANT, BISHOP WAS NEVER IN DANGER. HE WILL NEED TO BE OFF THE SET FOR AT LEAST A WEEK. HE WAS TAKEN TO THE STUDIO MEDICAL CENTER AND TREATED ON-SITE, AND LATER RELEASED TO HEAD HOME FOR REST.

WHILE THE REPORT OF HIS INJURY HAD MANY FANS CONCERNED FOR HIS WELFARE, IT WOULD SEEM MANY OF HIS FEMALE FANS WERE MOST UPSET TO HEAR BISHOP HAS A NEW WOMAN IN HIS LIFE. WHILE UNDER THE EFFECTS OF POWERFUL PAINKILLERS, BISHOP REPEATEDLY ASKED FOR ANDI PARKER, AUTHOR OF THE ORIGINAL BOOK SERIES ON WHICH RISE OF DAWN IS BASED. SPECULATIONS HAVE BEEN MADE ABOUT THE COUPLE'S INVOLVEMENT, AS ANDREA PARKER IS A BREAK FROM DAVID'S 'COMPANION' NORM AND A FAR CRY FROM THE STARLETS AND MODELS BISHOP USUALLY DATES. ANDREA PARKER WAS VIRTUALLY UNKNOWN BEFORE THE MASSIVE SUCCESS OF HER SCIENCE FICTION SERIES AND THE SUBSEQUENT MOVIE DEAL. ALTHOUGH NOT A PUBLIC FIGURE, PARKER IS KNOWN TO BE A DIVORCEE WITH A YOUNG SON AND IS SEVERAL YEARS OLDER THAN BISHOP.

WHILE PARTYING IN HOLLYWOOD LAST NIGHT, CO-STAR TAYLOR REISE WAS ASKED ABOUT THE RUMORS, TO WHICH SHE ANSWERED WITH A LAUGH "IF HE AND ANDREA PARKER WERE TRYING TO KEEP IT A SECRET, THEY WERE DOING A MISERABLE JOB." ANOTHER ON-SET SOURCE REVEALED THE TWO HAVE BEEN SEEN BEING VERY PHYSICAL ON THE SET, AND BISHOP HAS BEEN SEEN ENTERING PARKER'S TRAILER ON MORE THAN ONE OCCASION.

ONE HAS TO WONDER JUST HOW MUCH LOVING CARE AND ATTENTION BISHOP WILL GET WHILE RECOVERING.

Andi's entire body was hot, and a knot twisted in her stomach. It made them something illicit and secretive and made her feel ill. She understood with sharp clarity what David meant. There was nothing untrue in the article...yes, he'd asked for her. Yes, he'd probably been less-than-careful about his shows of affection when any eyes could see. Yes, he'd come to her trailer. But the voice of the article made her skin crawl.

She wanted to close the window and forget about the article, but something held her captive, and she scanned the words again.

A FAR CRY FROM THE STARLETS AND MODELS BISHOP USUALLY DATES...

Just when she thought she had the 'Why me?' voice shut down, it would whisper in her ear again. And it sounded strangely like Lawrence.

She rested her fingers again on the keyboard, ready to go back to work, when of their own accord they typed an entertainment database website URL Maggie had once shown her. She had told Andi anyone who was anyone—and a few who were no one—could be found on this site. When the page loaded, she typed *David Bishop* into the search box.

And swallowed against the guilty feeling she was spying on him.

Along the top of the page was his name, along with a row of thumbnail snapshots of him at different events and from different roles. Sometimes he stood alone, sometimes with women or cast members. Unlike Maggie, who always seemed to know who was with whom—who had left who—who wanted to be with whom—who had done what film and how many awards they did or didn't receive for it —who was on their way up—and on their way down—Andi had never been a celebrity watcher. She caught the occasional piece of information, but to say she followed anyone or anything, she didn't.

So, she knew things about 'the celebrity' David Bishop on a basic level only. He'd begun acting when he was eight years old, did his first major film at twelve, and once he hit his late teens, had become one of the fastest-rising leading men in Hollywood. He'd done action, he'd done romance, and he'd even done some romantic comedies. But, she couldn't list them all...she had just seen enough to know when the casting director told her they wanted him to read for the part—Andi had been all for it.

Beyond the basic outer shell of his bio, she knew nothing.

With a slight shake in her hand, she clicked on the biographical information listed on the site. She'd only guessed before at their age difference, but after seeing his birth date, she did the math in her head. Six years and eight months. Did that qualify her as a cougar? He was barely into his thirties and she was closer to forty than she liked to think about.

The information was generic. It listed his full name as David Daniel Bishop and said he was six-foot-two. He'd been born in Southern California, the first child and only son of a blue-collar family who took him to Hollywood when he was eight because he asked them to, simple as that. His parents divorced when he was ten, and his mother remarried the man she'd hired to be David's manager. There was a long list of every role he'd ever held, from the first commercial he did at eight for a major department store chain to his 'in 'production role in *Rise of Dawn*. Every award he'd ever been nominated for, and every award he'd won along the way.

Then came the more personal information. One by one, the site detailed every relationship he'd been rumored or confirmed to have had since he was sixteen years old. In his teens, he'd had a relationship with a young actress he'd met on the set of one of his first 'more adult-themed' films. Rachel Leighton. They'd been rumored to be talking about marriage, but no one had ever confirmed the stories, and they stopped dating when he was twenty. According to the site, they'd remained very close friends. There were several 'dated' names, many of which Andi recognized.

The final relationship entry was for Josie Connors, whom he'd been with for over four years and they shared a home on the California coast near Malibu. The entry only said the relationship ended—according to the date—just over a year earlier with no comment from either party. The only other notation was they'd seen each other at an event sometime after the break-up and while they'd appeared civil, there was visible tension between the two former lovers.

"Stop it, Andrea," she said to herself, shaking her head. "You aren't supposed to have a dirty laundry list on your new lover before you even start dating."

Her hand stilled over the mouse, and she sat up straighter.

"Holy crap..." She'd thought of David as her lover...

Andi jumped and squeaked when the voice chat program she'd left active earlier 'rang', telling her a call was coming in. Several people knew they could contact her that way, including her mother and her brother. She closed the celebrity page, revealing the chat program window. "David calling...'" ran like a marquee across the top, and her heart jumped.

She answered the call and turned on the webcam, but tilted her head when all she saw was a different angle of his bedroom. Ruffled blankets within the span of the camera told her the computer was probably on the bed, and beyond the sliding doors was the lit-up sky of the Hollywood Hills. But no David.

"Hello?" she called out.

"Oh, hey!" she heard a shout from somewhere in the distance and beyond the sight of the camera. "Hang on!"

"Okay."

The sound of bare feet running on a hard floor grew louder, and the room tilted briefly when he dropped to his knees beside the bed and turned the laptop to face him. His hair was damp and falling over his forehead, his jaw now freshly shaven. And he still wore no shirt... Andi's stomach fluttered and she swallowed.

"I wasn't sure if you'd answer, or not," he explained, huffing to catch his breath. "I tried about half an hour ago."

"I'm sorry. I was with Jake until a bit ago."

He smiled, wide and genuine. "I just wanted to say good night."

Pleasant warmth spread through her cheeks, pushing aside the tense anxiety she'd felt when she opened the article and looked him up on the web. "Get some more rest, okay?"

"I told you, sweetheart. I'm not risking tomorrow night." He winked.

Acting on a whim, Andi kissed her fingertips and touched her screen where his lips would be. She knew it wouldn't match up to him, but he'd understand the intent. "Good night, David."

"Good night, darlin'."

She disconnected the call first this time, and fell back heavily into her chair, huffing a breath. "You're crazy, Andrea. Insane."

"Damn straight if you're sitting here talking to yourself."

She spun her chair around to see Maggie standing in the office doorway, her shoulder against the jamb and a wide smile on her face.

"But you're not crazy for giving him a chance," she said with a nudge of her chin toward the now silent computer. "The boy is smitten."

*That's what I don't get...*she started to say but knew the arguments Maggie would counter with. For being a writer, Andi couldn't find the right words to make her best friend understand. How could she when she didn't understand herself? To be torn between the flattering euphoria that a man—a man like David Bishop—wanted to be with her, and the 'huh'-inspiring shock and confusion that demanded to know *why* a man like David Bishop would want to be with her. This was like a cliché storyline…gorgeous prince falls for an ugly duckling. Okay, so she wasn't an ugly duckling, but she wasn't a beautiful princess, either.

"Stop it," Maggie said sharply, yanking Andi back from the swirling thoughts that had temporarily seized her.

"What?"

"Overthinking it. Just…see where it goes. If nothing else, you'll have some great stories to tell when you're seventy and you can tell your grandkids how you had a wild love affair with David Bishop, the movie star."

Andi sank lower into her chair and groaned. "Sure, and write my tell-all autobiography?"

Maggie shrugged. "Why not? I could sell it in a heartbeat."

Whether it was Maggie's sharp wit—or Andi's inability to process the overload of thoughts in her head any longer—she burst out in laughter and laughed until she couldn't breathe.

CHAPTER SIX

The morning dragged, almost painfully. David had been up before dawn, having slept so much in the previous thirty-six hours his body had declared enough was enough. He'd sat on his balcony, drank coffee, and watched the sun come up over the Los Angeles skyline. But, once the sun rose and burned off the slight morning chill, he was ready to move on.

Five o'clock couldn't come fast enough.

He ran for nearly an hour on his treadmill, and put another hour in on his resistance trainer. After showering and making something to eat, he growled in his silent kitchen when he looked at the clock. Not even ten.

"This is pathetic," he mumbled, flopping down on his leather sofa, turning on the flat screen television mounted over his fireplace.

The KTLA morning traffic reported said something about a pile up on the 101 that had traffic backed up, but only some of the information actually made it into David's head. He was bored. Pure and simple. He wasn't used to just sitting around doing nothing. Even his 'vacations' had been working vacations for the last several years, and hiatus only meant an opportunity to work on some other project.

Lying around his house felt useless.

The house phone rang, and he reached behind the sofa to lift one of the handsets off the receiver, slumping further into the cushions as he put it to his ear.

"Hello."

"So tell me, sweetie. How much of it is made up? Is your face bashed in, forever destroying your career as Hollywood's Pretty Boy, or do you just have a boo-boo?"

David smiled at Rachel's gentle teasing, and he turned the television off. "Somewhere in between."

"So the title remains firmly in your hold?"

"Whatever..."

She laughed. "Good to know. What happened?"

"Oh, stupid accident. Ellen tripped over a cable and elbowed me in the face."

Rachel sucked in a breath. "Ouch."

"I think I probably used a few more colorful words."

She laughed again, and the itching boredom that made his feet bounce and his fingers twitch eased up. They hadn't been a couple for over ten years, but Rachel Leighton still had the ability to make him smile.

"I'm in Milan, and we just heard about it this evening when we returned from the shoot site. I would have called sooner."

David looked at his watch. "What is it, one a.m.?"

The question triggered a yawn on her end. "Yeah, thanks for reminding me. I was conveniently ignoring the clock, and the fact I have to be up and back outside the city in another seven hours."

"Milan in August. Must be brutal."

She groaned. "Awful. Give me dry desert heat any day."

"When will you be back?"

"Not for another three months. Why? You miss me?"

"Of course," he said, smiling. It only hurt a little, just around the eyes. "Call me when you get back. We'll do dinner."

"Just you and me?" she asked, her voice lifting.

"Are you bringing someone along?"

"Maybe, maybe not. I was wondering more about you. Your broken face isn't the only thing being talked about." She didn't give him a chance to deny or confirm anything. "So, your face falls somewhere between a boo-boo and scarred for life. Where do the stories about this writer—what's her name—"

"—Andrea Parker."

"Andrea. Very pretty name. So, where do the stories about Andrea Parker fall? All hearsay and innuendo? Or, should I be looking for a wedding invitation in the mail?"

"Somewhere in between," he answered again, not even attempting to disguise the smile in his voice. It wouldn't do any good. Rachel knew him too well.

"A writer, huh?"

"She's very good. Have you read her books?"

"No."

"You should. Wow. They're amazing."

"And I bet she's beautiful."

"Beautiful doesn't even—" He stopped short and chuckled, shaking his head. "Quit giving me a hard time."

Rachel laughed, but it quickly turned into a yawn. "Okay, I'll quit. But only because I'm exhausted. When I'm fully rested, you're in for more teasing than even *you* can handle."

"I can take whatever you dish out."

There was a small pause on the line before she said in a much softer voice, "For what it's worth, 'somewhere in between' sounds good on you."

Andi and Jake pulled into the driveway at 4:32, and she half-expected to see David sitting in his car at the curb. She grabbed the variety of bags from the backseat and did her best not to bolt into the house and make her son think she wanted to be free of his company.

She'd enjoyed the afternoon with him, even though neither of them liked shopping. It was more about time together and talking over lunch than the actual process of picking out jeans and tee shirts.

Jake had even helped her pick out—by convincing her she looked beautiful in it—a nice new dress to wear that evening. She wasn't sure about Jake's opinion of the whole 'date' thing. He'd just nodded, said "Okay" and poked at his pizza when she'd told him over lunch. He hadn't even acted surprised to hear was David Bishop she was going out with. She wasn't sure, because Jake sometimes kept his emotions carefully guarded, even from her.

They got into the house, and she handed all the bags but one to Jake. "Take those and get all the tags off, then toss them in the laundry. I'll wash everything before you wear them."

"Okay, Mom. Thanks."

Maggie came in through the sliding door from the backyard and set her empty glass on the counter. She looked at the clock over the stove and made a snarky sound. "Cuttin' it a bit close."

"Tell me about it. *Help.*"

Andi took the back stairs to the second level, with Maggie following behind, and kicked off her shoes before she was halfway across her bedroom. She tossed the bag on the bed and unbuttoned her dress on her way to the bathroom. "Get the tags off, will you? And find my black shoes?"

"I'm on it."

For the second time in three days, Andi took a shower in record time. She'd never been so happy to have short hair. The water hadn't even been on long enough to steam up the mirror before she stood in front of the vanity less than five minutes later, applying her makeup. A dollop of mousse and ninety seconds with the hairdryer, and her short waves were tamed into a reasonable evening style that settled around her face in soft curls. After a quick internal debate, she decided to stick with glasses and forego contacts. As rushed as she felt, she was likely to drop one down the sink or put them in the wrong eyes.

She hurried back to the bedroom wrapped in her towel and looked quickly at the clock beside her bed. Fourteen minutes until five.

"Crap," she groaned. For the first time, she actually prayed for a little light traffic to hold him up for five minutes or so. Just a little.

Maggie had laid the dress out on the bed and set her shoes on the floor. They were three-inch strappy black heels that all but screamed *broken ankle* to Andi, but she'd bought them on a whim a few months earlier. Andi shook her head, bending over to pick one up.

"No, not these."

"Those are the only black shoes I saw," Maggie said with a shrug.

"Don't be ridiculous. I have plenty of black—"

"Those are it, babe." She crossed her arms over her chest and raised an eyebrow. When Andi tried to move past her to the closet, Maggie sidestepped and blocked her way, tapping the watch on her wrist. "Tick tock." She turned away and headed for the door. "I wouldn't waste any more time trying to find something else." She winked and closed the door behind her. "I wouldn't bet on the boy being late!"

Andi made a mental note to sprinkle pepper in Maggie's coffee the next morning. But Mags was right, she didn't have time to spare. She didn't even have time to argue about the lacy black undies Maggie had left on the bed. She didn't look at the clock again until she buckled the last strap of the heels around her ankle. *Four minutes to spare.*

Just as she stood to take one last look in the mirror, she heard the crunch of tires on gravel in the driveway and her heart jumped into her throat. Giddy excitement like she hadn't felt since signing her first contract tumbled in her stomach and made her tingle. She should have turned and headed downstairs, but what would it hurt to take a quick peek at him before he saw her? *Probably saved her the embarrassment of drooling…*

Andi pushed aside the vertical blinds partially blocking the french doors leading onto her balcony, and wincing at the pop of the latch, opened the double doors. The air had already cooled some even though the sun was still up, and a wind came down off the mountains. Andi stepped gingerly on the stucco of the patio base and edged to the balcony wall.

A shiny black Audi sat in the driveway, sleek and elegant. It was a sports car, and the only reason she knew it was an Audi was because it said so on the back. Unlike her father who could name the make, model, and year of any car ever made just by the shadow of a profile— Andi only knew 'coupe' from 'sedan' from 'convertible', and sometimes even then it was sketchy.

She didn't realize the engine was still running until he shut it off, and the low hum faded away. Through the driver's side window, she saw his profile and the phone he held to his ear. He opened his door and stepped free of the car in one fluid motion, buttoning the front of his black suit jacket with his free hand. With some men, their suit wore them—but David Bishop 'wore' his suit—from the perfect way the crease broke over his shoes to the way the line of the jacket accentuated his height.

Heat flushed Andi's cheeks—well, more than her cheeks—and she moved a little closer to the edge to watch him unseen. As he shut the car door, he looked around the front yard, the phone still to his ear.

"I didn't call because I'm fine." He huffed and pushed the sunglasses up enough to pinch the bridge of his nose. "Ma…Ma…Ma! Listen to me," he said loudly, not shouting but Andi imagined whatever his mother had to say, she was saying it with such conviction was the only way she'd hear him. She smiled, somehow pleased at the thought his mother would call to check on him.

He chuckled softly and smiled. "I know you worry, Ma. Trust me, if I'd really been hurt I would have—" He paused, nodded. "Okay, fine. If I'd really been hurt, *I* wouldn't have called. But you would have known. I promise."

David walked to the front of the car and leaned forward, looking in the general vicinity of the front door, nodding his head for a conversation Andi couldn't hear. "Yeah. Yep. Ma? Ma." She must have taken a breath because he didn't pause. "Ma, I love you. I do. But, I've got to go." Pause. "I have a date."

Oh, this could get interesting…

"Ma, I told you, don't—*Yes*, with a *girl*."

Andi slapped her hand over her mouth, but not before her giggle carried down to the driveway. David spun around on the balls of his feet, seeking her out. She thought for a brief second about ducking behind the balcony wall, but the last time she looked in the mirror she wasn't ten, so she stayed her ground until he tipped his head back and saw her. A wide smile immediately spread his lips and he reached up to slip off his sunglasses.

"Yes, Ma. She's a nice girl. A very nice girl." The whole time he talked, he stared up at her and Andi drew in a deep breath to steady herself against the liquid warmth that swirled in the oddest places, like her elbows, and behind her knees. "And beautiful."

He chuckled. "Yes, it's Andrea Parker."

Andi crossed her arms on the balcony edge and leaned over, pulling her lower lip through her teeth as she looked down at him.

"We'll see," he said, his voice softer. "Okay. I'll talk to you tomorrow. I promise." One more pause before he added, "I love you, too, Ma." He tapped the screen with his thumb before slipping it into his pocket. All the while, he looked up at her.

"Hi," Andi said just loudly enough she hoped he could hear.

David smiled, and she loved how it changed his face—despite the dark bruising beneath his eyes. "Hey, yourself. You been up there long?"

"Since you pulled in."

He didn't say anything, just watched her, smiling. There was something about the way he watched her, like he was studying her, that made her skin warm and she couldn't help but smile back.

"What?" she finally asked.

He shook his head. "Nothing."

"I'll be right down."

Andi backed off the balcony and shut the doors, giving herself a final cursory look in the closet mirror to make sure nothing was hanging out that shouldn't be and Maggie had gotten all the tags. The dress was a departure from what she usually wore, with a sweetheart neckline it showed just enough cleavage to make her blush, and hug her torso. The fabric had a nice weight to it that let it drape around her hips and shift around her knees when she walked.

"Well, it's no yellow sundress…" she mumbled before swiping her evening bag—another detail Maggie had seen to while she broke speed records in the shower—and leaving the bedroom.

Voices carried up the stairs as she descended into the front hall. She had to take the steps carefully since her usual footwear consisted of sneakers and sandals, not three-inch heels. David's deep baritone mingled with Maggie's higher voice, but Andi couldn't make out any words. As she descended, Maggie and David came into view. David stood in the foyer with his back to the door, his sunglasses folded in his hands as he opened and closed the arms. Maggie leaned against the wall, grinning like the cat that ate the canary. She took the final step and her heels clacked loudly on the tile, or at least it sounded loud to her.

Both of them turned to look at her, and Andi did her best to keep her composure when David's gaze settled on her. The wide smile he'd worn since getting out of the car relaxed, and his eyes widened slightly. Andi slowed her steps, and her insides clenched at the sudden thought maybe the dress hadn't been such a good idea. She licked her lips and rolled them together, clutching harder on her purse. *Maybe that was why they were called clutches...*

"Hello again," she forced out, having to clear her throat.

He released a rough breath, his shoulders dropping a degree, and the smile widened again to dig twin dimples into his cheeks. "Andi..." he said, but nothing else came. She waited for him to say something else, and as each millisecond passed, her cheeks burned hotter.

Then he took a long stride toward her and laid a hand on her cheek, pressing his lips to the other, and her heart immediately jumped to a faster rhythm. His lips stayed there for several rapid beats before he whispered close to her ear.

"You're beautiful."

Andi turned her head, meeting his eyes. She swallowed and blinked trying to focus on speech as his thumb stroked the corner of her mouth, reminding her of the day they'd kissed on set. He'd spoken to Benton, but his hands had stayed on her face and his thumbs stroked her skin.

"Thank you."

"You two crazy kids go have some fun. No curfew tonight. Jake and I are going to make plans for Sunday and I'll probably let him gorge on junk food and soda until about one a.m., so don't rush back." Maggie pulled Andi from the moment with her 'Passive-for-Maggie' teasing. "Don't do anything I wouldn't do."

David slid his hand from her cheek down her arm to curl his fingers around her hand. "That leaves things pretty open, I'm guessing."

Maggie chuckled and pointed at them. "I knew I liked you."

David took a step toward the door, but she didn't follow. Not yet. "Where's Jake?"

Maggie shrugged and waved them off. "Probably putting those clothes in the laundry, just like you asked. Go on. Have fun. We'll be fine."

"I promise, Mom. I won't have her out too late," David said over his shoulder as they went out the door.

He held her hand as he walked her around the car and even after opening the door for her. Just as she was about to slide into the low-set car, David stepped close. With her hand still in his, he wrapped his arm behind her and pulled her to him. With the shoes on, she didn't have to raise her chin quite as far to look him in the eyes, but she still needed to tip her head back. He released her hand and ran his fingertips along her temple to her cheek, his eyes shifting to take in different parts of her face, returning to look into her eyes.

"This is going to be a long evening," he finally said.

"Why?"

"I made a promise, remember? I wouldn't kiss you again until after we'd had a real date."

"You kissed me inside."

His grin tilted wickedly and he shook his head. "Not the way I wanted to."

Andi leaned into him, feeding on the rush of confidence the look in his eyes gave her. "When do we go from 'having a date' to 'had a date'?"

He shifted his gaze to look past her to the sky, tipping his head as he contemplated her question. "I'm thinking we've got to at least eat dinner."

"There's a McDonalds around the corner."

He chuckled. "Sorry, sweetheart. We're not wasting this dress on McDonalds. I've got something a little better in mind."

David unwound his arm from behind her, and let her slide into the car. He made sure she was seated before shutting the door and jogging around the front of the car to get behind the wheel. Within minutes, they were headed south toward Los Angeles, and as soon as they were on the main highway, he reached across the console and took her hand, his fingers lacing between hers. He lifted their joined hands and kissed her knuckles before settling them on the center console.

They rode in silence for a while as he worked his way through afternoon traffic in the Valley, releasing her hand only long enough to shift gears, and quickly coming back to lace fingers again. Andi took the moments of quiet—which held no edge of the awkwardness she almost expected—to study him. He'd put the sunglasses back on to drive, but beneath the edges, she saw the shadows of the bruising around his eyes and nose. She'd noted the bruising when they stood close, but somehow it hadn't seemed important. It was his smile and his eyes that always held her focus; the way he always smiled wider when he looked at her and the way his gaze met and held hers.

She looked down at their joined hands, his thumb stroking across her skin, and stared at them like they belonged to someone else. Andi hadn't held a boy's hand since high school. Not really. She'd met Lawrence in college, and he'd informed her—with what she'd come to call his 'Educating Andrea' tone—that public shows of affection were juvenile and unnecessary. He told her he loved her and that should be sufficient.

Andi drew in a sharp breath and straightened her shoulders against the warm leather of the seat, shoving hard aside any thoughts of her ex-husband. He wasn't going to taint any part of the evening, and she wasn't going to listen to the growling whisper from behind her somewhere she was everything Lawrence said.

"I'm sorry," David said, pulling her from her thoughts. Before she could ask why he was sorry, he lifted her hand to his lips again. "I don't tend to talk much when I drive."

Andi smiled and shifted in the seat to turn a little more toward him. "It's okay. I'm usually a silent passenger. I do some of my best plotting in the car."

"Yeah?" He checked his mirrors before changing lanes, the low hum of the car increasing just slightly as he accelerated. "I'd love to hear about that."

"What, plotting a book?"

He nodded, settling into his new lane before turning his head toward her. The sunglasses hid his eyes, but she still 'felt' his gaze on her.

"I told you I read your books, right?" It was her turn to nod. "I've never known a writer—"

"You know scriptwriters."

David shook his head. "That's different, I think. When I read a script, I don't see it the way I did when I read your books."

Andi had done several book signings since her first book was released, and she'd attended conferences and conventions. No matter how many times a reader or fan praised her for her writing, she still felt the flush of embarrassment and amazement it was *her* books they talked about.

She cleared her throat and looked out the windshield at the passing highway signs. "Where are we going?"

"Burbank."

"You drove from LA to Santa Clarita just to double back to Burbank? David, I could have *met* you there to save you the drive."

"Are you kidding?" He squeezed her hand and glanced at her, his eyebrows bobbing over the top of the sunglasses. "And waste all that time alone in a car with you? No way."

She was beautiful.

David figured it was a good idea he had on the sunglasses, or Andi would see just how much time he spent watching her rather than the road. But, he couldn't keep his attention away. The simple sundresses she wore had always been enough to drive him crazy, but the dress she wore tonight was the stuff of sin. It clung to her shape in all the right ways and in all the right places, and even though the cut was modest by Hollywood standards, it had immediately left him speechless when she stepped into the hall.

He didn't have a garage full of cars, but when picking which one to take tonight he'd picked the S5 because the cabin was smaller and it allowed him to sit closer to her. He realized now his lack of foresight in recognizing his desire to hold her hand. Every time he needed to shift the car, he had to let go, and he didn't like it.

Afternoon commuter traffic slowed them down a little getting into Burbank, but once off the 14, it took no time to reach *Chez Nous*, his favorite restaurant when he wanted to fly under the paparazzi radar.

A small crowd of patrons stood on the sidewalk outside the two-story restaurant, which was typical for a Friday night. But, he'd called ahead to make sure they wouldn't have to wait. David parked just outside a circle of light cast by one of the parking lot lights and hurried around the front of the car to open her door. Her delicate hand slid into his as he helped her out of the low-profile sports car, and he did his best not to grin too wide at the extra inch of leg she showed when her skirt shifted above her knee.

"I think I've heard of this place," Andi said, glancing over her shoulder at the pale pink building. "Maggie told me about it."

David took the opportunity of her standing so close to wrap his arms around her and pull her against him. He loved how there was no resistance in her body and she leaned into him, her hands resting on his arms. She looked up at him and smiled, releasing a slow sigh.

"We're still 'having' a date, huh?" he asked.

She pulled her lips into a disappointed frown and nodded her head with a hum. "Yeah, afraid so."

His lips practically itched to kiss her, so before he broke the promise he'd made on a whim, he took a step back. But he indulged himself by letting his hands slide around her hips before taking her hand and leading her across the lot to the door. As they approached, the cluster of young people waiting on the sidewalk glanced in their direction. One of the girls—a twenty-something blonde in a dress that constituted little more than a long shirt—took a second glance and gasped, her eyes widening.

"Oh, my god," she whispered loudly, tugging on the sleeve of one of her friends. "Look! It's David Bishop."

The cluster turned their focus on him and Andi as a unit. Her hold on his hand tightened and she stepped a little further behind him.

"You've never done this before," he said sideways to her, slowing his step.

"Define *this*," she said with a nervous giggle. "Dated a celebrity? Dodged paparazzi? Beaten adoring fans off with my evening clutch?"

David laughed and released her hand to wrap his arm around her shoulder, bringing her close to his side. "All of the above."

"Nope. Never."

They reached the cluster, and the girl who first spotted him gasped and covered her mouth with her hand. "Oh, my god! You poor thing! Look at your face."

She—like too many fans—didn't understand the concept of personal space and practically threw herself against him, laying her hands on his face. Her thumbs brushed over his cheeks below his eyes, reminding him with an immediate throb of pain he was still bruised. He winced and pulled back.

"Oh, did I hurt you?"

David held up his hand, fending off another attempt at touching him. "It's fine, thank you for worrying."

He begged off on taking pictures with the blonde and her friend, outright ignoring her offer to 'kiss it and make it better.' Andi stood beside him, holding tight to his hand the whole time, not saying a word or pushing her way into the conversation.

"Not tonight," he said in answer to the photo request with his best public voice and looked down at Andi. "I'm with my girlfriend."

Her head snapped up and she stared at him, her eyes wide behind her glasses and her glossed lips apart. David smiled and slid his hand down her spine to the small of her back, bringing her closer. He wondered if she wore the flavored kind of gloss, and how slick her lips would feel against his. To keep from tempting fate, he slid his cheek along hers until he could whisper close to her ear.

"Do you have any idea how much I want to kiss you right now?" he asked low enough only she would hear.

The hottest blush he'd ever seen bloomed in her cheeks again and one corner of her lips tipped up in a smile. "I think I have a good idea."

David kissed her forehead, justifying to himself it was no more than the kiss he'd put on her cheek at the house. A camera flashed, and Andi jumped in his hold, but she didn't pull away. Ignoring the shouts from the group, he took her hand and led the way into the restaurant.

CHAPTER SEVEN

"Would you care for a glass of wine with your filet mignon, sir?"

"No, thank you. I'll stick with the soft stuff," he said with a grin, handing the menu to the young woman who had been assigned to their table.

"And you, ma'am?"

Andi ordered the Norwegian Salmon, and like David, passed on a glass of wine. She didn't know his reason for passing, but she just wasn't a fan. Which, she had been told by many people since moving West, was a shame since California produced some great vintages. As soon as the waitress walked away, David reached across the table through the stemware glasses and the small centerpiece maze to take her hand. The table was small, set up only for two along the back wall of the retro-style dining room, tucked away but within clear view of the grand piano situated centrally for the benefit of the entire dining room. A man wearing a tuxedo sat at the piano, playing a soft and easy tune Andi recognized but couldn't put a name to. In the subdued light, it was difficult to see most of the other patrons, and she wondered if that was intentional. The more she thought about it, the more she remembered what Maggie had told her about *Chez Nous*.

This was a place High Hollywood Society came to when they didn't care to be mauled by paparazzi. The occasional cameraman hung out in the parking lot or near the door, on the off chance someone note-worthy would come to eat, but most stuck to Los Angeles or Holly-wood—because more often than not, the pictures that paid the most money were the ones of the reclusive and troublesome celebs. And they either didn't care if they were seen, or made it a point to be seen, so the tucked-away restaurant didn't fit their needs, subconscious or otherwise.

"This is a cute place," she offered, taking in the décor. Whether it was 'retro' or just not updated, she wasn't sure but the wallpaper and paint colors would have been perfectly in place about thirty years earlier. Pinks and pale greens added lightness to the dimly lit space, keeping it from feeling too dark.

"I haven't been here in a couple of years. I miss the filet mignon."

"Why haven't you come?"

David shrugged, his thumb rubbing across her knuckles. "No reason." He leaned his other arm on the table, across the front of his chest, and shifted forward to bring his face into the soft glow of the low candle nestled in the centerpiece. "Where were you born?"

Andi arched an eyebrow and chuckled softly. "Quite the segue you've got there. Why do you want to know that?"

"Because I want to know about *you*, and I figure where you were born is a great place to start."

"Do you want my mini-bio? It's pretty boring."

He grinned wider. "Sure."

Andi set her chin in her hand. "Okay, I was born April 27th in Love-land, Ohio and—"

"What year?"

She shook her head. "Classified information. I was named Andrea Elizabeth—"

"Why won't you tell me?"

Andi sighed, leaning forward a little. "Are you going to let me finish?"

He cleared his throat and motioned for her to continue, but before she could, he plunged forward again. "How long were you married?"

A cold chill tightened the back of her neck, and Andi pressed her lips together, looking down at the table. His hold on her hand tightened slightly, but he didn't retract the question. It wasn't the asking of the question that made her balk—if this relationship, or whatever designation they decided to stamp on it, was going to happen, then he should know the best and worst of her—it was the fact Lawrence Bonherre had to invade their evening at all that bothered her.

"Nine years," she finally answered, raising her gaze to look into his face. Andi did her best to hide how uncomfortable the conversation made her by smiling and resting her chin on her hand again. "The talk of past relationships usually doesn't happen until the second or third date."

David's 'scoundrel' grin—she thought of it that way because it was always *that* grin inspiring her into trouble—touched his lips and she swore his eyes really did twinkle in the candlelight. "Yeah, and when I take a woman on a first date, I usually don't already know what her lips taste like." His voice was rough and low, and Andi swore it sent vibrations of sensation over her skin as his gaze settled on her mouth. "Or what she feels like against me."

The waitress arrived with their drinks, and as Andi slid her hand from his and sat back, she drew in a metered breath to counteract the thundering of her heartbeat. The waitress said something about their meals being out shortly, but Andi barely heard it as she sucked down a third of the cold soda to try and abate the heat radiating just beneath her skin.

As soon as the waitress stepped away from the table, David rose and came around beside her chair, holding out his hand. "Dance with me."

She looked up, then around at the empty floor around the piano. "No one else is dancing…"

"I don't care," he said with a small quirk of his grin.

There was something about the way he smiled at her that challenged her and empowered her at the same time. He could inspire her to flirt shamelessly, to kiss recklessly…and so it would seem…to dance. Andi laid her hand in his and scooted her chair back, following him onto the empty wood floor at the end of the piano. The pianist rolled from the end of one tune into a melody best suited for love ballads and slow dancing. David turned toward her and raised her hand over her head, turning her around once before he wrapped his arm around her waist and drew her to him. She rested her hand on his shoulder for only a moment before sliding it down his lapel.

"What makes you think I can dance?" she asked, smiling up at him.

"What makes you think *I* can? I just wanted an excuse to hold you." He ran the fingertips of both hands from her shoulders to the small of her back, parallel on either side to her spine. Up and down, he slowly stroked, threatening to make her shiver with the contact. "And to say I'm sorry. For making you uncomfortable."

Andi focused on the subtle black-on-black design of his tie. "No one likes to admit to their failures."

His hands splayed on her back and he pulled her closer, continuing to sway and step with the music. David bent his neck and turned into her, the tip of his nose grazing the side of her neck, and it was impossible for her to cover up the way her breath hitched at the subtle touch. She tingled and fluttered inside, tilting her head to elongate her neck, and swore she felt the warmth of his breath on her skin.

"Then I asked the wrong question," he said softly, but his lips were close to her ear. "I don't want to know what's gone wrong in your life. I want to know what's gone right."

"Well, that's easy."

David raised his head, but still held her so close she had to turn her face to the side to look him in the eyes. They looked dark—almost black—in the dim light. His fingers went back to following the line of her spine. "Yeah? Tell me."

It was hard to think, to keep her mind on the conversation, when her skin was alive and awake beneath his touch and her lungs burned from trying to breathe normally when he looked at her the way he did. Andi blinked and swallowed.

"I have a wonderful son in Jake and a wonderful friend in Maggie. I have a family who has always been behind me, no matter what. I have a career I once never would have even imagined. And…" She smiled, and let his grin inspire her again by tipping her chin toward him. Their mouths hovered not an inch apart, and she wondered what it would take for him to break his impromptu promise. "I *apparently* have a wonderful boyfriend."

His smile widened, but she couldn't carry off the moment and nearly choked on her own stifled laugh. Andi pressed her forehead to his shoulder and let her shoulders shake with the silenced chuckle.

"What are you laughing at?" he asked near her ear again, and she could hear the wide smile in his voice.

"I'm thirty-s-s-s—" She stuttered over the number, and stopped to clear her throat. He looked down at her with arched eyebrows. "I'm thirty-*something* years old. I'm too old to have a *boyfriend*. And I'm *way* too old to be *anyone's* girlfriend."

"Then what are we?" he asked. "We're not lovers."

Andi's breath caught in her throat as she looked into the intensity of his gaze. The word didn't have to be said, it slid between them without question. *Yet.* He smiled…a slow tipping upward of his lips, first one corner then the next.

"So, what did your son think of the fun park?"

Andi smiled and chuckled, her eyes lighting up as she wiped her lips with her napkin. "We got to the park, and after spending *three hours* walking around, he decided he was too old to have his birthday party there."

"Too old? How old is he?"

"He'll be eleven."

"Man, I would have *loved* a birthday party at a place like that when I was his age." He picked up his fork and poked at his baked potato to mix in the butter and sour cream. "Do you know where I spent my eleventh birthday?"

She shook her head, setting her arm on the table to rest her cheek against her curled fingers. Her smile was infectious, and he loved the way her eyes sparked with curiosity. "No. Where?"

David paused, thinking for a minute. He knew he'd been filming *something,* but couldn't remember what. Just it wasn't home, and it wasn't a party. "I don't know," he said with a chuckle and a shrug. "I just know it wasn't bowling and playing miniature golf. I don't think I've ever been."

"Maybe you can go with us sometime."

"I thought he was too old—"

"To have *birthday parties* there," she interrupted. "Going with your mom is okay."

The idea of spending a Saturday afternoon playing miniature golf with Andrea Parker and her son held more appeal to him than he expected, and he nodded. "I would love to."

She went back to cutting her food, and David enjoyed another brief moment of just watching her. Everything she did, every move she made even cutting her salmon, was graceful. Or maybe he just saw her through a softened lens.

"So, what does he want to do now?"

"He just wants a party at the house. Have a bunch of friends over and swim in the pool, that kind of thing. Grill burgers and hot dogs." She looked at him across the table, pausing for a moment with a piece of asparagus on a fork. "Do you want to come? It's Sunday afternoon."

"Wow. Bowling *and* barbeque?" he teased.

"You don't have to," she said quickly, deep color blooming in her cheeks. "I'm sorry. I didn't mean to put you on the spot."

"Sweetheart, I'd love to." He leaned forward, holding her eyes with his. "It sounds fun. What time on Sunday?"

"People are coming at eleven, and we're eating at noon. Honestly, David—"

"Can I come early to help?"

She stared at him for several moments before huffing a small breath and shaking her head, shrugging one shoulder. He wondered with the expression on her face, if she'd made some kind of decision she didn't say. Andi cleared her throat before saying "Sure. I'd love the help. Thank you."

He almost said he'd take any excuse to spend more time with her, but it wasn't the whole truth. David had never dated a woman who had children, though he'd had buddies who did. Nearly every one of them had warned against it. But, he was ashamed to admit, that most of his friends didn't have kids in mind when they asked their mothers out. The first time he kissed Andi, *really* kissed Andi, he hadn't known about her son. The fact did nothing to take away his impulse to be near her, with her. If anything, he realized with a grin as he focused again on his food, it had made her more appealing to him.

He wondered what his buddies would have to say about that.

And at the same time, he knew he didn't care.

They settled into silence for a few minutes, eating their meals while the piano music and subdued conversations filled the background. David had always thought of silence on a date as a sign things weren't going well, but just like the quiet they'd shared in the car on the way to Burbank, he didn't feel the uneasy edge of an uncomfortable date. It was natural.

Every minute he spent with her felt natural. Easy.

Real.

"Lawrence had an affair."

David paused with his steak halfway to his mouth, focusing on her. Before he could say anything, she cleared her throat and continued.

"Lawrence is my ex-husband," Andi talked more to her asparagus than him, poking at it with her fork. "He had several affairs. Shortly after Jake was born. Maybe before, I don't know."

With each sentence, her voice got a little softer until he barely made out the last. She still hadn't looked up, swirling the speared asparagus through the champagne sauce on her plate. Even with her head tilted down, he saw her work her lips nervously between her teeth and she flipped an errant curl behind her ear.

Before she could tuck the hand back under the edge of the table, David reached across and took it, curling his fingers around hers. And he silently thanked the restaurant owners for making their tables small and intimate so he could reach her. "Andi..."

Andi set the fork down with a clack, and he caught the slight shake of her hand. She drew in a deep breath before raising her head and looking at him, a nervous smile barely touching the corners of her lips. "You wanted to know how long I was married...I thought you should know why I wasn't anymore."

David squeezed her hand and she turned her palm into his, letting him hold it tighter. "Sweetheart, I—"

"Can I take those for you?"

He released her hand to sit back, nodding to the waitress as he watched Andi. She nodded as well, leaning back as she fidgeted with the napkin in her lap. Her gaze skimmed him but looked quickly away, focusing somewhere in the vicinity of the piano player.

The candlelight played over her features, making the subtle red of her hair come alive with each wave framing her face. Her glasses hid her eyes, but he thought maybe the shine he saw was more than a reflection from the candle on the lenses. She swallowed and drew a deep breath, her shoulders drawing back.

He recognized that moment…that deep breath she took whenever she needed to focus herself. Or when she needed to school her reaction. She'd done it after they kissed on the set that first time. That day he had thought it was just an actress shedding her character, only to learn it was because she had felt the effects of the kiss as much as he had.

"Sir?"

David blinked and looked up at their waitress. "I'm sorry. What?"

She smiled politely, balancing the dishes on her arm. "Would either of you be interested in seeing the dessert menu?"

Andi's attention snapped back to him, and whether she meant to or not, her gaze locked with his. Slowly, she smoothed her lips together pulling the lower one between her teeth. The gloss she'd worn earlier was gone, worn off by their meal, and he wondered if the taste still lingered on her lips.

In a flash, he wanted *nothing* more than to get *out* of the restaurant.

She didn't look away from him, but one corner of her perfect-for-kissing mouth tipped up in a subtle, sexy grin. David smiled back and shook his head, forcing himself to be polite and look up at the waitress. "Just the check, please."

The waitress either anticipated his answer, or it was near the end of her shift and she was ready to leave because she slid a black bifold from her apron pocket and set it on the table. David held up his hand so she knew to wait, and pulled his platinum card from his wallet. She took it immediately and came right back. By the time he filled out the tip and doted the 'i' in Bishop, he was ready to bolt to the door but managed a polite smile as he pushed his chair back and stepped beside Andi, offering his hand.

Andi's insides felt like she'd just taken a one-hundred-foot drop on a rollercoaster at sixty miles an hour. Exhilaration slammed hard into sheer panic. They'd teased each other all night, and when the concept of 'had a date' still hid behind 'having a date', she'd been able to flirt and smile.

Now, he led her from the restaurant with a firm but gentle hand holding hers, and even that touch was enough to make her insides shake. She was hot, wishing they'd turn the air conditioning up a little, yet gooseflesh prickled on her arms. Breathing with any kind of normality was nearly impossible, and her head felt light at the attempt.

"Thank you for coming, Mr. Bishop," said the manager as they approached. He stood at the door and pushed it open to let them pass. "Please enjoy the rest of your evening."

David paused in the doorway, and when she took her last step it brought her flush against his arm where she gripped his hand. He looked down at her, his devilish grin making his eyes spark. "Thank you," he said to the manager, but his eyes never looked away from her.

In her peripheral, she heard murmurs of his name and fought the urge to take a step back from him. It was a battle she still fought—being torn between accepting him when he said he wanted to be there with her and be seen with her, and the irrational voice that whispered she had no place there and she had to be insane to believe David wanted to waste his time with someone like Andrea Parker. The voice sounded so much like Lawrence Bonherre.

They stepped outside, and Andi took a deep breath of the cool evening air. The sun had gone down an hour before. The moon and the occasional lamppost lit the parking lot, and they moved past the few people waiting outside the restaurant to be seated. Out here, no one seemed to notice the man who walked beside her, holding her hand.

By the time they reached the part of the parking lot where he'd parked his car, there was no one else around except those they'd left behind. Andi's heart pounded in her chest like a frantic, caged bird.

"Are you cold?" David asked, his fingers working at the front buttons of his suit jacket. He stopped, turning toward her. "Here..."

"No, I'm fine." She hadn't *thought* about touching him other than to still his hands, but when she laid her hand on his lapel his eyes snapped to her. The lights cast strange shadows around them, close enough to let her see his face, but far enough away to diffuse his features. "I'll be fine once we're in the car..." she managed to say even though her throat was suddenly so dry it was hard to speak.

Beneath her hand, his chest rose and fell with breath that was just a little too fast. Without saying anything, he took her hand and they started across the lot again. The car was easily in sight, and he took the keys from his pocket, remotely unlocking the doors with a twitter and a flash of the lights. As they reached her door, he curled his fingers beneath the handle and she slid into the space between him and the side of the car. Before opening the door, he stopped and looked down at her. He stood so close she swore she felt the heat of his body against her cooled skin. Her nerves tingled and she couldn't quite steady her breath with the anticipation of wanting something, yet afraid of it at the same time.

"So..." he said in a low voice that scraped over her intensified nerves with a pleasant roughness.

She could only manage a soft hum in answer. Her fingers wanted to reach into the open jacket, to feel the warmth she knew would be trapped inside between his body and the smooth lining.

"We ate," he stated.

Andi nodded, raising her chin so she could look at him. His eyes shifted over her face, touching her with his gaze and she *had* to reach out. She had no choice but to let her hands slide over his shirt to his sides, releasing a shuddered sigh at the warmth she knew she'd find. An unfamiliar sense of satisfaction snapped through her when his body tensed beneath her touch and he turned to face her fully—his hands coming up to rest on the car on either side of her shoulders.

David leaned into her, his hips pressing hers back into the car and she let her hands shift from his sides to his back beneath the jacket. It fell open further and he stood so close the heat trapped inside warmed her arms. Andi couldn't catch her breath and knew her heart pounded so hard he had to see the jump of her pulse at the base of her throat. He bent his neck and the tip of his nose brushed the side of her neck, his breath hot on her chilled skin.

"Andi..."

The word reverberated against her and his lips brushed her skin when he said her name, his voice rough like gravel and honey. Her fingers curled impulsively into his shirt and she moaned low in her throat. Her knees liquefied and she slumped back against the car, but his arms came around her as his mouth pressed to the bend where her shoulder met her neck.

His mouth on her skin wasn't enough and she pulled at his shirt, bringing him closer and at the same time pulling away from him to find his mouth with hers. Then he was kissing her so deeply that the only thing she could do was open her lips to him and kiss back with the same need and intensity. His hands held her head, cushioning her against the edge of the car.

She couldn't touch him enough, couldn't pull him close enough, couldn't feel enough of him and when his hips pushed hard against her, she groaned into his mouth and the pitch of the kiss amped up another degree. One hand cupped her head, his fingers laced into her hair, and the other slid down her body to her waist and around to the small of her back, yanking her hard against him.

Andi wanted...that was all her mind could process. She *wanted* more...*wanted* to have him closer, *wanted* to kiss him deeper, *wanted* to taste him and breathe him and *feel* him.

She almost cried when he moved his mouth from hers and pressed his face into the hollow of her shoulder. David wrapped his arms around her, holding her so tight and the only sound she heard was their hard, rapid breathing as they both fought to find sanity again. Andi pressed her eyes closed and tucked herself against his chest, and after a few moments, his arms relaxed their hard hold. His hands stroked her back, and she focused on the contact.

Too soon he raised his head to look at her and touched her temple with his fingertips, curling her hair behind her ear. A small, sexy smile just touched his lips and he drew in one final long and deep breath, shaking his head.

"I don't think I'll ever be ready for what kissing you does to me."

Andi tried to smile, but everything felt weak and she was thankful he held her so close because she wasn't sure she could stand on her own. "I know what you mean," she managed to whisper and tipped her face toward him, wishing he'd go back to kissing her.

He cupped her face in his palms and pressed a closed-mouth kiss to her lips. She still wanted more, but better sense ruled. She knew she couldn't handle anything more, and suspected neither could David. He broke the kiss and rested his forehead against hers, their breath mingling in the space between them.

Then he took one hand away and opened the car door. Reluctantly, Andi stepped from the cocoon of warmth around his body and slid into the car. He shut the door and by the time he walked around to get in himself, her heartbeat was nearly back to normal.

"I feel like a teenager," Andi whispered, gasping for breath, even though she knew no one would hear them. "Sneaking home after curfew."

David chuckled against her throat, and she smiled against the buzz it created on her nerves. She threaded her fingers into his short hair, clutching it as best as she could while he kissed and sucked in tiny shots along her neck and shoulder. They had twisted awkwardly in the front seats of his sports car, the gearshift and console creating a cumbersome—and probably necessary—barrier between them. Through the progression of their 'good-night kiss' that had turned into a teenage-esque make-out session, Andi had twisted in her seat to face him with her knees drawn up beside her and David leaned half across the console so he could reach all the places he wanted to kiss…her lips, her cheeks, her throat, her shoulders. His hands had slipped beneath the hem of her dress, sliding it up her thigh, but his touch ventured no further.

That was a fact that both relieved and annoyed Andi.

His heavy breath against the exposed skin of her décolletage made her shiver, even though the breath was warm. David's hand left its resting place on her thigh to press his palm to her cheek, drawing her a fraction of an inch closer to her so he could run a trail of kisses from her throat to her jaw and finally to her mouth. His tongue brushed her lips and she opened her mouth, another one of many such groans escaping her throat.

She pulled at his shirt, his jacket having already been tossed in the back seat along with his wrinkled tie, and David shifted again to close the space between them. Andi heard a thunk and immediately felt the motion of the car.

"Damn," David cursed. He jerked back into the driver's seat, slammed his foot on the brake, and yanked the parking brake back into place. The car rocked, settling again in the driveway.

David looked across the small space, a wide and wickedness-inspiring grin on his lips, and Andi laughed. His deep chuckle followed and he dropped his head back on the high seat back, scrubbing his face with his hands.

"I think that's my cue to go inside," Andi said with a sigh and righted herself in the seat, tugging her skirt to her knees before smoothing her hands over her hair in a pointless attempt at returning order to the curls irreparably disheveled by David's fingers. She didn't bother to flip down the visor to look in the mirror, figuring she was better off not knowing how rumpled she looked.

He didn't verbally agree, but opened his door and swung his long body free of the car to come around and help her out. The night air was cold against her heated skin and she stepped against him, stealing his warmth as he wrapped his arm around her to walk her to the door. He walked her under the portico and stood behind her so he could rub his hands up and down her arms while she unlocked the door. Andi pushed the door open and took a step inside, but he didn't follow, stopping in the doorway with his arm braced on the frame.

"Do you want to come in?" she asked.

He reached his hand out and she took it without thinking, closing the space again between them. When she stood this close, she had to tip her head back to see his face and loved what she saw. Andi had put in her books one character 'saw' happiness in the eyes of the other, but it was a concept she only imagined and narrated, not one she had ever experienced. Until now. The warmth and what she could only describe as glee she saw in David's eyes made her smile and she stood up on her toes to kiss his chin.

"It's not a good idea," he answered just before touching a quick kiss to her lips. He pressed his hand to her back and pulled her against him. "Trust me, I *want* to. I really, *really* want to." He touched another kiss to her forehead, holding his lips there.

Andi released a slow breath, nodding into his touch. She understood what he meant. She didn't have to *like* it, but she understood it. David laid his hands on each side of her head and pulled back enough to look into her face.

"I will see you Sunday." He twisted his wrist enough to look at his watch and chuckled. "Correction. I'll see you *tomorrow*. I'll come early."

Andi nodded, and with one lingering kiss—a chaste kiss in comparison to the others of the night—he stepped away. She stood in the doorway until he was in his car and pulled out of the driveway.

Maggie cleared her throat from behind Andi, and Andi jumped with a yelp as she spun around. Maggie stood in the kitchen bundled in her favorite yellow chenille bathroom, her hip resting against one of the counter bar stools with her arms crossed over her chest. She arched her eyebrows in a terrible attempt at disapproval, but her smirk destroyed the effect.

"Oh, please..." Andi said with a toss of her hand as she shut the door. "You've come home much later after a much wilder night than mine."

"I don't know...he may *think* those car windows are tinted—"
"Mags!"

Maggie laughed and crossed the kitchen with her arms open. Andi could have kept up the annoyed personae but didn't want to kill the endorphin rush so she hugged her best friend back.

"About damn time," Maggie said, and Andi could hear the smile in her voice. "You deserve a little fun in your life, and hot *damn*, that boy is *smitten*."

Andi moved away to go to the refrigerator, taking out a cold soda. She wanted to tell Maggie how she felt, about how her blood felt like champagne in her veins and she felt like dancing around the house, but for once the 'writer' in her was absent and she couldn't find the words. She hoped the look on her face said enough.

She climbed into one of the barstools and popped the can open, letting the cold douse the heat beneath her skin. Maggie leaned on the counter to face her, resting her chin in her hands.

"I hate to spoil your evening, my dear, but I have to."

"Why? Did something happen?"

Maggie sighed. "Boner called."

The elation of the evening leaked out of her like air from a deflating balloon, and thick dread replaced it.

"Three times," Maggie added. She looked over her shoulder to the clock on the microwave. "And he'll probably be calling again any minute."

"What did he want?"

"You know Butthead," Maggie explained with a shrug. "He's not going to tell *me* anything. But, if I had to guess, I'd say it's about Jake's birthday."

Andi pushed the cold soda away and slammed her elbows on the countertop, hiding her face behind her hands. And on cue, the phone rang. Maggie picked up and answered with a short "Yeah." Andi's insides tensed when Maggie's frown tightened and she held the phone out to her.

"Hello, Lawrence," she forced herself to say without the slightest waver.

"Do you have any idea how late it is here, Andrea? I've been trying to reach you for hours and your *friend* wouldn't tell me where you were."

"I wasn't home."

"That much is obvious. My concern is where you're spending your nights while Jacob is left at home unsupervised."

Andi bit off her words, wanting to argue leaving Jake with Maggie was *far* from leaving him unsupervised, but she knew he wouldn't hear her or wouldn't care. "What do you want?"

"I'm picking Jacob up on Sunday for four days."

Andi shot up from the chair, gripping the edge of the counter. "What? Lawrence, you can't just—"

"The stipulations of the divorce are very clear, Andrea. Do you need me to explain them to you once *again*?"

"I am *very* clear on the stipulations of the divorce. They say with *proper notice* you can *request* visitation time with Jake, but as the custodial parent, I can say yes or no. You didn't *request* anything."

"I'm his father. I'm not going to ask permission to see him. Do you have a justifiable excuse why I can't take him for a few days?"

Andi slumped onto the stool again, bracing her forehead in her hand with her eyes closed. She could lie—tell Lawrence they had a trip planned and pack everyone up for a week—but they'd have to come back eventually. And if he ever found out she lied, he'd hold it over her head. Her stomach twisted at the thought of not being with Jake for four days. For four days he'd have to be alone with Lawrence. Not once had Lawrence ever raised a hand or threatened them in any way, but his abuse was the worst kind. Verbal. His words could sting worse than any punch.

"Andrea," Lawrence ground out.

"No," she finally forced herself to say. "But you can't pick him up until Sunday evening. We're having a party for him here."

"I'll come to the party."

"No, you won't," she snapped, slapping her hand down on the counter. It stung, but it focused her. "You'll come after the party."

The dead phone line was her answer.

CHAPTER EIGHT

"Is this what you had in mind when you offered to help?"

David was on his knees on Andi's lawn, surrounded by bits and pieces spread out on the grass around him that would eventually resemble something called a *Razor*, according to the instructions. Andi stood over him, her silhouette shielding him from the sun.

"I live to serve," he said with a smile

She lifted the hem of her sundress above her knees with one hand and knelt on the grass in front of him, holding out a glass of cola with ice. "For your hard work." He took it from her, but before he could drink, she leaned forward and kissed him.

The effect was instantaneous, and in a beat he'd forgotten the hot sun and the frustration over assembling the birthday gift and blindly set the glass down so he could hold her face in his hands, humming his appreciation against her mouth. It was like this *every* time he kissed her, and he hoped to God it always would be.

He opened his mouth and she matched him, her hands brushing his sleeves when his tongue touched hers. David didn't dare do more —didn't dare kiss her the way he *wanted* to—since her son could round the corner any minute. So he eased out of the kiss until they were still, their mouths pressed together. With a rough sigh, she moved away and sat back on her ankles, brushing her thumb across his lower lip.

"And that was for coming," she said softly.

Too softly. And her voice was too rough. It hadn't been right all day, and the spark he loved in her eyes was absent. Whenever he looked at her without her knowing, her lips were turned down it a poorly hidden frown she quickly forced away when he said something. She smiled now, but it was false and shallow—strained like she couldn't keep it up much longer.

David took a drink but didn't look away from her, watching her. After just a few brief moments, she slid her eyes away to look at her hands in her lap. With a sigh, she looked off across the yard to a fence running between the grass and a parking area beyond. Then she picked up a long screw from the grass and toyed with it. Fidgeting. Nervous energy.

"Andi," he said gently, reaching out to touch her chin and get her to look at him. She did, not fighting his touch, but her gaze only connected with him for a moment before dropping away. "What's wrong?"

Andi shook her head, moving back from his fingers, forcing the smile again. "Nothing. Just a lot to get done before the party and people will be getting here soon."

She started to roll back onto her feet to stand, but David grabbed her hands and shifted forward until his knees touched hers on the grass and they knelt face-to-face.

"Look at me. Please."

Andi swallowed and closed her eyes before she blinked them open again, looking him straight in the face.

"What are you trying to hide from me?"

Her lips wavered and she swallowed hard, her eyes shining brighter. David's chest clenched and he brushed his thumb across her cheek. She shook her head and scrambled away from him to her feet. Standing again, she swiped at her cheeks and sniffed, taking in a sharp breath as she brushed her dress with rough purpose. Heavy dread landed in his chest, and for a moment he wondered if coming had been a bad idea. Andi took one step away from him, then spun back and he rose on his knees in time for her to wrap her arms around him, which was interesting with the new angle. She touched his hair, leaning over to press a kiss to his forehead, and her entire body trembled like it was about to fly apart.

"I'm not hiding from *you*," she whispered roughly against his brow, sucking in a ragged breath before she kissed him again. "I promise. I'll tell you later."

David reached up to lay his palms along her jaw and drew her down for a kiss. "Okay."

Then she was jogging across the lawn to the back door of the house and disappeared inside. David sank back on his feet, staring at the back door. Part of him—a *huge* part of him—wanted to follow her and push until she told him. But, she said it wasn't him she was acting for...and that's what she was doing—acting...so, he hoped she would tell him when she didn't have to keep it up any longer.

He rubbed his face with his hands and stared at the remaining pieces of the gift. The thing was together, but he had extra parts. How did that happen? Giving up, he picked up the glass she'd brought him and drained the contents.

The rhythmic thump-thump of a basketball on cement echoed from the other side of the wooden fence. Followed by a *swish*.

Thump-thump.

Thump-thump-thump-swish.

He stood up and dusted grass from his slacks and set his empty cup on a table as he passed, heading for the gate leading to what he suspected to be a basketball hoop. Jake was on the other side, dressed in swim trunks and a tee shirt, and ready for the party. He bounced the basketball back and forth between his hands, hitting the same spot between his feet with each *thump*.

When the gate closed behind David with a clunk, Jake looked over his shoulder at him but never stopped the rhythmic bouncing.

Thump-thump-thump.

The area had been intended to park an RV or maybe a boat, like a lot of houses in California. But there was nothing parked, and a hoop had been hung against the garage wall. David held up his hands, with wrists together, and positioned to catch the ball.

"Send it here."

Jake didn't hesitate but brought the ball to his chest and tossed it straight at David, and he immediately started bouncing it as soon as he caught it. Without words, they settled into a game of H.O.R.S.E with David making the first basket. Jake was a tall kid for his age, and destined to bypass his mother in height probably in the next few months, but he was all knees and elbows. A decent build for basketball, and he gave David a challenge for each point.

After several baskets, David took a minute to hunch over and bounce the ball with one hand, wiping his forehead with the back of his other hand. "Looking forward to the party?" he asked.

Jake shrugged. "I was."

David went for the basket, and Jake sidestepped him, snagging the ball from his hand. He then started up the bouncing.

Thump-thump-thump.

"You're not now?"

Jake shook his head and shot for the basket. It was the first time he'd missed and David retrieved it, circling under the basket before coming back into the makeshift court.

"Is that why your mom is upset?"

Jake's attention shifted for a split second from the ball to David. He nodded and hunched again, ready to play.

"She won't like it you noticed."

"What's going on?"

Jake looked down and scuffed the toe of his shoe into the concrete. "My father is coming later today. He's taking me until Thursday."

David circled to Jake's right, but his attention wasn't really on the game anymore. "When did this happen?"

"Friday night, I guess. She told me yesterday."

David made his shot, but he didn't care anymore if it went in. It circled the rim before falling off without going through the ring. Jake caught it, tossing it between his hands before bouncing it off the back wall of the garage. David stopped playing, standing straight to put his hands at his waist. If Andi heard from her ex-husband on Friday night after their date, it helped explain why he hadn't been able to reach her on Saturday. Every call had gone to voicemail.

She hadn't provided details, but David had picked up enough from what she did say to figure out what she *didn't* say.

"She doesn't want you to go." It wasn't a question.

"*I* don't want to go," Jake added. He bounced the ball harder, the ball coming up nearly to his shoulders before he palmed it to slam it back down again. "I hate him. He's a jerk."

Well, that was one thing David could empathize with.

He watched Jake bounce the ball, watched the tight expression, nearly a perfect mirror of Andi's. The two of them were trying to put on faces *for each other*. David knew Jake was only eleven, but in the boy's face, he saw someone a lot older. And that was something he also understood. All too well.

"I know what it's like."

Jake pulled a 'yeah, right' face and softened the bounces so the ball only reached his waist. He had great control.

"No, it's true. My dad left us when I was ten. I probably saw him three or four times before I turned eighteen. And my first stepfather was a jerk, too."

"I don't care if I ever see him again." He turned sharply and threw the basketball at the stucco garage wall with such force David was surprised the plaster didn't crumble away. Jake caught the ball on the rebound, working it between his palms in front of his chest. His lips pulled tight and he only glanced at David before staring down at the textured surface of the ball. "He makes my mom cry *every* time he calls. Every time he shows up. She cried all the time before we left."

"You were pretty young, weren't—"

"I remember," Jake cut him off. He tossed the ball into the corner of the court and started for the gate, but David caught up with him, gripping his elbow.

"Jake, does he hurt you and your mom?" David asked, doing his damnedest to keep the snap out of his voice.

Jake stopped and stared at him, his lips pulled tight. "Like hit us?" He shook his head. "No." His eyes pinched and his lips pulled together. "But he still makes her cry, and I hate him."

David laid his hand on the boy's bony shoulder, patting it. He didn't know what he could offer the kid that would help. It sucked. All of it sucked, but the idea this ass made Andi—and her son—this upset, pissed him off and he hadn't even met the jerk yet.

"Are you the guy?" Jake asked.

David shook his head, not following Jake's switch in conversation. "What guy?"

Jake shifted his weight back and forth between his feet, licking his lips as he glanced toward the gate, and David wondered if he was worried *now* they'd be heard. "Maggie said there was a guy who thought my mom was pretty, but Mom was too chicken to believe him. You that guy?"

David drew in a slow breath through his nostrils, letting himself smile just a little bit. "Jake, I have no doubt a *lot* of men think your mom is pretty. But, yeah, I'm fairly positive I'm the guy Maggie was talking about." He leaned in closer to Jake. "But, I don't think your mom is pretty. I *know* she's beautiful. Don't you?"

Jake nodded, the tenseness around his mouth still holding his expression. "You're not going to make her cry."

It wasn't a question, wasn't an inquiry of any kind. It was a statement. Maybe even a demand. David squeezed Jake's shoulder. "No. I promise. I won't make your mom cry."

Jake nodded, accepting his answer, and stepped free of his hand to head for the gate. "It's kind of cool you're here," he tossed off with the best nonchalance an eleven-year-old can manage—which wasn't much. "A lot of my friends like you. You know, your movies and stuff."

"Yeah? So, it's cool with you I'm at your party?'

Jake shrugged and went into the backyard. Andi was back outside, and she stood at the patio table setting out bowls of chips. She looked up and saw them both, and smiled. It was far more genuine than any of the other half-attempted smiles he'd seen that day, but it was far from perfect.

"Yeah, it's cool." Jake looked up at him, a crooked smile on his face. "You think any photographers are gonna jump out of the bushes or anything?"

David grinned. "It could happen."

"Cooool," Jake said with a nod.

Maggie opened the slider from the house to the backyard and led a couple of kids about Jake's age into the yard with their parents in tow. "Jake, Juan and Eric are here."

"Hey!" Jake called out, raising his hand in a wave.

Both boys and their parents, turned in his direction with their hands raised in waves. Then their expressions shifted to shock and then shouts of "Holy crap! Jake's got David Bishop at his party!"

"Cool," Jake said again, lower this time so only David heard.

He laughed and laid his hand against the back of Jake's neck, walking with him toward the first guests.

Andi looked out the slider to the backyard and warmth like hot honey spread through her chest. David and Jake were still in the backyard, sitting on the grass with handheld computer games that battled each other. They both swayed and twisted as if their bodies could somehow affect the game, their shouts and laughter at whatever had happened on their screens loud enough to carry through the closed glass door.

Jake shouted, "Yes!" and held his game over his head. David simultaneously groaned and slapped his hand to his forehead, falling back on the grass. "Oh! You killed me," he moaned, and Jake laughed louder.

Her heart was confused, that was the only way she could categorize the battle of emotions that threatened to have her crying one second and laughing the next. Seeing her son so at ease with David settled a pleasant kind of ache in her chest, and if she let herself turn completely whimsical and self-indulgent, she imagined days like today lasting for a long time. At the same time, tears burned in her eyes because Jake had never had something so simple—something so many of his friends took for granted. Even in divided homes, her friends had their fathers in their lives. Interested in their lives. She was terrified of the day he lost even this short glimpse of a normal life.

Andi blinked back the tears, refusing to let anyone see them. Later, alone, she'd indulge in the breakdown that had threatened to knock her down since Lawrence called. He had never asked to take Jake overnight, let alone for several days. *What if he wanted to share custody? What if he wanted to take Jake to Chicago? What if…what if…*

It was the *'what ifs'* that had kept her up all the night before, and what had remained of the night after David brought her home. And it was the *'what ifs'* that had her stomach twisted into tight knots and her head hurting so bad she could barely stand the sunlight. It had been over a year since a migraine had crippled her into hiding in bed for two days, and Maggie would say it was no surprise Lawrence had been around then, too.

Maggie set a prescription bottle of prescription migraine pain reliever on the counter near her hand. "Take them before you can't walk straight."

Andi shook her head, and the simple action made her head split and her stomach roll. "No. They knock me out. I can't until after Lawrence gets here."

Maggie snorted and looked at the microwave clock. "How many times did he call today to make sure you would have Jake ready on time? And the bastard is half an hour late."

It was a fine line Andi walked between being thankful he hadn't come yet, and wishing he would just get there and get it over with. But that would mean Jake would be gone.

Her throat tightened and she pressed her hand to her stomach, mentally demanding her body to not be ill. Not now. Not with Lawrence arriving any minute. Not with David here to see how her ex-husband could tie her in knots even now…six years after leaving him.

She drew in a slow breath as the nausea backed off, and looked out the sliding door again. David and Jake now sat on one of the lounges, side-by-side, with David hunched forward resting his elbows on his knees. They were talking, but she couldn't hear them or see their faces to gauge what kind of conversation they had. Then David patted Jake's shoulder and jerked his head in the direction of the backyard, and Jake nodded. They stood and disappeared from her line of vision, heading toward the basketball court behind the garage.

The knock at the door made her jump, and she gripped the edge of the counter to keep from tipping over.

"Oh, joy," Maggie mumbled, crossing the space to the front door. "Bonehead is here."

Andi sucked in several sharp breaths, panic pounding in her chest, which just made her mad. He was *nothing*. He was her past. He had *no* control over her life!

Except he was the father of her son, and for that reason alone she'd never be free of him.

Maggie opened the door with a flourish. "Larry," she said, her voice dripping with sarcasm as she used the name she knew he detested. Which is exactly why she used it. "About damn time."

Lawrence said nothing, pushing past Maggie into the foyer with a deep scowl.

"I've been great, thanks for asking, Larry," Maggie continued as she let the door shut with a bang slightly softer than a full-on slam. "How's the little lady?"

"Once again, your lack of propriety amazes me, Margaret."

Maggie tipped her head back and laughed. "I think that's the best compliment you've ever given me, *Larry*."

Andi stayed behind the counter, using the edge as support while she categorized her ex-husband. He hadn't changed in the year or so since she'd seen him last, hadn't even changed much since they divorced. Lawrence was average in height, not even hitting five-eleven, but most women would probably say that was where 'average' ended for Lawrence Bonherre. Dark blonde hair that never seemed out of place and striking blue eyes that had caught her attention across the University of Illinois' on-campus library. They had looked warm then, attractive and inviting. But just a few years later, the same blue was cold and distant. Like ice.

"Andrea..." he said by way of greeting, and he smiled. His gaze shifted over her, not even attempting to hide his assessment, and settled on her face. "You look...good. I liked your hair longer."

"Wow, Andi. Don't let all that sweet talk go to your head. Larry is really making an effort."

Andi blinked and swallowed, disconcerted by his display of pleasantries, as limited as it was. But, it was exceptional for Lawrence. Especially in the last few years.

"I'll get Jake," she forced from her restricted throat and pushed away from the counter edge.

"No. Wait. I want to talk to you for a minute."

The migraine edged tighter into her line of vision, twisting her equilibrium, and she rubbed her forehead with her fingertips to attempt to ward it off. "Do we have to do this tonight, Lawrence? I know where you're staying and how to reach you, what else is there?"

Lawrence looked over his shoulder at Maggie, who stood near the door with her arms crossed. She arched her eyebrows and shrugged.

"What?"

"As much as you've infiltrated Andrea's life, this has nothing to do with you."

Maggie looked to Andi, and she gave a small nod letting her friend know it was fine to leave them alone. Maggie huffed and flipped her hand in the air, walking to the living room area on the other side of the open space. She dropped into her favorite chair and picked up a magazine from the coffee table, flipping randomly through the pages.

"What is it you want?"

He walked toward her and laid his hand on the edge of the countertop furthest from her. Regardless, her skin crawled just having him close. It amazed her that at one time she let this man touch her and now, the idea of being within ten feet of him made her squirm. Whenever he even came close to contact, she thought of all the women he'd been with while still married to her. Women he'd had sex with and came home to her, sometimes taking her to bed, too. The idea made her twitch and greased her stomach.

"I'd hoped we could have a civil conversation. We were married for nine years, after all."

"Bringing up the disaster that was our marriage isn't the wisest thing if you want to have a *civil* conversation, Lawrence." She had to force the words through clenched teeth and tight lips to keep from getting sick.

"But our marriage is what I need to talk about. Andrea, I've been thinking about some things. I've decided I need to make some changes in my life. Which is why I asked to spend some time with Jacob. I've been too absent from his life—"

"That's just fine with us."

His smile slipped, but he swallowed and the unsettling expression returned. "A boy needs his father. I want to make sure he has one. Especially as he grows older. He needs to learn how to be a man."

Maggie snorted from the living room.

Cold terror hit her veins as every fear that had kept her up all night collided in one staggering slam to the center of her chest. "What are you saying?"

He rounded the corner of the counter and moved toward her, and she fought the urge to scramble over the counter to the other side. But she refused to let him see her shaken. She refused to let him know he had any kind of power over her. So, she crossed her arms and clenched her teeth, glaring at him so he never saw her look away. Never saw her flinch.

"I made a mistake letting you leave so easily, Andrea. I shouldn't have let you go six years ago. I should have made you stay."

Maggie barked a laugh from the other room.

Lawrence scowled again, looking across the living room where Maggie still sat shaking her head. By the time he looked at Andi again the forced smile had returned. "My mistake was not fighting the divorce."

"No. Your mistake was sleeping with any slut who could stand you long enough to get her skirt up."

Maggie snickered, and the sound gave Andi a small modicum of strength. She wasn't alone in this. The day she'd found out about Lawrence's affairs, she'd felt isolated. Her parents lived three hundred miles away, and she had no friends to speak of because everything was about appearance rather than companionship. She had no one but her son.

Until Maggie opened her home to them. Gave them a place to be, a place to recover and gather strength. It wasn't a typical home, but she and Jake had a home with Maggie O'Connell. She could be abrasive, sometimes even crass, but Maggie was Maggie and Andi loved her for it.

"I understand now why it hurt you so much when you found out,"

Lawrence went on, ignoring the peanut gallery. "I should have been kinder."

"You shouldn't have slept around," Andi snapped.

"This is all the past, we've talked about this. The reasons—"

"Don't you *dare* try to put it on me again."

"I'm not," he said, raising his hands in a pathetic symbol for surrender. "I'm saying I understand now." Lawrence sighed, his shoulders slumping. "Leslie—"

"Oh, please *God* tell me she cheated," Maggie roared from the other room and followed it up with loud laughter, throwing her hands up in a victory cheer as she stomped her feet. "Yes! There *is* a God and He's got a *great* sense of humor."

Some small part of her wanted to automatically say "I'm sorry," just like she would for anyone who told her they knew the feeling of betrayal she knew. But it was a very small part, and the angry ex-wife beat her down until she shut up without even a whimper.

"Are you getting to some kind of point, Lawrence?" Andi made sure her annoyance was more than obvious in her tone.

He took another step toward her, and despite herself, she pushed back against the edge of the counter until it cut into her lower back.

"I know now, Andrea. I know I made a mistake, and I understand you were the best thing that ever happened to me. My life was good when we were together."

"*Your* life, not mine."

"We were good *together*, Andrea." He reached for her hand, pulling it free of where she had it tucked in the bend of her arms. "I want to talk about being a family again. You. Me. And Jacob."

"You have got to be friggin' kidding!" Maggie declared from the other room, practically leaping from her chair.

Andi yanked her hand free of Lawrence's hold and sidestepped him, taking a deep breath when she found air he hadn't tainted with his expensive aftershave. The room tipped and vice grips grabbed the back of her head, squeezing so tight she wondered if her eyes would pop out. She used the edge of the counter to get around to the other side and spun around to face him again.

"Who the hell do you think you are to even *comment* on any of this?" Lawrence shouted at Maggie, jabbing his finger viciously in the air. "This has nothing to do with you. If it weren't for you, Andrea wouldn't have left me at all!"

"Well, then *hall-eh-luh-jah* for me."

"Lawrence, stop—" Andi tried, but they both continued.

"You filled her head with all that bull about being a writer. Do you have any idea how embarrassing it was for me when my partners learned my wife wrote smut?"

"Look who's laughing now, *Larry*. I'd say a movie deal and four books on the Bestseller's List deal trumps your whiney, stick-up-their-ass partners any day."

Lawrence spun around on Andi. "Is this the kind of influence you allow around our son? What the hell kind of examples does he live with? A bitch and a—"

"If you don't like it, get the hell out," Maggie cut him off.

"Who do you think you are?" Lawrence demanded. "Get out of here and leave us the hell alone so we can talk like civilized people."

Maggie closed the space between them in three long strides and came toe-to-toe with Lawrence, jabbing her finger against his chest. "I'll tell you who I am and I'll tell you where the hell you are. I am the witness to the life Andi has made for herself without *you*. And you are in *my* house. My house. Andi's house. And Jake's house. If *anyone* is getting out of here, it's *you*."

"Please..." Andi begged, her stomach twisting. She curled her fingers around the back of a barstool, her knuckles white and aching. "Please just stop this. Jake will hear, and it's already bad enough—"

"What's bad enough? Doesn't he want to spend some time with me? What the hell have you been saying?"

"Nothing Jake doesn't already know. That you're a jerk and a horse's ass," Maggie tossed over her shoulder as she went into the kitchen, putting the counter between herself and Lawrence.

Andi had no doubt it was to prevent herself from hitting him. Maggie was Irish to the bone and her temper was like a match to kindling, especially when it came to Lawrence. Lawrence sucked several deep breaths in through his flared nostrils, his hands clenched at his side. Andi closed her eyes and dropped her head forward, begging the migraine to hold off just a few more minutes before putting her on her knees.

The sliding door opened behind her, and a gust of cooler evening air hit the back of her calves. David and Jake talked casually, their voices tinged with laughter that just for a moment pushed aside the tension gripping her.

"Can we go when I get back?"

"Absolutely, as long as your mom…" David's voice fell away, and Andi drew in a slow breath, lifting her head as she opened her eyes to look at them.

She did her best to smile, but even though she couldn't see her face, it felt more like a grimace. "Jake honey, your dad is here."

"Hey, Jacob," Lawrence said with way too much false enthusiasm. "You ready for some fun?"

David's gray-blue eyes were locked on Lawrence, and any semblance of a smile was gone. It didn't surprise her because the tension in the room was tangible. It was thick and heavy, choking her. He raised his hand and rested it on Jake's shoulder, squeezing slightly.

Jake frowned. "I'll go get my bag."

Jake walked past his father, swinging wide so there was no chance their bodies would touch. As Jake disappeared up the stairs, David bent close to her ear to whisper. "What's wrong? You're pale and I can feel you shaking."

Andi turned to the sound of his voice and raised her hand to rest it against his cheek. His hand immediately came up to hold it, his eyes shifting to study her. She had to look worse than she felt.

"I'm just—"

"Who the hell are you?"

"Don't get out much, do you, Larry?" Maggie snarked from the kitchen, and despite the sick pain in her head, Andi smirked just a little bit.

David's attention didn't waver from her, and he started to raise his other hand to touch her face, but when the room tilted and she felt herself sway, his palm came to her back. It was all the support she needed to keep herself on her feet.

Keeping her eyes open was something altogether different. Just the light from outside burned through her retinas into her brain.

"Andrea, I want to know who else you're exposing my son to as if she isn't bad enough." He indicated Maggie with a jerk of his head. "Who are you?" Lawrence demanded again.

David's jaw shifted, and he seemed to take a moment before looking away from her. He stepped forward enough to extend one hand toward Lawrence, the other maintaining the comforting pressure against her back. She wanted to turn into him, lean against him, but that would just be fuel for the fire Lawrence had started before he ever arrived.

"David Bishop," he said.

Lawrence glared for several moments and Andi thought she saw the flash of recognition in his eyes before he consented to grip David's hand. His wrist flexed as he tightened his hold, a familiar power play she'd seen him use many times. Then his frown flinched and he tried to pull his hand away when David did the same.

Maggie drew in a deep, dramatic breath through her nose and let it go with a long "Aaaaaaaaah. Smell the testosterone." She leaned forward. "Just so we're clear, Larry…I was referring to David. You have to be a man, after all."

"You fu—"

"Hey!" David bit out, and Lawrence's attention snapped to him. "There are ladies present."

Jake came back into the kitchen from upstairs, his duffle bag slung over his shoulder. David dropped Lawrence's hand and took a step back. He stepped just slightly behind her so his hands could settle at her hips. She wondered if the positioning was more for her benefit, or Lawrence's. The pain was almost unbearable now, stabbing her eyes and filling her line of vision with equal amounts of color and black spots. Her knees didn't want to hold her up anymore, and she leaned into David just enough to keep her standing. His hand pressed firmer to her hip, giving her more support.

"Bye, honey," Andi said, trying her best to keep her voice level. "I'll see you on Thursday."

Jake nodded and dropped his bag by the door, moving wide

around his father again to reach her. She wrapped her arms around him and held on tight, hoping he didn't feel the tremble in her body. "I love you, sweetheart," she whispered near his ear and kissed his cheek.

"I love you, Mom."

She let him go, leaving a chunk of her heart with him—the rest stuck in her throat. David held his hand out to Jake, but instead of shaking hands, they slapped their palms together and gripped each other's thumbs for a second before sliding their hands apart with enough force their fingertips snapped off each other. They curled their hands into fists and bumped their knuckles together.

"Later, buddy," David said with a wide, genuine smile. "Next time we play, I'm not letting you off so easy."

Jake grinned, waving David off. "Whatever, old man."

Maggie met Jake at the end of the counter, hugged him just as tight as Andi had, and said something in his ear no one else could hear. He nodded and stepped away.

Without a backward glance at them, Lawrence walked past Jake's bag and stormed to the door. Jake slung the strap over his shoulder again and followed his father from the house, his head hung low. By the time the door closed, Andi couldn't stop the choking sob that had built up in her chest since Lawrence came through the door. She shook so badly, that she felt like she was going to fly apart, and her head wanted to split apart to relieve the pressure.

David wrapped his arms around her from behind, pulling her back against him with his lips near her ear. He whispered and kissed her cheek, but it was all coming down around her and she couldn't even see anymore.

Maggie grabbed a glass from the cabinet and filled it with water from the sink, setting it near Andi with the bottle of migraine pain pills. "She only gets these damn things when that son of a bitch shows up and stirs the pot."

"Migraine," David said, no inflection of question in his voice.

Andi tried to nod, but the motion threatened to turn her inside out and she floundered to grip the back of the nearest barstool.

"Do you take any kind of triptan?" he asked, but the question took several seconds to trigger in her pain-fogged mind.

"Yes, but they're upstairs," she managed through clenched teeth.

David moved around to face her, his hands never leaving her until he cupped her face in his palms and gently urged her to look at him. She shook violently now, so violently it felt like her organs moved on their own accord. Silence and darkness it was all she wanted.

"I can help with this. Do you trust me?"

"What, do you have healing hands, boyo?" Maggie asked.

He grinned just slightly, but never took his attention from Andi. "Something like that. I learned a few things about getting rid of migraines when my sister Caroline had them. She stopped having them after my niece was born, but as a teenager, she had them once or twice a week."

"I just want to lie down," Andi whispered, hearing the tears in her voice.

David bent at the knees and swept his arms behind her back and legs, lifting her off the ground to hold her against his chest. The sudden change in position made her groan, but she kept her lips tightly shut to keep from being ill. Their voices were muffled like Andi was listening to them through water. She turned into David, pressing her face into the side of his throat, enjoying the warmth of his skin as chilled gooseflesh prickled on her arms. This was when she knew it was bad…when she felt more like she had the flu than a headache. She closed her eyes and prayed for dark silence.

CHAPTER NINE

The interior of Andi's bedroom was in almost complete darkness when David nudged the door open with his foot, even though the sun was still up outside. Heavy drapes covered french doors to his left, and he figured that would be the balcony she had watched him from two nights before. There were no other windows, and only a sliver of sunlight came in through the drapes. Only a small nightlight from an attached bathroom cast any artificial light, and David wondered if Andi knew this was coming…the migraine Maggie said only happened with her ex came around.

He'd met the man for all of five minutes, and already Lawrence Bonherre set David's teeth on edge. Even if Andi hadn't shared what little she had, and if Jake hadn't told him how much he hated his father —and *why*—David wouldn't have liked him the minute he walked into the same room. The guy screamed asshole, plain and simple.

He crossed to the bed against the far wall and set Andi down close to the pillows stacked near the headboard. She moaned softly and pressed her face into the curve of his neck, her fingers curled tight into his shirt.

"You just need to sit here for a couple minutes, sweetheart. I promise."

If he'd known, things never would have gone this far before he stepped in. David only hoped now he could still help.

He pressed a kiss to her forehead before crouching in front of her. Andi had her head down, her hair falling across her cheeks, with her eyes closed. Her fingers stayed curled in the fabric of his shirt at his shoulder. He tried not to shift his position, knowing he was probably the anchor keeping her upright and slipped her glasses off her nose. He set them on the bedside table in front of her phone charging stand and ran his hands down her calf to unbuckle her sandals. Tight lines framed her eyes and her lips were pressed together in a thin line, but she didn't blink and barely seemed to take a breath.

"You still with me, sweetheart?" he asked.

She just nodded. Slowly. Barely.

Maggie followed them into the room, a cup of water in one hand and the bottle of pain pills in the other. She set them on the small table beside the bed. "What else do you need?"

"Do you know where she keeps the triptan?"

"Probably in the bathroom. I'll check."

"Thanks. I want her to take those."

"Sure thing, doc," Maggie said with a salute before going into the adjoined bathroom. She flipped on the light, and Andi winced even though her eyes were closed.

The migraine may have gone too far.

David finished with the sandals and stood, laying his hand on Andi's shoulder as Maggie came back, the medication box in her hand. Maggie held the box up, trying to read in the dim light.

"Says she can take one when the migraine starts, and one an hour later if it doesn't go away."

"Get two out, please. We're not going to mess around."

Andi swayed and raised a shaky hand to her forehead. "Please..." was all she managed to say.

David nodded toward the box, and Maggie complied by dumping the blister pack into her hand and popping two small pills into her palm. He toed off his Birkenstocks and took his hand from Andi's shoulder to pull his phone, wallet, and keys from his pockets. Tossing those on the bedside table, he undid the buckle of his belt, tugging it free from the belt loops of his shorts. Andi swayed but set her hand on the mattress beside her to keep herself upright. Maggie stopped, the blister pack in hand, and stared at him with arched eyebrows.

"Honey, just what do you think you're doing?"

David grinned and shook his head, tossing his belt aside. "Just getting comfortable."

He held his hand out, trying to talk as little as possible. She dropped them in his hand, then reached for the water and pain pills.

"Just the water. If this doesn't work, I'll give her the pain pills."

"She's in pain," Maggie argued with a sharp snap.

"I know, but let me try this. I swear, I won't let her stay this way if it doesn't work."

Maggie pursed her lips and stared at him for several moments before huffing out a breath through her nose and handing him the glass. "You sure as hell better take care of her."

"I will." David crouched again in front of Andi and took her hand to turn it over, dropping the pills in her palm. "Andi? Take these."

Without opening her eyes, Andi put her palm to her lips and tipped her head back. Her other hand reached out blindly for the water, and he pushed it to her fingers. The water sloshed in the cup with the tremble of her hand, and he supported the bottom as she raised it to her mouth and sipped. Taking the glass from her as soon as she was done, he held it out to Maggie.

"Sweetheart, I need you to help me, then I promise, you can relax."

Andi tried to open her eyes but only managed to squint at him. Even in the limited light from the bathroom, he saw the lines of pain around her lips. David moved quickly to rearrange the pillows against the headboard, and Andi immediately leaned sideways to lie down.

"Not yet. Hang on."

She groaned but shifted back to a sitting position, her hands over her face. Maggie scowled at him, her arms crossed. When he had the pillows the way he wanted, he turned to Andi's friend and set his hands on her upper arms. "I know this looks weird, but I swear, I know what I'm doing." He met her glowering stare. "I'll take care of her."

Maggie stared him down, not blinking.

"It's okay, Mags," Andi said softly from behind him, and Maggie looked past him to where she sat. Her voice was so soft it almost didn't carry enough for him to hear her. "I'll take the pain pill if I have to."

"Fine," Maggie said through tight lips. "I'll be here if you need me." She pointed a finger at David's nose. "No funny business, boyo."

She twisted out of his hands and marched to the door, giving them one last look before closing it behind her. David took his position at the head of the bed with the pillows behind him for support.

"Okay, sweetheart. I need you to come to me."

With a gentle touch, he eased Andi with him so she reclined between his legs with her back to his torso. She moaned with each movement and her fingers fisted into the bedding. If her migraines were anything like Caroline's, he figured she fought against her equilibrium at this point, and as long as she was still the world didn't spin around her. Every movement probably twisted her stomach and set her off kilter.

David raised his knees so his legs bracketed her and positioned her so her arms draped over his thighs and she was cradled against him. Caroline had told him once when the room was spinning, even with her eyes shut, she felt 'secure' when she felt her brother hanging on to her. It grounded her and helped her relax enough to let the massage work.

"I used to do this for my sister," he said softly, so Andi would understand what he was doing. "It's a massage technique to relieve the tension of the migraine. It might take a while to get rid of the pain completely, but we should know in a few minutes if it's going to work."

Andi didn't answer but nodded her head a slight degree. Taking a deep breath, David slid his fingers into her hair, angling the tips toward his chest as he pressed against her scalp. His thumbs found the base of her skull, and he edged around until he instinctively found the spot he needed.

"Take in a breath," he instructed. She did as he asked, her ribs expanding against him as she drew in. "Now, let it out slowly."

As she did, he applied gentle but firm pressure.

"One more time."

It took a good thirty seconds before he felt the almost imperceptible change beneath his fingers, and he released the touch.

"Oh, god..." Andi practically purred and a small tremor shifted through her.

David closed his eyes and swallowed. Okay...so having Andi Parker lying against him—reacting like *that* to the massage—was about ten thousand kinds of different from his sister.

"Good?" he asked, keeping his voice level as he shifted his focus from the base of her skull to the hairline along her forehead.

She just hummed.

David rested his cheek against her soft hair, the scent of strawberries and some other fruit mingling in his senses. He set his thumbs just below her temple, right above her ear, and used the tip of his index fingers to search her forehead for the next sweet spot. Finding the right ridge, he guided her through her breathing until he felt the release and she sighed.

"Feeling better?" he whispered against her ear.

She tilted her head to the side, exposing the long line of her throat to him. Any other time, he would have pressed his lips to her skin. He still remembered with painful clarity the way her skin tasted from their teenager-esque make-out session in his car, and the flash of memory shot through him. David clenched his jaw and either relieved some of the pressure—or added to it—but indulged in the small pleasure of letting his lips brush her jaw and the lobe of her ear.

She hummed...whether it was in answer to his question, he didn't know.

David massaged her shoulders, working his thumbs in small circles on the back of her neck, for a few minutes before sliding his hands down her bare arms to her hands. He raised her right hand from where it rested and sandwiched it between his hands. Her fingertips were cool, but her palms were warm. David massaged her hand between his, rubbing gently from her wrist toward her fingertips. Pinching the soft skin between her thumb and index finger, he worked the flesh between his fingertips until he found what he needed.

This had always been the telling point of whether the massage would work or not...at least with Caroline. He never quite understood why it worked so well, but the pressure on the hands did the most to relieve the pain. David shifted so he could look at Andi's profile without disturbing her position, and applied the pressure. She already understood the rhythm of the breathing and drew in a long breath. As she released it again, he took away his fingers.

Andi gasped and her eyes flew open. "What was *that*?"

David smiled, allowing himself another small indulgence of smoothing his hand across her stomach, pressing her back against him. "Accu-pressure. Don't ask me how it works, I don't know. I just know it does. Give me your other hand."

He repeated the massage on her left hand, garnering almost the same reaction with just a little less surprise. With each new spot he worked on, the tension abated from her body. Where her spine had been almost rigid when they first settled, she now let her body relax against him. She drew up her knees, matching his position, but in doing so the hem of her sundress slipped up her legs, giving him a temptingly pleasant angle of view. After repeating the course of pressure points two more times, her breathing had deepened and he suspected she was either near sleep or already there.

When he finished with the second hand, he draped her arms across her body and wrapped his arms around her. With just the slightest shift, he settled down into the pile of pillows he'd situated to support them, giving him the chance to let his head rest back on the stack. She sighed and turned within his embrace onto her side, tucking her hand between his chest and her cheek.

The room was in almost complete darkness. The sun had set and the only light came from the crack in the bathroom door and the night-light Maggie had left on. In the darkness, unable to see her face, David closed his eyes and smoothed his hand up and down her bare arm. Gooseflesh rose under his fingertips and he tugged at the blankets until he could flip them over the two of them, wrapping her in a cocoon.

It had been a *very* long time since he'd held a sleeping woman in his arms. Rachel had probably been the last since Josie didn't like being touched when she slept, let alone being held. David rolled his head against the pillow, forcing aside the thoughts of old girlfriends and past mistakes. Right now, Andrea Parker slept against him, the smell of her shampoo drifting around him and the warmth of her body sinking through his clothes.

David brushed her hair from her cheek and pressed a kiss to her forehead before he closed his eyes.

The first sense that registered for Andi was the unfamiliar but pleasant weight of an arm draped over her waist, and the warmth of a hand against her stomach. The second was the whisper of a warm breath against the back of her neck, and the slightly rough bristle of an unshaved cheek just touching the side of her throat.

The third was the distinct lack of a headache or the muzzy, groggy, thickheaded feeling she always woke up with after drugging herself into a healing sleep.

She blinked her eyes but tried to stay as still as possible, not wanting to move away from David's embrace. The sun had come up again, shining in a thin slit down the crack in her drapes, but the room was still mostly in darkness. They were curled together at a strange angle across the bed, almost horizontal to the headboard. Instead of being beneath the blankets, David had managed to flip the duvet around them, wrapping them together inside it. His back was to the pile of pillows and she was nestled against him, his chest expanding against her spine with each breath he took. His extended arm was her pillow, and the sleeve of his short-sleeved shirt had shifted up so her cheek rested on his upper arm. Andi was bundled and warm, and the scent of David wrapped around her.

She closed her eyes again and drew in a slow breath, smiling.

She could get used to this.

Very used to this.

And that was probably not a good idea.

Oh, who cares? You're here now!

Andi slid her arm from within the warm cocoon of blankets to touch her fingertips to the inside of his exposed elbow. A prominent vein ran from his triceps to his lower arm, and fine light hairs flecked his skin. Just a few inches from his wrist there was a small scar, no more than half an inch in length, slightly paler than the tan skin of his arm. With a smile, Andi wondered what he might have done to earn it.

David stirred, sucking in a deep breath through his nose, inhaling the morning. His hand splayed against her lower stomach and pulled her firmer against him, and Andi's eyes fluttered closed. She barely stifled the low moan that purred in her chest at the flutter that spread beneath his hand.

She didn't stifle it nearly as well as she thought because she heard his low chuckle and his lips brushed her shoulder. The arm supporting her head curled around to cross her chest, and he wrapped his fingers around her shoulder, wrapping her in his arms as snugly as the blanket.

He ran the tip of his nose along the side of her neck, brushing her hair aside, making her shiver, and his lips brushed her ear when he whispered, "This could be habit forming."

Andi turned her head toward him, able to focus on his face without her glasses because he was so close. "I was just thinking the same thing—"

Before she could finish, he raised his hand to her cheek and turned her into him, his open mouth covering hers. Just like every other time they kissed, everything inside Andi came to life in a dizzying flash that stole her breath and made her heart pound. She rolled within his arms to face him, never breaking contact with his lips and he shifted over her, the weight of his hips against hers enough to make her groan against his mouth.

He rose over her, bearing his weight on his elbows, and his leg slid between her thighs, sending an erotic rush through her. A silver chain slipped free of the shirt, a Star of David dangling between them. Andi curled her fingers into his shirt, tipping her head to follow his kiss. The blanket twisted around them, finally falling away, and the brush of cooler air on her bare legs made Andi gasp. They'd been so cocooned in the covers the room air felt almost chilly.

All thoughts of a chill vanished in a flash when he laid his hand on her leg and slid it up her thigh, taking the hem of her dress with it. His fingers curled against her hip, scorching her through the thin fabric of her cotton panties, and Andi instinctively raised her knee, curling her foot behind his knee. The warmth of his calves, and the bristle of sparse hair against her ankle, brought images of him over her—skin-to-skin—making love to her, and she closed her eyes, clinging to fistfuls of his shirt. David shifted over her, his hips bucking against her, his teeth grating gently against the skin below her ear.

The cool air of moments before was now stifling, and her clothes restricted every breath. His kisses were both rough and soft, his morning beard abrading her skin, but making her nerves come alive. Andi couldn't breathe right, couldn't pull in enough oxygen to abate the dizzying effects of his body over her, couldn't get enough or touch enough.

David growled, the vibration shifting over her throat, and pushed his hands into the bed, sliding his body down hers. His lips still brushed her skin from her throat to the 'v' of her dress, but he didn't kiss. Andi opened her eyes, watching him, trying to make her brain work past *want* to catch up with the change in him.

David rose over her, bracing himself on his arms, and looked down at her. Even that movement, his body brushing her in all the best places, sent shivers of arousal skimming over her and melted her insides. Heavy lids hooded his eyes and only the tiniest of grins touched the corners of his wet lips.

"I'm sorry," he said, taking in deep breaths. "I can't seem to control myself with you."

"You make it sound like a bad thing." Andi couldn't control her urge to shift beneath him, tilting her hips against the not-so-subtle sign of his arousal behind the zipper of his shorts.

David groaned and dropped his head forward, resting his perspiration-slicked forehead against her lips. Andi kissed him and raised her arms to push her fingers into his mussed hair. Slowly, by degrees, her breathing leveled until she felt less like she'd been dropped at the top of the Himalayas without an oxygen tank.

"Oh, it's not a bad thing at all," he said, his breath skimming across her throat. "It just makes it very hard for me to be the gentleman my mom raised me to be."

Andi smiled, combing his hair with her fingers. He settled his weight, partially on her still but mostly on the mattress beside her so they were nose to nose. Her skin still craved him, her body still screamed to shift against him and pull at his clothes until she found more of *him*. But, she drew a long, slightly shuddered breath and tried not to think about how much she wanted him to…

"Every time I kiss you," he said softly, drawing her away from her dangerous thoughts. Sometimes it didn't pay to have a vivid imagination. Didn't pay at *all*. "It's like…" David laughed and curled his hand against his temple to support his head, tucking her beneath him just a little. "I can't think of any way to say it that doesn't sound stupid."

"I'll forgive you," she encouraged with a grin.

He slid his hand over her hip to the small of her back, pulling her against him. His small grin had grown into a full-fledged smile—dimples and all—that made her heart jump all on its own.

If she wasn't careful, she could fall completely and totally in love with this man.

"Okay," he grinned. "You asked for it."

"I did. Tell me."

David's gaze shifted down to focus on her lips, and Andi's breath caught at the way his eyes darkened. She *saw* it happen. That was another one of those turn of phrases she—and half a gazillion other authors of romance—used in her writing…the way arousal darkened his gaze. Another one of those things she wrote, imagined, but never experienced.

Until *right now*.

"I want you."

The simple statement sent butterflies free in her stomach.

"It's not just…I don't just want to make love to you. I *do*, believe me. I do want to make love to you."

Andi smirked, feeling just a little devilish. "Oh, I believe you…" She settled her hand at his hip and slid it back to rest on his backside, tugging him just a little closer.

David growled low in his throat and kissed her. But, this time he pulled away before neither of them were thinking clearly again. He laid his palm against her cheek, his thumb stroking her lip.

"I want to be with you, Andi. Just *with* you. Around you. Near you.

I want to touch you *all the time*." He looked down at their bodies, where they touched almost everywhere from chest to knees and curled his fingers around hers. David lifted her hand to his mouth, kissing her fingertips and her palm. "I want to hold your hand. I want to feel your skin. I want…"

He trailed off, finally lifting his gaze to look at her.

Tears prickled in her eyes, and Andi had to swallow against the intense rush of emotion—what emotion was this?—that hit her. She blinked harder because she knew what it was…love. It was too late. She had *already* fallen in love with him.

It might have happened…right then…right there…at that moment.

"So far, I'm not hearing anything stupid," she whispered through her tight throat and blinked hard against the tears she didn't want to fall.

But they did, sliding from the corner of her eyes across her temples. David smoothed his thumb across her skin, wiping the tear away. Andi curled up to press her lips to his this time, cradling his face in her hands as she held the simple kiss. When she settled onto the bed again, his eyes held an almost mischievous twinkle. She loved it when he smiled and his eyes sparked like that…it was the smile that inspired her to do outrageous things. It probably should worry her he could get her to do things she never would have done before with just a smile, but it didn't worry her. It thrilled her.

Just as easily, his face sobered and the smile relaxed without completely disappearing. "Do you remember what you said in your trailer last week? What did you call it…TS…TS…"

"TSTL," she provided. "Too stupid to love. I was rambling."

He grinned again. "You said you weren't going to assume anything, you would ask me if you wanted to know something. And you didn't want me to assume anything."

Andi nodded against the pillow. "I remember."

"Okay…" He huffed a breath and took her hand, holding it against his chest as he stared down for a moment. When he looked up again, Andi knew instinctively by the intensity of his eyes that whatever he had to say was important. Her nerves tingled, anticipating either something good…or the worst.

"Every time I kiss you...well, you know how it is every time we kiss."

She nodded.

"Andi, I don't want..." He stopped again, and smiled—but it was a self-deprecating kind of smile that spoke of uncertainty...something she'd never seen in him before. "I don't want to ruin this."

"If we made love, we'd ruin it?"

David shook his head. "No. Not if we..." He laughed, humorously, and rubbed his hand over his face. "I've never had a conversation like this. I feel like a teenager—"

"That seems to happen a lot with us," she said, letting her voice stay light.

This time, when he laughed, she knew he meant it.

"Yeah, it does."

She waited for him to continue. Andi was fairly sure what he wanted to say, what he was trying to say, but like she'd promised him...she wouldn't assume anything.

"Andi, I want this...us...for a long time. And, I don't want to rush into it—even though it probably seems that way because we've been going at top speed since that kiss in your trailer—I don't want to—It's too important, you're too important to me to—"

Andi took pity on him and laid her finger against his lips. "I understand."

"I don't know how long I can hold out," he said against her touch, pulling her hand away so he could lean toward her, his lips hovering over hers when he spoke again. "Especially if I wake up again with you in my arms."

"I don't know...I kind of like tempting fate."

She felt his smile just before his tongue slid past her teeth to tease the inside of her mouth with a slow, seductive kiss that instantly revived every butterfly that had fallen dormant during their conversation. But as he pulled back from the kiss, he shifted onto his knees and backed off the bed, offering her his hand. Andi took it and let him draw her to her feet.

He rested his hands on her hips, drawing her against him. "There's temptation, and there's waving a steak in front of a hungry lion," he said with a smirk.

Andi pulled a face. "Are you calling me a piece of meat?"

Before he could defend himself, he was interrupted by a knock at the door.

"Everyone decent?" Maggie called.

"Yes."

Maggie opened the door, peering cautiously around the edge before stepping inside. David didn't try to move away, and Andi was fine with that.

"How are you feeling?"

"I probably should have asked you that," David said with a chuckle against her temple. Then with comical interest, he dipped his knees and looked her level in the eyes. "How are you feeling?"

"I feel great." Andi smiled, turning to Maggie but looking at David from the corner of her eye. "David is very good with his hands."

"Oi!" Maggie declared, throwing up her hands. "I just asked if your headache was gone, not about anything *else* that might have happened! Besides, that's a conversation for later over Cherry Garcia and hot fudge." Maggie wagged her eyebrows.

"Yes, my headache is gone." Andi left the rest hanging, not feeling like justifying anything else that might or might not have happened.

"You still feel up to the book signing this afternoon?"

Andi slapped the heel of her hand against her forehead. "Oh, crap! It's Monday! I completely forgot with—" She stopped short, not even wanting to mention *his* name.

He was like the evil wizard in *Harry Potter*…He Who Shall Not Be Named.

"I can still cancel if you're not up to it."

"No, it's fine."

"You have a book signing?" David asked, looking between Andi and Maggie.

"In Valencia," Maggie provided. "She's got them scheduled all over Southern California over the next few months, helping to hype the movie a little. When the studio starts running trailers, she'll be doing a book tour. Nationwide."

"Mind if I tag along? Today…can't promise the nationwide part."

Andi looked up at him, squinting because she hadn't put her glasses on yet. Lying nose-to-nose in bed, she didn't need them to see his face…but now, both he and Maggie were kind of blurry. Without her saying a word, David took a sideways step and picked up her glasses from the bedside table, handing them to her.

"Thank you."

He just grinned.

"Are you sure you want to come? They're not all that exciting. I've sat at a book signing for two hours before without a single person coming to the table."

"What she doesn't tell you is that was three years ago before anyone knew the names *Andrea Parker* or *Rise of Dawn*. Nowadays, people get in line hours before she shows up."

"It's not—"

Maggie silently cut her off with a high arch of her eyebrows…all but daring Andi to argue with her. Andi sighed and turned to the bed, tossing the blankets back into some semblance of where they belonged.

"Okay, fine…they can get crowded. But, there wouldn't be much for you to do but—"

"But watch you beat off adoring fans?" He grinned. "I can't wait."

"Awesome!" Maggie said with a clap of her hands. "Take a shower, whatever, and then I say we need breakfast." She pointed at David. "You're buying."

CHAPTER TEN

"Come right this way, Ms. Parker."

A young girl, probably no older than twenty or twenty-one with a gold name tag that read 'Beth', led the three of them through the middle display area of the massive bookstore toward a table David saw set up along the back, near the in-store Starbucks. Maggie had called it at the house...there was already a line of at least four-dozen people lined up outside the store doors, the line stretching down the sidewalk past the Ben and Jerry's and Baja Fresh restaurants in the same plaza. Most of them already carried bags of books or held books in their arms. For those who didn't have their own, a massive display was set up right inside the store doors with all four books in the series set up and ready for the taking. Some of the *Rise of Dawn* books had the original cover art, and some had the movie-themed covers—whichever the readers preferred.

"Our manager asked I send his apologies for not meeting you. But, we've made sure everything is ready for you." The girl looked past Andi to him, where he walked on the other side of her. "I'm sorry, but we didn't realize there would be other...guests...with us."

"Oh, I'm not here," David said with a grin, waving the hand that wasn't holding one of Andi's. "I'm a tag-along."

The girl smiled nervously and nodded, focusing again on Andi as they reached the table. It was a long table, draped in a green and tan cloth, with stacks of books on either end. A large poster board set in a metal easel was positioned at one end, announcing *'Andrea Parker – Author of the Award-Winning Insurgence series'* would be signing books from noon until three. A studio shot of Andi showed her with a long braid of her beautiful red hair hanging down the front of one shoulder, and the beautiful grin he'd learned to love.

David turned his attention to her, taking in her profile. She wore a yellow gauze top with a neckline that scooped low enough in the front to drive him crazy, and far enough in the back to make him imagine running kisses along the edge to the back of her neck. The yellow made her skin glow and highlighted the red of her hair. A simple yellow headband held her short, wild curls away from her face and David decided he much preferred the curls to the long braid in the picture. And today she wore faded jeans that hugged her in all the right places. David couldn't decide what he preferred…the sundresses that whispered around her and let him see her legs or the jeans that hugged her hips and showed off her backside.

"Thank you very much, Beth," Maggie said, setting her bag on the table. She set her hands at her waist and scanned the area. "It all looks great. You've done a good job."

Beth blushed and smiled, her eyes consistently shifting to Andi. "It's our pleasure to have an author of your caliber in our store, Ms. Parker. If there's anything you need, anything at all, just let us know. Feel free to ask for anything from the café, and if there's anything you'd like that we don't have in the store, we'll be happy to get it for you."

Andi smiled, looking directly into the girl's bright eyes. "Thank you so much, but I'm sure we'll be just fine. Maybe just some water?"

"Yes, ma'am."

Beth hurried off to the café as Maggie set in on adjusting the stacks of books and displays. David had done autograph sessions a few times, at conventions or events his manager had put together, and Maggie reminded him of Avi. Of course, Avi was more bristle than smile and wasn't nearly as pretty as Maggie Connelly.

"So, boyo," Maggie said turning to him. "I relinquish my standard seat beside Andi to you for the afternoon. It's your job to make sure her Sharpie markers never run out, and she's well hydrated, and if any fans bring gifts, it's your job to politely collect them and set them aside. Generally, keep the author happy. Can you handle that?"

David grinned and looked at Andi. "I will do my best."

"You don't have to," Andi said as she turned to him, and instinctively, David set his hands on her hips to draw her closer. "You've probably got someone who does all that for *you*."

David shrugged. "Yeah, but it'll be fun."

Beth returned with three bottles of water, setting them on the table, and nervously rubbed her hands together. She kept looking at Andi, and then away, looking for anything like she couldn't look Andi in the eyes. "We're about ready to let people in, Ms. Parker."

"Great. Thank you."

David moved around the table and pulled her chair out, scooting it in for her when she sat, and she smiled up at him. The smile lit up her face and made her eyes spark, and David drew in a satisfied breath. He could look at that smile for the rest of his life.

He took his seat beside her, smoothing his hand down the front of his shirt. Right now, he was damn thankful he kept a change of clothes in his trunk. He'd taken a shower with Spiderman Shampoo and Body Wash in Jake's bathroom, and he smelled faintly like bubble gum, but at least he didn't look like a schmuck beside Andrea Parker…Award-Winning Author and Hot Mama Extraordinaire. Andi took a deep breath and let it out, puffing her cheeks, and tucking her hands beneath the table.

David scooted his chair closer to her so he could slide his arm across the back of hers. She leaned into him, and he pressed a kiss to her temple. "Are you nervous?" he asked. "You've done these before, right?"

She smiled and laughed softly, shrugging her shoulders. "I can't help it. I still remember the days when I couldn't get an editor—or agent, for that matter, before Maggie—to look twice." Andi shifted to turn a little more toward him so their legs pressed together and they were eye-to-eye.

David smiled and fought the urge to lean in *just* a little more and run his lips along the side of her throat. "Why? Your books are amazing."

"And you're prejudiced."

"Not true. I loved your books before I ever..." He let his attention shift down to her lips, nearly groaning when she pulled her lower lip through her teeth. "...kissed you."

Andi drew in a slow breath, releasing it with a soft shudder as she moved away again. She set her elbow on the table and rested her head against her curled fingers, looking at him. "I was told romance readers didn't want something so heavy on the science fiction, and I was told readers who liked hi-sci-fi wouldn't want to read books with as much romance as I put into them. I had almost given up when Maggie took me on as a client."

David looked up and spotted Maggie a few feet away, talking with some of the store patrons who were inside, but hadn't come looking for Andi.

"Maggie is a smart woman."

"Or foolish, depends on how you look at it," Andi said with another soft laugh. Another one of her traits when she was nervous, he'd noticed. That and the talking fast. "Either way, I guess it paid off."

"In more ways than one..."

She shifted her gaze to him, and when he smiled—hoping she understood what he meant—she smiled back, warm color blooming in her cheeks. "Yeah, in more ways than one," she repeated.

David leaned toward her and had just enough time for probably one of their most chaste kisses ever before Beth opened the store doors and let in the line of Andrea Parker fans.

Andi surreptitiously looked at her watch and tried not to yawn.

Thirteen minutes to go.

The line had finally started to wane around two when she could see the end of it and people were waiting inside the door of the store rather than out in the sun. Andi felt bad for the poor people who had stood without shade for at least a couple of hours to get inside and had even asked the store to offer cold water to everyone. She supposed the ice cream place next door made a killing today.

Andi had half expected a mob of fans to descend on the store once anyone heard David Bishop was there. But, it hadn't happened. The people who came in line first pointed and spoke amongst themselves, and the news carried down the line, so as it moved people were no longer surprised when they came through the door. A lot of people already had cameras with them, and some dug out their camera phones. Anyone with a camera asked for her photo, and his...and theirs. They asked the next person in line to take their photo with Andi and David, or they snagged Maggie whenever she came near enough to the table to be asked. Each time, David was more than willing to comply. He whispered in her ear once he'd take any excuse to put his arm around her...cameras or not.

But he refused to sign autographs. He'd been polite about it but insisted this was a book signing and he wasn't part of the venue.

"I have to admit, these are the first romance novels I've ever read."

Andi forced herself to focus on the next person who stood in front of her, signing her name in his book. A tight tingle went across the back of her hand, making her flex her fingers as she set the pen down. Three hours of signing her name paid a toll on her hand. She closed the flap, looking up at the man. He was probably about sixty, gray around the temples, but had a nice smile.

"I like hearing I've introduced someone to a new genre. Just as many people tell me they'd never read a science fiction novel before as tell me they've never read a romance before."

"Well, you've got a real talent, Miss Parker."

"Thank you very much, Sam," she said, managing to remember the name he'd given when he came to the table.

He turned his attention to David, and Andi almost laughed at the serious, stern expression that replaced the smile. "I heard they're makin' a movie out of them. Heard you're Jason." With a small jerk of his chin toward David, he said, "You'd better do it right."

David cleared his throat and folded his hands on the table, taking on the same serious expression although Andi saw the mischievous glint in his blue-gray eyes. "I'm doing my best, sir."

"Good."

With that, he turned and left and Andi managed to wait until he was out of earshot before she laughed, hiding her mouth behind her hand. David chuckled. "Your fans are vicious."

Andi laughed as the final person in line came to the table. She saw in her peripheral vision a customer come through the store doors. She probably wasn't more than twenty-two or twenty-three with dark blonde hair hanging in waves around her face from a center part. She wore denim shorts accentuating endless legs and a tight baby tee leaving little to the imagination. Andi usually wasn't one to notice people in great detail, but the girl was absolutely stunning. She took a few steps toward them, stopped short, and took a sharp right turn into the magazines and travel section.

The last customer approached the table with bright red cheeks, and her hands shook as she set the four books on the table. Andi offered her usual smile and greeting, but the woman barely looked at her, staring down at her hands instead.

"Would you like me to make it out to anyone special?" Andi asked, dipping her head in an attempt to look the woman in the eye. The poor thing looked like she was about to fly apart.

"Audrey," she managed to say, although her voice shook as much as her hands. "Ms. Parker, I-I can't believe I'm meeting you. You're just… you're amazing," she gushed.

No matter how many times her readers complimented her, Andi always felt a rush of heat to her cheeks and had to fight off the urge to look around and make sure they were talking to her. "Thank you so much. Are you Audrey?"

The woman nodded.

Andi tried some more to pull the woman into conversation, but she was too nervous to speak. When Andi signed the last book and slid them across the table, Audrey swept them up and stuttered a quick "thank you" before heading for the door. Andi sat back with a huff and flexed her hand again. She could sit at a desk and type for hours without any problem, but let her sign her name a couple hundred times, and the ache almost reached her elbow.

David twisted in his chair to face her and took her hand in his, immediately started on a slow but firm massage working from her knuckles back toward her wrist. "Relax your hand."

Andi wasn't sure what she moaned at…the instant *zing* that shot up her arm at the simple, non-sexual contact, or the instant easing of the ache in her fingers. Movement at the door drew her attention, and she glanced over to see if the new customer approached the table. She wore a yellow halter-top sundress that spread over her belly, she had to be at least seven months pregnant, and the poor girl looked ready to melt. Dark blonde hair was stacked on her head and held in place with a large clip, and she led a kindergarten-age girl in blonde pigtails by the hand.

As soon as she was inside, she glanced toward the table and smiled. But, immediately, she turned sharply to the right, looking for the entire world like someone had just called out to her. Pulling the little girl behind her, she headed into the magazine section.

Andi tried to ignore the small sense of relief the woman hadn't come to the table. David's gentle ministrations were far too nice to be interrupted.

He leaned slightly forward with his elbows resting on his knees with her hand held in both of his. His head was down and his focus was on the circles he made with his thumbs on the back of her hand. His fingertips worked her palm and the heel of her hands.

"Have you ever considered being a personal masseuse?" she asked.

David raised his head and looked at her, kissed her knuckles, smiling as he spoke against her skin. "Are you offering me the job?"

"Could be."

David titled his head and grinned the kind of grin that inspired her to insanity. He shifted forward, setting one hand on the table and the other on the back of her chair. Andi smiled, watching his lips approach.

"I leave the two of you alone for three minutes and you're already back to the kissing. You're almost making me jealous."

David stopped short of her lips, his eyelids sliding over his eyes as he held her gaze, shook his head just enough to silently say *'That Maggie Connelly'* and kissed her. He broke the kiss as he stood, laying a hand on her shoulder.

"Do you want anything from the café?"

Andi barely stifled her yawn, nodding. "A latte, please. Venti. Sugar-free vanilla syrup."

David nodded and kissed her cheek before loping back to the café. Andi watched him over her shoulder for a moment before turning back to her agent and friend. Maggie leaned one hand on the table, the other on her slim hip.

"How are you doing, my dear?"

Andi sighed and slouched lower in her chair. "Exhausted."

"You drew a great crowd."

Beyond Maggie, Andi saw three faces peering at her around the end of a bookshelf stacked with recent releases; the pretty young blonde who had come in a few minutes before and the pregnant woman with the little girl. As soon as they made eye contact, all three ladies came out from behind the shelf and headed for the table. Andi watched, trying to figure them out, as she shifted forward in her chair again. Maggie saw them coming and stepped aside, but only to the end of the table so the women could approach. The younger woman took the lead, reaching the table first with a wide grin and an enthusiastic, "Hi!"

"Hello," Andi answered, looking between all of them, settling last on the little girl who hid partially behind her mom. High pigtails held ringlets of chestnut brown hair so the curls brushed her cheeks and shoulders, and pretty blue-gray eyes stared at Andi wide-eyed. "What's your name?" Andi asked.

"Katherine," she said softly, so softly Andi almost didn't hear her.

"Hi, Katherine," Andi said with her best 'Honest, I don't eat children for breakfast' smile. She focused her attention again on the women. "Thank you for coming."

The younger woman picked up the first book in the series from the depleted stacks on the table and opened it, thumbing through the pages. "Well, I don't usually do stuff like this, but when Mom speaks… Anyway, these are great books."

"Thank you."

Andi looked between the three. If the two women weren't sisters, they had to be some other form of close familial connection. The pregnant woman stepped around the younger, leaning her hand on the table, looking so tired Andi was tempted to get up and offer her chair.

"What my sister is so ineloquently trying to say while avoiding the point like it's an angry bee hive, is our mother asked us to come down. The whole family has read the books, some of us more than once."

"The word you're looking for is obsessively…" the younger sister mumbled, garnering a glare from the older.

"I'm glad to hear it. We're working on the film adaptation now."

"Yeah, we heard," the younger woman said with an undeniable twinge of sarcasm.

"*Sarah*," the older woman hissed.

Andi looked between them. *What the heck was going on here?*

"What?" *Sarah* hissed back. "What am I supposed to do? It's a little late for subtle, isn't it? Mom's well-laid plans have been shot to—" She looked down at the little girl, stopping short. Then she smiled wide, a million-dollar smile to be sure. "We can't exactly stand here and chat for half an hour to find out if she's as wonderful as we hear."

"Sarah!" the older snapped this time. "She's going to think we're all psychotic before we have a *chance!*"

Sarah huffed, rolled her eyes, and then turned a saccharine smile on Andi. "Sorry. My siblings are constantly reminding me of my manners, and my severe lack of them."

"Lack is putting it mildly," her older sister grumbled. Then she sighed and looked past Andi with a nervous smile before meeting her eyes again. "Let's try this again since I'm sure any second now we're going to be called on the carpet for our snooping—even though we were *sent* and it wasn't our idea." She extended her hand. "Hi, I'm Caroline. This is my sister Sarah and my daughter Katherine."

Andi shook the woman's hand, sliding a sidelong look at Maggie. Who just shrugged and swirled a finger near her temple. *Some help she was.*

"Hi," Andi said again, taking the woman's hand.

"As Sarah also implied, we were sent here to meet you face-to-face.

Especially in the light of certain...um...reports, our mother has concerns."

"Your mother..." Andi arched her eyebrows and tilted her head. "Do I know your mother?"

"No, but I'm sure you will if *she* has anything to do with it."

Katherine, who had spent the majority of this conversation peeking at Andi over the edge of the table, suddenly jumped up with a brilliant smile and wide eyes. "Mama! Mama! Look!" She pointed past Andi in the general direction of the café. "It's Uncle Davey!"

Andi snapped her attention to Maggie, who already stared back. Then Maggie grinned and followed Katherine's exuberant pointing. "Look, Andrea...it's *Uncle Davey*."

Katherine scrambled past her mother and bolted around the end of the table in a dead-on run. "Uncle Davey! Uncle Davey!"

Andi stood, turning to see the little bundle of enthusiasm plow straight into David's legs as he desperately tried not to drop the coffees in his hands.

"Whoa, Katie," he laughed as the little girl dropped to sit on his foot and cling to his right leg, her arms and legs wrapped around him like a spider monkey. She giggled as he attempted to walk the final steps to the table, looking between Andi, Sarah, Caroline, and Maggie. "Hi..."

Andi took mercy on him and relieved him of the coffees, setting them on the table before she folded her arms and winked at him. "I'm going to go out on a limb here, make a wild guess, and assume these ladies are your sisters?"

David untangled Katherine from his leg to pick her up and she immediately planted a loud kiss on his cheek. He walked around the table to hug Sarah first, shifting Katherine onto his hip to do so. "Yeah, and I'm wondering how the heck you knew I was here."

As he moved on to hug Caroline, Sarah answered with a snide, "Typical David Bishop, thinking we're here for *him*. We came to meet Andrea." With a slight pause, she added, "Mom's orders."

"How would she even know—"

"Oh, *puh*-lease." Sarah rolled her eyes and crossed her arms, cocking one slender hip. "You aren't exactly attempting to hide anything. The fact you called out her name after your..." She smirked. "Little accident

—nice shiners, by the way—was enough to make Mom curious. And then today—"

"Sarah, don't get into that just yet—" Caroline cut her off.

"And why do you smell like bubble gum?" Sarah continued, not even pausing to acknowledge her sister. They just kept plowing over each other.

They seemed to do that a lot.

Another customer approached the table, the *Rise of Dawn* books held to her chest. She scanned the small crowd warily and Andi motioned her forward just as David set his hand on Caroline's shoulder and led both his sisters away from the table.

"Hi. How are you today?" Andi asked, trying to focus on the young girl. She couldn't have been more than seventeen or eighteen years old, and stared—in turn—between Andi and David where he stood clustered with his family.

"I'm glad I caught you," she said in such a soft voice, Andi almost didn't hear her. "I got out of school at two-thirty and rushed over here. Is that...is that David Bishop?"

Andi took her books from her, opening the first as she glanced at them again. Diverting her attention again, she saw Maggie watching her with an annoying smirk. Clearing her throat, Andi looked at the girl. "It is, yes."

"Who is he with?"

"His sisters," she answered absently. "To whom?"

"Oh, sorry." The young girl blushed bright red and giggled nervously. "Joni. J-O-N-I"

Andi signed the books, forcing herself not to glance in their direction. Even when she heard David's voice rise high enough to carry to her. She couldn't make out what he said, but he didn't sound very happy. Not angry, just...not pleased.

"I've been watching online for photos from the movie shoot. Do you get to be there because you wrote the books?"

"Yes. I think everyone will be pleased with the film. I'm very happy with the adaptation."

Another girl rushed in the store door, running down the short space to them, obviously joining Joni. She was flushed and breathing heavy, but smiled wide. "Oh, I'm glad we made it!"

"I just told her that," Joni said. "Check it out. David Bishop is here."

The new girl looked to where Joni pointed. "He's so hot."

Andi grinned, capping her pen, but chose not to comment.

"Miss Parker just told me she gets to be on set when they film," Joni told her friend, sounding almost proud for being able to share that bit of information.

"Well, *duh*. Of course, she's on set. They're…you know…*together*."

"Oh, but, I—" Andi started, raising her hand.

But Joni had already gasped loudly—actually, it was more like a squeal—and covered her mouth with her hands. "Oh. My. God! Seriously? How do you know this and not me?" she demanded of her friend.

"Hello? Google Alerts."

Andi caught David's shift of attention back to her at the girl's outburst. He still held his niece on his hip, but his eyes met hers, and he raised an eyebrow. Andi smiled and shrugged, just a tiny movement, and he smiled.

"Do you think we could, Miss Parker?"

Andi blinked and looked away from him, back to the girls. "I'm sorry. What?"

"Could we take a picture? We'd like one with you if we can…but…" Joni's friend blushed. "Do you think we could take a picture of you and David Bishop together?"

"Here," Maggie offered. "I'll even take the picture."

Andi walked around the table and stood between the girls, putting her arms behind their backs—feeling suddenly short because these teenage girls stood a good two to three inches taller than her—and smiled as Maggie snapped a few pictures; some with just them, some with the girls holding up their books and putting on exaggerated grins.

"Come on, boyo," Maggie called over her shoulder, and David looked their way. "Get over here and show us your million-dollar smile."

David set Katherine down, said something to his sisters, and bounded over. The girls were thrilled to have their pictures taken with them, and Joni giggled until she was beet red when he put one arm around her shoulder, and the other around Andi. When the unnamed girl whispered something about getting these on the 'Net before anyone else, Andi didn't have the heart to tell them at least two dozen similar shots had been taken throughout the day. Finally, when she couldn't see straight from all the flashes, Joni retrieved her phone from Maggie.

"Thank you *so* much. We thought we'd miss you, and this ended up being the best afternoon *ever*."

David hooked his arm behind Andi's neck, pulling her to him to press a kiss to her forehead. "My sisters want to go to dinner. Feel free to say no." He said it quietly, so it was between just them.

Andi leaned back to see his face, hoping to see what answer he wanted to hear. But as soon as she tipped her chin upward, he captured her lips. At first, it was just lip-to-lip pressure, but then he drew in a sharp breath and his hand cupped her jaw. The pad of his thumb teased the corner of her mouth and she opened for him. Andi's insides quickened and her fingers curled of their own free will into his shirt. Had only been a few hours since he'd kissed her like this?

Which one of them initiated the slowing of the kiss, she wasn't sure…maybe they didn't need one or the other to be the 'strong one'. After what he'd told her that morning—she was too special to him to rush anything more than kisses that made her toes curl and her breath short—they didn't need to explain anything anymore. David punctuated the long, deep kiss with several short ones before moving across her cheek to her ear and finally leaving one lingering kiss below her ear.

Andi raised her arms to wrap them over his shoulders, lacing her fingers into the short hair at his nape. "I don't think I'm ready to say goodbye yet," she said softly, and he tightened his arms around her.

Another flash went off, but Andi found she didn't care.

Not until someone cleared their throat did Andi feel the need to move. Since she knew the distinct sound of Maggie drawing attention this way—and knew it wasn't Maggie—that left few possibilities. David loosened his arms to look but held her close to him still.

"Yes?" he asked with a grin.

"You're drawing a crowd and pretty soon we're going to charge admission," Sarah snarked. "Are we going to dinner, or what?"

David arched his eyebrows and Andi nodded. Maggie had drifted off to thank the store staff, and two clerks already worked on breaking down the table and display. As they walked to the parking lot, they discussed where to go, and since Caroline and Sarah were in one car with Katherine—and the three of them had come in Andi's big RX— the Bishop sisters would follow them to a local restaurant. The place they chose was fairly common, nothing special, but Andi had recommended it because the booths were high and tended to allow for more intimacy.

Since it was Monday and only mid-afternoon, the restaurant was nearly empty and they were seated immediately in a large, horseshoe-shaped booth. Andi slid in, following David and Maggie sat on the outside of one end. Katherine scrambled into the booth to sit between David and her mom, and Sarah was the other placeholder to close the semi-circle. It took all of about fifteen seconds before Katherine scrambled into David's lap and launched into a story. All Andi could catch was it was about Katherine's best friend Stacy and a rabbit named Mr. Fluff. David nodded frequently, prodded with questions when Katherine paused to breathe, and laughed with her descriptions turned into a form of six-year-old interpretive dance.

All the while, he held her hand on his thigh and Andi watched him with his niece, enjoying the sensation of warmth that spread through her chest.

"Your boy is every woman's dream. Even the youngest fall beneath his charm," Maggie said, leaning toward her.

"Oh, I think it's David who's fallen beneath Katherine's charm."

"Hey." Maggie nudged Andi with her elbow until she turned and looked at her friend. Maggie smiled, setting her chin on her palm. "Have I mentioned lately how I like that glimmer in your eyes?"

"What glimmer?" Even as she asked the question, Andi smiled.

Maggie chuckled. "*That* glimmer. But, you know what the best part is?"

Andi shook her head.

"He's got the same glimmer."

"When are you going to show me the real reason you came out here?" David asked, pushing his plate away from him. "You said at the store mom read something that fired her up."

Andi looked up from her plate, glancing between him and his sister. "Your mom is upset about something?"

"We didn't say upset…just *fired up*. Which, for Mom, can mean a lot of things."

David leaned back and slid his arm behind Andi so it rested in the warm space between her back and the seat. She shifted just slightly closer to him, settling against his side, and David smiled. But he kept his attention on Caroline while watching the smirk Sarah didn't attempt to hide.

"I talked to her on Friday night about the accident on set. What's happened since then to would set her off?"

His sisters exchanged glances, and without a word Caroline opened the large bag she'd been carrying around, pulling out a folded newspaper. If it could be called a *newspaper* because he immediately recognized the name of the publication emblazoned across the top in large yellow block letters. A gossip rag. They reported every dirty, gory, and embarrassing detail they could dig up on any celebrity with even the smallest amount of recognition. And if they couldn't dig up facts, they made them up. Whatever sold a paper. More than once, David had been forced to endure their scathing reports and outright lies. He'd been everything from a drunk to a drug addict, anorexic to gay. And everything in between.

He mumbled an abbreviated curse—for the sake of young ears sitting beside him—and reached for the magazine. But Caroline moved it out of his reach.

"No, hang on. I waited to show you for Andrea's sake." She looked directly at Andi and tried a smile. "I don't know how you handle this stuff, being in the public eye and all. It would drive me nuts. It's bad enough watching them do it to my brother."

"I can't handle it," Andi answered with a shrug. "Authors don't draw hordes of paparazzi and screaming fans. They come to our book signings, they post comments on discussion boards, but we're pretty much faceless."

"Not anymore," Sarah said before loudly draining her glass of soda with her straw.

This time, when David held out his hand, Caroline relinquished the folded rag. David took his arm from behind Andi to unfold the paper. Andi immediately gasped and her hand flew to her mouth.

"What?" Maggie demanded.

Taking up almost the entire front page was a grainy but unmistakable picture of David and Andi. In the parking lot of *Chez Nous*—*after* the date. The only word he could think of was *erotic*. In a heartbeat, his mind remembered the moment—of having her body pressed against him, her hands beneath his jacket pulling him closer, the sweet sound of her hitched breath when he tasted her neck, the thrust of arousal that had shot through him at holding her so close—and his body immediately responded. He couldn't deny *then* how much he'd wanted Andrea Parker any more than he could deny it right now.

And just as quickly, the arousal turned into fury at the headline.

BISHOP HELPS NOVELIST WITH HER SEX SCENES

"Son of a bitch."

The paper disappeared from his hand when Maggie yanked it free. "Damn."

At the same time, a distinct twitter came from Andi's purse and she scrambled for it, her hands visibly trembling. He studied her face as she avoided his—and everyone else's—eyes. "Jake," she whispered before finally retrieving the phone.

She took a sharp breath and curled her hair behind her ear before putting the phone against her cheek. "Hi, honey." He commended her. The tremor in her voice was barely audible. The shimmer in her eyes, on the other hand, couldn't as easily be hidden.

"Mom, has something happened?"

The volume on Andi's phone was high enough that David heard

Jake's voice carrying to him. He didn't know if his sisters could hear, but there was no doubt both he and Maggie could.

"Why, sweetheart?"

"Mom, he's really mad about something. He's been slamming stuff around downstairs, and I keep hearing him say your name. Did you see him since last night?"

Andi hunched forward, putting her elbow on the table to support her forehead against her shaking hand. "No, I haven't seen or talked to your father since he picked you up. What's he saying, honey?"

"I don't know. I can't tell. Oh, crap...it sounds like he's coming."

"You don't have to worry, Jake. You can call me whenever you want, he can't—" There was a shuffling sound on the phone, and Andi sat up again. "Jake? Jake?"

"What the hell are you exposing Jacob to, Andrea? What the hell kind of debauchery and whoring around are you involved in since you came out here? How can you look your son in the eyes when he has to see crap like this?"

Andi closed her eyes, and while he watched everything change in her expression—the angry ball in his gut growing bigger by the second—he caught the exchange of glances between his sisters and assumed they could hear the conversation as well.

"Lawrence—"

"Don't even try to justify this, Andrea. You and I are going to deal with this. How the hell are we supposed to rebuild our family when you're slutting around?"

"We aren't—" She had to stop when her voice cracked, and a tear squeezed from her closed lids.

David laid his hand on her knee, not knowing what else he could do at the moment that didn't involve telling Lawrence Bonherre to rot in hell. Despite his burning desire to do so, he knew it wouldn't help anything. Not right now. But, God help Larry the next time they came face to face and he tried to speak to Andi like that.

"We have nothing to *discuss*, Lawrence," Andi said through clenched teeth, the words practically a hiss. "You don't get to 'deal with' anything in my life. It's *my* life."

"We'll see about that."

Then David heard nothing, and Andi lowered the phone from her ear.

"Andi—"

"Let me out," she suddenly demanded, practically shoving Maggie out of the way to be free of the booth. "Let me out!"

Maggie stood and Andi scrambled from her seat, heading for the front of the restaurant. David moved to follow.

"No." Maggie held up her hand to stop him. "I'll go to her."

"I can't just let her go!"

"I know." Maggie offered a sympathetic smile, but it did nothing to calm him. "But, I've been picking up these particular pieces for a few years now. Just give her a little time to breathe. Then we'll figure out things."

David drew in a breath, forcing himself to ease back into the seat as he released it. Maggie nodded, picked up both her purse and Andi's, and headed out of the restaurant. David watched her go until she rounded the corner and disappeared.

"Your friend looked sad, Uncle Davey," Katherine said softly, shifting closer so she could reach up and touch his cheek. "Was she sad?"

"Yeah," he managed to say without his entire face cracking with the force it took to smile at his niece. "She was."

"What an A-S-S-H-O-L-E," Sarah spelled out. "Who the hell was that?"

"Andi's ex-husband. Well, first it was Jake…her son." David forced himself to take another breath. "He's eleven."

"David." The tone of Caroline's voice made him look at her, and he caught the glimmer of tears in her eyes. Not enough to spill over, but enough to make her blue eyes shine. She smiled, small and shaky, but with sincerity. "Do you love her?"

David looked back through the restaurant to where Andi had disappeared. He swallowed and nodded his head in answer before he could make his mouth form the words. "Pretty sure I do, yeah."

"Then that's all Mom wanted to know."

David slumped into the booth, scrubbing his face with his hands.

CHAPTER ELEVEN

Andi managed a cursory glance in both directions before she leaped from the sidewalk and ran across the parking lot toward her SUV, offering a perfunctory wave to the one car that had to slow in order to keep from hitting her in her mad dash from the restaurant. She wasn't sure what would overpower her first: the tight knot of nausea in her gut that threatened to make her sick, the vice-like pressure at the base of her skull, or the war waging in the center of her chest between vicious rage and gut-wrenching humiliation.

The tears didn't hit until she reached the driver's door and realized she'd left her purse inside. All she carried was her phone, clutched in her fist like a grenade minus the pin. If she let go, she'd be blown away. The first tears were slow, slipping from her eyes to blur her vision. She stared at the display on the phone, the screen blurring more with each blink.

That bastard.

Andi choked around the sobs lodged in her chest, threatening to rip their way out of her. She closed her eyes and slammed her forehead against the door, pressing her palms to the warm glass, forcing down the sounds of her weeping. She couldn't do this. Not here. *Not here.*

"Andi…"

She spun away, giving Maggie her back, and wrapped her arms across her hurting stomach. The sobs were more like heaves because she refused to let them free. Until Maggie's hands smoothed over her back to squeeze her shoulders. Andi folded like a crushed cardboard box, and Maggie dropped with her, not letting her hit the ground. The cries escaped but were lost—muffled—by her knees as she curled in on herself.

Maggie said nothing, just crouched beside her with her arms around Andi's shaking frame.

She wasn't supposed to cry over Lawrence Bonherre ever again. She'd sworn more than once she'd never let another tear fall over him.

"This isn't *over* Larry, my dear," Maggie said softly, and Andi realized she'd said the self-condemning statements aloud. "This is *because* of Larry. Because he's a self-righteous bastard who believes the world revolves around his pimply, pasty white ass."

Andi raised her head and took off her glasses, the lenses now spotted by her tears, to wipe her fingers across her cheeks. "I don't know what's worse, Mags. I'm so *angry* with him right now for believing for one *millisecond* he has *any* say in my life. I'm angry because the truth of it is he *does* have a say in my life as long as Jake is a minor. He can pull this power trip whenever he wants his way, and I have to bend or face his wrath in court. I'm angry he reduces me to *this*!" She slammed the palm of her hand against her chest, shaking her head. "And I'm angry because every time, *every* time something good happens in my life, he has the *uncanny* ability to suck all the joy right out of it!"

She shouted now, but she didn't care anymore. What other humiliation could be worse than sitting in a restaurant with her—her—*whatever* David was—and his sisters, and having her ex-husband call her a whoring slut? Even if they didn't hear, how could she just sit there unaffected?

Andi was on a tangent now.

"I had a baby...he had his secretary. I get an agent and a book deal...he tells me his *affairs* are *my* fault because I'm as attractive and sexy to him as a dead fish. I get a movie deal...he marries the woman I caught him having his last affair with, and tells me now that he has a 'family' atmosphere perhaps Jake should spend more time with him in Chicago. He lorded *that* over me for a good year. And now…"

She dropped her head forward, unable to finish the rant. To finish would be to admit David Bishop might be a *good* and *permanent* thing in her life…or could be…and to say it was to doom it.

"Larry is all bull and no crap if you know what I mean," Maggie stated, sitting on the cement beside her so they were hip to hip, facing each other. "Larry likes to throw his weight around when it comes to Jake, but he never follows through. He demands a visit, and then you don't hear from him for a year or so. He's huffing and puffing, that's all."

Andi shook her head, sniffing loudly. "I don't know, Maggie. He's furious. And when Lawrence is angry…" She shook her head again.

Maggie tipped sideways, bumping Andi's knees with her shoulder. She grinned. "Good thing you're not alone then, yeah? You got me. You got Jake. You got David—"

Andi snorted.

"Which one are you snorting at?"

"Which do you think," Andi answered, swiping viciously at her cheeks.

"You've been trying to rule out that boy since the first time he kissed you. Cut it out."

Andi snuffed her nose and leaned against the side of her truck. Her mind kept flipping back and forth between the embarrassed, humiliated girlfriend—even mentally, Andi cringed at the word—who wondered just how much her sexy new boyfriend would take before he ran for the Hollywood Hills…and the romance novelist who looked at everything as a plot and refused to be the TSTL heroine who wallows in self-pity rather than just talking to the man she loves.

But she was also a realist. That was part of being a writer, knowing what was fantasy and what would and could happen. Romance readers always love to say they want stories that *could* happen, but they don't. They want the fantasy with just enough reality to let them believe it could happen. The man always sees the beauty in the woman she can't see in herself. She always gets him at the end of the book, no matter how many stupid mistakes she makes. It doesn't matter how many women he's been with, or how many men she *hasn't* been with, he only wants *her* for the rest of his life.

If she looked at her life—as it currently seemed to be unfolding—like a romance novel, she'd see all fantasy. Gorgeous, sexy movie star falls for older divorcee with son. All is beautiful until…enter the dastardly, bastardly ex-husband designed to add conflict. But the handsome hero and his ladylove prevail over all the hardships to live happily ever after. After all, a book has to have a happily ever after, no matter how ridiculous and unlikely it seems.

Reality didn't come with a Happily Ever After guarantee. If it did, the mystical 'they' wouldn't have coined the phrase 'Life isn't fair.'

At that moment, she felt as far from fair as one could get.

"So, are you going to sit here all night and hide from him? Or are you going to get yourself up, dust yourself off—"

"And start all over again?" Andi finished with a thick, wet sigh. "I don't have the energy quite yet. Just give me a few minutes to put on my game face again, okay?"

Maggie patted her shoulder and gave a short nod, gaining her feet with a moan and grumble about being 'too old to be sitting on the ground'. Andi listened as Maggie's footsteps moved away and faded, and waited another ten-count before pulling her knees to her chest again and dropping her head to her folded arms. The tears were done, but the choking, smothering weight in her chest hadn't eased. It didn't matter Lawrence's opinion of her meant nothing to her, his words had cut deep and bled hard.

Andi jumped when the phone she still gripped in her hand rang again. It was Jake's ring, and for a split second, she considered not answering. What if it was Lawrence again?

But, it would more likely be Jake. Andi refused to ignore her son to spite his father.

Andi swallowed and flipped the phone open, bringing it to her ear with a shaking hand. "Hello."

"Mom…"

Jake spoke so low and soft she had to strain to hear him, and probably wouldn't have been able to hear him at all inside the restaurant with all the ambient sound. "Yes, honey. Are you okay?"

"Yeah. He's back downstairs and told me to stay in my room like it was some kind of punishment. I don't want to be around him anyway."

"He didn't hurt you, did he? He didn't say anything?"

"Not about me, no. But, Mom, he said a lot of really awful things about you. I know you don't think I know stuff yet, but I know what he called you." His young voice took on a sharp, rough edge and Andi easily pictured her son with tight lips and clenched fists. "I wanted to hit him, Mom."

"No, honey," she said quickly. "Don't do that. It's okay."

"No, it's not," he nearly shouted, but his voice dropped again. She assumed he didn't want his father to know he was on the phone with her again. "It's not, Mom. Because he's wrong."

Andi sucked in a sharp breath, trying to quell the tears that returned with a vicious vengeance. She blinked and looked up at the cloudless sky. "I'm sorry, Jake. I'm so sorry."

"Mom, where are you?"

She blinked at his question, releasing more tears, and rubbed her nose. "I'm in Valencia. I had a book signing today."

"Is Maggie with you?"

"She's here, yes. Just not *right* here."

Andi dropped her glasses on the cement beside her, covering her eyes with her shaking hand. It took her several deep breaths and the sheer power of will to speak again. "Are you okay? Do you want me to come get you?"

"No. He leaves me alone pretty much. I don't want you to see him."

The sob in her chest burned like a ball of acid, and she pushed her curled hand against her sternum, willing back the overflow. What kind of mother was she that her eleven-year-old son had to worry about her like this? What had she exposed him to that he couldn't just be a kid

"Is David there?"

Andi swallowed, forcing down the lump. "I-I'm not sure. He was, but he might have left."

"Was he there when I called?"

She nodded, then realized she was being stupid. "Yes. Why?"

"I don't want you to be alone." The conviction in his voice broke her heart into a thousand shards that jabbed at her chest when she took a breath.

"I'm not alone, honey."

"But is David there?"

Andi sighed. "Here? Right now? No, honey. I don't know where David—"

She stopped short when a shadow fell over her and a familiar pair of brown Doc Martens stepped beside her. Andi couldn't say anything as he crouched beside her, his blue-gray eyes focused on her face—which had to be a wreck since she'd been crying.

"Mom? Where's David?"

David took the phone from her with one hand, and laid the other against her cheek, his thumb smoothing over her skin. In a beat, Andi was so tired she could barely move. She let her head settle against the vehicle door, watching him.

"Jake…" he said into the phone.

"David, you're with Mom, right?"

With a flash of heat to her cheeks that made her eyes water, Andi realized just how easily and clearly she heard every word her son said. And if she could hear him so easily, there was no doubt in her mind not only had *David* heard every vicious word Lawrence had said, but mostly likely Caroline and Sarah as well. She closed her eyes, taking the coward's way out, unable to look him in the eye now she knew for certain he'd heard.

"Yeah, I'm here."

"Don't leave her, okay? My father said some stuff—"

"I heard him. And I won't."

There was silence for a moment when she didn't hear either one speak, but she couldn't open her eyes yet to see why. Then she heard Jake again.

"I saw…I saw the picture he was mad about."

"Not the best thing to see, I guess."

"I don't care. I mean…I don't mind. Just—can you tell her that?"

"I'll tell her, Jake."

"Tell her I love her, okay? She's really upset, David. Just…take care of her, okay?"

"I will. I promise."

Jake said goodbye, and Andi heard the distinct beep of the call ending. She wanted to run again but figured she wouldn't get any further than last time, and she didn't like the whole idea of running to begin with. Never helped. The knot in her stomach made her feel ill, and the sun had shifted enough to take away the shade, and the heat made her skin crawl even worse than before. But she couldn't open her eyes.

…whoring around…slutting around…

Only Lawrence could take something that made her feel so good and make it ugly and vile. The man had slept with more women than he could truthfully admit to—had come home to their bed and tainted her with his cheating body—and had the nerve to say what she had shared with David was something dirty and wrong.

"Andi, open your eyes, sweetheart."

She swallowed hard and blinked several times before she could bring him into focus. He took her hand and rose, helping her to her feet so she stood between him and the driver's door. He retrieved her glasses from the ground and folded them, putting them in his shirt pocket. David stroked her cheeks with his thumbs, his gaze following his touch, skimming over her features. Andi curled her shaking fingers around his hands and looked down, focusing on one of the buttons on his shirt.

"Let's go home," he said softly and leaned forward to kiss her forehead.

Andi tucked herself against his chest, her hair brushing the underside of his chin, and absorbed the feeling of his arms wrapped around her. She didn't want to think or believe the worst, but she wanted to enjoy his embrace as long as possible. He rubbed her back and shoulders and kissed her brow, and Andi slowly felt some of the knot ease and the sick feeling of humiliation abated enough that she could think and speak with coherency.

As her thoughts cleared, she remembered the promise she'd made him just the week before—had they gone from acquaintances to *this* in less than two weeks?—in her trailer at the set. And she ran through all the arguments and rationalizations she'd made sitting on the pavement, wishing for the world it would open up and swallow her.

She could wonder and doubt and wait for the end...or she could just find out now.

Andi pulled away from his embrace, stepping back until her hips bumped the driver's door. "Are you leaving?" she asked before she lost her nerve.

He smiled. "Not on my own. You're my ride, remember? I left my car at your—" He paused, and the smile slipped away. "You don't mean right now...leaving here."

Andi shook her head, managing only a sharp jerk. She crossed her arms over her body to disguise the shaking that worked through her so hard it made her insides hurt.

"I'm not demanding you stay, or asking you to go," she forced herself to say with a relatively level tone. "I just want to know."

David stepped to her again, setting his feet on either side of hers so he stood as close as possible, and laid his palms against her cheeks, tipping her head enough she had to either close her eyes or meet his stare. His brow pulled down over his eyes, creating a small line of furrows above his nose and any hint of a smile was gone.

"I'm not leaving."

"I mean it, David. You can do whatever you want, no guilt. No pressure. No—"

His mouth pressed to hers, stopping her argument. Andi tried not to breathe, tried not to melt into him, tried to brace herself against the glorious feeling of David. Still holding his lips to hers, he tugged her arms free from across her body and shifted closer, urging her to wrap her arms around his neck. When his hands moved over her sides to her back and pulled her closer, she whimpered and lost the battle. His lips parted, and she matched him, pushing her fingers into his hair. His teeth grazed her lower lip before his tongue slowly and thoroughly filled her mouth, drawing another small sound from the back of her throat. By the time his lips moved from her mouth, and he pressed his face into the side of her throat, tears ran down her cheeks again and she clung to him.

David hugged her hard, pulling her so firmly against him she had to toe up to keep her feet on the ground. He kissed her throat—short quick kisses that curled warmth inside her with each peck—to her cheeks and finally her mouth again.

When he pulled back, he was smiling again, and the spark had come back to his eyes.

"I'm not leaving." He kissed one cheek, then the other. "I'm not leaving."

Andi nodded.

"Say it."

"You're not leaving," she whispered.

He kissed her. "That's right."

David wrapped her in another breath-stealing hug, and she sank into it.

"I need you at the studio no later than six."

David groaned into his phone, offering Andi his hand to help her from the SUV. "Avi, I'm supposed to be resting, remember?"

"Yeah? Is that why you were spotted at your girlfriend's book signing today?"

David smiled, looking at Andi, but the smile quickly fell away. Her eyes were cast down and her lip was a fine, straight line. Not a frown, but far from a smile. She took his hand as they walked to the house, but her fingers were loose and limp in his hold.

"I'm not doing a circuit. One. That's it."

"David—"

"One. That's all they need. Everyone will see I'm alive, I'm not scarred for life, and we move on. I don't want to tie up my whole morning with this."

Andi pulled free of his hand as soon as they stepped inside the house, heading for the staircase leading upstairs. "I'll be back in a few minutes," she said quickly over her shoulder before she disappeared up the stairs.

"Three."

"One," David said firmly and hung up.

He watched Andi go and shoved his hands into his pants pockets to hide his clenched fists. Touching Andi—holding her hand—was the only thing that kept him from curling his hands up into tight balls...or worse yet...punching a wall. Lawrence Bonherre was a lucky bastard he wasn't anywhere around, or David wouldn't work so hard at restraining himself.

Maggie dropped her purse and bag on the kitchen counter, heading directly to the refrigerator. "Can I get you something? Water? Soda? Juice? I might even have a beer in here somewhere."

"Whatever you've got. No beer."

Maggie slid him a glance over the top edge of the open refrigerator door before disappearing behind it. She came out with a glass pitcher of juice and took two tumblers from an upper cupboard, coming back to him. David did his best to divert his attention from the stairs, but knew he failed miserably...and found he didn't care.

Andi hadn't said a word on the way back to the house. David had left the driving to Maggie, and sat in the back seat beside Andi, holding her hand on the seat between them. Her fingers laced through his, but her attention remained out the window.

Maggie slid the glass toward him, and he swallowed three-quarters of the contents before setting it down on the counter a little too hard.

"Don't let her fool you," Maggie said after several minutes of silence.

David pulled his gaze from the stairs. "How's that?"

"She's going to come down with a big smile on her face, a spring in her step, and acting for all the world like she hasn't got a care. She needs these few minutes to get on her game face. Andrea Parker is one hell of an actress when she needs to be."

"I saw yesterday. For Jake."

Maggie nodded. "She does a lot for Jake's sake. Some day she'll realize she's not fooling anyone, let alone her son. But, if she knew how much he understands, it'd break her heart."

"Can I ask you something?"

"You can ask," she said with a shrug, lifting her glass to her lips. "Whether you get an answer or not will depend on the question."

"I asked Jake if his father ever hurt them…hit them. He said no."

Maggie pressed her lips together, and she rolled her head slightly as if working out tension or a knot in her neck. "What Larry does is worse than that. If someone hits you, you've got physical proof. You can show someone and they believe you. Larry's abuse was indifference. He didn't care. He just didn't care if what he did or said hurt her."

"He wasn't always like that…" David couldn't imagine Andi willingly entering into a marriage with a man like that. She was a strong woman. Losing control when things got intense wasn't a lack of strength…it was just 'enough'.

"Not by what she tells me, no. According to her, he was…" She made a face and tipped her head back and forth. "Nice. He wasn't Prince Charming, but he wooed her and properly courted her, all that happy horse crap. Based on some of the things she's let slip, Larry was always a self-centered butthead. She just didn't see it at first."

David glanced at the stairs. A huge part of him wanted her to come down, just so she was there with him. But, another part of him hoped to hear more before she did. He understood bad marriages and rough family life, and he understood putting on a good face. What he didn't understand were the people who set out to make their lives miserable for everyone around them.

"I'm going to clue you in, boyo, on the stuff our beloved Andrea wouldn't tell you if her life depended on it. Yeah, she's told you Larry is an ass. What she hasn't told you—and never will tell you—is to what extent. I know because I lived through that part with her."

"So, *you* tell me."

"I only know the Larry who came after Jake's birth, and after Andi wrote her first book. That's when it changed. He cheated on her—"

"She told me that."

"He cheated on her *a lot*. With any woman—and I mean *any* woman —who'd pull up her skirt or drop her panties for him. He told her after she had Jake, he didn't find her attractive. He told her she let herself go, and having sex with her turned his stomach."

David gritted his teeth together and curled his hands around the edge of the counter, the knot in his chest bursting into righteous rage.

"Larry has this idea he's some great male catch, and if he wants *it*, he gets *it*. As much as he insulted her, he didn't have any problem coming home to their bed and taking more from her after screwing around with his bimbos. She'd already left him and come here when he threw that fact at her as one of his final parting barbs. Andi threw up for three days. It's a miracle she came out of the marriage *alive* and *healthy*. You understand me?"

David nodded. When she told him her husband had been unfaithful, he had assumed he understood her pain. And to a point, he did. But his experience hadn't been *this* cold, this biting, this spiteful and heartless.

Maggie had paused, and he looked up, wondering if there could possibly be more. She leaned into the corner of the counter, her arms crossed over her body and her expression tight. "She'll deny it and say she refuses to let the opinion of Lawrence Butthead affect her. She *wants* to not let it affect her, but it does. How can it not when someone who tells you they love one day tells you the next you are nothing to them."

For that, David had no answer. When it ended with Josie, things had been hard—on both of them—but as hurt and angry as he had been, he never lashed out to purposefully hurt her. Despite what she'd done, he cared too much to do that. She hadn't been his wife. She hadn't been the mother of his child.

"This is a lot to hear," Maggie stated, pulling him out of his thoughts.

He met her eyes. "Tell me more."

"In the six years she's lived here, she's been on maybe half a dozen dates." Maggie paused, staring hard at him. "You're the first man she's let touch her."

The reality of that statement sank in, and David dropped his shoulders.

"I tease her about you, but I do it so she won't panic and bolt. She deserves you."

David had to swallow before asking his next question, knowing Maggie's answer would be nothing short of the truth. "Do I deserve her?"

Maggie stared at him, long and hard, for several moments before offering a small nod. "The verdict is still out. So far, I'm on your side."

David drained the glass and looked back to the stairs. "She thinks I'm going to leave."

"Are you?"

"No," he snapped before looking at her again. Then he took a slow breath and tried again. "No, I'm not. Why does she think I would?"

"She hasn't figured out why you're here, yet...and you wonder why she thinks you'll leave?"

David started to defend himself—or maybe it was just to rail on someone or anyone to relieve the knot of tension in his chest—but Maggie cut him off. She pushed away from the counter and crossed to him, stepping close enough that she had to tip her head back to look him in the eye. "Hurt her, and I hurt you. She and Jake are my family, and I love them."

David nodded, making sure she saw the same conviction in his face. "I won't hurt her. I've already promised Jake, and I'm promising you."

"Tell her I told you any of this—"

David raised his hand. "Understood."

Just as Maggie predicted, Andi came bouncing down the stairs moments later with a smile on her lips, her skin glistening and glowing like she'd washed her face. The red was gone from her eyes, and when she picked up Maggie's glass to steal a sip, the shake was gone from her hands.

Except for the very distant sound of traffic—so far away it was no more than white noise—the only sound David heard was Andi's breathing and the gentle creak of the double hammock they held each other in, swaying in Andi's backyard. The sun had set, and the cooler desert night air had set in, but with Andi curled against his side, he wasn't cold at all.

His arm circled her shoulders, and she rested her cheek on his chest, her hair brushing his jaw as her fingers toyed with his Star of David pendant. The touch was *damn* distracting, but he wouldn't still her hand for the world.

She shifted closer, rubbing her cheek against his shoulder, and drew in a long breath. He could get used to this damn quick.

"I suppose you have to go home soon," she said softly after probably a good half hour of silence. If he hadn't slept beside her the night before and listened to her breathing, he might have thought she'd gone to sleep.

David ran his thumb up and down her arm and turned his head slightly so when he spoke it was against her hair. "Eventually. But not yet."

"I suppose it would be selfish of me to want you to stay." She continued to talk to the buttons of his shirt, not raising her head to look at him.

He shook his head, chuckling softly. "No." He sighed and looked at the stars again. "But, I have a meeting with Avi tomorrow at six downtown.

"Is that who you were on the phone with earlier?"

He nodded. "My manager. He had a television interview set up for one of the LA Morning shows. Damage control." She tensed. "Because of the accident on set," he added.

"What is there to control now?"

"He wants me to do some live interviews so people can see I'm alive and well and not hiding some disfiguring face injury," he said with a chuckle. "I told him one and one only. I have no interest in running the gauntlet. Though I should warn you…"

She lifted her head, looking up at him, and David realized with a flash of warmth from head to toe, he rather liked looking at Andi Parker from this angle. Lying down, her in his arms, looking up at him with bright eyes and ruffled hair…it was an erotic image.

"Warn me about what?" Her forehead creased into a deep worry line and she frowned.

He touched her cheek and ran his thumb over her lips before curling up enough to press a kiss to the lines on her brow. "Don't look so serious. I'm sorry. I should have worded that differently. I should *inform* you when I do the interview, that your name is going to come up."

Andi's eyes rounded and she pulled back. "Why would they care about me?"

David laughed, his voice echoing back from the stillness of the evening. "Okay, I'm going to try very hard not to sound conceited when I say this, but they're going to care because *I* care. Because you and I have been—and forgive the bad phrasing, but it's not mine—*seen* together in public. We've been connected, and neither one of us has made any denials when we are together. So, I'm going to get asked."

"What are you going to say?"

"Depends on what they ask…"

She scowled, and he practically heard the wheels turning in her head. "What kind of things will they ask? I've never really…" Andi shrugged, as best she could in the position they were in, and shook her head. "I've never paid attention to celebrities and their love lives." She pulled a face somewhere between a grimace and confusion.

David chuckled. "What was that face for?"

"I'm trying to figure out when you went from being David Bishop the sexy movie star—Mr. Top Ten Most Eligible Bachelor—to David, the man who danced with me before dinner. David, the man who came to my son's birthday party. David, the man who…" Then her lips curled up slowly, into a provocative grin, and she shifted up his body until she leaned over him, her lips just brushing his. "The man who kisses me in my backyard hammock and slept in my bed last night."

He pushed his fingers into her hair, holding her head so he could slide his tongue into her open mouth. She hovered over him, letting his tongue taste her, returning the touch with their breath mingling in the space between. Andi tilted her head and angled her lips over his, and he wrapped his arms around her, pulling her against him. His body screamed to pull her over him, to satisfy his need to have her thighs wrap around him, to feel her slight weight on him, but he forced himself not to indulge and curled his fingers into her yellow blouse.

Andi pushed herself away and shifted onto her side beside him, her lips glistening in the moonlight. Fighting the groan in his throat, David shifted with her until they were face to face and the hammock creaked and swayed with their movement.

"Have you figured it out?" he asked.

Andi shook her head, smiling. "No. Sometimes, I don't think you have. I look at you sometimes and wonder what the heck you're doing here…with me…and that's when I remember who you are."

David touched her cheek, something he found himself doing often, and something he found himself enjoying more and more each time. "I'm just a man, Andi."

"Oh, I know," she said with that same sexy smile. "Trust me."

"You're tempting fate again…"

She smiled wider. "So, what would they ask you? And what would you say?"

David folded his hands under his cheek, matching her. This was another position he could get used to very easily. "Well, they'll ask me if the rumors are true we're seeing each other. And feel free to correct me if I'm wrong, but I *believe* the answer is yes."

She smiled and nodded. "I think that's a safe answer."

"They might ask if you are my girlfriend." He chuckled at her grimace, the exact reaction he'd known he'd get from the dreaded term. "Hey, their word, not mine. And since it's their word, I'm going to have to answer yes."

"Ugh. I told you, I'm too old to be anyone's girlfriend."

"And just how old is that?"

Andi shook her head. "Nope."

"You know I'll find out eventually, right? There are vays to vind out deez tings…" he teased, pulling an awful evil spy accent. "In fact, the proverbial 'they' probably already know. Do you want me to hear on live television?"

"That's evil, and I don't like being manipulated."

David closed the small space between them and said, "Yeah, but is it working?" just before he kissed her. She returned the kiss but was still scowling when he settled back on his folded hands. "Oh, come on, sweetheart. It can't be nearly as bad as you think—"

"Thirty-seven."

David figured he did a damn good job at hiding his response. He just arched his eyebrows and protruded his lower lip, trying to look like he contemplated her. "Well, not quite cougar territory…"

She smacked his arm and he laughed. "See, that didn't hurt too much, did it?"

"It hurt…a lot…painfully so," she huffed. Then her face sobered and her gaze shifted away from him. "They're going to ask you why you're dating a divorcee with a young son. They're going to want to know why you'd choose to complicate your life like that. Especially since said person's ex-husband is a bastard and will always be around, being a pain in the ass."

"And I'll answer them."

Her eyes shifted back to him, but she didn't say anything. David shifted closer to her so their noses almost touched, but held her gaze. "I'll tell them I'm not dating her ex-husband, I'm dating her. I'll tell them her son is great. I'll tell them she is worth it. And then some."

Andi laid her palm against his cheek, stroking his skin, and he turned into her touch to kiss her warm palm. "As the *reason* I'm dating her…well, any blind fool could see why. I'll tell them I admired her before I ever met her. I'll tell them as soon as she walked onto the movie set, I couldn't stop thinking about her." She drew in a sharp breath. "And I'll tell them from the moment I kissed her, even if it was on set to demonstrate a scene, I was a lost man."

"You were?"

David nodded and pulled her to him for a kiss. It seemed he couldn't go much longer than a few minutes around Andi Parker without kissing her or touching her. Oh, yeah…from Kiss One, he'd been lost. No going back. No choice.

"Do you want to go with me?" he asked, not pulling back enough to break contact. He tilted his head, letting his chin brush her skin, and inhaled her scent.

"To the interviews?" Andi practically gasped.

He nodded. "You don't have to be *in* the interview, just go with me."

She didn't answer right away, curling herself against his chest so her face tucked into the side of his throat. David had to draw a slow, metered breath to remind himself of his gentleman status.

"I'm afraid," she finally said.

When he tried to see her face, she curled tighter into him. So, David relented and wrapped his arms around her, holding her as close as she seemed to need. "What are you afraid of, sweetheart?"

She shook her head, her hair whispering against his skin. Andi drew a quick breath, the kind she took whenever she wanted to convince everyone she was fine. "Nothing. I refuse to be afraid. I'll go if you want me to, David."

"I'd be proud to have you there," he whispered across her ear.

"When? Tomorrow?"

"The interview won't be until after ten. I'll write down the address before I go."

"Okay."

It was his turn to sigh. "I hate to, darlin', but I've got to go."

She nodded against his throat, and he held her for another indulgent moment before they disentangled themselves. They managed to get out of the hammock without flipping it over, and without dumping either one of them on the grass. But it involved a lot of laughing and more than one startled squeal from Andi. Finally, on their feet, he took her hand and they walked back to the house. Maggie shouted a farewell from the living room as they passed through. They paused long enough for David to write down the studio, and they continued out the front door to his car. Standing beside it, David turned to her and she slid easily into his embrace.

He kissed her deep and thoroughly, letting the desire flare to life now he felt less likely to take advantage of the setting. Even then, in moments, he leaned Andi against the car and relished the feeling of her body against his. Images of the tabloid photo came to mind, and as much as he wanted to be angry at the photographs, they captured a moment that would be engrained in his memory for the rest of his life. Pulling in deep breaths, David rested his forehead against hers and laced his fingers into her hair.

"I'm an addict," he admitted. "I've spent one night holding you, and I don't want to sleep alone."

She nodded, curling her fingers into his sides. David took her face in his hands, tipping her chin up so the moonlight played across the curves and planes of her face. He drew a breath, and the scent that had wrapped around him all night filled his senses. "You are so beautiful," he said, but found it hard with the sudden restriction of his throat he didn't understand. He stroked her cheek with his thumb, brushing the corner of her lips. "I can't believe how beautiful you are."

Andi wrapped her arms around his neck and pulled him to her again. Her body trembled in his hold as she kissed him again. Letting her go and getting in his car was one of the hardest things he could ever remember doing. Andi stood at the top of the driveway and watched him go, lifting her hand in a wave.

CHAPTER TWELVE

"What time did he say you should be there?" Maggie's shout echoed up the stairs.

Andi ran from the bathroom into her bedroom, wincing as she stuck an earring in her right ear. That's what she got for wearing earrings once every six months. She paused long enough in front of her closet to take in the full view, and winced again. What did one wear to her celebrity boyfriend's live television interview at which she would not be seen? The only thing she knew for sure was it *wasn't* a sundress. So, she'd opted for white linen pants and a form fitting pale blue blouse with capped sleeves and a fluttery hem. As a last ditch effort to dress up the outfit, she'd draped a gold link belt around her hips, with the jingly ends dangling down her thigh. With a shrug, she lifted her leg and slipped on a pair of beaded sandals.

"Andrea Parker! What time did David say?"

"He said after ten," Andi shouted back, already out her bedroom door and heading for the stairs.

"Honey, it's already eight. If you want to get there in time, you've got to go *now*."

"I know, I know," Andi mumbled as she rushed down the stairs into the kitchen. Why was it whenever she *needed* to be somewhere, she couldn't get out the door on time? If she hadn't needed to be at the studio until two in the afternoon, she would have been up and dressed by seven. She swept up her purse from the counter, took a quick swallow of the orange juice Maggie had left on the counter and headed for the door.

Maggie already stood in the foyer, briefcase in hand, ready to head out herself. "I hear there's an accident on the five, traffic is backed up for forty-five minutes. You might want to take the two-ten."

Andi groaned. "I hate going the back way. I'm terrified I'll take a wrong turn and end up in Pasadena before I realize I'm in the wrong place."

"That's why your phone has GPS, my dear."

Maggie led the way to the door, pulling it open, and Andi dug her keys from her purse to lock the door behind them. She walked forward, her head down, rummaging in the small bag. "How can a set of keys get lost in one tiny compartment?"

She caught in her peripheral that Maggie stopped short. "When you left Bonehead's name at the security gate, did you say he might be back?"

"I did. Why—" Andi looked up.

"You were forever misplacing your keys," Lawrence said with a smile that made Andi's stomach clench with actual nausea. "Do you remember our first Christmas together? I bought you that key chain that beeped when you clapped your hands."

"How precious. And cheap," Maggie mumbled, continuing out of the house

"What are you doing here, Lawrence?" Andi asked, pulling the keys from her purse. She glanced down the driveway to his rental car as she turned to lock the house door. "Where is Jake?"

"He's at the condo I rented for the week—"

"Who is with him?"

"I'm sure he's fine, Andrea. And we're not far from here. I told him I wanted a chance to speak with you." His gaze shifted to Maggie. "Alone."

"Yeah? Did you have to tie him down when you told him that?"

Maggie said with an arch of her eyebrow. "Had to have, or he wouldn't have let you out of the house."

Lawrence looked away before Maggie finished, leveling his gaze on Andi in a way that made her chest tighten. She had learned his looks, his expressions, and this was his Charmer face. He'd used that same smile at every dinner party they'd ever attended, and years later she realized, while they were dating. He'd used it the night he took her to bed the first time. The orange juice in her stomach turned to acid, and she swallowed hard at the nausea induced by the memory of Lawrence Bonherre touching her.

"Could we talk?" he asked, and she noticed the small nosegay in his hand. "About yesterday. And Sunday. I didn't handle things very well."

Maggie snorted. "Oh, don't get down on yourself too much, Larry. You handled in typical butthead style."

"I don't have time," Andi said firmly, taking a step forward.

He sidestepped to stop her. "Just five minutes."

"I have someplace to be, Lawrence."

He held his empty hand out, palm up, and offered his best grin. "Please. I want to smooth things over for the sake of our son."

Andi drew in a slow breath, releasing it through her nose. Lawrence had strategically managed to park his car behind Andi's Lexus, so she wouldn't be able to leave until he let her go. Or...she could run him over. The idea had merit, but it would involve filing a police report and creating impossible delays. She looked at her watch. "I can't spare more than three minutes."

"It's a start, Andrea," he said in his calmest voice.

Maggie scowled.

"Go ahead, Mags. I know you've got to go. You can't avoid the five. I'll see you tonight."

Maggie glared at Lawrence, held her hand up to her cheek like a mock phone, and headed for her red Mustang convertible. "Don't forget, Andi. David needs you there," she offered with a wink.

Andi tried to hide her grin, knowing Maggie had thrown David's name out purely for effect. And while Lawrence's smile didn't waver, she caught the slight twitch at the corner of his left eye that spoke volumes to the effect of Maggie's ploy. As soon as Maggie pulled down the driveway, Lawrence took a step toward Andi, holding out the flowers.

"I came to apologize for my behavior both Sunday and yesterday. I was rude and lost my temper, but, Andrea—"

"An apology doesn't come with a 'but,' Lawrence." She walked past him toward her car, clicking the automatic lock as she walked. The doors beeped, she pulled the driver's door open and tossed her purse on the passenger seat. "If you're sorry, you're sorry. Leave it at that."

"You have to understand how upsetting this was for me, Andrea. I came here to see my son, but also to find a way to reconcile…to bring our family together again."

"A fifty-percent success rate isn't too bad. You saw your son."

"We're a family—"

"No!" Andi snapped, twisting around so fast to face him that her sandals ground into the gritty cobblestone of the driveway. Yesterday he'd caught her off guard and had gotten the better of her, but Andi would be damned if he did it again. "We *were* a family before you decided things like wedding vows meant nothing. It's over, Lawrence. Visit with Jake, and then *bring him home*. The sooner we get this annual visit done and over with, the better for everyone." She turned her back on him to get in the SUV. "Now, move your car. David is waiting."

It felt good to throw out the last bit, and she hid her smirk by reaching for her sunglasses on the dash. Lawrence's fingers wrapped around her elbow and Andi jerked free.

"Don't. Touch. Me," she barely hissed through clenched teeth.

His Charmer smile wavered, but he maintained it and dropped his hand away. "I've decided not to head back to Chicago for a while. It's more important I'm here."

Andi gritted her teeth, pressing her lips together before speaking. She needed to, otherwise her words would most likely start more trouble than they could avoid. "Jake comes home Thursday. If you decide to stay and want to see him, you'll have to give me a full forty-eight hours' notice before any further visits. We have a life here, Lawrence. One that doesn't involve you."

She climbed into the Lexus without giving him the chance to say more and slammed the door. He stood beside the car for several moments as she started the vehicle and purposefully put it in reverse. When he didn't make any move to approach his car, she let the car roll backward. Lawrence held his hands up and jogged to the car, getting it out of the way before she changed her mind about the whole 'backing over it' idea. Andi watched in her side mirrors until he cleared the end of the driveway. She pressed the accelerator hard enough to kick up a cloud of dust and make a satisfying squealing sound. She backed into the street and turned the car in the direction of the fourteen, not looking back to see which direction he was headed.

The morning only got worse from there. Her feeble attempt at avoiding the traffic on the five got her stuck in another bumper-to-bumper commute three miles from the studio. The drive should have taken an hour—easily getting her to the studio before the show began — but turned into an hour and forty-five minutes. As it crept closer and closer to ten, Andi tapped her hands harder and faster on the steering wheel. She forced herself to breathe and not get hysterical. She hated traffic, hated driving in traffic, and hated being late. But more than that, she hated disappointing someone as important to her as David.

Finally, the traffic opened up and she thrust the car forward. The parking gods were with her and she found a spot near the entrance of the studio building, giving herself one final check in the rearview mirror as she smoothed on a touch of lip gloss. She forced herself not to jog into the building and up to the security desk.

"You don't make my job easy, David."

David took a long drink from his latte, hoping the espresso would energize his system. He set the paper cup down on the ready-room table and shifted forward to rest his elbows on his knees. "You manage my career, Avi. Just how have I made that hard?"

Avi laughed and crossed his legs, smoothing his hand down the creased front of his dark trousers. Like usual, Avi was impeccably dressed in a dark suit and deep plum shirt with a tie. "I shouldn't learn the important details in the news along with the rest of the unenlight-ened masses."

"What? I called you as soon as I could talk."

"The accident on set isn't what I'm talking about."

David rubbed his eyes and drained the last of the latte. He was torn between either making Avi *say* it was Andi he referred to, or just acknowledging he'd waited for Avi to bring it up all morning. In the end, he decided he wanted Avi to say it. Avi had been his manager since he turned eighteen and fired his step-father/manager, and David credited much of his adult success to Avi's guidance and hard work, but that didn't mean he wanted Avi 'managing' his private life—no matter what spin he wanted to put on it.

So, he sat silent and watched his friend…and waited. Avi eventually huffed and shook his head.

"Okay, fine. You want me to spell it out? I will. I would have liked a heads-up about Andrea Parker before pictures of the two of you making out like two teenagers in the parking lot of *Chez Nous* popped up in every two-bit gossip rag in the state. Before 'insiders' on the set tell stories of you visiting her trailer and screaming for her while they tried to fix your face."

"At what point exactly am I supposed to report to you?"

"Is this thing serious?"

"I hope so," David answered honestly.

Avi stared at him, and David stared back. Finally, Avi shook his head. "Damn, man. It's written all over your face."

David smiled and stood, pacing to the far wall. The caffeine had finally kicked in, making him antsy to move. If he continued sitting, he'd start fidgeting and if he started now, he wouldn't be able to quit in the interview. He checked his watch again—nine thirty-eight—and shoved his hands in his pockets.

"Okay, fine. I'm not going to get an apology—"

"What am I apologizing for? Not telling you I kissed a girl? Avi, we *aren't* teenagers and I'm not going to tell my best friend when I've made it to first base with my girlfriend."

"I'm just saying certain information should be released slowly."

"You make it sound like any of this is *bad*. I'm dating Andrea Parker, big deal. I kissed her in a parking lot, big deal."

"You're dating a woman who divorced her husband for cheating a year after breaking up with your long-term girlfriend for doing the same thing."

David's neck heated and he pushed his hands deeper into his pockets, gritting his teeth. "The only people who know that are you and Josie, so what does Andi's divorce have to do with anything? I didn't even know she *was* divorced when I..." He realized with humor he didn't know how to classify the whole process that brought them together. When he what? Kissed her to clarify a scene? When he sought her out for another? Or did things start when he asked her to dinner and ended up kissing her again? "I didn't know she was divorced when I met her, and I didn't know *why* she was divorced until after we went out. So, none of that has *anything* to do with us."

"Okay, okay. Didn't mean to piss you off."

"You didn't," David mumbled, pacing again so he wouldn't look at his watch. "I'm just worried. She said she'd be here before ten."

He felt Avi watching him but didn't look at his manager. David wasn't being completely honest, he was pissed...a little. Public scrutiny was a part of his life. He didn't rue his fate because of it, he didn't become a hermit, but he didn't work at being in the public eye. Photographs and autographs were part of the deal, and so were screaming fans and gossip rags looking to sell copy. David loved what he did, always had, even when his stepfather nearly ruined it all while bleeding David dry. He'd loved it since the first time he stepped on a commercial soundstage at nine years old. He couldn't imagine being or doing anything else.

That didn't mean he wanted his love life under the public microscope.

"Are you just going to pace, or are you going to tell me about her before she gets here?"

At least the scolding tone had left Avi's voice. He was maybe fifteen years older than David, which made him feel just old enough to think he could put David in his place when needed. It worked when David was eighteen, but not at thirty-one. David smiled and sat again, his foot immediately bouncing with the after-effects of the espresso.

Before he said a word, he smiled. "She's amazing, Avi. She's beautiful and sexy, and she's so smart. I could sit and *talk* with her for hours, or listen to her. I went to a book signing with her yesterday—"

"Yeah, I know," Avi interjected, but David continued without pause.

"And for three hours, I sat there and watched her. And listened to her talking to these people who came *hours* ahead of time just to see her. They'd ask her questions about her books, and when she answered, I *had* to listen. Her mind is just..." He waved his hands on each side of his head, trying to find the right words and to express everything he'd felt the day before. "And she's so damn beautiful."

"You mentioned that." Avi chuckled.

"And Jake—"

"Who's Jake?"

"Her son. He's a great kid."

"Damn, David. You're going from zero to sixty in two seconds flat with this woman. Spending time with her kid is dangerous. Women get vicious when their kids are involved, especially when things end badly."

"Who says things are going to end?"

Avi's eyes popped open and he adjusted his black silk tie. "You were with Josie for three years, and I never heard you talk like this once."

David scowled and slumped into the couch. "Andi isn't Josie, and Josie is no Andi. I don't even like comparing them."

"Well, there's no doubt about it. You're in love."

A soft knock interrupted any response David might have had, and the door opened slowly toward him. "Hi. I'm looking for David Bishop—"

David jumped up from the couch and yanked the door open. He swept Andi into a hug just as she looked at him, surprise registering on her face. Andi raised her arms and wrapped them around his neck, laughing softly in his ear as he lifted her feet off the floor.

"I thought you wouldn't make it," he said as he let her go, already smiling like a fool and he knew it. David looked her over from head to toe, sucking in and releasing a breath as he took in the white linen pants and the sky-blue blouse that accentuated her curves just enough to tempt. A gold chain belt hung low around her hips, drawing his attention. "My god, woman. You're beautiful."

Andi smiled, a sexy color blooming on her cheeks. "I'm sorry I'm late. I tried avoiding the traffic, but just got myself caught in more. And…" She stuttered over words she didn't say, blinking with a sharp shake of her head. "I was delayed leaving."

"Everything okay?" He ran his hands up and down her bare arms.

"Absolutely. Just…had to take out the garbage," she said with an unreadable smile.

He slid his arm across her shoulders, drawing her against his side to turn her toward Avi. "Sweetheart, this is Avi Siegal, my manager."

Avi stepped forward, hand extended, with a wide smile of perfectly straight, white teeth. "As much as my man here has gone on about you, I don't need an introduction. It's nice to meet you, Andi." He took her hand and clasped it in both of his.

Andi nodded, but her attention barely registered on Avi. She looked up at him, and David noted for the first time her quick breathing like she'd run to the room. "I'm not too late, right?"

"Nope. I'm heading out in a few minutes. Avi had them save a seat for you in the front row."

"Oh. I thought I'd be back here waiting for you."

Within his embrace, he felt the slight tensing of her back and shoulders. "Don't worry. Brooke promised she wouldn't point you out or anything. You're just there to see the interview."

"Although, Brooke's interviews are a hoot. You might have fun—"

David shot Avi a warning glance, shaking his head slightly.

"Or…not. Maybe another time," Avi amended.

"Can I come back to you when it's over?"

Just the way Andi asked the question sent a shot of quicksilver through David's bloodstream, and he decided no more than thirty seconds should ever pass after seeing her before he kissed her. He touched her cheek and turned her to him, meeting her with a kiss. Her lips were slick, letting his slide across them easily, and the faint taste of something sweet – like honey and raspberries – touched his tongue.

David opened his mouth, letting his tongue follow the taste. Andi's hands slid over his stomach to his sides and thoughts of couches and kicking Avi out almost pushed out everything else.

A brush of air across his cheeks preceded the soft clearing of someone's throat. "I wanted to say hello before the show, but looks like someone beat me to it."

David smiled against Andi's lips and drew his lips together in a last kiss. He took her hand as he turned toward the door. Brooke Halle, an actress-cum-celebrity talk show host who did a live Monday through Friday morning program, stood in the doorway with one hand on her hip and the other on the knob. She grinned, looking between Avi and them. Brooke was the only interview David okayed with Avi because he'd interviewed with Brooke before, and she always kept things light. He didn't need any third-degree interviews—just wasn't in the mood. Knowing how long Brooke had been 'in the business', David put her in her late forties, but her young face said otherwise. In Hollywood, one could never tell if a person just aged well or had a very good surgeon.

David stepped away from Andi but kept her fingers wrapped snugly in his as he extended his free hand to Brooke, leaning in to kiss her cheek. "Good to see you, Brooke."

"Good to see you too, David. Bruises and all." She pointed at his face. "You don't look nearly as bad as the reports say. Last I heard you and Dr. 90210 were going to be good friends."

She and Avi greeted each other the same way, then turned back to them. "Andrea Parker?" she asked, extending her hand.

Andi had to let go of David's hand to take Brooke's. "Yes. Hi."

Brooke winked and smiled. "Nice to meet the woman behind the hullabaloo."

"Forty-five seconds, Ms. Halle," called from the hall a young man wearing a head mic and carrying a clipboard.

"Thanks," she answered, already halfway out the door. "See you out there."

"Do I need to go?" Andi asked.

"Not a big rush. I don't go out until after the first commercial break. Avi can take you to the seats, though." Andi nodded and smiled up at him, the kind of smile that made his chest expand with pure pride over the fact this gorgeous woman would look at him like *that*. He raised his hand to touch her cheek. "Avi will bring you back the next commercial break after I leave the stage."

When he spoke, the lingering taste of honey and berries danced on his lips and he ran his tongue along the inside of his lower lip, tasting the gloss she'd left behind.

"Okay, lover boy. Let the young lady go so we can get to our seats without being too obvious."

Avi took Andi's elbow to lead her away, but David needed one more taste before she was gone. He pulled her back, and she came into his arms without hesitation, her hands sliding up his arms to rest behind his neck. He angled his lips over hers and kissed her slowly, deliberately, taking the sweet taste from her lips. Her mouth opened beneath his, and he delved inside, his entire body coming more alive than a dozen cups of espresso could ever accomplish.

David slid his cheek across hers to whisper near her ear. "I love how you taste," he said softly enough only Andi heard.

She shuddered in his hold, her breath warm against his jaw. Reluctantly, David let her go and she walked out with Avi, smiling back at him over her shoulder before disappearing into the hall.

David rubbed his lips together, letting the faint taste of honey and berries settle on his tongue. He'd felt the slickness of Andi's gloss with the first kiss, but the delicate taste had taken time to register. When he ran his thumb over his lower lip, the gloss still slicked his skin. David looked at the pad of his thumb and smiled.

The same young man who'd called Brooke to the stage stuck his head in the door. "Mr. Bishop, if you'll please follow me."

David snatched up the sunglasses he'd set on the arm of the waiting room couch and slipped them on, following the man. Avi had discussed with Brooke, and then with David, about wearing the sunglasses until he was on stage to cover the remaining bruises. It was a gag, but it was humorous, and that's why he liked Brooke's show. She had celebrities and well-knowns on every day, but her interviews were light and fun and never too serious. He also knew he could trust her to bring up Andi without making her a point of gossip.

He smiled as he followed the stage manager to his entrance door.

Andi, even just the thought of Andi, invariably and inevitably put a smile on his face. Brooke's voice carried through the false walls that separated her set from the back area, and he heard her monologue as he waited to enter.

The soundstage was dimly lit, with most of the lights focused on the simple, permanent set of the Brooke Halle morning show. The background looked like a mock-up of a simple home with part of a kitchen visible. Brooke had a desk set center stage, with a chair and couch side-by-side adjacent to it. In the background, a black baby grand piano sat near the faux set wall.

Avid led her by the elbow through the maze of cameras and cables taped to the floor to two empty chairs in the front row. Andi sat and said a brief hello to the woman seated beside her. The middle-aged woman smiled brightly, clutching a quilted bag in her lap.

"You got here just in time," the woman said with enthusiasm. "I heard there was a last-minute change to the show schedule." She whispered, but her voice seemed loud to Andi. "I heard some big celebrity is going to be here." The lady smiled, pride in her knowledge obvious in her bright eyes. "I heard it might even be David Bishop."

"Oh, that would be wonderful," Andi replied, letting the woman enjoy the chance to pass on the news she believed no one else knew.

The woman nodded and extended her hand. "I'm Lucille."

Before Andi could answer, the stage door opened and Brooke Halle stepped onto the stage, raising her arm in a high wave as the audience burst into loud cheers. She made a show of pointing at certain people in the audience and waving, even blowing kisses, before sitting behind her desk. Her first few minutes of chitchat didn't register with Andi, but she did her best to pay attention. Her thoughts slipped again and again to David's final kiss before she left the ready room.

"So, we all heard about the terrible accident that happened on the set of David Bishop's new movie *Rise of Dawn*…You saw the papers or the reports on television that said everything from he had a hangnail to he's disfigured for life, right? Well, David is here today to set the record straight—" Whatever she said after that was lost in the roar of the studio audience.

The door at the back of the stage opened, and David came out wearing dark sunglasses that hid much of the remaining bruises. They were nearly gone now, nothing in comparison to those first couple of days after the accident, but with the glasses they weren't visible at all. Now, seated with the rest of the crowd, Andi could take him in and appreciate just how good he looked. Except for their dinner, David often dressed more casually in slacks and button-down shirts, or shorts and a tee shirt, when not on set. But today…today he played the role of celebrity interviewee. He wore perfectly tailored dark dress slacks with a matching three-button vest over a dark gray dress shirt. His shirt-sleeves were rolled to his elbows, revealing his muscled lower arms, and the collar remained unbuttoned to expose the base of his throat. Andi had to lick her lips and draw in a slow breath. If she inhaled deep enough, she swore she could smell the scent of his cologne—or shampoo—or whatever he used to give him the earthy, spicy scent she associated with him.

David raised his hand just as Brooke had, greeting the crowd. Brooke came around to the front of the desk and chairs, meeting him in a quick embrace and exchange of cheek kisses, motioning for him to sit. The crowd hadn't calmed yet, but as he settled into the chair, bringing one foot up to rest his ankle on the other knee, they finally quieted enough for Brooke to speak.

"So, how you doin'?" she asked with a grin.

David chuckled. "Good. Enjoying a few days off."

He scanned the crowd, and Andi knew the moment he found her because her breath caught and her heart jumped. She didn't have to see his eyes, just the way his lips ticked up at the corners in a slow smile. Lucille sighed beside her, touching Andi's arm. "Isn't he just the handsomest thing ever? I mean, I know I'm practically old enough to be his mother, but that doesn't mean I can't enjoy the view, right?"

"Right," was all Andi managed to say.

"You know, there are easier ways to get a day off," Brooke joked.

"Are you going to end the suspense and let everyone see how badly things are—or aren't—as the case may be?"

David obliged and took off the sunglasses, squinting against the lights. The stage lighting emphasized the remaining bruises, but even then, they didn't look very bad. Another day or so, and they'd be nothing but shadows and he'd return to work. The thought made Andi sad. She'd enjoyed these days with him and knew being with him on set wouldn't be quite the same.

A series of gasps, moans, and "Oh" sounds shifted through the crowd.

"See? Not so bad."

"So, what happened?" Brooke asked.

David shifted in the seat, setting his elbow on the arm. He rubbed his thumb across his lower lip and for just a moment, he looked directly at Andi. She couldn't help but grin...just a little. With a flush of heat from her toes to her hairline, Andi realized why he'd kissed her so thoroughly before letting her go. He'd kissed her gloss away and now tasted it on stage. A sweet tumble shifted through her stomach, and she sat back just a little further in the seat.

David told the story of the set accident, with Brooke slipping in questions and statements to instigate a laugh or reaction from the crowd. David laughed along, joked with her, and shifted almost nervously in his seat. When he stilled for a moment, his foot bounced until he shifted again.

"So, you're enjoying some time off..." Brooke let the statement trail off.

"Yeah. But, it's back to the set on Thursday." He rubbed his lip.

They talked another minute or so about not much of anything. She asked questions about the movie, and he provided carefully scripted answers designed to not give too much away. The plot was no secret to anyone who'd read the books, but some of the movie effects and whatnot were purposefully being kept under wrap to build more interest in the release.

"Speaking of the movie, and the woman who penned the best-selling novel that inspired it..." Brooke let the sentence fall away as she cleared her throat. She turned to pick up a pile of papers near her elbow. "You know we just had to ask, David."

An immediate rush of panic slammed into Andi's chest and her cheeks felt so hot she figured they could use her face as a source of backup lighting.

"Yeah, yeah…" David shifted to see what the host was about to show the audience. "I know, Brooke."

She smiled and held up a blown-up shot similar to the one Caroline had shown them the day before. This one was slightly different, probably taken a second or two before or after the other, but the effect was the same. A better, more erotic-looking kiss couldn't be and had never been staged for any movie ever, as far as Andi was concerned. As embarrassed as she was such a private moment was caught on film, and as much aggravation the exposure caused with Lawrence, the effect of the shot was intense and immediate for her. She remembered the kiss with clarity, every touch of his lips, and every smooth stroke of his hands. In the image, Andi's eyes were closed, her head tilted back with her lips parted to accept his kiss as his tongue filled her mouth. Her fingers were just visible beneath the back hem of his jacket where her hands had slid down to his waist. He cradled her head, his fingers laced into her hair, leaning her back against the car.

David shifted again. He tilted his head, released a long sigh, and rubbed his lip. "I'm thinking about having that framed," he said with a smile.

Brooke laughed, angling the photo toward one of the nearby cameras so the large LCD screen above them enlarged the image to ten times life-size. Andi stared for a moment, pressing her hand to her chest to still the sudden pounding of her heart. When she lowered her head, her breath caught as she discovered David staring at her. Andi smiled slowly, and he did the same, winking.

"Oh, my…" Lucille said beside her. She turned slowly and looked at Andi. "Oh, my."

Andi shook her head, leaning toward Lucille. "Please don't say anything."

Lucille shook her head. "Oh, I won't. Are you…you're Andrea Parker?"

She nodded. "Yes."

Lucille flushed bright red. "Oh, my. You lucky, lucky woman."

Andi smiled genuinely. "I know."

"These made the rounds yesterday," Brooke continued. "Hitting all the major and not-so-major magazines and entertainment news shows. And just to make sure we have it right, this lucky young woman would be Andrea Parker, right?"

David nodded, still watching Andi. "Yes, that would be her."

Brooke cleared her throat and snapped her finger, forcing David to shift his attention. "Over here, David," she said lightly, then looked out into the audience. "We promised David we wouldn't put her on camera, but Andrea is in the audience today. It seems we can't hold David's attention with her around."

A murmur went through the audience, and Andi had all she could do not to slouch. But, that would surely draw everyone's attention. Lucille patted her hand and nodded, her expression saying Andi's secret was safe.

"So, if we judge by this photo, I'd say you and Andrea are... dating?" Brooke raised her brows and tilted her head, intentionally adding a sarcastic lilt to her voice.

David nodded. "Yeah, that's safe to say."

"Uh huh, uh huh…" She set the photo face down. "Do you care to elaborate?"

David glanced at Andi and held her gaze for just a beat before looking back to Brooke. "I've spent enough time with Andi to pick up some of her writer terms, and all I'll say is we're a work in progress."

Brooke protruded her lower lip and tipped her head side-to-side in a variation of a nod. "Okay, I can take that. But let me just say, if this is the work in progress—" She held up the photo again, "I'm buying the final copy!"

The audience erupted in a unison bout of laughter, and David chuckled.

"Now, we invited you to bring Andrea out here with you, but you said no. Why is that?"

David drew in a breath, his shoulders rising and falling, and he tilted his head slightly to the side. Just before he spoke, his gaze connected with her again and Andi's heartbeat jumped. There was something so dark and intense about his eyes today…just his gaze made her flush.

"Andi—"

"So, it's Andi and not Andrea?"

David nodded. "Andi is still getting used to her fans lining up for hours just to say hello and get her autograph in a book. Live interviews might be a bit much right now."

"Maybe next time, then?"

"Maybe…" He didn't look away.

If he wasn't careful, everyone would figure out where she was just by following his eyes. Andi knew the thought should—and would usually—make her panic, but this time it didn't. Instead of panic, warm pride bloomed in her chest and she realized *she* was the woman David Bishop looked at like that…with desire. With a smile. No one else but her.

"You allow me to bring up an interesting point, David," Brooke said, pulling Andi from her thoughts. "I read in one of the *many* articles that have come out in the last week about you, and about Andrea—I'm sorry. Andi, right?—Since your accident when you and she were connected publicly—that's another topic altogether—but, anyway, this article described the two of you as a bit of an odd couple. Since celebrities don't often…well, let's be honest…you don't often date outside of your kind."

Andi had a hard time following the scattered, rambling point and chuckled softly when David stared at Brooke with a single eyebrow arched. It looked like he had the same problem.

"I never quite heard it put that way before," he finally said when she finished circling her point.

"It's true, though." Brooke looked out to the audience, nodding her head and holding her hand out as if asking for affirmation from the crowd. A few people mumbled, and many nodded. "Except for the few big names who have been married *forever*, and probably to someone they married before everyone in the world knew their names, most celebrities end up married—more than once, I might add—to another celebrity. If not married, then at least dating. Right? Isn't that usually the case? Even with you?"

David shrugged, keeping his focus now on Brooke. "Generally speaking, yes."

"So, anyway, this article tried to make you two an odd couple, like I said. But, the way I see it, you're not. I mean, *hello*! Who hasn't read or doesn't know about the *Rise of Dawn* books? Cave dwellers, maybe, but I bet even some of *them* have downloaded it to their Kindle. But otherwise, Andrea Parker is nearly as much a household name as…well… David Bishop."

The crowd clapped and cheered, and Brooke encouraged it was an enthusiastic "Am I right? I'm right, aren't I?" She looked out into the general audience, her focus quite clearly directed away from where Andi and Avi sat. "So, Andrea honey, when you're ready for an interview, you come on up. My couch is your couch, and you can bring your boyfriend if you want."

Andi closed her eyes and heard David's chuckle. She didn't have to look to know he was grinning ear-to-ear and confirmed it when she opened her eyes again. He watched her, one arm slung across the back of the chair, the other hand rubbing his lower lip.

"What's so funny, David?" Brooke asked, leaning on her desk to make eye contact. "And do you need a tissue? You've been working at something on your lips there…oooooh…" She winked at the camera. "I get it now. I caught David and Andi back in the ready room." She pursed her lips and made a kissing sound. "It's a good thing she doesn't wear bright red lipstick, my friend."

His tongue ran across his lip before his smile widened, and he winked. Andi knew the giddy, warm feeling in her stomach was something best left to love-struck teenagers—and if she tried to describe it, she'd sound like a blushing virgin in a romance novel—but she was tired of denying it, and tired of trying to convince herself otherwise.

"Now, just a little more serious," Brooke said, clearing her throat as she tried to *look* more serious with an obvious theatrical flair. That's what you get when you have an actress who'd taken the talk show route. "She may be a celebrity in her own right, but I understand a lot of people have been surprised you two would date because there *are* some marked differences between the two of you."

As soon as she started with the new angle of discussion, the warm feeling disappeared with a snap and her stomach clenched like someone had thrown ice water on her insides.

"Andrea—I'm sorry. *Andi*—is divorced with a son. That's not a surprise or news to anyone who is inclined to look her up."

David nodded. "True."

"And she's older than you…"

He didn't blink, didn't look away from Brooke, and didn't shift. "Yes," he answered simply.

Brooke stared at him, arching her eyebrows, obviously waiting for more of an answer. "Okay…" she said after a moment. "I guess that answers the unasked questions then, doesn't it?"

David smiled and looked into the crowd again. "I guess it does…" he said in a softer, lower voice as his gaze settled on Andi.

CHAPTER THIRTEEN

The front door flew open and Jake bolted into the house, dropping his duffle on the floor as he sprinted into the kitchen. "Mom!"

Andi set down her casserole pan, turning just in time to catch her son in a firm hug, squeezing him hard. "Oh, I missed you," she whispered against his hair, doing her best to blink away the tears. It felt like an eternity had passed since he'd left, instead of just four days.

She heard the front door close, and looked up to see Lawrence standing in the entryway, his hands pushed into his pants pockets, a forced smile on his face. Andi much preferred when he scowled, because at least then she knew what to expect. When he smiled, anything could happen.

Jake looked at the pan and grinned. "Are you making chicken?" She nodded. "The way I like it?"

Andi nodded again, grinning. "Yep. With broccoli and cheesy rice."

"Awesome!"

She kept her arm around him, not quite ready to let go, and took a quick inventory. He looked the same as he did on Sunday, but she still needed to know he was okay. Her chest hurt from a mixture of heartache that he'd been gone and joy he was home again.

"And we're having chocolate cream pie for dessert. Maggie is making homemade whipped cream, just for you."

Jake hugged her again. Past him, Lawrence watched silently. He still smiled, but it was strained and tight…disapproving. Andi kissed her son's hair and rubbed his back. "Why don't you take your bag to your room? Maggie will be home soon."

Jake darted away and snatched his bag from the floor near the door. He stopped short of the stairs, looking back at Andi with only a brief glance toward his father. "Mom?"

"Yes, honey?"

"Is David coming for dinner?"

Andi smiled, drawing in a slow breath before she answered. She didn't look toward Lawrence at all. "He had to return to the set today, but he's going to try and make it."

Jake grinned wide. "Great. I told him I was going to beat him good next time we played *Super Mario*." Then he was gone, bounding up the stairs.

"Home safe and sound, and none the worse for wear," Lawrence said once silence settled in the kitchen.

That's debatable.

Andi drew in a fortifying breath, leaned back against the edge of the counter, and turned her attention to him. He'd taken a few more steps into the kitchen, standing at the end of the counter near the tall stool chairs. It took her time to get used to being around her ex-husband. She had to build immunity to the nausea and revulsion. Sunday had been the worst, followed very closely by Monday, but only because he'd caught her off guard so soon after learning about the photographs. But, in five days, she'd built up the walls again—brick by brick—until he was just an annoyance.

Still, an annoyance guaranteed to make her insides crawl and her stomach clench.

She turned away from him, retrieving the package of thawed chicken breasts from the cold water in the sink. Andi sensed him move closer but refused to turn. With the chicken washed, she set to making Jake's favorite meal…a concoction she'd created in a desperate attempt at having something 'different'. Lawrence cleared his throat.

"Did you need something else?" she asked, not looking up from her task.

When he didn't answer after several moments, Andi looked up and stilled. Lawrence stood just a couple of feet away from her, his head tilted slightly with a strange smile on his face as he watched her. A chill moved up her spine and the hair on the back of her neck stood up, making her skin tingle. It was all she could do not to twitch.

"What are you looking at?"

"You…" he answered, his voice softer. "I never stopped long enough to watch you when we were married. To watch you move, doing something as simple as making dinner. You can be very graceful, Andrea."

A sneer threatened to pull at her lips, but she didn't allow it, going to the sink to wash her hands. "I have things to do before dinner. You didn't answer me. Is there something else you need?"

"You."

Andi spun around, water dripping on the counter and floor from her wet fingers. She stared at him, unable to process an adequate response. Lawrence took a step toward her, and she sidestepped him, retrieving a paper towel to dry her hands.

"Andrea, I meant it when I said I wanted to make us a family again. I didn't handle it well. Margaret Connelly has a way of digging at me, you know that, and I wasn't expecting another man to be at my son's birthday party."

"Kind of like I wasn't expecting to find you mid-fellatio with Leslie?"

Lawrence blinked slowly, lowering his head in a slow nod. "I deserve that."

"You deserve more, but I find as of late I don't care enough to expend the energy required to tell you exactly what you deserve to hear." Andi walked around him to throw the paper towel in the trash, turning with one hand on her hip and the other on the counter. "The fact of the matter is, Lawrence, I don't give enough of a damn about you or your wife or anything about your life to comment. You are my son's father, and for that reason and that reason alone, I tolerate you."

His smile slipped away but came quickly back into place. "I'm not going to give up easily, Andrea."

"I don't care if you give up easily, or give up hard, just give up."

She was exceptionally proud of her ability to keep her voice level. In fact, it wasn't all that hard.

He pressed his lips together and looked at the plate of chicken. "Should I assume then I won't receive an invitation to dinner?"

"I didn't make enough," she ground out.

When he looked at her again, the smile was still firmly in place but his eyes had taken on a cold edge. In that, Andi was either blessed or cursed. She recognized the edge. His opponents in the courtroom might not be able to see past the charming smile, but she'd been the recipient of those cold stares enough to recognize them. Despite her previous pride in remaining unfazed by Lawrence, her blood chilled just a little.

"You made enough for David Bishop, though."

She didn't answer, just stared back. Lawrence drew in a slow breath through his nose, releasing it just as slowly. He touched the counter with his manicured fingertips, rubbing at the granite as if removing a spot. "I've been doing some research on him since we met the other day."

"Let me help you out," she said with her most pleasant smile before rattling off the website address she'd used herself to read about him.

"Oh, I've looked there. Several other places, too. Your David has had a very colorful life…filled with plenty of beautiful women."

Andi crossed her arms over her body, pressing her lips together. She didn't know where he was going with this line of conversation… and yet, a cold lump formed in her chest because she feared where it might go.

"I have to wonder what he's doing with…" He trailed off and moved his gaze over her from head to toe. Today she'd returned to the comfort and coolness of her sundresses, knowing David seemed to like her in them. But, under Lawrence's cold stare, she immediately felt like the frumpy, unattractive lump he'd reduced her to before she finally left. "Someone as simple as you, Andrea. Don't get me wrong, you're not too hard on the eyes, but in comparison to Josie Connors and Rachel Leighton…" Again, he let what was left unsaid sink in.

She had nothing to say in return, and the fact he'd left her speechless sat in her throat like a chunk of ice. Andi had thought it early on, and wondered why David would want her, but he'd come a long way in convincing her he did, so the reasons hadn't mattered. Until this moment. And she *hated* Lawrence for making her question it all over again…no matter how hard she tried not to. She looked away, using sheer willpower to keep back the tears that threatened to fill her eyes

"Andrea, I would hate to see you hurt."

"Bull," she snapped, looking at him again. "You'd love to see me hurt. Liar."

"No, you're wrong." He took a step toward her and Andi straightened, holding her breath. "I never intended to cause you pain, and if I can save you from it, I will. Just think on this, Andrea…and I truly don't bring this up to be cruel…but, you know our sexual relations were less than satisfying."

The statement sliced through her with the ferocity of a knife. Her heart hurt, and he hadn't delivered the worst of his words, she knew that much.

Lawrence took a step closer and leaned in, dropping his voice so there would be no chance of anyone else—even if someone *had* been in the room to witness his 'act of kindness'—to hear his words. "I can only assume the two of you are not lovers. Because, Andrea, how long do you think a man like David Bishop will stay once he takes you to bed?"

"Get out," she hissed through clenched teeth.

Lawrence took a step back, a false expression of sympathy painted on his face. "I'm willing to accept your shortcomings, Andrea, because I know your strengths and I'm willing to take the good with the bad. Can David Bishop say the same? *Will* he?"

"And am I to take the good with the bad?" she forced herself to ask. "I'm supposed to graciously crawl back to my position as your wife because you *accept* me, and in return what am I to accept?"

"You had a good life with me, Andrea. You can't tell me it wasn't, because then *you* would be the liar." He turned away and walked nearly to the door before turning again. "Think about what I said…and look at your boyfriend with a realistic view. Look to the future. What do you see?"

Then he left, closing the door carefully behind him. Andi closed her eyes and tried to swallow against the desert now in her throat. With shaking hands, she put the pan of chicken in the refrigerator to cook later and forced herself to drink a glass of water. It would be another hour before she needed to start dinner. A good hour to gather herself again and bury the bitter doubt Lawrence had once again managed to harvest in her. She didn't know what she hated more…that he stirred up the dark thoughts in her, or that some part of her believed him.

Lawrence was the only man she'd ever been with intimately. She was twenty when she gave up her virginity…she didn't lose it, she knew exactly where it was going. At the time, she'd believed it was out of love he urged her to bed. Maybe it had been, maybe not, so many years later she couldn't be sure. After leaving him, the idea of being touched by another man nauseated and terrified her for a long, long time. When she finally accepted not every man was Lawrence Bonherre, it had been easier just to ignore that part of herself. Besides, no man had made her think about that kind of intimacy.

Until David.

She finished cleaning the kitchen and decided to attempt a diversion. Andi turned on her computer and stared at the end of her latest chapter. It only needed another three or four paragraphs to wrap things up and move on, but the words wouldn't come. She read emails, responded to some fan mail, and then found herself unoccupied once again. Only forty minutes had passed. Wandering without any real purpose, she went into her bedroom and stared back at herself in the closet door mirror.

The sundress she wore just barely cleared the middle of her knees, and she'd put on sandals with a slight heel, just enough to define her calves a little. The dress had a princess cut with a low V-neck and buttons down the front, letting it hug her body and fall around her hips. As she stared at herself, she drew in a shaky breath. There was nothing *wrong* with her body. She wasn't too heavy, wasn't too thin. Her body curved into her waist, and swayed into her hips…and wasn't that what a woman's body was supposed to do? Andi didn't dislike anything she saw, but she didn't see anything that made her proud. She just…was.

So, what *did* make David look at her the way he did?

Andi turned sideways and ran her hand over her stomach, pressing into the slight swell beneath her waist. It wasn't much, but after Jake had been born no amount of crunches completely got rid of the little bit that refused to go away. Her breasts were fuller and larger now than they had been before she had a baby, and for that, she supposed she was thankful. The short hair made her look a little younger, enough she thought she registered a small bit of surprise in David's eyes when she'd finally admitted her age.

She wasn't the type of woman who examined her reflection to find the imperfections, she hadn't ever considered fixing this or lifting that, and even now nothing came to mind she'd wish to change. After leaving Lawrence, a part of her figured there was no reason to bother.

A soft rap at her open bedroom door made her look over her shoulder, and her breath caught in surprise. David stepped in, a wide smile on his lips as he shut the door. "Hey, sweetheart. Jake let me in, and said you were probably up here."

"Hey…" she said softly, smiling. "You got out on time."

"I didn't mess around today," he said as he crossed the room. "I wanted to get home."

"You went home first?"

David stepped behind her and wrapped his arms around her, his hands sliding over her stomach. Her dress shifted beneath his touch, raising the hem just above her knees. He rested his chin on her shoulder and met her gaze in the mirror. "I meant here."

Andi's breath caught, and the tears she'd forced away when Lawrence threw his venom tingled in her eyes again…but the rush of emotion that caused them was like night and day. David tipped his head and kissed the curve of her throat where it met her shoulder, and the warmth of his breath on her skin spread through her. She watched him in the mirror as his gaze moved over her reflection.

Not once, not ever in nine years of marriage, did Lawrence look at her with the heat she so blatantly saw in David's eyes. Not by half. He drew his hands across her stomach to her hips, his touch a delicious pressure. Andi watched, her arms hanging at her side. His large hands spanned her waist and moved up to her ribcage. Her breath caught when his thumbs barely brushed the underside of her breasts before he pressed her back against him, his palms flattened again on her stomach.

"You are so beautiful," he said near her ear, and the weight of his voice made her heartbeat leap into a staccato rhythm.

"Why?" she asked before she realized the question had formed in her mind.

He rested his chin on her shoulder again and looked at her in the mirror. "Why are you beautiful?"

Andi nodded, holding her breath.

David smiled, wrapping his arms completely around her until he held her snugly against his chest. "Do you want a random list, or should I just start at the top of your head and work my way down?"

Andi didn't answer, just watching him.

He chuckled softly, kissing her shoulder. "You keep asking me to put everything into words. I'm not good at it."

"That's okay," she answered, having to clear her throat before she said anything more. "It's what you say, not how you say it."

"Easy for you to say, you're the writer."

Andi shrugged. "I just write down what I hear in my head. You're the actor. You know how to say all the right things—"

"When someone writes them for me." He grinned.

"Try?"

David sighed and straightened so his chin rested on top of her head. As he stared at her in the mirror, his smile widened until the dimples she loved to see popped in his cheeks. "You have the best smile," he finally said, and she had to smile because she had just been thinking the same thing about him. "Especially when you talk about Jake. Your whole face changes when you look at him or think about him."

She smiled wider, and David pointed at the mirror.

"There it is. That's the smile I love."

They stared at each other for several moments, and Andi's heart pounded almost painfully in her chest. David swallowed, his eyes drifting from the mirror to look at her directly. Andi tipped her head back so she could look at him. He touched his fingertips to her jaw and angled her face toward him just as he had the morning she'd woken in his arm.

"Sometimes," he said, his voice rough and he swallowed again. "You smile at me like that, and I think, 'I could live the rest of my life looking at that smile'."

"See," she whispered. "You know what to say."

He turned her toward the mirror again and ran his finger from her jawline, down the side of her throat, to the hollow of her collarbone. "This spot…right here…is beautiful. I can see your pulse, and I can see when it beats faster when I touch you." He leaned down and let his lips hover over the spot he touched. "Like now." He touched his tongue to the spot and followed it with a long kiss that pulled at the sensitive skin.

Andi closed her eyes and let her head fall back to rest on his shoulder.

"Your body is beautiful," he whispered against her ear. Andi didn't try to hide the shiver that ran through her, and it was only intensified by the low moan in David's throat. "That's why I love you in these sundresses. They don't hide any of your curves." His hands ran over her again, across her stomach to her waist, and then down over her hips. "I watch you walk, the way the skirt flips around your legs, and I think about—"

Andi twisted in his embrace and circled her arms around his neck, cutting off his words with her lips. He moved with her, wrapping his arms around her to pull her hard against him before their lips ever met. When he kissed her, all air rushed from her lungs, and she pushed her fingers into his hair, holding on when his tongue filled her mouth. He cupped the back of her head, holding her in place as he kissed her with an intensity that liquefied everything inside her.

"Oh, god…Andi…" he growled against her mouth.

He bent at the knee and wrapped her in an embrace, lifting her feet off the ground to carry her to the bed. They fell together, and Andi gasped at the rush of arousal that shot through her, making her shake from the inside out. At the same time, raw panic choked her. David's warm, strong hands pushed up the hem of her skirt, and her body practically hummed. His hips pressed hard into hers, sending another jolt through her, and she gasped for breath, pulling at his shirt until she freed it from the waist of his pants and found the warm skin of his back. He kissed her lips, her cheek, her throat, and the exposed skin dipping into the valley between her breasts.

Andi closed her eyes, trying to lose herself in his touch rather than Lawrence's parting words. David wanted her, and he touched her like Lawrence never had. He made her feel alive.

She didn't realize she was crying until David's lips lingered at her temples and he softly whispered her name. He moved off her to lie beside her, folding her against his chest. "Shhhhh, baby. It's okay. It's okay."

"Damn bastard," she cried, curling her fists into his shirt.

David tightened his hold, laying his cheek against hers. "Sweetheart…I hope you're not talking about me."

The joking lilt to his voice made her smile despite the anger now crushing her chest, replacing the panic of moments before. She sucked in a sob and shook her head, burying her face into the warm curve of his throat. His pulse pounded against her lips.

"I'm sorry," she forced from her tight throat.

"There's nothing you need to be sorry for, Andi."

Finally, she was able to release the vice grip she had on his shirt and slid her arms around him. With just a slight tug, she pulled him toward her so they rolled together and he pressed her into the bed with his weight. It felt good to be cocooned between him and the mattress, and she released a shuddered sigh He shifted to brace himself on one elbow to hover over her, his gray-blue eyes studying her face. The smile was gone, not quite a frown but his expression had turned serious.

"Did your ex talk to you when he brought Jake home?"

Andi blinked. The tears had stopped, but the remaining moisture still blurred her eyes. David raised his free hand and tugged off her glasses, now hopelessly spotted by her tears. He leaned so close, she didn't need them to see the details of his face.

"Did he?" he asked again.

"He came inside." Her voice sounded small and unconvincing, even to her.

He touched her temple and ran his fingertips below her eye, down her cheek to the corner of her lips. She felt the slick of his touch left behind by her tears. His eyes hardened and he pressed his lips together before speaking.

"What did he say?"

Andi shook her head.

"Andi, what did he say?" he asked more sternly. "I want to know what he could say to make you weep when I touch you."

She swallowed and closed her eyes briefly before looking at him again. "Please, David. Don't make me repeat it."

"I want to know—"

"I know you do," she cut him off gently. "But I don't think I could stand it."

David wrapped her in his arms again, his cheek against hers. "I'm beginning to develop a deep hatred for that guy."

Andi managed a chuckle. "Talk to Maggie. She's the president of the *Lawrence Bonherre is a Butthead* club, but she might let you be vice president."

With a groan, David shifted off the bed and pulled her with him until they stood. With a gentle touch that made her heart ache, he smoothed his hands over her clothes to right them and brushed her hair back from her face. He cupped her cheeks in his hands and tilted her head back so she looked at him. The angry sternness was gone from his face, but the smile was also gone.

"If you won't tell me *what* he said, tell me what you need to hear to make you forget. I will say it all day every day—forever if I have to."

Andi stared up at him, trying to find an answer. What could he say that he hadn't already that could void out Lawrence's words? He told her she was beautiful, she was sexy, and he thought she was amazing...but those were platitudes saved for lovers—or would-be lovers. What could a man like David Bishop say? She'd stopped seeing him— somewhere along the way—as the almost ethereal, worshiped sex-god celebrity who somehow existed above everyone else. Perhaps it was when she watched him assemble a toy for her son, or when he grumbled the day before about spilling marinara sauce on his favorite Aero- smith tee shirt.

He wasn't the untouchable movie star anymore, but he was still so near perfect it made her break into gooseflesh when she thought about him, or looked at him. His thumb stroked her cheek near the corner of her lips, just as he'd done after kissing her that first time on set, while he waited for her to answer. Andi drew in a slow breath, her body trembling as she released it.

"Tell me I'm not perfect, but I'm good enough for you."

He leaned in to kiss her, just pressing his lips against hers in a restrained touch. Then touched his forehead to hers before pulling back only enough to look her straight in the eyes. "I'm not perfect, but I *hope* I'm good enough for you."

"I meant—"

He laid his thumb on her lips. "I know what you meant."

David scraped his fork across his plate, picking up the final remains of his dinner. He had to remind himself it was bad manners to lick a plate and fork clean as he took the last bite. "This is great," he declared, finally setting down his utensil. "What's it called?"

"Mom's amazing cheesy chicken," Jake said with a wide smile, looking at his mom. "She made it up."

"Mom's amazing cheesy chicken," David repeated. "I don't suppose it'd work to tell *my* mom I want 'Mom's amazing cheesy chicken' the next time I'm home."

Jake shook his head. "Secret family recipe. Only Mom can make it this good."

David looked across the table, and let the now-familiar feeling of warmth settle in his chest when he saw the smile on Andi's face as she looked at her son. A tint of pink stained her cheeks, making David wonder if even her son's compliments were enough to make her blush. She caught him watching her and paused to glance back, her smile ticking up just a little more.

"Did you save room for dessert, boyo?" Maggie asked, pushing her plate away.

"Dessert? No one said there was dessert!" David declared, throwing up his hands. "I'm about to bust now."

"That's okay," Jake said quickly. "We have a rule. We have to wait half an hour after dinner before we eat dessert."

David leaned back in his chair, patting his stomach. "Good. What's for dessert?"

"Homemade chocolate cream pie," Jake answered, his eyes practically sparking. "Mom makes that, too. *Real* chocolate pudding she makes on the stove, *not* from a box. And Maggie makes fresh whipped cream."

David arched his eyebrows and looked at Andi. "*Real* chocolate pudding, huh?"

"Just wait until you try it, David. It's awesome."

He smiled at Jake and set his hands on the boy's shoulder. "Let's say I beat you at *Mario* in the meantime."

"Not gonna happen."

"Oh, brother…the boys are ready to play," Maggie grumbled with a playful grin as she stood. "Time for the womenfolk to do the dishes."

David stood quickly, taking the plate from Maggie as he picked up his own and stacked it on Jake's. "Let me help. Jake and I can play after."

"Nope." Andi walked around the table and added her plate to his stack, taking them all from him. "You two have fun. This is why we have a dishwasher."

David followed her into the kitchen anyway, grabbing the empty casserole pan and rice dish as he walked. The table sat near the front of the house, tucked into a dining area off the open living room and kitchen. Much of the main floor was open, one space leading into the next. Maggie and Jake stayed at the table, gathering the last of the dishes as Andi set the ones she carried in the sink, and turned on the water to rinse them.

He stepped behind her, bracketing her body with his arms as he braced his hands on the counter edge. He shifted to rest his chin on her shoulder, kissing her quickly on the side of her throat.

"If I didn't know better, I'd say this is Jake's favorite meal."

Andi laughed. "What gave him away? The way he devoured it, or the way he wouldn't stop saying 'this is my favorite'?"

"Tough call. He's very subtle." He caught her glancing toward Maggie and Jake, then quickly at him before picking up a plate to rinse off. "Is this okay?"

"Is what okay?" she asked.

"PDA." She glanced at him again but didn't say anything. "My public shows of affection," he clarified with a grin.

"I know what it means…"

"Every time I've touched you or kissed you since Jake came down-stairs, you've looked to him to see what his reaction would be. Just now, you looked over there to see if he's watching. I don't think it bothers him, Andi."

"I don't think it does, either. But, I think it has a lot to do with *you*."

"Me?"

She nodded, smiling at him over her shoulder before running a handful of utensils under the water. "I think he likes you a lot. He asked if you'd be here tonight."

David felt the smile grow on his face, finding deep satisfaction in the idea Andi's son accepted him and might even like him. Memories of his stepfather barreling his way into the family skirted on the edge of David's thoughts, but he ignored them.

"Dating isn't new to just me," she said with a shrug and a small smile. "My dating is new to Jake, too." She tilted her head and looked out the window over the sink. "Okay…that's not completely true. I've gone out, but…"

"But, you've never had someone here for dinner. Someone who can't keep their hands off you for more than ten minutes." He smiled when he saw the bloom of color in her cheeks again. "Someone who wants to take you and your son somewhere on my next day off."

She looked sideways at him. "Where?"

David shrugged, straightening so he could wrap his arms around her and stand close while she rinsed the dishes. "Tell me what he'd like."

She hummed, setting aside the plate she'd rinsed. "He loves

Disneyland, but I can only imagine what kind of chaos that would create."

David didn't agree aloud but did agree.

"He's been talking a lot about wanting to go to an aquarium…"

"Great! We'll go to the Aquarium of the Pacific. If you're going to go to an aquarium, go to an *aquarium*." David stepped to the side and opened the dishwasher, loading in the dishes she'd rinsed.

"Oh, don't do that. I can."

He ignored her and kept stacking. "So, should we go? How about Monday?"

Andi stopped, her hands still dripping with water, and looked at him. She smiled and nodded her head. "I'd like that. And I think he'd like it, too."

"How about Maggie?"

"How about Maggie *what*," Maggie said as she set the last dishes on the counter by the sink.

"I want to take everyone to the Aquarium of the Pacific on Monday."

Jake lit up. "Cool!"

"As cool as that sounds, some of us *do* have regular day jobs," Maggie answered. "We can't all be famous movie stars or bestselling novelists."

David let the snark go with a shake of his head. "How about Sunday, then?"

"Are they open on Sunday?" Andi asked.

"I don't know, but I'll find out."

"This is awesome!" Jake declared again. He leaped to Andi and threw his long, lanky arms around her, hugging her so tight Andi groaned, but smiled all the while. "Thanks, Mom."

"Don't thank me. It was David's idea."

Jake let Andi go and stepped toward David, his arms open like he meant to hug him, too. Then he hesitated, and David caught the waver in his expression. Before he could take a step back and renege on the hug, David pulled the boy to him. It was all the encouragement Jake needed. After the speech Jake had given him on Sunday, he had to remind himself Jake still was just a kid. At eleven, David would have liked a few more hugs from his mom...and especially his dad. He ruffled Jake's hair and caught a tremble in Andi's lip as she turned away on the pretense of loading the dishwasher.

With his arm still around Jake's shoulder, David looked at Maggie. "Aw, come on, Mags," he teased, using the nickname he'd heard Andi use with her friend. "It wouldn't be the same without you."

Maggie squinted her eyes and pursed her lips, looking between him and Andi. Then her eyes settled on Jake and she smiled.

"Yeah, Maggie. Come on. We always do stuff together," Jake pleaded.

She huffed, but David knew by now most of Maggie's attitude was all show. "Fine. I only had one appointment on Monday anyway."

Jake cheered again.

"Why don't you go get the game," David told the boy, squeezing his shoulder. "I've got just enough time to beat you before dessert."

"You wish, old man," Jake yelled over his shoulder as he bolted from the room.

David laughed but caught Maggie watching him. When he met her gaze, she just smiled and nodded and turned to go.

"I'll be back in a few minutes to make the whipped cream," she said as she walked away. "I'm sure you two can keep yourselves occupied."

Andi closed the dishwasher door and pushed start, the beep of the machine almost covering up her soft sniffle. David gripped her elbow and turned her to face him. No tears marred her cheeks, but her eyes glistened with them.

"You've been crying way too much for my liking," he said softly.

She smiled and chuckled. "Yeah, but these are good tears." Andi stepped to him and he instinctively wrapped his arms around her waist. He never missed an opportunity to hold her. She kissed his chin, then his cheek, and finally whispered a kiss to his lips before laying her forehead against his jaw. "I could fall in love with you, David."

He drew in a slow breath and closed his eyes, pulling her closer. David smiled, letting the liquid warmth she inspired spread through him.

"I could fall in love with you, too, sweetheart."

CHAPTER FOURTEEN

" Can we go see the Monsters of the Abyss show next?" Jake asked around the mouthful of hot dog in his cheek. He practically bounced in his seat, his eyes still wide and bright from three hours of walking the aquarium.

Andi set down her sandwich to hand her son a napkin, but before she had a chance, David held one out to Jake. "You've got mustard on your chin, buddy."

Jake scrubbed at his face, swallowing his bite so he could talk without mumbling. "Can we?"

"It's fine with me. How about you, Mom? Can you handle the monsters?" David asked, winking at her with a grin.

"Oh, I think I can handle it. As long as I have a hand to hold on each side."

"I'll hold your hand, Mom."

David slid his arm across the table, his palm up, and Andi laid her hand over his. "I have no problem holding your hand, Mom."

Maggie returned to the table after taking a phone call and picked up her bag. "Sorry to leave the fun, kids, but I've got to step away for a bit."

"Is something wrong?" Andi asked.

"Nothing a new contract negotiation and a bottle of Prozac won't fix." Maggie looped her arm through the strap of her purse and dropped her phone inside. "Brian Cavanaugh is having a hissy fit over some clause in his contract. I've got to talk him down before his head explodes or something." She shook her head, rolling her eyes. "Authors."

Andi arched her eyebrows and chuckled. "I was never that bad, was I?"

"Honey, do you think I'd live in the same house with you if you were?" Maggie ruffled Jake's hair. "Save a seat for me in the show, okay, Jake?"

He shook his head, his cheek already full of hot dog again. He mumbled something about being fine and having fun, but most of it was lost around the food.

"Dude, don't talk with your mouth full," David chided.

Jake swallowed and took a sip of his soda. "Sorry."

Maggie sighed and waved, heading out of the café. An entire day without Maggie receiving some kind of frantic phone call had been too much to wish for, but they'd given it a try. They'd spent the morning wandering through the galleries and petting the stingrays, and Andi couldn't remember a day she'd had so much fun. Jake talked animatedly about what it'd felt like to touch the stingrays, and how he wanted to go back to the shark lagoon again before they left. David managed to occasionally throw in a comment, but for the most part, Jake talked non-stop. The conversation was the two of them, and Andi leaned back in her chair to observe.

Watching the two most important men in her life laugh and talk together made her heart grow in her chest until she thought it would burst right through her ribs.

Jake slurped at the remains of his coke, poking at the ice with his straw. "Can I go to the bathroom, Mom?"

"Sure, go ahead."

"Do you want me to go with you?" David asked.

Jake rolled his eyes. "I'm *eleven*," he said as if that was all the answer required.

"Oh," David said with a chuckle, winking at Andi. "Sorry."

Jake bolted from the chair and headed for the restrooms at the back of the café, easily staying within Andi's line of vision. Being the mom of a growing young man who could no longer sneak into the ladies' room with her, Andi always chose seats that allowed her to see the bathroom. As soon as Jake disappeared through the door, David turned to her and reached for her hand again. He leaned forward, smiling.

"I'm very proud of you."

"Oh? Why is that?"

"You haven't tried to hide once from the photographers."

Andi immediately sat up straighter and scanned the restaurant. "I didn't even see them."

David smiled and raised her hand to press her knuckles to his lips. "I thought as much. And no, I'm not going to point them out to you."

Andi slanted her eyes at him. "Then why tell me?"

"Like I said…I'm proud of you."

She tilted her head, taking him in not for the first time that day. He looked like any other man at the aquarium in his faded jeans, sneakers, and a white button-down shirt rolled to his elbows. Andi loved that look on him. She wanted to run her hands over his forearms and feel the strength of his muscles, feel the bristle of the short hair on his arms, and study the contrast between his tan skin and her fairer tone.

It had only been a couple of weeks since the kiss on set that had catapulted her into this relationship with David. They'd gone from on-set acquaintances—with him being the untouchable, infamous 'David Bishop'—to *boyfriend* and *girlfriend*, as much as the words still made her cringe—at a speed that made her dizzy. But, it was the best kind of dizzy.

"What?" he asked after several moments of her silent study.

Andi shook her head. "Nothing."

David stood, pushing his chair back with his legs, to pull her to her feet. He wrapped his arms around her, his hands pressed to her back, to bring her against him. Andi smiled up at him, resting her hands on his arms above his elbows. He kissed her, but kept it simple and restrained, even though he hummed with satisfaction against her lips.

"Was that for the benefit of the paparazzi?" she asked when he pulled away.

He kissed the end of her nose. "Sweetheart, I don't do *anything* for the benefit of the paparazzi."

He let her go and they gathered the trays of garbage as Jake ran across the restaurant toward them. He pitched in, gathering up his garbage, and after cleaning up they left the café. What Jake wanted to see was downstairs, and they had a good thirty minutes until the next show, so they walked through the Baja Gallery again. Just as excited as their first trip through, Jake stared into the massive aquariums with fascination.

Andi walked hand-in-hand with David, staying a few feet behind Jake as he made the rounds. She hadn't stopped smiling all day, from the minute David arrived to pick them up. Jake hadn't stopped talking the entire hour or so drive to Long Beach. And despite the fact Andi knew David tended to be a 'silent' driver, he'd carried the conversation with Jake the whole way.

"I'd be willing to bet Jake is going to clear six feet before he's done growing," David said randomly as they traversed the winding gallery toward the first floor.

"Why do you say that?"

"Look at him now…" He motioned toward Jake with the hand not holding hers. "He's got to be a good head above other kids his age. I saw it at his party. We're not going to be able to keep him in pants, he'll be growing out of them so fast. And if he's anything like I was at his age, we won't be able to keep food in the house."

Andi looked at him, but his attention was on Jake, a wide smile on his lips. She wondered if he even realized what he'd said…

"I can't keep food in the house now," she said, fighting against the rasp in her throat.

"Let's get moving, buddy," David called to Jake. "We want good seats."

"If I didn't know better, I'd say you're as excited about being here as Jake."

David squeezed her hand and looked down at her. "I am. I never got to do stuff like this when I was a kid."

They walked down the slight incline leading to the first floor. Jake was twenty feet ahead, his hands and nose pressed to the thick aquarium wall, talking with a redheaded boy who stood beside him. The young boy had to share the same enthusiasm Jake felt because they both had the same excited expression as they pointed to various things in the tank.

Jake turned and motioned to them. "Mom! David! Come check this out."

The boy with Jake turned to look as well, and his mouth fell open. They walked just close enough that she heard the boy whisper, "Is that David Bishop?"

Jake looked back over his shoulder, grinned, and shrugged. "Yeah. He's my mom's boyfriend."

"*Coooolll.*"

David chuckled. The two boys ran ahead, talking like they'd been lifelong friends. Andi always loved the ability of children to make friends. Later, if she asked, Jake probably wouldn't even know the boy's name. But it didn't matter, because they were here now and they were having fun. It was hard to believe at Jake's age David was already working. He was Davey Bishop then, and most likely not a single person had any idea how far he would go, but he was already a paid actor. Who never went to an aquarium or had a birthday party.

"Do you regret going into acting so young?" she asked as they rounded a corner and caught sight of Jake and his friend again. They were nearly through the gallery to the Great Hall of the Pacific.

David's attention was ahead of them, watching Jake, and he broke into a wide grin before looking at her. His smile was the kind that reached his eyes and made her heart expand in her chest. "I don't know if regret is the right word. I wish some things had happened differently, like my parents' divorce, but I always knew acting was what I wanted." He lifted her hand and kissed the back. "I've got a whole theory on life, though"

"What theory is that?"

They crossed the great hall before he could answer, to where Jake stood with his friend and who Andi assumed to be his friend's parents.

The woman held a small child on her hip, a little girl with strawberry blonde ringlets encompassing her head like a halo.

"Mom, Connor is going to see the show, too. Can we sit together?"

"It's okay with me. Just remember to save a seat for Maggie."

The boys shouted "Cool!" in unison. The man, with bright red hair like Connor, held out his hand. "Duncan. This is my wife Ellyse."

David released her hand to take Duncan's, shaking it firmly. "David."

Andi raised her hand. "Andi. Looks like our sons have hit it off."

"Well, Connor isn't exactly a shy kid." Duncan's gaze kept sliding to David, and finally, he smiled, looking slightly embarrassed. "I'm sorry. I don't mean to stare. But you're—"

"Duncan," his wife admonished, blushing profusely.

"It's okay," David offered, holding his hand up. "It's hard for me and my girlfriend to go anywhere and relax, so if I could just stay David, that'd be great."

When he said *girlfriend*, his hand found hers again and he squeezed it gently. Andi caught the glint in his eyes. He threw that word around now just because he knew it'd get a rise out of her. It was a few more minutes yet before the beginning of the show, and a small crowd gathered in the great hall to wait. They talked with Duncan and Ellyse, learning they were from Burbank and the little girl's name was Corinne. Duncan and Ellyse only seemed aware of David—the David she no longer saw—for the first couple of minutes, but then the unease slipped away and the conversation was no different than any other she'd had at a playground or movie theater.

The doors opened a few minutes before the show was supposed to begin and they all entered. The crowd wasn't nearly enough to fill the theater and they picked a row halfway down the ramp, with everyone filing in. As promised, Jake made sure he sat beside her even though Connor was already on his other side and they still talked non-stop. David sat on the end of the line on the other side of her, with Duncan and Ellyse on the other side of Connor. As soon as they settled, David took her hand and pulled it toward him so it rested on his thigh and he laced his fingers through hers.

"So, what is the theory?" Andi asked while they had a couple more minutes before the show.

He leaned toward her until their shoulders touched. "My theory on what?"

"Life. You said you had a theory."

He grinned, his gaze shifting down so he could focus on her mouth. "My theory is if you're happy with who you are, and where you are, then you can't regret anything before today."

"Why is that?"

His lip ticked up a little more when she spoke, and slow warmth spread through her. Andi had read about men who could excite a woman with their glance, and women who felt an erotic rush when a man looked at them with hooded, dark eyes—she'd even written similar things in her own books because it was a common ploy—but never once had she experienced it until David looked at her *that* way. Like he enjoyed every move she made, every smile she gave, and every word she spoke.

"Because everything from your past brought you to where you are. Good. Bad. Painful. Wonderful. All of it brought you here."

"What if you're *not* happy?"

His eyes shifted up to look into hers, and her breath caught for a moment. Then he reached across with his free hand and touched his fingertip to her chin, tilting her head just a little bit. "It's just a moment to bring you to something better later."

"I like your theory."

David leaned in closer, his breath warming her cheek. "So, what is today?"

"Today?" It was getting hard to think, he was too close and the lights dimmed in the theater…just enough to hide a quick kiss…

He changed the question by asking, "Is this something better?"

The weight of his voice moved over her like a wave of warm water. Andi drew in a hitched breath and nodded. "Yes," was all she could manage, even though a thousand different answers ran through her head.

She leaned into him and pressed her lips to his just as the music for the show rolled. David's lips opened and his tongue brushed hers. His hand squeezed hers and with a final quick, and painfully inadequate as far as she was concerned, kiss they settled in for the movie.

"I say we put in another hour or so, and then head back north. Catch dinner on the way home."

Andi nodded, settling beside David on one of the benches facing the shark lagoon. "That sounds fine to me. I don't know if Jake will make it home," she said with a chuckle, watching her son with Connor as they pet the small sharks in the lagoon. "He's played hard today. I give him until we hit the highway to be out like a light."

"He'd better wake up for dinner," Maggie said. "I love fish and chips as much as the next person, but I'm ready for a nice steak."

David leaned back and draped his arms across the back of the bench, one behind Andi and the other behind Maggie. "I can't argue with that logic."

Andi settled against him, resting her head on his shoulder. The mid-afternoon sun was bright and warm, and she figured she probably gained some color today. Unlike David and Maggie, she could just look at the sunshine and get pink. But for now, it was nice. She closed her eyes and released a long, slow breath.

The heart-piercing sound of Jake's scream snapped her from her repose. Andi sat up and blinked her eyes open, trying to find him. But David was already gone, leaping the bench in front of them to reach Jake where he sprawled out on the wet concrete around the lagoon. Andi rushed to the end of the aisle, Maggie right behind her, to jog down the steps.

"Ow! Ow! Ow!" Jake cried, his knee pulled to his chest so he could hold his lower leg.

"What happened?" Andi demanded when she reached David, who already knelt beside her son.

"He slipped on the wet concrete," David explained, his expression tight.

"It hurts, Mom! It hurts!" Jake cried.

A wide and long scrape ran from his knee to just a few inches down his leg, but it was only a surface scratch barely drawing any blood. The way he held his leg, she figured the scrape was the least of his pains. He held his foot at an angle, rocking on his tailbone.

"Is it your ankle, honey?"

Jake nodded, hissing. "It hurts!"

David shifted on his knees so Jake could lean against him, rubbing his hand up and down Jake's arm. "How bad is it?"

Andi gingerly took Jake's foot in her hand, thankful he had on sandals so she could see the ankle without having to remove a sneaker and sock. He had another scrape on the outside of his ankle, and it looked like it had swollen slightly, but when she carefully moved the foot the movement only garnered a sharp hiss from Jake and not a scream. It was probably nothing more than a slight strain.

"You just twisted your ankle, honey. You'll be okay."

"Are you sure?" David asked. "Should we take him to the ER?"

Jake looked from David to her, a look of sheer panic on his face.

"No, that's not necessary."

"If you think it could be broken—"

Andi reached out and touched David's hand, cutting him off. "David, it's okay. He'll be fine. But, I think we're done for the day."

"Aw, man. That stinks," Connor declared from nearby with a stomp of his foot.

"I'm sorry, Connor. Maybe you and Jake can get together some other time."

Jake blinked his eyes hard, fighting the big tears that threatened to fall. "It really hurts, Mom," he said softly, his voice rough. "And my knee hurts, too."

"Well, that I can take care of right now." Andi turned her purse, which she had worn across her chest, and dug into it for the small first aid packet she always carried. Just enough triple antibiotic ointment and bandages to fix up minor dings and scrapes.

"I'll head back to the café and see if I can get a small bag of ice," Maggie offered, standing.

"Thank you."

"Are you sure it's not swelling too much?" David asked as she smoothed the ointment on Jake's scraped knee. "You can't be too careful with ankles."

Andi looked up from her task and started to say something light until she saw the tight line of his lips and the way his eyes pinched at the corners. He still supported Jake against his chest, his hands rubbing the boy's arms, and Andi wondered if the act of comfort was more for Jake...or David. She smiled, trying her best to look convincing.

"I'm sure. It'll be fine. He's just going to have to stay off it for a day or two."

When David's expression didn't relax, Andi felt a small tug at her heart. She couldn't remember a single time Jake's father showed a fraction of the genuine concern David showed now for a boy who wasn't his son. When Jake was little, Lawrence was more worried about how quickly Andi could stop the crying than *why* Jake might be crying. She focused on lining up the cartoon character bandages over the scrape, crumbling the wrappers in her hands as Maggie returned with a small bag of ice in one hand and a milkshake in the other. Andi arched an eyebrow and Maggie shrugged.

"There's nothing ice cream won't cure. But, I figured a milkshake would be safer in the car."

"Do you think you can walk to the car, honey?"

Before Jake could whine an answer, David scooped her slight son up in his arms, swinging him effortlessly onto his back to carry him piggyback. "No need. I've got him."

By the time they reached the doors leading to the parking lot, Jake's tears had dried. But, David's expression was still tight and dark. He set Jake in the back seat of his car—a four-door SUV today—and when he shut the door, Andi touched his arm.

"David."

He turned to look at her and she reached up to lay her hand against the side of his face, smoothing away the lines at the corner of his eye with her thumb. "Thank you."

"For what?"

Andi smiled and toed up to kiss his cheek before walking around to the passenger side.

Andi unlocked the house door and pushed it open to let David in. She tossed her keys on the counter and headed into the kitchen.

"Could you take him upstairs? I'll just get him some ibuprofen and be right up."

"Yes, ma'am." David winked at Jake and he chuckled. He seemed to get a kick out of being carried around, so David turned a little sharper than required, lifting Jake higher, and Jake chuckled.

He carried Jake up the stairs and waited while Jake leaned over to turn the doorknob. Just inside the room, he turned so Jake could flip on the light switch. The room was large, big enough for a full-size bed, long bureau, desk, and drum set in the corner with more than enough room to move around. Dirty clothes littered the floor and the bed was unmade. A door on the left wall opened to an attached bathroom. The walls were painted blue with a sea theme border and one wall had a massive mural of a blue whale painted across the entire width of it.

"When your mom said you liked the aquarium, I get the impression that was an understatement."

"I want to be a marine biologist."

David made an effort to look impressed as he kicked aside a pair of pajamas on the floor and laid Jake down on the bed with a purposeful bounce. Jake laughed. The ankle wasn't bothering him so much anymore. David sat down beside him, bouncing the bed again.

"I'll help you with your sandals."

"Thanks, David."

His ankle was cold to the touch from the bag of ice—which was a bag of cold water by the time they got home—and the skin was red, but there was no swelling. The bandages Andi had put on the ankle scrape had fallen off on one end, flopping to the side with the pad tinted yellow by the antibiotic ointment. David finished peeling it off while Jake's skin was probably still numb from the cold and tossed the sandals on the floor.

"Do you want more ice?"

Jake shook his head, settling back into the pile of pillows behind him. The sheets and blankets had fish and whales and dolphins, and one of his pillows was a giant walrus. Yeah, *like the aquarium* was definitely an understatement. At least he knew what to get the kid for the holidays.

David smiled at the idea of being there.

"I had fun today," Jake said, stretched out with his fingers laced over his stomach. "Mom smiled a lot."

"She knew you were having a good time."

Jake shrugged. "I guess." He stared at David, and for a moment David saw the same boy who had informed him just over a week earlier he *wouldn't* make Andi cry. The boy who dreaded seeing his father and who didn't want to leave his mother alone. "Mom smiles a lot when you're here."

"I hope so," David answered honestly.

"I like it when you come over."

"Why? Because you always beat me at *Mario Brothers*? Because I've been practicing at home, and eventually, I *will* win."

Jake laughed. "No. I just like it when you come over."

"Good." David leaned sideways so he rested his hand on the other side of Jake, leaning in like he was imparting some secret. "I really like being here with you and your mom."

Jake smiled, but the smile quickly disappeared into a serious expression. He drew in a long, slow breath before saying, "My friend Travis' mom has a boyfriend."

David glanced down to see Jake working his fingers together nervously. His face was calm, but there was something more going on in the statement. "Does Travis like him?"

Jake shook his head against the pillows. "He told Travis if he doesn't do what he says, he's going to send him away to a school where he would have to live. He couldn't even come home on weekends."

"That must be pretty scary for Travis."

"He doesn't want to go. His dad is dead."

David nodded, swallowing. Somewhere in another part of the house, a phone rang. He looked down, watching Jake's hands, hoping like hell he said the right thing. "Do you worry something like that will happen to you?"

Jake's fingers stilled, and David looked up into the boy's face. Jake nodded slowly. David lifted his hand and laid it on top of Jake's. "Buddy, I care a lot about your mom. I think you know that already." Jake nodded. "But, I also care a lot about you. I would never, ever send you away from your mom because I know how much you love each other."

"Never?" he asked, his voice cracking a little.

"Never," David reiterated. "Besides, who would I play *Mario* with?" he said with a chuckle as he ruffled Jake's hair.

The soft sound of someone clearing their throat preceded Maggie's entrance into the bedroom. "I've got something that should make you feel better, Jake-my-boy."

Jake pulled a face when Maggie handed him a small dosage cup half-filled with a thick, orange liquid. "Can't I just take the pills?"

"This is what your mom sent up, and this is what you get."

Jake squirmed, but took the cup and knocked back the goo, following it up with a drink of water. David slid off the bed and headed to the door, leaving Jake with Maggie with a final wave and promise to be back for a rematch. As he stepped into the hall, Maggie called his name and he waited for her to join him.

"Is Andi downstairs?" he asked, pointing in the direction of the stairs with his thumb.

"Yeah. Boner called." Maggie didn't even attempt to hide the disgust on her face. Course, David doubted Maggie *ever* tried to hide her true opinion of anything.

"Oh." The immediate need to get downstairs hit David, and he turned to go.

"David," Maggie called again and he pulled up short. She took the step needed to reach him, her arms crossed over her body. She stared up at him, lips set firm, for several moments as he waited for her to say whatever it was that was obviously on her mind. "The verdict is in," she finally said.

David drew in air through his nose and pulled his shoulders back. "And?"

"I don't know if you deserve her or not, that's something you've got to know for yourself, but you've earned her. So far."

He swallowed, forcing himself not to ask what had convinced her. Instead, he just nodded and cleared his throat. "I'll make sure it stays that way."

"Good." She turned to go back into the bedroom.

"Why do I feel like I just got parental approval?"

Maggie laughed over her shoulder. "Big Jake and Erica Parker are nothing compared to me, boyo."

David took the stairs that led directly into the kitchen and heard Andi's voice as he neared the bottom of the steps. "I told you last week, you have to call two days in advance."

As he took the last step onto the kitchen tile, she turned to see him, offering a tight smile. Then she shook her head and dipped her chin, sighing.

"That's just too damn bad, Lawrence. And keep in mind during your extended stay in California, school starts in a week and a half and you're not going to have the option of taking him during the week."

David crossed to her and leaned into the corner of the counter where it turned into the breakfast bar. From there, he could watch her without hovering, and he could know if the conversation took a turn he didn't like. Her eyes flicked to him for a moment and she pressed her lips together.

"No, that won't work." *Pause.* "No." *Pause.* She huffed. "How many ways do you need to hear it, Lawrence? No!"

David hated watching her when she spoke to her ex-husband. Her entire body changed, curling like a bowstring tightened too far. Much more and she'd snap. She walked around the bar to the other side and sat on one of the tall stools, her forehead held in her hand.

"Fine, you want a reason? I'll give you three. One, if you'd thought to check before you pre-purchased tickets you'd know we took him to the aquarium *today.* Two, he hurt his ankle playing and needs to be off it for a few days. Three—and here's the *big* one, Lawrence—I told you very clearly and precisely that you must ask forty-eight hours *in advance* if you can see him. Last I checked, calling me at five o'clock on a Monday night to take him on Tuesday does *not* constitute two days' notice."

David followed her path around the bar and stepped behind her, laying his hands on her shoulders. In less than fifteen minutes, tight knots had taken over her shoulders and neck. He pressed his thumbs to the base of her skull and ran them down the side of her spinal cord, beginning the slow process of easing away the tension. Unfortunately, what took a quarter-hour to cause would probably take an hour to work out.

Standing this close, he heard Larry Bonherre's voice through the phone, not as clearly as he'd heard in the restaurant a week earlier, but clear enough to hear Bonehead's arguments.

"I don't understand why you're being so difficult about this, Andrea. I'm trying very hard to build a relationship with my son, and if I didn't know better, I would say you're sabotaging my attempts."

"If I didn't know better, I'd say you're purposefully ignoring my specifications just to anger me and make me appear difficult," Andi snapped back.

"Why would I want to anger you, Andrea, when I've made it quite clear since I arrived my primary goal is to bring us together again as a family?"

David's hands stilled. Andi hadn't said anything about Bonherre's wish to reconcile. For a moment, a flash of panic hit him she might consider it. Then she leaned back into him, resting her head against his chest, and tilted her head so she could see him. He didn't have to look very deep to see in her eyes there was no chance she would go back to Bonherre. David smiled and pressed a kiss to her forehead, urging with his touch that she face away from him again so he could work the knots from her shoulders.

"Andrea? Are you going to answer me?"

"No, Lawrence, because I gave up trying to figure out any of your motivations over six years ago. The answer remains the same. No to the aquarium and no to tomorrow. Just to make it clear, Jake won't be able to go anywhere until later in the week when I am convinced his ankle has had sufficient rest. Beyond that, maybe."

David heard Bonherre's sigh. *"I would like to take him Friday night."*

Andi rubbed her forehead, and under his constant massage, David felt the tension pull again at her neck. "Just overnight," she finally answered. "I want him back by noon on Saturday. I have to take him to finish his school shopping."

"Thank you, Andrea. I appreciate your willingness to allow me this time—"

"Noon on Saturday, Lawrence. You can pick him up after five on Friday."

Andi hung up the phone before Bonherre could say more, slamming the handset down on the granite countertop. She groaned and held her head in both her hands. Almost as quickly, she moved to stand.

"I need to check on Jake."

David held her in the chair, wrapping one arm around her to keep her from standing. "Mags is upstairs with him. He's fine. Isn't a fan of liquid medicine—" Andi chuckled and he smiled, wrapping his other arm around her. "But, he's fine. Just sit for a minute and let me work at those knots."

She relaxed in his arm and he went back to work on her shoulders. Andi let her head drop forward, stretching the long column of her neck. She groaned when he found a particularly tight area and pressed his thumbs into it. After a few moments of quiet, as he worked, she finally spoke in a low voice—so low he almost didn't make out everything she said.

"He didn't ask how Jake hurt his ankle."

David had realized as much by listening to the conversation but had no idea what to say when she pointed it out. He just kept working, moving down her spine as far as he could with the barstool back in the way. Andi raised her head and released a long breath, her shoulders slumping a little.

"You wanted to take him to the ER," she continued a small chuckle that lacked any humor following her statement. "You carried him so he wouldn't have to walk on it. And you never once told him to stop crying about it. His father didn't even ask what he did or how bad it was."

Larry Bonherre is an ass.

That was the simplest explanation, but David figured Andi didn't need him to confirm anything to her about her ex-husband. So, he kept rubbing and working at the tension the man created instead. Maggie came down, glanced at them, and went to the refrigerator for the milk. She opened a cupboard and took out a package of cookies, putting four on a plate, and poured a glass of milk.

"Same old crap from bonehead?" she asked as she put the milk away.

Andi nodded. "He wanted to take Jake tomorrow. To the aquarium of all places."

Maggie snorted and kicked the refrigerator door shut as she picked up the milk and cookies. "Loser," she mumbled as she headed back up the stairs.

"You're filming tomorrow," she said, not asking.

David knew she kept track of the filming schedule, and grinned because he remembered Andi's ranking system Maggie had explained to him. "Tomorrow is what…a one or a two?"

She chuckled. "A two. I planned on being there."

David leaned down and kissed the small hint of skin at the base of her throat where it curved into her shoulder. "Good."

"I might have to bring Jake with me. I don't want to leave him on his own with a hurt ankle."

"He can hang out in my trailer if he wants."

"I've got a trailer, too, you know," she said, looking over her shoulder at him.

"Yeah, but does your trailer have a Meta Quest 3 system?" Andi's eyes popped open, and David laughed. "One of the perks I guess Maggie forgot to get in your contract."

"I'm going to have to talk to her about that…" She folded her arms on the counter and slumped forward, resting her head on her arms. A low hum shifted through her, vibrating against his hands.

After a couple more minutes of massage, David cleared his throat. "Did Larry want anything else? Other than taking Jake?"

She nodded against her arms. "Yeah, but I wasn't paying much attention."

He stopped the massage and stood beside her stool, leaning on the counter. "Can I ask you a question?"

Andi turned her head on her hands so she faced him, a lazy, relaxed smile on her lips. "Of course."

"Does he want to reconcile?"

Andi sat up and set her elbow on the counter, bracing her head against the heel of her hand. "He wants to, yes. He told me last week when he came to pick up Jake." She shook her head against her hand. "He's had this epiphany—he says—about how much better *his* life was when we were married. It would seem Leslie, his wife—and the woman I caught him cheating with, by the way—has turned the tables on him."

"She had an affair…"

"Yep." Andi sat back, rolling her head. "He still hasn't taken any of the blame for our life falling apart, but he's convinced getting me back will…" Andi trailed off, her eyes darting to him. Before she said anything more she reached out and curled her delicate fingers into his shirtsleeve, pulling at him until he unfolded his arms and turned to her. "It's not going to happen in this lifetime, or any other."

David took her face in his hands and leaned down to kiss her. He stroked her hair from her face when he pulled back, looking into her eyes. "I didn't think so, but it's nice to hear it."

She shook her head in his hold. "Even if you and I weren't together, he'd have a snowball's chance in hell of getting me back. David…" Andi raised her hand and touched his face, her lips ticking up in a small smile as her gaze skimmed over him. "You've done more for Jake and me in less than a month than Lawrence has done in eleven years."

David leaned in for another kiss, but before his lips could touch hers, Maggie shouted down the stairs. "Hey, boyo! Jake is waiting for his rematch!"

David tilted his head toward the stairs and arched his eyebrows. Andi smiled and nodded. "Good luck. You're going to need it."

CHAPTER FIFTEEN

DANDI TAKES A FAMILY OUTING

DAVID BISHOP AND ANDREA 'ANDI' PARKER—THE HOTTEST, FRESHEST, MOST ADORABLE COUPLE TO HIT THE HOLLYWOOD RADAR—WERE SPOTTED EARLIER THIS WEEK SPENDING WHAT APPEARED TO BE 'FAMILY' TIME WITH PARKER'S SON AT THE AQUARIUM OF THE PACIFIC (TOP LEFT INSET). FIRST REPORTS OF THE <u>RISE OF DAWN</u> SET ROMANCE SURFACED JUST THREE WEEKS AGO AFTER BISHOP SUFFERED AN ON-SET INJURY AND WITNESSES REPORTED HE ASKED FOR PARKER WHILE BEING TREATED. SINCE THEN, BISHOP AND PARKER HAVE MADE LITTLE OR NO ATTEMPT TO HIDE THEIR RELATIONSHIP, AND BISHOP CONFIRMED IN AN INTERVIEW WITH BROOKE HALLE THEY WERE DATING—ALTHOUGH, HE REFUSED TO COMMENT FURTHER ABOUT THE SERI-OUSNESS OF THE RELATIONSHIP OR IF THEY WERE EXCLUSIVE (CENTER).

ONE ON-SET INSIDER STATED THEY BELIEVED THE AFFAIR DIDN'T EXIST BEFORE A 'STAGED' KISS THE TWO SHARED WHILE FILMING A SCENE. THE INSIDER REPORTED THE SUPPOSEDLY 'FOR DEMONSTRATION ONLY' KISS WAS INTENSE AND "VERY REAL," AND PARKER IMMEDIATELY EXCUSED HERSELF TO HER TRAILER…BISHOP FOLLOWING NOT FAR BEHIND. IT WAS THE FOLLOWING WEEK

WHEN RUMORS OF THEIR ROMANCE SURFACED, AND THE QUOTED INSIDER WENT ON TO SAY, "WE WERE ALL WITNESS TO THEIR FIRST KISS. AND IF THAT WAS THEIR FIRST KISS...WOW...I CAN'T IMAGINE WHAT FOLLOWED IT UP!"

DAVID BISHOP, 31, IS SIX YEARS PARKER'S JUNIOR—WHICH, WHEN CONSIDERING THE AGE GAPS THAT HAVE OCCURRED IN HOLLYWOOD, IS NOTHING. WHAT HAS INTRIGUED SOME 'BISHOPITES' IS PARKER'S DIVORCED STATUS AND THE FACT SHE IS THE SINGLE MOTHER TO AN ELEVEN-YEAR-OLD BOY. PARKER HAS ALSO SHARED A HOME WITH ANOTHER WOMAN—MARGARET CONNELLY, HER LITERARY AGENT—SINCE HER DIVORCE SIX YEARS AGO. MANY HAVE QUESTIONED WHETHER BISHOP IS SEEKING A PRE-FAB FAMILY AFTER RUMORS SPREAD FROM HIS BREAK-UP WITH JOSIE CONNORS JUST OVER A YEAR AGO. SOME REPORTS SAID THE BREAK-UP WAS A RESULT OF UNFAITHFULNESS IN THE RELATIONSHIP, WHILE OTHER RUMORS IMPLIED BISHOP WANTED A FAMILY AND CONNORS WAS UNWILLING TO PUT HER CAREER EVEN TEMPORARILY ON HOLD TO HAVE A BABY. STILL OTHERS QUESTION THE SCHEMATICS OF A RELATIONSHIP THAT MAY INCLUDE BISHOP, PARKER <u>AND</u> CONNELLY.

MOST ANYONE WHO HAS SEEN THE COUPLE OUT AND ABOUT ONLY COMMENT THEY APPEAR EXCEPTIONALLY HAPPY IN EACH OTHER'S COMPANY, AND THEIR AFFECTION IS ENOUGH TO GIVE JUST ABOUT ANYONE THE 'WARM FUZZIES'. AFTER ALL, THE FIRST PUBLIC PHOTOS OF THE COUPLE INVOLVED A HEATED KISS AGAINST BISHOP'S CAR (BELOW RIGHT). AFTER THAT, WHO <u>WOULDN'T</u> FEEL ALL WARM AND FUZZY?

STEP FATHER POTENTIAL?

IN A CITY WHERE MOST WELL-KNOWN ACTORS GO OUT OF THEIR WAY TO HIDE FROM THE SCRUTINY OF THE PUBLIC EYE—DAVID BISHOP DOESN'T SEEK IT, BUT HE CERTAINLY DOESN'T HIDE FROM IT. HE DOESN'T EVEN ACKNOWLEDGE THE STALKING PAPARAZZI OR CURIOUS EYES AS HE GOES ABOUT HIS LIFE LIKE YOUR AVERAGE, EVERY DAY MAN.

THIS PAST WEEKEND, DAVID WAS ONCE AGAIN SPOTTED WITH HIS NEAR-CONSTANT COMPANION AND GIRLFRIEND ANDREA PARKER, AND HER SON. THIS TIME, BISHOP AND YOUNG JACOB BONHERRE — PARKER'S SON FROM A PREVIOUS MARRIAGE — WERE SEEN PLAYING AGAINST EACH OTHER ON A MASSIVE VIDEO GAMING SYSTEM ON DISPLAY AT THE LOCAL BEST BUY. BETWEEN SHOUTS, CHALLENGES, AND LAUGHTER, NEITHER SEEMED TO CARE NEARLY EVERY MOVE WAS BEING CAUGHT ON CAMERA (SEE IMAGES ABOVE).

AFTER FINALLY BEING GENTLY SCOLDED BY 'MOM', THE THREE LEFT THE STORE TOGETHER AFTER BISHOP ORDERED THE ENTIRE SYSTEM. AS THEY CROSSED THE PARKING LOT (SEE LOWER LEFT IMAGE), THEY LOOKED LIKE ANY TYPICAL FAMILY…DAD WALKING WITH HIS ARM AROUND HIS WIFE AND HIS HAND ON HIS SON'S SHOULDER.

WHICH INSPIRES THE QUESTION…IS DAVID BISHOP APPLYING FOR THE ROLE OF STEPFATHER? COMING FROM A BROKEN HOME HIMSELF — HIS FATHER AND MOTHER DIVORCED SHORTLY AFTER HE BEGAN ACTING AT THE AGE OF 10, AND HIS MOTHER WENT ON TO MARRY HIS MANAGER; THE SORDID DETAILS OF THEIR MALFUNCTIONING RELATIONSHIP WERE REVEALED WHEN DAVID TURNED 18 AND FIRED HIS MANAGER/STEPFATHER — AND HAVING BEEN A BACHELOR FOR MUCH OF HIS ADULT LIFE, IS DAVID READY TO SETTLE DOWN AND BE A FAMILY MAN?

REPRESENTATIVES FOR BOTH DAVID BISHOP AND ANDI PARKER HAVE DECLINED COMMENT.

BISHOP FINALLY SNAPS AT PAPARAZZI

AFTER WEEKS OF EFFECTIVELY IGNORING THE PAPARAZZI WHO STALK HIS EVERY MOVE WHEN OUT WITH HIS GIRLFRIEND — NOVELIST ANDREA PARKER, CREATOR OF THE <u>RISE OF DAWN</u> SERIES IN WHICH BISHOP STARS IN THE MOVIE ADAPTATION — DAVID BISHOP FINALLY LASHED OUT AT A PHOTOGRAPHER WHO GOT A LITTLE TOO PUSHY…AND A LITTLE TOO PERSONAL.

SUNDAY EVENING, BISHOP AND PARKER ATTENDED A PRIVATE PARTY AT THE HOME OF BAXTER BENTON, AWARD-WINNING DIRECTOR OF THE FILM <u>RISE OF DAWN</u>. MANY OF THE KEY PLAYERS IN THE MAKING OF THE FILM WERE IN ATTENDANCE, INCLUDING PRODUCERS JERRY HENTON AND HELLENE STANWICK, CO-STARS TAYLOR REISE AND ELLEN ROTHSCHILD, AND SEVERAL OTHER BACKERS AND CONTRIBUTORS TO THE FILM.

AT THE END OF THE EVENING, AS BISHOP AND PARKER LEFT THE MANSION, AN UNNAMED PHOTOGRAPHER LEAPED FROM THE HEDGES TO SNAP PHOTOGRAPHS OF THE TWO IN WHAT HAS COME TO BE KNOWN AS THEIR USUAL HEATED EMBRACE. AS THE STORY GOES—BASED ON EYEWITNESS ACCOUNTS— THE PHOTOGRAPHER STARTLED PARKER, CAUSING HER TO STUMBLE BACKWARD AND NEARLY FALL DOWN THE MARBLE STEPS LEADING DOWN TO THE DRIVEWAY. BISHOP CAUGHT HER; HOWEVER, HE IMMEDIATELY TURNED ON THE PHOTOGRAPHER. WITNESSES ALSO SAY THE PHOTOGRAPHER PROVOKED BISHOP BY MAKING A LEWD COMMENT ABOUT ANDREA, AT WHICH POINT DAVID BISHOP SEIZED THE MAN'S CAMERA EQUIPMENT AND TOSSED IT INTO A NEARBY FOUNTAIN. NO BLOWS WERE EXCHANGED, BUT THE PHOTOGRAPHER WAS HEARD SHOUTING THREATS OF LEGAL ACTION AS BISHOP AND PARKER CONTINUED DOWN THE STEPS TO THEIR WAITING CAR.

DANDI BABY BUMP?

THREE MONTHS INTO THEIR RELATIONSHIP—AND YES, DAVID BISHOP AND ANDREA PARKER HAVE OPENLY AND VERBALLY ADMITTED THEY AREN'T JUST CASUALLY SEEING EACH OTHER, THIS IS A SERIOUS RELATIONSHIP—COULD THAT BE A BABY BUMP ON ANDREA PARKER? WITH THE FILMING OF <u>RISE OF DAWN</u> COMING TO A CLOSE, PERHAPS THERE WILL BE A NEW BISHOP BY THE PREMIERE? (SEE IMAGE LEFT).

"Are you *kidding* me?" Andi held the grocery store gossip rag closer to her face, tilting it slightly sideways to get a different angle on the picture. "That's my *purse*."

The newsprint magazine disappeared from her hands with a snatch as David tossed it on the grass. He grinned and looked down at her. "Move over, sweet cheeks."

Andi squealed and laughed, clinging to the edge of the hammock as David practically threw himself into it, the ropes creaking precariously with the sway. They nearly flipped twice by the time he settled beside her, throwing the blanket over them he'd gone into the house to retrieve. Once the sun went down, the October evenings had a definite bite.

They swayed like babies in a cradle and Andi smiled, nuzzling her nose against the side of his throat. She pulled back, focusing on his face in the semi-darkness. "Did you just call me *sweet cheeks*?"

"Yep. I'm trying it out…sweet*heart* is so…bland," he said, frowning.

"Sweet cheeks *isn't* happening."

"No?"

Andi shook her head. "Not unless I get to call you stud muffin."

David tilted his head, seeming to consider the name. "I could live with—"

She cut him off with a tap to the chest, and he grinned before pulling her closer to kiss her. Andi didn't wait for the intensity of the kiss to build, but opened up to it and slid her hands beneath his shirt to feel his warm skin. It was a dangerous game they played. He hummed against her mouth.

"How long do we have before Bonehead gets here?" he asked against her mouth before drawing her into another kiss. She waited until he paused in the kiss to answer.

"Probably five minutes." Andi didn't comment on David's mimicking of Maggie's name for Lawrence. After three months of being together—and nearly three months of dealing with the temper tantrums and power trips Lawrence pulled—she figured David had earned the right to call her ex-husband 'Bonehead', just like the rest of them.

David's expression grew serious and he tilted his chin, looking her in the eye. "Are you ready to tell me what happened this afternoon?"

Andi sighed, rolling partially on her back so her head was still cradled on his arm. She settled against his chest so she could look up at the stars. An evening breeze fluttered the tree leaves and stirred her hair, and David adjusted the blanket over them. Today hadn't been all that different from the last half-dozen confrontations she'd had with Lawrence. He'd lengthened his stay in California to three months already, with only intermittent trips back to Chicago when the partners demanded it. She had to wonder how long old man Hackman—senior partner at the law firm where Lawrence had worked for the last ten years—would put up with his absence. Apparently, being a thorn in her side was more important right now than something so trivial as keeping his job.

"Nothing to tell." Andi curled closer into David, inhaling his cologne and the scent of night air. "It was just Lawrence being Lawrence. He started with the excuse he wanted to confirm pick-up time, and ended with veiled hints about my uncooperativeness and my sabotaging of our family." She shook her head, letting her nose rub against his throat. "Lawrence is relatively intelligent. I don't understand why he won't let this go."

"I understand."

Andi pulled back, and the hammock swayed with the motion. She focused on his face, tipping her head back to see him through her glasses. "You do?"

David slipped his arm from beneath the edge of the blanket and touched her cheek. He traced a line along her jaw to her lower lip, smiling when she playfully drew his finger between her teeth. "He screwed up, and he knows it. He lost you. If I lost you, I'd be pretty damn persistent in trying to get you back, too."

"Well, you're not going to lose me."

David smiled, a slow curving of his lips before he slid his hand behind her head and pulled her to him for a deep, open-mouthed kiss. She expected the instant and breath-stealing onslaught of want that hit her whenever he kissed her—or touched her—or sometimes even looked at her. That didn't mean she was prepared for it, only that she knew it would come. He hummed a deep groan against her mouth and shifted, his weight angling just slightly over her. The hammock creaked and swayed, an erotic sound all on its own but when mingled with the throaty rumble of appreciation from David, Andi's insides fluttered.

Just at the edge of her hearing, Andi registered the sound of the sliding door. She stilled her lips, waiting for the inevitable interruption.

"Sorry to break it up, kids, but Butthead is growling at the door," Maggie called across the yard.

"Very classy, Margaret." Lawrence's voice carried from inside, and just the sound grated on Andi like a steel file on her spine.

"Oh, sorry. Didn't mean to bruise your tender sensibilities…Boner."

David smiled and kissed the end of her nose before tilting the hammock enough to set his foot on the ground, steadying it so she could get out without tumbling. Although the faux-pained expression on his face as she lingered for just a moment over him, her hands on his chest, was worth the gymnastics required to keep her off the grass.

"Do you want me to come with you?" he asked, the hammock swaying again.

"Nah," Andi said, waving him off as she took a step toward the house. "I can handle Lawrence. I'll be back in a few minutes." She winked. "Keep a spot warm for me."

His chuckle followed her across the lawn to the patio door. Maggie had left it open for her, but no conversation drifted outside. It was easy to see why once she reached the door. Maggie stood in the kitchen behind the counter, a coffee cup in front of her with her arms crossed defiantly over her body. Her eyes practically sent sonic death beams across the small space to where Lawrence stood against the back of a couch, his hands shoved into his pockets. Jake sat on his duffle bag, his attention set on his handheld game. The only sound in the room was the beep and whistles coming from the game.

Lawrence barely waited until she had the glass door shut before he launched into his latest diatribe—thinly veiled by his plea for reparation. "Andrea, honestly," he hissed through clenched teeth and tight lips. "What kind of example are you setting when you're practically having—" He slid his eyes sideways before dropping his voice even lower. "—sex with your *whatever* you want to call him with your son right here."

Andi clenched her fists, the flash of anger hitting her cheeks. Jake didn't look up, but she caught the slight shift of eyes that told her he'd heard. She didn't bother to lower her voice. That would just give him credence. "Get your mind out of the gutter, Lawrence."

Maggie snorted, but Andi shot her a look before she could say anything. The verbal banter between the two of them had become full-out screaming matches more than once in the last few weeks. Maggie shrugged. "What?"

"Boys his age are impressionable, Andrea. We need to be a strong moral example for him."

"Like *you*, Boner?" Maggie came back, followed by a loud snort. "Yeah, boffing your secretary was a *great* moral example for him."

Jake shifted on the duffle but still didn't look up.

"Can we change the subject, please?" Andi begged. She took a deep breath, letting it out. "Jake has a homework project due on Monday, so he needs to be home no later than six tomorrow night. We have to pick up some supplies, and he'll have Sunday to work on it."

Lawrence waved her off, dismissing everything she said. He took a step toward her. "Andrea, we are returning to Chicago in three weeks."

"Hallelujah," Maggie muttered.

Andi did her best not to wish him a hearty farewell. She bit down and crossed her arms.

"We've wasted too much time fighting," he continued, barely acknowledging Maggie. "We have a lot to accomplish before then. We need to get Jacob registered in school. I've found an excellent boarding and day school just thirty minutes outside the city. Now, I know it'll be a mid-semester move, but I've already spoken to the headmaster and—"

Dread—like a bucket of ice water—hit Andi's stomach and it clenched painfully. His actual words registered. *We.* "What are you talking about?" she forced herself to ask.

"The same thing I've been talking about for the last three months. You and Jacob returning to Chicago with me so we can rebuild our family. Honestly, Andrea…"

"I don't want to go to Chicago!" Jake shouted, immediately coming to his feet. He was across the foyer in three long strides, standing in front of Andi with his back to his father. "What's he talking about, Mom? I don't want to go to Chicago! I don't want to go to a boarding school! I don't want to leave California!"

Andi drew Jack to her, hugging him, but she spoke directly to Lawrence. "You're not going to Chicago, honey. Not now and not in three weeks."

Lawrence huffed and turned away, pinching the bridge of his nose. "Of course he is. And you are. We all are."

"Oh, me too?" Maggie tossed in.

He continued without acknowledging her. "That's the whole *point* of me being here!"

"It may have been your point, Lawrence, but the rest of us weren't listening."

"That's quite obvious!"

"You'll stop shouting," Andi said in her best 'Mom means business' voice, as David called it. "Or you'll leave."

"Fine. We'll talk about this tomorrow. Jacob, go to the car. I'll be there in a minute." The level calmness of Lawrence's tone battled with the set of his jaw and the crimson color creeping up his neck.

"I don't want to go," Jake snapped.

"You'll go because I said so."

Jake tensed in her arms at the harsh edge of his father's words. Andi's heart pounded and she felt sick—the gut-sick that told her things were wrong. More wrong than usual. She licked her lips and did her best to school her features before turning Jake to face her. She set her hands on his shoulders and waited until he pulled his stubborn stare away from his father to look at her.

"Jake honey, just go outside. I'm going to straighten this out once and for all."

"I don't want to go," Jake said again, his young face twisting into a grimace. "Mom, tell him I'm not going with him today."

"Okay. Just go outside."

"I'll go with him," Maggie said, throwing a fierce look at Lawrence. "Before I decide to hurt someone."

"Thank you," Andi said after her.

"Get in the car," Lawrence ordered as Jake turned to go.

Jake gave Andi a look over his shoulder, and she shook her head a small degree. She didn't care she'd agreed to the visit, it was her right to change her mind. Jake looked between her and Lawrence and headed for the door, Maggie joining him as she slid her arm across his shoulders. As soon as it shut behind them, Lawrence gripped her elbow and turned her to face him.

"I've about had it with you, Andrea. I've put up with your dalliances because I figured I owed you that much. But, it stops today. You and Jake are coming back to Chicago and we're—"

"No!"

"Don't you dare—"

"No, don't *you* dare," Andi hissed through her teeth. "Get your hand off me *right now*, Lawrence." He stared at her, his lips pressed together in a thin, white line but he dropped his hand from her elbow. She wouldn't give him the satisfaction of seeing her rub at the ache he'd left. "Jake isn't going with you today. And get this through your *thick* head. We are *not* mending anything. I am *not* ever going to be your wife again. You live in Chicago and we live here. I've been gracious with the visitation stipulations, but we're done. You can go back to Chicago whenever you want. Don't worry about waiting three weeks. You're going back alone. *Alone*, Lawrence."

"Who do you think you are to—"

"Who do I think *I* am? I've been wondering the same thing since you showed up three months ago, throwing your weight around like you expected us to bow at your feet and thank you for coming back. We don't need you. And more to the point, we don't *want* you back, Lawrence."

"We're still married, Andrea. We entered a covenant, Andrea."

"And you *broke* it!"

"You break it *now*!" He tossed his hand in the direction of the back door, and her gaze involuntarily shifted to settle briefly on the swaying hammock.

"Get out, Lawrence," she forced out, turning her attention back on him. "I've had it. I've had enough of the arguments and the passive-aggressive attempts to get your way. I'm done. Get in your car and go."

David folded his hands behind his head and stared up at the starry night. Another breeze came through the backyard, rustling the paper he'd tossed in the air earlier. He maneuvered the hammock enough to pick up the nearest pages, attempting to sort them into a neat pile. The photos of Andi were on the top of the stack, upside down, and he flipped them over to take another look. In the dim light, he could barely make out the photograph, but the words set out against the white of the page.

DANDI BABY BUMP

David smiled and chuckled, even though he knew he probably should be righteously enraged by the story, especially on the tail of some of the others that had surfaced recently. Gossip rags and entertainment news seemed to be at either one end of the spectrum or the other when it came to Andi and himself. Some stories were hurtful and vicious, twisting truth into something unpleasant or making up whatever they thought would sell copy. Others made them look like Cinderella and Prince Charming or Couple of the Millennium.

He wasn't sure where this story fell, but either way, it just didn't bother him.

The muffled sound of the house door slamming shut carried around to the backyard. He lifted his head and looked toward the patio door, but Andi didn't come back out. Voices carried on the breeze, and the tone made David's skin prickle. He sat up, the hammock swaying, and listened.

"Get in the damn car, Jacob."

"No! I'm not going!"

"Lawrence, so help me—"

"Shut up, Andrea!"

He was halfway across the backyard before he registered his feet moving. He yanked open the wooden gate to Jake's basketball court.

The court led around the back of the house and opened up to the driveway. The voices bounced off the house walls, and David broke into a jog.

"Let go of me!" Jake shouted. "I don't wanna go!"

"Try it, Andrea, and see how far you get. I'm his *father*, and I have rights."

"Get your hands off them, you slimy pencil-penised bastard!" Maggie shouted.

"I said let him go and *leave*."

David rounded the corner and took only half a second to take in what he saw. Lawrence Bonherre had Jake by the arm with his car door open, trying to shove the boy inside, and Jake was fighting. Andi stood in the space between Jake and the open door.

That's all he needed to see.

Bonherre was on his back against the hood of his rented Lexus with David's arm across his throat before he had a chance to throw another order. "Let me go, you son of a bitch," Bonherre choked out, struggling against the grip.

He sputtered and thrashed, but David said nothing, holding him in place. When Bonherre finally stopped, David leaned in a little closer. "Are you paying attention?" he ground out through his clenched teeth. David gave him a jerk. "Do we have your attention now? Because I'm pretty sure the lady told you to do something."

Lawrence glared, his entire face flushed crimson. "Can you say lawsuit, golden boy?"

"I sure as hell can, bonehead," David hissed with a jerk of his hand that clutched the ass's collar.

Andi touched his shoulder, and he felt the tremble in her hand. "Let him go, David. He's not worth it. Please…"

He took a step back, releasing Bonherre who practically crumpled on the driveway before standing.

"Get in your car and go," David ordered, staring down Bonherre.

He tugged on his shirt, smoothing out the wrinkles left by David's fist. "You don't have any rights here, golden boy. You can't tell me to go—"

"But I can," Andi snapped, moving around David to meet Bonherre toe to toe. She stood firm, but David saw the tremble in her clenched hands. "And I did. Get in your car and go," she repeated. "Go back to Chicago, go back to your wife, just go."

Bonherre huffed air through his nose and stared them down for several moments before slamming the passenger door shut and rounding the back of the car to get in. He started the car with a roar of the engine and tore out of the driveway, kicking up stray bits of gravel in his wake. As soon as he was gone, Andi sucked in a shaky breath, a tiny sound caught in her throat. David touched her arm and turned her back to him, his gut clenching at the tears glistening in her eyes.

He laid his hand against Andi's cheek and she closed her eyes, the tears spilling.

"Are you okay? Did he hurt you?"

She nodded, then shook her head and covered her face with her hands. David bit back the curses running through his mind and leaned in to press his lips to her forehead. A small choking sound made him turn.

Jake stood at the edge of the driveway, his back to them with his shoulders hunched and his head down. His body shook and another small, smothered sound came from him. David stepped to him and dropped to his knees beside Jake.

"Hey, buddy," he said softly, setting his hand on Jake's back. Jake jumped. Andi stopped beside him, her hand hovering over her son's head before she stroked his hair. "I'm sorry. I didn't mean to scare you."

Jake turned, and David was reminded once again even though Andi's son put on a mature face at times, he was still just a kid. Barely more than a little boy. Tears ran down his cheeks and his nose ran, his mouth twisted in a frown. He sucked in a sharp breath, his chin shaking as he tried to talk.

"Dads aren't supposed to do that," he managed to say between choking sobs that made his shoulders hitch. "They're not supposed to make moms cry and they're not supposed to scare their kids. I know!" He jabbed his chest with his finger. "He does it *all* the time and he's not supposed to. I know!"

Andi cried beside him, but David didn't dare look away from her son. He fought the tightness in his throat as he laid his hand on Jake's wet cheek. "No, they're not supposed to."

"Then why does he?"

David shook his head. "I don't know."

"*You* don't make Mom cry. *You* don't say mean things," he sobbed.

"And I never will. I promised you, Jake. I meant it."

David rose on his knees to pull Jake into a hug, and the boy broke down into harder sobs. "Why can't you be my dad?" he cried into David's shoulder.

David closed his eyes and held on tight. Andi wrapped her arms around both of them, curling her trembling body around them. David wanted to tell Jake how much he wished the same thing, but the words stuck in his throat. No matter if he felt it, or not, he couldn't just toss something like that out there—not right now when Jake was so torn up. When Lawrence Bonherre had torn apart any last resemblance he may have had to a decent father.

But he wished it. Oh, how he wished it.

And that reality was more comforting than frightening.

David rose, lifting Jake with him so the boy wrapped his legs around David's waist, not lifting his face from David's now-damp shoulder. David wrapped his free arm around Andi and pulled her to him, holding both mother and son. Maggie stood just a few feet away, her arms crossed over her body. David met her eyes and her lips twisted into an agonized frown before she turned away and wiped her cheeks.

"No good son of a motherless goat," she mumbled as she headed for the house.

"Come on," he said softly, taking Andi's hand. "Let's get inside."

"He's finally asleep," Andi sighed as she hit the bottom of the stairs.

David sat in the family room, a small fire burning in the fieldstone hearth. He looked over the back of the couch, and as she approached, he held out his hand. Fighting the lump in her throat, Andi took his hand as she walked around the couch. She sank into the cushions beside him, settling against his side.

"Poor kid," Maggie said from the chair facing them. She shook her head, and Andi watched the play of emotion shimmer just beneath Maggie's tough expression. "Do you think he'll leave?"

Andi shook her head, focusing her energy and attention on the slow stroke of David's thumb up and down her arm. It was meant to soothe, but it gave her a focal point...something to fill her thoughts other than Lawrence Bonherre and his...there weren't enough adjectives to describe his actions.

"I doubt it," she finally answered. "He's a dog with a bone."

"He's a stupid dog with a rotten, half-eaten, blanched-out chicken bone he's going to choke on if he keeps gnawing at it."

Andi grinned and lifted her head from David's shoulder, looking at Maggie. "Wow, that's quite the metaphor. You should be a writer."

Maggie snorted. "Not likely." She pushed herself to her feet with a long, tired groan. "I'm calling it. I'll poke my head in on Jake to make sure he's asleep."

"Thank you," Andi said softly as Maggie passed, pausing to pat her on the shoulder.

Maggie flipped off the kitchen light as she climbed the stairs, leaving the fireplace as the only source of light. Orange flicks of color danced on the walls, and in the still quiet of the house, the wood crackled and popped. David pressed his lips against her forehead, inhaling deeply.

Andi closed her eyes and laid her cheek on his chest, letting the steady rhythm of his heartbeat sooth away the heartache that twisted in her chest. Anger, frustration, disbelief, and black sorrow battled to be the dominating emotion—leaving her exhausted and drained and unable to process more than the slow stroke of David's hand on her skin. Lawrence had hurt her when he cheated, he'd bruised her and nearly broken her with his words and his accusations. He'd left her hollow for a long time.

Tonight...he broke her heart.

Not for anything he said to her, or for anything he'd done, but because he had taken whatever remained in his son's heart that saw him as a Dad—more than just a man who said he was his father—that glimmer of worship that may have been rekindled—and he destroyed it. Never had she seen her son cry like that, never had her heart broken into so many pieces she wondered if it could ever be put together again.

She didn't realize she wept until David's arms closed around her.

CHAPTER SIXTEEN

David slammed the heel of his hand against his steering wheel, his cursing echoing back to him inside the empty car. The car jerked, and he righted it on the road. Once the car cruised down the highway again, he rubbed a hand over his face and tried to quell the rolling, boiling anger in the center of his chest. He'd wanted to break Lawrence Bonherre's nose...or choke him until his eyes popped out... or both. But he hadn't, and for the last four hours he'd been fighting the rage. And the urge to break something...

The only thing that had kept him calm was Andi...and Jake. He couldn't let Jake see him angry like that; the kid was already scared out of his skin. It had been fifteen minutes after Boner's disappearance before Jake could take a deep breath, and before he let go of David. Jake needed the calm after the storm.

Andi needed his silence, not his anger.

Now, driving home at midnight, his only outlet was speed. He accelerated and slammed the car into fifth gear, the performance engine humming as he zipped around a semi.

His cell phone twittered and an immediate, intense wave of panic hit him. He was already plotting how to turn around before he ever pushed the Bluetooth button on his steering wheel.

"Andi?"

"Nope. Sorry to disappoint."

David squinted, listening to the voice. "Rachel?"

"Yeah. Am I calling too late? Did you give up your night owl ways?"

"No, it's fine. Are you back in LA?"

"Yeah. I landed this morning, but I've been sleeping all day. Now I'm wide awake and hungry. I wondered if you were up to a trip to Canters."

David let some of the tension roll off his shoulders and swallowed down the adrenaline that hit his throat when he thought it was Andi on the phone. He took a deep breath and let it out.

"Hey, you okay?" Rachel asked. "If you're not up to it, no big deal."

"No, I'm not okay," he admitted. "I'll tell you about it when I get there. Give me half an hour," he said, glancing at the dashboard clock. "I'm north of the city."

"Okay, I'll see you there."

David hung up and hit the gas, roaring down the deserted highway. He made it to Fairfax Avenue in just under thirty minutes and pulled into an empty spot along the curb outside Canter's Diner. Lights shined from inside the old Jewish deli that had been around a lot longer than David had been alive, but he and Rachel used to come here in the middle of the night for Reuben sandwiches and Mishmosh soup. Half a dozen patrons sat inside by what he could see through the window. He pulled the door open and the small bell overhead rang, announcing his arrival.

Only one person other than the single waitress took notice of his entrance. Rachel Leighton stood from one of the booths along the back wall, and with a small squeal, ran across the diner into his open arms. Her long, loose brunette hair swung around them, and she hung on tight when he lifted her off the floor. Rachel kissed him hard and loud on the cheek before he set her down.

"It's so good to see you," she declared, holding his face in her palms. Taking his hand, she led him to the table and resumed her spot.

David sat down across from her. "You look great. Milan agreed with you."

"Thank you." She took his hands across the table. "Enough of that… tell me what's wrong. You're still with Andi, yeah?"

David nodded, dropping his head forward with his eyes closed. He swallowed against the lump in his throat that had been choking him all night. Anger. Frustration. The need to help, but not knowing how. Wishing he could just fix it all…

"Hey," she said softly, trying to wedge her fingers into his tight fists. He released the clench and wrapped his hands around hers. "David, you're scaring me. What's going on?" She gasped. "Is it true? I mean, I never believe any gossip rag stories until I hear it from the source. Is Andi…is she pregnant?"

"No." David chuckled, a humorless sound even to his ears. "If only a baby were the greatest complication in my life right now."

"I don't know if I hear regret or wishful thinking."

"Here you go," the waitress said, setting two glasses of water on the table. "Been years since I saw you two in here."

David raised his tired head and looked at the woman. She was probably close to fifty, and if she recognized them as customers, she had to have been at the diner for at least ten to fifteen years. But she wore a bright smile and had friendly eyes, and David was thankful tonight he didn't have to beat off news hounds. He smiled and read her nametag, and immediately remembered.

"Anne. It's good to see you." He tried not to let the fatigue drag his voice down, but it went so far past just being tired that he couldn't help it.

"You want the usual?" Rachel nodded for them both. "Mishmosh soup with a Cosmo for her. Hot Reuben and Guinness for him. I don't forget my regulars, even when they're not so regular anymore."

David raised his head. "I'll skip the beer. Coffee please."

Anne crossed out the Guinness on her notepad and nodded. "You got it. Give me five minutes." With a wink, she left them alone again.

"Have I mentioned how proud I am of you?" Rachel asked when Anne walked away. "How many years has it been?"

"Seven years, four months, nine days."

Rachel crossed her arms on the table and sighed. "Okay, back to business. You said on the phone you weren't okay. Andi's not pregnant, though I'm thinking if she *were* it wouldn't be a problem. And by the way, you're tapping your fingers on the tabletop, I'm guessing you could take on a grizzly bear and win right now."

David stopped the tapping he hadn't realized he'd started and curled his fingers into his palms.

"Does this have something to do with Andi?"

David scrubbed his face with his palms, growling out his frustration. "Yes, but...*she* isn't..." He rubbed his forehead, trying to find a way to explain. "Damn it," he cursed, slamming his fist down on the table so hard the salt and pepper shakers bounced.

Several heads turned to look at them but immediately looked away again. Rachel grabbed his hand and held it down. "Talk to me, David. What is it? I thought things were good, you loved her—"

"I *do* love her, and that's why I'm so damn pissed off."

Rachel's expression shifted to something between horror and dread. "Oh, god," she choked out.

David shook his head and raised a hand, stopping her thoughts. He knew exactly where her assumptions led. She'd been there for him through the end with Josie. "No. Not that." He huffed, trying to find something to do with his hands that didn't involve banging something or breaking something.

"David..." She left the 'what the *heck* are you talking about' part of the question unsaid.

Didn't mean he didn't hear it.

By the time Anne returned with their food, David had laid out everything in painful detail. Everything from Bonherre's first phone call to Andi weeks before that had left her embarrassed and ashamed, to the events of that afternoon. He couldn't tell her everything— couldn't tell her how Jake had sobbed and shook in his arms—or how David had seen the heartbreak in Andi's eyes—if he tried to put words to it, he wouldn't have been able to finish.

"I don't think I've ever wanted to hurt someone so badly in my entire life. I've been mad, but this was...visceral."

"You can't love someone and not get angry when someone hurts them."

David set his arms on the table on either side of the Reuben plate, wondering if he had enough appetite to eat. He lowered his head again, closing his eyes. "It practically killed me to leave her."

"So why did you?"

"I don't stay," he said, raising his head with a tired sigh. "I've only stayed at the house once, and Jake wasn't home."

"Really?" she said, scooping a matzo ball from her bowl. "Not even when..." she trailed off, arching an eyebrow for emphasis.

"We aren't..." David cleared his throat. Funny, if there was anyone he should be able to talk to frankly about sex, it should be the first woman he was ever intimate with. "Andi and I aren't lovers. Not in the physical sense, anyway."

Rachel choked on her broth and had to take a sip of her drink.

"You don't have to act so surprised."

"Sorry." Rachel sat back and studied him while he attempted eating the mile-high sandwich. Once he bit into it, his stomach remembered how much he loved Canter's Reubens. She waited until he chewed and swallowed, wiping mustard from the corner of his mouth. "You've changed, David. It's been—what, a year and a half?—since I saw you, and you're so different."

"A lot of things were different then." The last time he saw Rachel, she had helped him move into his house on Mulholland and out of the house he'd shared with Josie in Malibu. Only a handful of people knew the real reason he'd left...that he'd wanted more than just a live-in girl-friend...and Josie's answer was to have an affair.

"I heard it on the phone that time I talked to you after the accident. But, I thought maybe it was the new relationship euphoria." She shook her head. "It's not, is it?"

"I love her," he said without hesitation and ignored the crack in his voice when he said the words. "I want to be with her for the rest of my life."

"It won't be easy with this butthead of an ex constantly sticking in his nose."

"Nothing worth having comes easy."

Rachel laughed out loud. "Wow. So philosophical."

David shrugged, feeling some of the weights lift off his shoulders. The more he told Rachel, the more he knew it was true. At the same time, he wondered why he could tell Rachel this—tell his sisters, tell Avi—but he hadn't told the one person who probably needed to hear it the most. The person he should have told *first*.

Like a punch to the gut, David realized how wrong he'd been.

He tossed his napkin on the table, covering the sandwich he'd barely touched. "I've got to go."

"Now?" she asked, staring up at him as he stood.

David took out his wallet and tossed enough money on the table to cover the food and give Anne enough of a tip to make up for a few of the missed years. "I've got to take care of something I've put off way too long."

Rachel grinned, her eyes sparkling. "Promise me we'll have dinner soon…you, me, Andi…"

"Absolutely." He leaned over and kissed her cheek before leaving the diner.

Andi sat nestled in the corner of the couch, staring at the glowing embers from the fireplace. She tugged the chenille throw around her legs and wrapped her arms over her body, fighting the chills even though the house was not cold. She'd tried a hot shower, tried putting on her favorite flannel pajamas, and even tried warm milk to chase away the chill rooted in her gut—but none of it helped.

She picked up her phone from the coffee table parallel to the couch and looked at the time. Nearly two in the morning, and sleep wasn't anywhere in sight. She felt alone, even though Maggie and Jake were upstairs. Tonight, more than any other night, she wished she'd had the guts to ask David to stay. Even if just to hold her like he had that night so many weeks before.

Andi no sooner set the phone down than it vibrated across the smooth surface. She picked it up and tapped on the new text message icon.

Hey Beautiful

Hey, yourself. I thought you'd be in bed
by now.

How'd you know I was still up?

Call it intuition

Before she could respond, his next message hit.

Where are you?

She smiled.

In the living room. Did you make it home okay?

Yes. I miss you

I miss you, too.

Come to the door.

Andi scowled, staring at the screen. She jumped and gasped when a soft knock sounded, echoing like a gong through the quiet house. Throwing back the blanket, she padded barefoot to the door and released the deadbolt. When she opened it, David stood with his shoulder propped against the side of the house, a tired but still wonderful-to-see smile on his lips.

"What are you doing here?" she asked softly.

"I forgot to do something earlier."

"What?"

He stepped into the house, and in one easy move, took her face in his hands and kissed her. Andi melted into him and he wrapped her in his arms, lifting her feet off the ground to step inside and kick the door closed behind him. His mouth never left hers. Andi wanted to be embarrassed because she wore her favorite baby blue flannel pajamas with little clouds, wanted to ask what brought him back two hours after he left...but mostly she wanted him to never stop kissing her.

The deep, thorough, toe-curling kiss eased into smaller, lingering kisses until he finally left one brief touch to her lips and pulled back to look into her face. David smiled, one corner of his perfect mouth ticking up to be followed by the other.

Andi drew in a breath, not even attempting to hide the way her pounding heart made her voice shudder. "I'm pretty sure you kissed me before you left," she managed to say.

"That's not what I forgot," he said with that grin that made her blood race. "That was just an added benefit of coming back."

"Okay. What did you forget?"

His gaze shifted, smoothing over her face and down to the collar of her pajamas. This had to be the most dowdy, 'housewife frump', pair of pajamas she owned, and yet the way he looked at her made her feel like a sultry woman wearing black lace lingerie.

"I forgot to tell you something."

She waited, holding her breath as he traced his fingertips along her jaw and down the side of her throat. His fingertips rested at her pulse point, which she knew had to be jumping beneath his touch, then returned to her face. His thumb stroked her chin and her lower lip, his eyes watching the path his fingers took. Then he shifted his gaze up and looked her in the eyes.

"I love you, Andi."

She blinked, trying to keep him in focus. Her glasses were upstairs beside her bed, but he was close enough she easily saw his expression in the light cast by the fire. Andi realized her mouth was open when his thumb brushed the inside of her lip and he leaned in to kiss the same spot.

"I should have told you a long time ago."

"You should have?" she managed to ask, swallowing against the sudden dryness in her throat. Her heart pounded so hard she felt lightheaded.

"I should have told you when I knew." He chuckled softly, grinning. "But I thought telling you I was in love with you two days after our first date might seem too fast."

Andi blinked again, wondering if she were still on the couch and this was a vivid dream. Of course, last time she'd assumed she was dreaming David had kissed her in her trailer and sent her life into a crazy, amazing, wonderful tailspin. "You've loved me since then?"

"I've *known* I loved you since then. I loved you before that." His thumbs stroked her cheek and he curled a bit of damp hair behind her ear. The small touches were almost distracting, only in that they sent small jolts of warm energy through her. "I got so used to thinking it I forgot I hadn't said it."

She could only stare. Somewhere in her befuddled, tired, stressed mind she knew she should say something—quite specifically "I love you, too"—but another part didn't want to let her believe this was real. That she wasn't curled up on the couch dreaming of him.

"Do I need to say it again?" he asked, leaning in close enough his breath brushed her cheek.

Andi nodded within the gentle touch of his hands. His thumbs stroked the corners of her lips, and his day's stubble abraded her skin, succeeding only in heightening the contact. "I…" He kissed her. "Love…" Another kiss. "You…" He punctuated the words with a deeper, longer kiss that pulled a soft sound from the back of her throat. "Andi."

By the time he said her name, she believed him and knew not even the most vivid dream could come close to this moment. Andi raised her arms and held his rough cheeks, opening herself up to the rush as his hands pulled her closer and his tongue slowly slipped past her lips. When she looked into his face, she had to blink against the tears blurring her vision. Andi thought for sure she had cried enough there couldn't be any left…but this was a different kind of tear.

David smoothed away the moisture from her cheek, studying her.

"I love you, too." She finally found the ability to speak and smiled beneath his touch. She let a breath go from so deep in her soul that she thought she must have been holding it forever.

David hugged her, pressing his face into the curve of her shoulder. He held on so tight she had to toe up, but she didn't want to let go any more than he did. He kissed the side of her neck, her jaw, her cheek, then her lips again. Then he stepped back and slid his hands down her arms to link their fingers.

"Well, now that we've got that out of the way—" Andi gasped, trying to look affronted. David just chuckled. "Come on. We both need some sleep."

As if on cue, Andi yawned and tried to stifle it behind her hand. David chuckled again. He led her toward the stairs, giving her a sidelong glance. "Nice pajamas, by the way."

"I didn't know I was going to have company."

"I'm not complaining. Darlin', you are the sexiest woman in flannel I've ever seen."

Andi stopped halfway up the stairs, and David turned to look down at her. The stairwell was dark, and she could barely see his face in the light cast from above. "Are you staying?" she asked.

He came down a step so they were closer to the same level, and smoothed his hand over her hair. "Is that okay? I just want to hold you."

Andi moved closer, aligning their bodies so she could run her nose along his rough jaw. "Are you sure?"

He drew a long breath, letting his mouth hover over hers. When he spoke, his lips brushed hers but he didn't complete the kiss. "I'm sure I love you. And I'm *absolutely* sure I want to make love to you…but tonight, I need to hold you more."

He brushed a kiss across her lips and moved up the stairs again. In her bedroom, they moved in silence as Andi pulled back the blankets of the undisturbed bed and slid between the cool sheets. David shucked off his sneakers and shed his jacket and shirt. She turned away when she heard the click of his belt bucket, closing her eyes against the erotic rush that slammed into her. Then he lifted the blankets and lay down beside her, his arm draping her waist to pull her back against him.

In one moment, in one beat of her heart, she felt all the tension of the day dissipate and her body relaxed into the soft bed. David sighed and settled into the pillows with his lips hovering near enough to her ear that she felt his warm breath. Her heavy eyelids slid closed, and within moments, Andi was asleep.

Andi stood at the top of the driveway, raising her hand in a wave as David backed into the street. He stopped when he'd straightened the car and kissed his fingertips, tossing the kiss to her as he drove away. She waited until he was out of sight before heading into the house, and was greeted by the smell of roasting coffee as she opened the door.

"About time you came back in. I figured I'd have to brew another pot before the two of you got done saying goodbye." Maggie made kissy-face noises and followed up with a wink and grin.

Andi smiled and sank into one of the kitchen chairs, hunching over the steaming cup Maggie had already set on the table for her. Maggie sat, humming in satisfaction as she sipped her cup.

"So," Maggie said after a few companionable minutes. "He stayed the night."

"Sort of," Andi answered, setting her cup down. "And not the way you think." She chuckled at Maggie's eye roll. Her cheeks hurt from smiling, but she didn't care enough to stop. "He left around midnight." Maggie just arched her eyebrows, in a Maggie-esque way of demanding more information. "He came back." Andi paused. "To tell me something."

Maggie leaned on her hand. "Had to be good if he couldn't call or text…or wait."

"He came back to tell me he loved me."

Maggie broke into a wide grin and slapped the table. "About damn time!"

Andi drained her cup and stood. "I'm going to work on that chapter this morning. I might even have it done before Jake gets up. What do you want to do today since we're all home?"

"Sorry, hun. I've got lunch plans with Phillip."

"You've given up on Nicco, huh?"

Maggie took both their cups and headed for the sink, shrugging her shoulder. "Nicco was a child in a man's body. Granted, an amazing man's body. I got sick of feeling like I should be cutting his meat for him." She chuckled. "At least with Phillip, I'm not afraid to let him have sharp utensils."

Three hours later, Maggie had left and Jake had finally rolled out of bed. Andi finished chapter twenty-two and moved on to a healthy beginning on twenty-three before she decided to head downstairs for something to eat. Jake was on the couch where she'd curled up the night before, his handheld game beeping and whirring as he fought for the next level.

"You hungry, honey?" she asked.

"Nah," he mumbled, not looking up.

Before she could try again to pull him into conversation, someone knocked at the door. Andi set down the bowl she'd intended to use for cereal and crossed the foyer, peeking out through the peephole. Her gut clenched and she immediately felt sick. Lawrence stood on the other side, a deep scowl twisting his features. The façade of pleasantness was gone.

Andi took a step back from the door. "Jake, honey, I need you to go upstairs."

He looked up. "Why?"

"Please, just go upstairs. Your father is here."

He rolled off the couch and bolted up the stairs, his face already blanched a stark white. It was a pathetically sad state of things when a boy got that look on his face at the mention of his father. Lawrence knocked again, harder this time, but Andi waited until she knew Jake was safely in his room before she opened the door.

"What do you want?" she demanded.

Lawrence pushed past her, not waiting or expecting an invitation to come inside. "I think I've made that abundantly clear, Andrea."

"And I've made it abundantly clear you're not getting it. If that's why you're here, leave now and save both of us all that wasted time."

Lawrence turned to face her, and the coldness in his eyes made her breath hitch. He'd worked hard for the last three months to hide the coldness from her, and the fact he didn't try anymore frightened her more than she wanted to admit.

"I agree. With this self-centered attitude of yours, frankly, I don't want you as a wife—"

"Which is convenient, since you *have a wife*, Lawrence," she snapped off. "What does Leslie think about you spending so much time away from home?"

"The sad part is how Jacob will suffer for it," Lawrence continued as if she hadn't spoken at all. "Unless I do something about it."

Andi laughed. How so like Lawrence to take her decision and turn it around to make it seem like his idea all along. "*My* self-centered attitude? Lawrence, having an affair is about as self-centered as you can *get*. You did what *you* wanted, took what *you* wanted, and expected everyone else to just fall into line. Hmmm…kind of like your *wife*."

"What you're doing is just as self-centered, Andrea."

Andi smacked her hand against her forehead. "Part of me wants to tell you to go to hell, and yet, part of me is dying to know what I've done to garner this opinion from *you* of all people."

"David Bishop."

Andi squinted at him, wondering when the second head would spring from his shoulder. "David…I would ask you to explain, but I know you will anyway."

"He's a bad influence."

"How?"

"Oh, come on, Andrea. Don't play naïve with me. We both know it's useless. David Bishop is a Hollywood playboy. Next to Las Vegas, Hollywood *is* Sin City. His type has no moral compass, no self-restraint, and no discretion."

"Takes one to know one." Andi almost turned to see if Maggie were in the room, or if she'd said the words herself.

"Damn it, Andrea…" He dropped his voice and his eyes slid back and forth as if he hoped no one else might be here. "He's a Jew, for God's sake."

Andi blinked, staring at him. "You screwed Hannah Berger in her father's office," she said, forcing herself not to clear her throat of the foul taste the words left behind. For just a second, Lawrence's eyebrows shot up. He didn't know she knew his Jewish partner's daughter had been on the list of conquests. "You had sex with almost the entire secretarial pool. You f—" She forced herself to stop, biting down on her lip to keep from saying words that would foul her mouth more than affect him. "You can't even *tell* me how many women you had sex with before I found out. And you want to judge me based on the faith of the man I love?"

Lawrence slammed his hand down on the counter, making the cookie jar lid rattle. Despite herself, Andi jumped and took a step back. But he followed, closing in on her with his finger pointed in her face. "It's being around people like David Bishop and Margaret Connolly that has changed you, Andrea. Your attitude and your focus are wrong for the mother of a young boy."

"You're deluded, Lawrence. Maggie has been nothing but wonderful for Jake. She loves him. She treats him like her own son."

"You're proving my point. What kind of family values will he garner from living with two women—two women, I might add, who consistently have men coming and going? Staying the night. What are you teaching him?"

"What are you *talking* about?" she shouted.

"David Bishop spent the night here last night—"

"How do you know that!" she demanded. "My God, Lawrence. Are you stalking me?"

"The point isn't how I know, it's that he was here. And who knows what kind of men Margaret brings through here."

"She doesn't bring *any* men through here!"

"She's just part of the problem, Andrea. I refuse to allow someone like David Bishop to influence my son when I can't be here to guide him myself."

"You don't have any say over the matter. You don't get to dictate whom I spend my time with. You lost that right the first time you went outside our marriage."

"With you at home, no man would blame me."

Andi pulled back, clamping down her jaw. It didn't matter how many years had passed, the truth of it was Lawrence Bonherre was the only man she'd ever been with intimately, and no matter how much she tried to remember the way David looked at her—or the way he told her he wanted her—Lawrence's words hurt deep and tore at old wounds.

"And this is where you're wrong, Andrea." Lawrence moved in on her again, cornering her against the counter edge and the patio door. "I can dictate who is in my son's life, and I fully intend to practice my rights to do so."

"Why are you so afraid of David?" she demanded, cursing at the weakness in her voice.

Lawrence smirked. "The only thing I'm afraid of is what influence that golden boy punk will have over my son, and I won't have Jacob turning into a morally corrupt mama's boy because his mother falls for the first wick thrown in her direction. Once the court sees how pitiful you are, I'm certain they'll decide the boy needs proper male guidance, and not the kind some Hollywood hotshot can give him. Not that I expect him to stick around long."

Andi crossed her arms over her body and gripped her elbows to hide the tremble in her body.

"If you couldn't keep me, what makes you think Bishop will settle when there's so much more…"He looked her up and down, his eyes lingering at her breasts long enough to make her skin crawl. "…satisfying fish in the sea. You're just a convenient diversion."

"Do you ever get tired of hearing yourself speak?" Andi hissed.

"Am I using too many big words, Andrea? Let me make it simple for you. Remove David Bishop from Jacob's life or I remove Jacob from yours."

CHAPTER SEVENTEEN

"I don't know, Ma. I'll ask her tonight."

"Honestly, Davey. The way you've avoided bringing her out here, you make me think you don't want Andrea to meet your family."

David wedged his phone between his ear and shoulder so he could lift the pot of pasta off the stove. He chuckled at the astonishment in his mother's voice. "Ma, she's already met Caroline and Sarah. And if Sarah didn't scare her off, no one will."

His mother made a sound of admonishment laced with too much laughter to be effective. He chuckled with her and dumped the pot of angel hair into a colander.

"We've been wrapping up the film. Makes it tough to get away, and we'd want to come at least overnight."

"Sounds like you've talked about it…"

David grinned. He could almost see the gleam in his mother's eyes. "Yes, we've talked about it." He shifted the phone again. "We were going to come for Yom Kippur, but…" He trailed off, not finishing the excuse. Bonehead had messed up their plans, as usual. "When things are calmer, we'll come. I promise."

"Davey…" The weight of an unasked question in his mother's voice made him pause before rinsing the pasta.

"No, Ma. She's not pregnant," he said before she asked. His mother always claimed she didn't believe anything she read, but she almost always asked about it.

She tsked. "I know. You would have told me."

David straightened so he could hold the phone, getting it out of the bend of his shoulder. "You're right, Ma. I would. So, what do you want to know?"

"I've read a lot about her ex-husband. I don't think I've read *anything* nice."

"Well, on that..." He turned on the sink to rinse the pasta, swirling it with his fingers. "They are right. And frankly, Ma, he's part of the reason we haven't come. When I bring Andi to meet you, I want to bring Jake. Her ex-husband is making it hard for us to plan anything." He had to fight from grinding his teeth just talking about Bonehead.

"I guess if you're still trying, she's worth it." There was only the slightest hint of an actual question in her statement.

"Absolutely, Ma. She's worth it." He smiled when he said it.

The doorbell chimed, and David glanced at the front entrance. "Ma, someone is here. I gotta go. I love you." He clicked off the phone and set it on the counter. Jogging barefoot across the wood floor, he reached the door just as the chimes rang again. David didn't bother to look outside to see who it was since only friends and maintenance people had the code to the front gate.

Andi stood beneath the overhang of the front door, dark glasses covering her eyes with her arms crossed over her body. With the coming of fall, she'd given up the sexy sundresses he loved so much, but she still managed to flirt with his libido by wearing V-neck sweaters with a tendency to slide to the side, exposing her collarbone and throat for impromptu kissing, and jeans that hugged her in *all* the right places.

"Hey, sweetheart," he said, not even trying to hide his happiness at seeing her. "Were your ears burning? I was just talking about you." He laid his hand on her arm and pulled her inside, kissing her cheek as she moved past him. She turned into him, her lips brushing his cheek, but almost immediately stepped away. David squinted, watching her with a sudden and undeniable sense of dread. "Did I get the plan wrong? I thought I was coming to the house tonight for dinner."

She nodded but turned her back to him, leaning into the back of the couch. Even with the space between them, he saw the tension in her body. "I needed to talk to you before tonight," she said softly, her voice too rough and too low.

The dread expanded through his chest.

"Andi, what's wrong…"

She sucked in a sharp breath that came out as a bitter laugh. "What gave me away?" she asked, her back still to him.

David crossed to her and laid his hands on her upper arms. Her entire body tensed and she arched her body away from him to avoid contact. He didn't drop his hands. "Just tell me."

She turned to face him, but in the same motion moved out of the space between him and the couch, walking several feet away before she stopped and crossed her arms over her stomach again. A tremor shifted through her body and she bowed her head. David took a step, but she stumbled back from him as soon as he moved, bumping into the wall leading to the kitchen.

"Don't. Please," she begged in a painfully low voice.

"Andi, honey, you've got to tell me what's wrong." What could be wrong to make her move away from him with near panic? "Did something happen?"

She chuckled humorlessly. "Yeah, I guess you could say that." She wouldn't look right at him, even though the dark glasses hid her eyes, the kind designed to look like sunglasses but slid seamlessly over prescriptions. The problem with those types of glasses was they were designed to hide everything beneath even more effectively than regular sunglasses. He couldn't see her eyes at all.

David tried one more time to take a step toward her, and once again the wall stopped her. She made a small, desperate sound, her breath coming in short jerks. He raised his hands and reached for the sunglasses. A similar scene from months before played through his mind…and he remembered what she said.

"If this were a bad romance novel, then you'd assume I stepped away from you because I didn't want you to touch me. Which would be wrong, I just

stepped back because I need to think, and I don't do very well when you're touching me."

"I'm just taking off the glasses. I want to see your face, sweetheart."

She didn't relax her tense stance, but she didn't try to stop him when he reached again for the glasses. He slipped them off, swallowing hard. Her eyes were closed tight, but he didn't need them to be open to see the results of her tears. Her cheeks were streaked, her skin flushed, her eyes red.

"Andi, look at me. Please."

Her eyes fluttered open, and a tear ran free from one, sliding down her cheek to her throat. She made no attempt at wiping it away. David raised his hand to brush the tear away, and she bolted. Before he could turn around she was back to the couch again, bracing herself against the back as if it were the only thing holding her upright.

"Damn it, Andi. *Please*. Tell me what's going on!"

Her head snapped up, and she took several heavy, almost painful-sounding breaths. "We're over, David." The last words came out so strangled he barely heard them…but their meaning was far too clear. "We have to be."

He couldn't say anything, his ability to ask simple questions like "What?" and "Why?" was suddenly gone. David's arms dropped to his side and he stared at her for several moments. She looked away and ran the back of her hand across her streaked face, still using the other hand to brace herself. Half a dozen scenarios ran through his head that could explain this, the foremost being his late-night trip to Canter's with Rachel. Could someone have told Andi and she misunderstood? Did she think he'd gone to Rachel because—

He immediately shook off the idea. For her to do that would be breaking her own cardinal rule—assuming anything without just asking. She wouldn't end what they had over a suspicion. Over a story in a paper or some picture. She might ask, but she wouldn't jump to such a drastic conclusion that it would drive her to this.

Finally, he found his voice, but even then it was hard to force the word out. "Why…"

She laughed again, the same stilted, grim laugh she'd used since arriving. Andi tipped her head back, looking toward the ceiling and then off to the side, only meeting his eyes for the briefest of moments. This time when she drew in a breath, he watched the transformation he'd seen before as she took control and pushed down whatever emotion she didn't want him to see. She'd done it when he kissed her on set, she'd done it when Bonehead pushed too far. Andrea Parker had somewhere along the lines learned to master the art of smothering her emotions until she could hide them behind a thinly veiled mask.

But today was different. The mask had slipped before she ever arrived. And she was having a hell of a time putting it back in place.

"I ran through no less than a dozen ways to answer that question on my way here. I thought of every bad—and good—novel I'd ever read when the heroine had to end it and had to come up with any reason other than the truth."

"You can't tell me the truth?"

"The truth is too pathetic," she tossed over her shoulder as she moved away from the couch to pace the distance between the sitting area and the staircase leading down to the guest bedroom level. She shrugged and shook her head, her red curls bouncing. "I read this story once about a woman who told the man she loved she didn't love him at all. That even though they'd made love, and she'd told him how she felt—she lied and said it wasn't true. And he believed her. I never understood how he could just believe her. If he loved her as much as he said, how could she have given so much to him to have him just swallow a pile of horse pucky like that."

She rambled, talking so fast the words bunched up into one long word. Andi hadn't been like this around him in weeks, so nervous or wound up she couldn't keep her voice calm.

"Why did she lie?" he asked, hoping her ramblings would eventually lead to the truth.

"Oh, well, in this particular case, she was being stalked by a killer and she ended it to protect him. Which is the epitome of TSTL. Here's a hint to women…if you're being stalked, tell the man you love. Especially when he's ex-FBI and has an arsenal the size of Texas."

"I'm going to assume you're not being stalked by a killer." He was doing his best to keep his voice level and to not push her, no matter how much he wanted to get to the point.

"No," she said with a vehement shake of her head. "I'm also not dying of a rare disease, I'm not part of the Witness Protection program, and I haven't decided I'm just too much of a screw-up to allow you to love me. Although, that last one does seem like a viable option."

He wondered if her fast-talking was the only way—in this case— she managed to keep herself talking at all. "None of that answers my question."

She walked, her arms wrapped over her body. Andi kept her face down, and her hair fell forward to hide her eyes. David shifted his jaw, turning his focus toward the far corner of the room because watching her tear herself apart was too much. The silence was like a pressure cooker, any minute the top would blow. David drew in a long, slow breath through his nose before looking at her again. It hurt to clear his throat, but he managed to force his next question.

"Last night, you told me you love me." When he said 'you love me', her eyes slid closed and her nervous pacing stopped with a jerk. David swallowed hard. "Are you not sure? Has that changed? Or have you changed your mind?"

She spun around then, her eyes wide as she shook her head. "No! No…" Her lips twisted into a frown she tried to make into a smile, and failed miserably. Andi tilted her head, looking at him. "I love you." She sucked in a breath, saying the words again as she let it go. "Don't— Please don't—Just know I love you."

"I love you, too."

His admission almost seemed to hurt her. She pressed her hands against her stomach and bowed her head, drawing in a shaky breath. After a moment, she raised her head again, unshed tears glistening in her eyes. "I almost wish you didn't." She clenched her fists and dropped her hands to her side, squaring her shoulders. One more time, she tried to rein it all in.

The words stung more than he wanted to admit.

"Why don't you want me to love you?"

Andi raised a trembling arm and pressed the heel of her hand to her forehead. If he had to bet, he figured she was minutes away from another migraine…if she wasn't already there and pushing through it, just like she had tried so many weeks before.

She dropped her hand, bracing it against one of his shelves to keep on her feet. "For someone who lives by the word, I'm doing a terrible job," she half mumbled to herself. "Give me a computer and I could be out of your life in five paragraphs or less."

"Andi—"

She snapped her attention to him. "It's a sick paradox," she said, cutting him off. "I *want* you to love me...but this...this would have been so much easier if..." Andi closed her eyes and tilted her head, her hand fluttering in the air as if she needed to wave off her thought.

Her voice was thick, choked by the tears he knew she held back. "I've been expecting this day almost since the beginning. But, I figured you'd be the one telling *me* it was over and we were through. I didn't think I would have to be the one to find the words." When she met his eyes, her gaze softened for just a moment and the smile looked almost genuine and complete. "Then you told me you loved me, and for a few hours I thought this might be..." Andi couldn't finish. She pressed her lips together and swallowed hard, shaking her head.

She'd completed another circuit of the living room and returned to the couch. Andi sank onto the arm, weary fatigue dragging her down. David took a hesitant step forward, and she didn't jerk or move away. He forced himself to remember what she'd said in her trailer weeks before. If she moved away it was because she had to think. He had to let her think...so he could convince her not to go.

"If you love me, why are you leaving me?" he asked in a gentle voice. "The real reason, not some badly written romance novel."

She almost smiled. "I'm rubbing off on you."

David ticked his head to the side. "I hope so."

Her strong façade slipped for a moment and her eyes filled with tears, but she huffed a breath and looked away. David waited, his hands pushed hard into his pockets just so he wouldn't be tempted to reach for her and make her skitter away again. Andi swallowed, rolled her damp lips together, and looked at him again. "I can't lose my son."

Her words sucker-punched him, but David clenched his jaw to keep what he hoped was a calm expression. In an instant, he knew exactly who was behind her tears and her decision—Larry Bonherre—he just needed to wait out the details.

"As much as I love you, I can't lose my son," she said again, maybe trying to convince herself the two facts had to be exclusive of each other.

"Sweetheart, you're not going to lose Jake."

She crumpled like a rag doll, her hands covering her face as a wrenching sob ripped through her. David lunged forward and caught her before she hit the hardwood floor, lifting her in his arms to set her on the couch. Andi curled forward, her face still covered, rocking as she cried. He knelt in front of her, lost as to what to say or do because he still didn't know what he was dealing with—other than the fact Andi's heart was being ripped out and he had absolutely no doubt who was doing the ripping. He tried to stroke her hair, touch her face, to get her attention on him but as soon as his fingers touched her, she tried to scramble away. This time, David didn't let her go. He knelt right in front of her, holding her hands in her lap.

"Andi, sweetheart, look at me."

She shook her head and tried to free her hands. "Don't touch me. I can't—if you touch me, I won't—I-I—"

"You won't be able to leave me? Then damn it, I'm never letting go." He heard the edge in his voice and hated it made her entire body tense beneath his touch, but he wanted to shout 'No!' and this was the most restraint he could manage.

She wouldn't look at him until he took her face in his hands and made her meet his gaze. David stroked her cheeks, waiting for the moment when her eyes shifted to him and her shoulders relaxed a small degree. "Andi, *I love you*. You may have been waiting for the day we ended, but I've been waiting for the day we begin."

She sucked in a shaky breath. Her cheeks were slick beneath his touch, and her glasses were spotted by her tears. David risked letting her go long enough to slip the glasses off and set them on the table behind him.

Andi clenched her hands in her lap, but when he touched the tight fists she immediately gripped his fingers. "He's going to take Jake if I don't..." Andi hesitated and swallowed, rubbing her lips together.

David hissed through his teeth. "If you don't *what*, Andi."

"If I don't take you out of Jake's life—if I don't end our relationship

—he's going to file for amended custody and says he'll take Jake away from me."

"On what grounds?"

Andi shook her head. "It doesn't matter," she practically screamed with frustration. "He'll make them up. He'll make them stick."

He almost laughed at Bonherre's audacity. "Sweetheart, I don't care who he thinks he is, he can't just take your son away from you. You're his mother—"

"I can't risk it."

"Andi—"

"No," she said firmly. Andi pulled her hands free of his and scooted a couple of inches away, but not so far away she left his reach. She snuffled her nose and let out a shaky breath. "When we divorced, my attorney told me I was damn lucky to get custody. Lawrence was gracious in not fighting for Jake because he could have and won."

"On what grounds?"

She hung her head, staring at her hands. "I left him and took our son, she said that didn't look good. I had no guaranteed form of income beyond my royalties, and I shared a home with Maggie."

David squinted, shaking his head. "What kind of moron lawyer did you have?"

Andi's laugh returned to the satirical chuckle. "The kind I could afford. I'd been here a year, and I'd been living off the advance Maggie negotiated for me for *Rise of Dawn*. It wasn't much, but living with her, we could do it."

David shifted closer to her again, kneeling in front of her legs. "Regardless of what she said then, things are different now. Andi..." She kept her attention on her hands, worrying the hem of her sweater between shaking fingers. "Andi, sweetheart, look at me."

She swallowed and blinked, heavy tears rolling down her flushed cheeks. But she did as he asked and raised her head, looking him in the eyes.

"Things are different now," he said gently, offering the best smile he could manage. "Sweetheart, I don't know the exact numbers but I'm willing to bet you made more money off the royalties and movie deal for *Rise of Dawn* than Bonehead has made in ten years. Am I right?"

She ticked her head to the side with a single-shoulder shrug. Her smile was anything but happy, edged with cynicism. "It's not my ability to take care of Jake financially that's being contested."

"He's just—" David huffed and dipped his head for a moment. "Okay, you want to talk bad storylines? This is the old 'If I can't have you, no one else will either' scenario."

"I know what it is," she said in almost a whisper. "I know exactly what it is. But that doesn't change the fact if I haven't ended my relationship with you—if you're not out of Jake's life—by Monday morning, he's filing a petition with the California Family Court to take Jake away from me."

Her voice was calm, too calm. She teetered between hysteria and this robotic monotone, and David wondered just how long it would be before she cracked. Andi tried so damn hard not to show weakness she had no idea she was the strongest woman he'd ever known. It was her recovery from those moments when it just became too much that showed her strength. She just didn't see it in herself.

"You're letting him win."

"Then so be it," she said softly, her lower lip trembling. The seesaw started its slow tip in the other direction. "It doesn't matter what he does to me, as long as I have Jake."

"Your happiness doesn't matter?"

"I can't lose Jake," was her only answer.

"I can't lose *you*." As soon as the words left his lips, he was sorry. He refused to turn this around to him—but, damn it!—he *couldn't* lose her! She closed her eyes, fresh tears squeezing free. David drew in a long breath and sat back on his calves, dropping his head into her lap. He held her hands in his, resting his forehead on their joined fingers.

"I'm sorry." He raised his head and sniffed, not surprised or ashamed of the tears burning in his own eyes. "But, sweetheart..." David shook his head, not knowing what else to say. He couldn't promise her she wouldn't lose Jake. He didn't know. He rose on his knees again to be eye level with her, taking her face in his palms. "I can't just let you go. I can't."

"Do you think this is *easy* for me?" she cried. "This is *killing* me!"

"I know. I know." David rose on his knees and urged her toward him so he could kiss her brow. She leaned into his lips, her body trembling. "I know, sweetheart." He squeezed his eyes shut, tamping down the raw panic in the back of his throat—and that's what it was—panic at the thought of losing her.

He leaned back but didn't take his hands from her face. Her skin was hot and flushed, damp and clammy from her tears. "Okay, listen to me. He said Monday morning?"

She nodded in his hold. "Monday he'll file, but he gave me until tomorrow to decide.'

"Give me until tomorrow."

"To do what?"

"To help you decide." David stood and went to the kitchen where he'd left his phone. He unlocked it and opened his contacts, finding the number for Joe Canning, Attorney at Law. "To give you all the facts and all the truths." He dialed, listening to the ringtone as he returned to the couch. David sat beside her and took her hand, holding it against his leg as he waited for an answer. He didn't bother with the office line, going straight for Joe's house. "All you've heard is what Larry wants you to hear."

"Hello?" answered a woman after three rings.

"Hey, Barbara. It's David Bishop."

"Hi, David," Joe's wife said, the smile in her voice carrying through the phone lines. "Hang on a second, I'll get Joe."

Andi watched him, curiosity digging deep lines between her eyebrows. She swiped at her wet cheeks with her free hand, snuffling. He glanced around to see if there were any tissues within reach, but there weren't and he wasn't ready to let go of her hand quite yet.

"Who are you calling?" she asked, her eyes shifting as she looked at his face.

"Joe Canning. My lawyer."

"David—"

He leaned over and kissed her, finding a small degree of victory in the fact she didn't move away. Her lips were wet and tasted of her tears, and he swore to himself eventually Bonherre would pay for every tear he made her cry. A shuffling sound on the line preceded Joe's booming voice.

"David, how the hell are you? What kind of scrap have you gotten into that you're calling me on a Saturday?"

David attempted a laugh but figured he failed miserably. "No trouble, Joe. But I need some help. It's important."

"Sure. What do you need?"

"The name of the best Family Law lawyer in Los Angeles. For a friend."

Joe laughed. "You'll eventually fill me in on why you need this, right?"

"Sure thing. You're my lawyer, Joe…you know everything."

Another chuckle from Joe. "Why don't you let me make a call? I've got a name in mind, but I don't know if she's taking on any cases right now."

"If she's the best, convince her, Joe," David said with as much weight as he could manage in his tone. "I meant it when I said it's important."

Joe sighed, some of the joviality slipping from his voice. "Okay, David. You want to see her…what…Monday?"

"Today."

"Today? What the hell could be so damn urgent—"

"Today, Joe."

Joe huffed. "Okay. Give me ten minutes. I'll call you back."

David confirmed and hung up. Andi was already shaking her head. "David, I can't fight him on this. He's a lawyer himself, he knows—"

He kissed her, satisfied again that she didn't skitter away like a frightened bird. David kissed her lips, then her cheek, and lifted her hand to kiss her knuckles. Taking a deep breath, he slid off the couch to kneel in front of her again, holding their hands in her lap.

"Listen to me, okay?" She nodded. "Joe isn't going to fool around. When I ask for the best, he's going to give us the best. We're going to talk to her and find out the truth."

"And if the truth is he has a chance…"

David swallowed against the intense lump in his throat and bowed his head. The next words he spoke were probably some of the hardest he ever had to say. "If we talk to her, and she says Larry has a viable chance at taking Jake away from you, I swear to you I will—" Even then, he choked on the words. "I won't be the reason you lose your son. I love you—I love you *both*—too much to let that happen."

"So, your ex says he has grounds to contest custody of your son. The question is…does he?"

Andi took yet another breath to push down the nervous twittering caterpillars in her stomach, licking her lips before she answered. "He says he can because he doesn't like the type of people I have around Jake. The type of people who influence him."

She tightened her hold on David's hand.

"Who specifically?" Attorney Theresa Rodriquez asked, arching one perfectly shaped eyebrow.

"My best friend Maggie Connelly," Andi said, clearing her throat. "She's also my agent. And David."

Theresa's eyes shifted from Andi to David and back to Andi. "I'm going to ask you a bunch of questions. You're probably not going to like them, but it's better I ask and know the answer than not in hopes of protecting your feelings."

Andi nodded. She dared a glance at David and found him watching her. When their gazes connected, he smiled just a little and his hand squeezed hers.

"I'm going to want to talk to Ms. Connelly. You two live together, correct?"

"We own a home together."

Theresa arched an eyebrow. "Is this a sexual relationship?"

Andi almost protested, but realized these were the types of questions Theresa said she had to ask. And they would probably get much worse from Lawrence, especially if he represented himself. *If* it went that far. "No. Never. Maggie and I are best friends, and she supported me when I left Lawrence. It started with Jake and me staying with her, and eventually, we decided nothing needed to change. Except for buying a bigger house. But, no…Maggie and I are not…" She shook her head, leaving the last of the statement unsaid.

"You consider her a positive influence on your son." It was a statement, not a question.

"Without a doubt. She loves him as if he were her own."

"Does she make any lifestyle choices your husband or the court might find unsavory?" When Andi didn't answer right away, Theresa qualified. "Does she drink to excess? Does she use drugs? Is she promiscuous? Does she have a criminal record?"

Andi shook her head. "No."

"What about her past? Anything in her past that might be brought up?"

Andi sighed, lowering her eyes as she thought. The truth of it was she knew very little about Maggie before they became friends. Maggie tended to hold her past close to her chest, and if it came up, she blew it off saying 'The past is the past'. Andi said as much to Theresa, adding, "She's a widow. She was married in her twenties, and her husband died after just a couple of years. I don't know how. It's one of the things she doesn't like to talk about."

Theresa nodded and hummed, making a note on her legal pad. "The two of you…you're involved?" she asked, only glancing at them over the rim of her glasses.

"Yes," David answered this time.

Her response was just a small sound in the back of her throat. "Serious, I take it."

Andi opened her lips but no sound came out. David answered instead. "Absolutely." He lifted Andi's hand enough to kiss her knuckles, but kept his attention on the attorney who had come into Los Angeles at the request of Joe Canning just to talk with them. Joe said Theresa was the best Family Law attorney in the county, and during the drive there, David told her he'd never had any reason to doubt Joe's word or advice.

When Theresa raised her head, she looked directly at David. "You're going to be more of a challenge, Mr. Bishop. If this goes to trial and character is brought into question, we're going to have to be completely honest with the court. The judge is going to have a perception of you—whether it be true or not—based on what he or she has read or seen about you, and how much weight they give entertainment news reporting. If we put everything out there from the get-go, with complete honesty, they're more likely to accept what we say. Whereas if we wait for them to dig out the skeletons, they're going to wonder what else we're hiding."

David nodded. Andi watched his profile and caught the almost indiscernible tensing of his jaw. His thumb stroked a constant rhythm across her knuckles. "What do you want to know?"

"You tell me," Theresa said with a shrug. "I could rattle off all the things I can remember, and we can put them in the true or false column, but that'll take awhile. What are your skeletons?"

David shifted, tugging his jeans down his thighs before he lifted one leg and rested his ankle on the opposite knee. He rubbed the fingers of his free hand across his lips, clearing his throat. Andi held her breath. She hadn't thought about the man he had once been, because that wasn't the man she knew. The man she knew was considerate, affectionate, and kind, and he loved her.

"David respects women and likes kids, whereas my ex has no use for his son, treats all women as whores, and lives to grind us beneath his heels," Andi said, watching David. He smiled, a quick tug of his lips, but he didn't look at her. Andi drew in a slow breath and released it, looking to Theresa. "Who do you think is the better influence?"

"I'm not the one you need to convince, Andi."

"I'm a recovered alcoholic," David said abruptly, halting anything Andi might have said in reply to Theresa. He flicked his gaze in Andi's direction for only a brief second and cleared his throat again. "Over seven years."

Theresa hummed and wrote, seemingly unsurprised by his revelation. "Do you still have a sponsor?"

"We exchange Christmas cards these days, that's about it."

"You say recovered, not recovering…you consider it behind you?"

"Absolutely."

Theresa quirked a smile. "You say that a great deal, Mr. Bishop."

"Only when I'm without a doubt."

She nodded. "Good. We want that kind of conviction. Anything else? Drug use?"

"Not since I was twenty-two. It wasn't a problem, more recreational. I preferred alcohol." His voice was flat and emotionless, he could have been reading off a grocery list. But each time he paused, Andi caught the clenching of his jaw.

"Arrests?"

David released a slow breath and almost let go of her hand, but Andi tightened her hold, refusing to let him. He looked at her, and she dipped her chin with a small smile. This was all new information to her, but she wanted him to see it didn't matter. Yes, she'd read some things about him online, but she hadn't dug in deep. She hadn't gone far enough to know any of this.

He cleared his throat again. "One DUI when I was twenty-four. That's it."

"Did you enter rehab afterward?" Teresa said, glancing back at her notes.

"Yeah."

"Didn't take much to make you change your ways."

"With a mother like mine, the straight and narrow tends to be pretty straight and narrow. I strayed too far, and she slapped me back in line."

Theresa nodded. "So, nothing since then? Not even a parking ticket?"

David chuckled. "I didn't say that…"

She grinned, setting her pencil down. "I got all this information from public records before you got here, I just wanted to make sure you were being honest with me."

They hashed out everyone's dirty little secrets for the next hour. Beyond her divorce, and her chosen profession, Andi didn't seem to have any marks against her that raised Theresa's flags. They talked about Lawrence, specifically the multiple affairs and the reason for the divorce. When Andi filed for divorce on the grounds of adultery, Lawrence hadn't contested and hadn't denied the claim. Theresa explained that might work in their favor and made more notes. By the time they were done, she had five or six pages of notes jotted down.

"Let's revisit the past with you, David," she said, shifting in her chair to face him. "In cases like this, where Bonherre is using a former spouse's current lover as grounds to claim custody, I've seen the petitioning spouse drag up said lover's past relationships in an attempt at finding dirt. Do you think any of your past relationships could come to bear here?"

David swallowed, jerking his head. "No. Other than casual dating, I've only been with two women who could…*comment*," he added with a wry quirk of his mouth. "One was and is still one of my best friends, Rachel Leighton. She's been in Milan until recently. The other is Josie Connors. We split well over a year ago."

Theresa arched her eyebrows. "As I recall, the events leading to the break-up have never been discussed in a public forum."

"We want to keep it that way." His voice was firm, without question. Andi watched him, realizing with surprise her heart pounded…wondering…waiting. They'd never talked about Josie, although he'd talked about Rachel more than once, and always with a smile. The same kind of smile he had when he talked about his sisters.

"I'm not the public forum," Theresa said with as much authority.

David's mouth twitched like he fought a frown, and he sighed. He looked to Andi when he answered, not Theresa. "I left when she slept with her co-star."

"So, Bonherre doesn't like David…why?" Theresa asked, apparently satisfied with David's answers.

"He gave a list of reasons. All just…prejudices," Andi said with a shake of her head and a shrug. "He believes anyone associated with Hollywood must be morally corrupt deviants. And he won't have his son exposed to that. And…" Lawrence's last complaint stuck in her throat, and she realized of all the reasons he gave, his final blow was the one she found most offensive.

"And…" Theresa urged.

Andi shifted her hand within David's hold, weaving her fingers between his, and met his curious gaze. "David is Jewish," she finally said, embarrassed by the rough scrape of her voice. "Larry has a problem with it. He didn't *explain* why he has a problem, but he said it like it was…a disease or something."

"So, we add anti-Semitism to the list." Theresa added a note to the third page in her pile. It amazed Andi how unaffected Theresa seemed by most of what they said. She must have seen and heard some horrible things as a family lawyer to think nothing of their ever-unfolding drama. She raised her head with a sigh. Theresa met Andi's eyes, holding her gaze for several heartbeats before asking the next question. "Did Bonherre ever physically abuse you?"

"No—"

"Andi," David said softly, stopping her rote answer.

Theresa looked between them. "Speak."

Andi swallowed and slowly pulled her hand free from David's. He wanted her to tell Theresa about the confrontation the day before, but she could do better than that. Except David hadn't seen the evidence yet. He watched her, a hard line digging into his brow, as she pushed the loose sleeve of her sweater up her arm, exposing her elbow and the dark bruise wrapped around her arm just above it. The clear impression of four fingers and a thumb met above the bend.

"Damn it," David cursed, cupping her elbow gently as he twisted to get a better look. He shot her a sharp look, but she knew it wasn't for her as much as for the man who wasn't there. "When did he do *this*?"

"In the house. Before…"

David pulled back and scrubbed his hands over his face, groaning into his palms. Theresa opened her desk drawer and took out a digital camera, coming around the desk. She motioned for Andi to stand, and took several pictures of the bruises from different angles, asking Andi about the events of the previous day.

"So, this was the first time he's been physically violent?" she asked, returning to her desk.

Andi sat, and David immediately reached for her hand again. His jaw was still set firm, that same deep line digging into his brow.

"Violent, yes. He grabbed me once before, a few weeks ago, but it wasn't rough and he let go as soon as I said to get his hands off me."

"Did you report what happened yesterday to the police?"

Andi swallowed and bowed her head, realizing now how stupid she'd been to say nothing. She'd hoped—obviously in error—he'd just go back to Chicago.

"Well, that makes things tougher. I don't know how to play that quite yet."

Andi nodded, stealing another glance at David. His knee bounced in a frustrated rhythm and he ran his fingers across his brow. Tension emanated around him like a force field. Andi swallowed, looked down at their joined hands, and then looked to Theresa again.

"Okay, so you said he claims he'll file on Monday if you don't break up this little affair of the heart," Theresa said, motioning between Andi and David with the eraser end of her pencil. Andi nodded, the lump of fear she'd managed to swallow for two hours choking her again with a vengeance. "This is going to play one of two ways. First, you call his bluff and he backs down. If he has half a brain, that's exactly what he'll do. He'll concede defeat and go back to Chicago, and you'll have to put up with him on the random holiday. Second, you call his bluff and he goes through with the filing."

"What happens then?" Andi managed to whisper.

"Then he makes a damn fool of himself in front of the court."

"He told me—"

"He's blowing smoke," Theresa said, cutting her off. "He's making a power play, trying to make you think he can do whatever the hell he wants because he's got *esquire* after his name. The truth of it is this is *LA*, and in *LA* we eat little minnow attorneys like him for a mid-afternoon snack." Theresa sat back, popping her feet on the edge of the desk. "Truth be known, I hope he does. I'd love to see the look on his face when the judge gives him a solid dressing down."

"So, what you're saying is he hasn't got a snowball's chance in hell…" David leaned forward in his chair.

"That's what I'm saying. He can huff and he can puff, but he's not going to blow your pretty little house down unless you hand him the matches and jug of gasoline."

"And if I don't call his bluff?"

Andi's question snapped David's attention to her, but she didn't dare look at him. Her insides waged a battle between bubbly ecstasy and unbelieving dread.

"You do what he says, you mean?" Theresa tipped her head to the side and made a dismissive face. "Then he's got you by the back pockets until your son turns eighteen."

A new thought hit her, but to ask it she had to pull her hand free of

David's. "You said the question of character might be brought up. Ultimately this is about Jake."

"Yeah," Theresa said with a nod.

"Will Jake have to testify or give his opinion or anything?"

"Are you worried about what he'll say?" Theresa sat up, picking up her pencil again.

"I just don't want him to be involved unless he has to be."

"The judge may ask him what he wants…who he wants to be with. Do you think he'd say he wants to be with his father?"

"No," Andi answered with unwavering conviction. "There's no doubt in my mind."

"We'd try to keep him out of it," she said, tapping her pencil against the pad. "But, he's of an age the judge would value his opinion if he feels he needs convincing one way or another."

Andi clenched her hands in her lap and pressed her lips together to fight the panic. Theresa stood, holding her hand out to each of them. As she shook Andi's hand, she held it for a moment longer. "You tell me what you want to do, and I'll take care of the rest. If you call his bluff, make sure you hand him my card when you do it."

Andi nodded and took the proffered cards, tucking them into her purse. They left the office, walking through the silent and dark building to the bank of elevators. Theresa had agreed to meet them at her office, and since it was Saturday afternoon, the building was almost completely empty otherwise. Only the lights in the hall closest to the exterior doors of *Rodriguez, Santovalle & Smith – Attorneys at Law* were lit. Moving away from the elevators, the stretch of hallway dimmed into darkness.

Once she'd let go of his hand in the office, David hadn't tried to take it again. A tense muscle jerked along his cheek and his lips formed a straight line. He only took his hands from his pockets to push the button for the elevator.

Andi's insides shook, but she knew her decision. Once Theresa had laid everything out, there was no doubt in her mind. The doors opened and they stepped inside. Not until the doors closed again could Andi take a breath. David remained silent, and she knew her question had hurt him—or angered him—or both, because she knew what he wanted to hear. What he wanted her to do.

The elevator gave a small jerk when it began its descent, and David leaned back against the handrail defining the perimeter of the cabin. He had his head down, jaw muscle twitching. Andi couldn't control the small tremors in her hand when she reached for him, using both her hands to pull his free from his pocket. He didn't resist, and when she stepped close to him, he curled his fingers around hers to hold them against his chest. His long breath stirred her hair.

Andi swallowed, raised her head, and looked into his face. A deep line dug into his forehead between his eyes—not quite a scowl, but evidence of the thoughts she knew had to be running through his mind. She almost couldn't breathe correctly, each breath a ragged jerk in her lungs. She was terrified to make the decision, and could only pray it was the right one.

"I'm sorry," she said softly.

David closed his eyes and dropped his head forward until his brow rested against hers. He released her hand and brought his palms up to stroke her hair and touch her cheeks, his eyes slit closed. Andi blinked against hot tears when he whispered a curse before wrapping his arms around her and pulling her so hard against him her breath caught.

"I had to make sure," she said against his shoulder, holding on. Another ragged breath shifted through him and she felt it when she pressed her hands against his back. David nodded into her neck. "But now I know."

Andi pulled back, and at first, he fought against releasing her, but finally let her shift enough that she could see his face. She touched his cheek and he turned into the contact.

"I won't let him win."

David's eyes snapped open, and the sheen clouding them jerked at her heart. "What?"

She shook her head. "I won't let him win. I won't kowtow to him anymore. I refuse to let him destroy my chance at..." She smiled. "At something so much better than I ever—"

She never finished the thought. Andi reached for him the same instant he reached for her, and the hard kiss stole her breath. David wrapped his arms almost completely around her, nearly lifting her toes off the ground with the intensity of the embrace. He twisted them, putting her back to the wall, and shifted to take her face in his hands.

"I love you," he whispered against her mouth before kissing her again. "I love you."

Only the gentle jerk of the elevator and the ding of the opening doors stopped them.

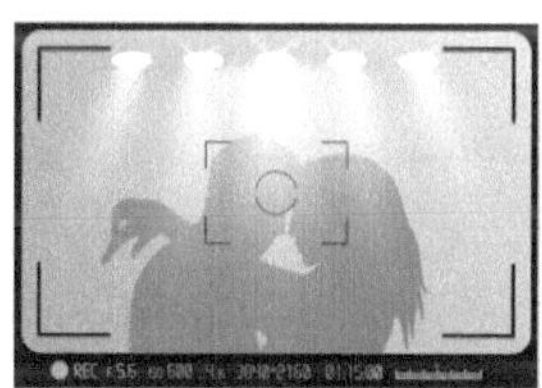

CHAPTER EIGHTEEN

"*Y*ou're amazing, and I want to know just how amazing. And you're ten kinds of sexy. I think the better question is why *wouldn't* I want to be with you.*"*

Andi glanced sideways across the cab of David's car, using her sunglasses to her advantage to watch him drive. Desert hills flashed by past his profile, but they were a blur. She studied him…the line of his jaw sprinkled whiskers too long to have been shaved this morning. Perhaps he hadn't bothered after returning to his house. She shifted her gaze over the firm set of his lips and the ridge of his brow over his sunglasses. He was beautifully made. She almost smiled, but suppressed it because it might give her away.

He tilted his head, checking his mirrors to pull around a car in front of them, and she watched the way the muscles along his neck flexed with the action, and the way his throat moved when he swallowed. He had on a dark shirt, and it made her think of the tee shirt he'd worn that day in her trailer when he'd asked her to go to dinner. When he'd told her he wanted to be with her.

Andi drew in a long, slow breath so she wouldn't draw his attention. On a day like today, she was glad he was a silent driver focused on the road. It gave her the chance to think.

This was the car he'd driven when they went to dinner. The car he'd walked her to with the energy around them so intense it'd practically sparked a mid-summer wildfire. A thousand butterflies took flight low in her stomach as she remembered that evening in exquisite detail.

David leaned into her, his hips pressing hers back into the car and she let her hands shift from his sides to his back beneath the jacket. It fell open further and he stood so close the warmth trapped inside warmed her arms. Andi couldn't catch her breath, and knew her heart pounded so hard he had to see the jump of her pulse at the base of her throat. He bent his neck and the tip of his nose brushed the side of her neck, his breath hot on her chilled skin.

"Andi..."

The word reverberated against her and his lips brushed her skin when he said her name, his voice rough like gravel and honey. Her fingers curled impulsively into his shirt and she moaned low in her throat. Her knees lique-fied and she slumped back against the car, but his arms came around her as his mouth pressed to the bend where her shoulder met her neck.

His mouth on her skin wasn't enough and she pulled at his shirt, bringing him closer and at the same time pulling away from him to find his mouth with hers. Then he was kissing her so deep the only thing she could do was open her lips to him and kiss back with the same need and intensity. His hands held her head, cushioning her against the edge of the car.

She couldn't touch him enough, couldn't pull him close enough, couldn't feel enough of him and when his hips pushed hard against her, she groaned into his mouth and the pitch of the kiss amped up another degree. One hand cupped her head, his fingers laced into her hair, and the other slid down her body to her waist and around to the small of her back, yanking her hard against him.

Andi wanted...that was all her mind could process. She wanted more... wanted to have him closer, wanted to kiss him deeper, wanted to taste him and breathe him and feel him.

"Are you plotting?"

David's question snapped Andi out of her thoughts and she jumped. He chuckled, shifting his attention only momentarily from the road to look in her direction. Or, she assumed he looked in her direction since he had on sunglasses just like her.

"Kind of," she answered.

"New book?"

Andi smiled. "Maybe the best love story ever told."

"Science Fiction?"

"Well, the whole plot is pretty implausible." His eyebrows quirked, and she imagined his expression of interest behind the glasses. Andi smiled, enjoying the sense of calm that had settled over her since talking to Theresa and the sense of warmth that had wrapped around her since they left the attorney's office. She was still afraid, but it no longer smothered her and stole her ability to breathe, think, or live.

She shifted so she was partially turned toward him, her back against the door, and drew up her left leg to set her foot on the edge of the seat. The car was compact inside, but because of the low profile, it made it easy to practically fold herself up in the seat. *Not so practical for midnight make-out sessions.*

David's lips quirked up in a grin. "Must be a good story. Based on that smile."

She let it spread and pulled her lower lip through her teeth. "I'll let you know how it turns out."

David took his hand from the steering wheel and curled it around her raised knee, his thumb stroking the denim. Warmth spread from the touch and Andi inhaled. She laid her head on the back of the seat, no longer trying to hide the fact she watched him. She ran her fingertips along his bare forearm, enjoying the feel of tiny, crinkly hairs beneath her fingertips.

"Do you want to go eat? We could swing over to—"

"No," she answered, gently cutting off his suggestion. "Let's just..." Andi drew a breath. "Let's just go back to your house. I'll call Maggie and tell her what's going on. I'm just not hungry right now."

David nodded, his fingers squeezing her knee gently. They fell into silence again as he navigated the city highways. It wouldn't take long to get back to his house since it was barely on the outskirts of Los Angeles, but the Saturday afternoon traffic was thick enough to slow them down. Andi let her mind drift again in the companionable silence. Driving from David's house to the lawyer's had been in a strained silence, with Andi fighting just to breathe. Now, she was more angry than anything else. Angry at Lawrence for—even for a few hours—convincing her he had the power to take away her happiness. Angry at herself for letting him.

She didn't realize she'd reached out to touch David until her fingertips slipped through the shorter hair behind his ear and he turned. He just smiled and went back to his driving. For just the briefest moment, Andi's thoughts flashed back to the early years of her marriage to Lawrence. When they first married, he was affectionate within the walls of their apartment. Outside, he said it was inappropriate and once actually scolded her in the hallway of a business associate's home because she'd reached for his hand. As time went on, she learned to keep her hands to herself. It was difficult at first because, despite his coldness, she had loved him and wanted his nearness. She told herself he was right and she had to learn to school her actions. As time went on, touching Lawrence never crossed her mind.

Now, the thought of *ever* touching Lawrence Bonherre left a bitter taste in her mouth. Andi focused instead on the man beside her...a man who had never once moved away from her touch.

"I want to be with you, Andi. Just with you. Around you. Near you. I want to touch you all the time. I want to hold your hand. I want to feel your skin. I want..."

The smile David gave her curled heat in her stomach, and at that moment she wanted to kiss him more than she'd ever wanted to kiss him. Just the thought of his arms around her and his lips on hers made her breath catch and her skin flush. She glanced out the car windows to determine where they were. He'd gotten on the 405 without her noticing, but it took her a few moments to figure out just how far they were from Mulholland. The way her blood skimmed beneath her skin, it wouldn't be soon enough.

By the time he pulled through the security gates at his home and parked the car, Andi had plotted half a dozen ways to kiss him between the car and the front door. After that, she was pretty much open to any surface he chose. She could almost hear Mags in her head. *"You've turned into a hussy! I'm so proud."* Andi curled her lips between her teeth to hide her snicker.

David parked the car in the wide driveway, not bothering to put it back in the garage. He turned it off and pulled the keys, turning with his lips open as if ready to say something. Instead, a synthesized rendition of *Hello, Dolly* filled the small space and whatever David intended to say disappeared on a huff. He opened the door and climbed out of the car, snagging his phone from the console cup holder.

"Hi, Ma."

Andi opened her door as he came around to her side. He offered his free hand and helped her from the car, smiling at her as he held the phone to his ear. He nodded his head, humming in affirmation to whatever his mother might be saying on the other end.

"Ma, I told you I'd talk to her."

Andi tilted her head and he winked at her, drawing her against him with his free arm to place a kiss on her forehead. Not what she wanted, but it was a start. David huffed, a sound intended to sound exasperated but it was laced too strongly with his smile to be convincing.

"Okay, Ma. Okay." He tilted the phone beneath his chin so his mother could hear him, but he wasn't speaking directly into it. "I know it's a good month away, but my mother wants us to go there for Thanksgiving. Maybe stay until the weekend. I told her we'd have to talk about it but *she's being pushy*." He said the last directly into the phone, but again any edge to his voice was lost in his grin.

Andi smiled, chuckling softly at the easy teasing she'd seen before when David talked to his mother. She hadn't met Dolores Masters yet, but based on her children, Andi already imagined she would like the woman. "I…I think so. I mean—" The words 'I don't know what Lawrence will want' stuck in her throat.

David nodded and shifted to take her hand, leading her toward the house. "We're going to work on it." Pause. "Ma, that's all I can say. We don't know."

He let go of her hand to dig out his keys and unlock the house door, pushing it open to let Andi enter first. The house was still, the light subdued with the blinds partially shut in the huge living room that encompassed three-quarters of the main level. Andi understood the concept of the house but hadn't been any further than the main level. Most often, David preferred coming to her house in Santa Clarita. He'd never explained why or said as much, but whenever plans were made he wanted to be there instead of his house in Hollywood. The house was several decades old and spoke of Classic Hollywood from the outside despite its unique architecture. The inside was more modern, bright, and clean but still with the Mid-Century Modern style. The kitchen ran along the back of the house, with doorways entering it from the open living room space. To the left of the kitchen area was an open staircase leading downward to the bedroom levels. He'd told her briefly once the lower level was divided. Half was set up with two guest bedrooms and bathrooms with another sitting area. The other half was his bedroom. A second staircase in the opposite back corner of the house—not readily visible from the front door—led to the master bedroom.

David was still talking to his mother as he shut the house door. He motioned toward the kitchen and tipped his hand to his mouth, asking her if she wanted a drink. She shook her head, smiling as he walked to the desk along one wall.

"I'm trying to find it, Ma. Hang on."

Andi smiled, remembering the evening she eavesdropped on him talking to his mother in his driveway. *Yes, Ma. She's a nice girl. A very nice girl. And beautiful.*"

Andi leaned against the back of his couch and tried not to dwell on earlier that day. She'd come here with such resolve—and such a broken heart. In hindsight, she had panicked at Lawrence's threats. She'd let him once again intimidate and manipulate her.

She curled her fingers into the couch back. Never again.

"I can't find it. I think it's downstairs." David looked over his shoulder at her and pointed toward the stairs. "I'll be right back, sweetheart."

She nodded and watched him go. His conversation with his mother continued until his voice faded down the staircase. Andi strolled around the open space, letting her fingertips run along the back of the couch and along the edge of photographs he had on display along the fireplace ledge. Pictures of his family—his mother, his sisters, his two nieces now Caroline had given birth a few weeks before—some together, some individual. Some he was in, some she thought perhaps he was the photographer. She stopped at the window and looked back at the couch. Her body flushed hot again when she remembered an evening here, just a few weeks before, when their kissing and cuddling had accelerated so fast they might very well have made love right there on the couch. Clothes hadn't come off, but David's warm, gentle, and strong hands were inside her sweater and had caressed her body until she had been ready to scream.

That night, it hadn't been David who stopped them. That night it had been her.

She remembered now the cold panic that had cut through the languid heat his touch had created. She hadn't asked him to stop, but David had stilled over her, and she knew the tension in her body had said more than anything she might have said. He'd apologized...he'd actually *apologized*...for letting it go too far. Andi had been angry then, and she was angry now because she knew the real reason.

No matter how much she fought it and wanted to deny it, Lawrence Bonherre had infiltrated every aspect of her life. Even down to her relationship with the man she loved...a man she wanted to be with forever. In every way.

"Having sex with you is like screwing a rag doll!"

"...how long do you think a man like David Bishop will stay once he takes you to bed?"

"If you couldn't keep me, what makes you think Bishop will settle when there's so much more satisfying fish in the sea? You're just a convenient diversion."

Lawrence's words buzzed in her head every time she came close to that final step of intimacy with David. She wanted to be with him, not just to relieve some primitive itch, but because she loved him. Just like he'd told her more than once—she craved David's touch. She craved being near him and with him and beside him, and just...part of his life. She loved he knew Jake got an A on his last science project, and he had been the one to help Jake make a 3D model of an ocean ecosystem. She loved that when he looked at her, he always smiled. She loved that he wanted to do things right...forever.

She loved he fought for her.

She loved she knew he would have done anything to keep her son with her.

And she loved him because nestled amongst all the photos of his family was a new photo. David sat with his arms extended on either side of him, with Andi on one side and Jake on the other. It was on her couch at home, and she now vaguely remembered Maggie taking the picture. He must have asked for it from her. Andi blinked and smiled.

She loved him for loving them.

Andi touched the photo, then walked with purpose across the living room to the camouflaged staircase he'd disappeared down minutes before. Taking a deep breath, Andi took the first step.

His voice was distant, so she didn't expect to find him when she reached the bedroom. The stairs opened directly into the room and she recognized parts of it from the webcam conversation they'd had weeks before while he recovered from his on-set accident. The bed sat against the interior wall, made but not meticulously so, with pillows tossed haphazardly against the padded headboard. She stopped one step short of reaching the floor, which was a light bamboo just like upstairs with a large rug in rich brown rolled out beneath and around the bed. To her left was a sliding door that opened onto a large patio with an amazing view of Hollywood. The sun had begun to set, daylight just dim enough to let her see the lights of the city.

Ahead of her was a wall with built-in bureau storage spanning half the length, with a large mirror set up in the center. To the left appeared to be the entrance to an open bathroom with a partial glass-block wall. The right end of the built-ins had a desk where David crouched with his phone wedged between his ear and shoulder while he shuffled through one of the desk's file drawers.

"Okay, here it is," he said, pulling something from the desk as he straightened his head and held the phone properly. He stood and bent over his desk, reading whatever paperwork he'd just found. Andi couldn't help but admire the view. He rattled off a number. "Caroline can just reference that number when she calls. They'll tell her. Right. Okay, I'll talk to you later. Love you, too."

He turned as he hung up the phone, and Andi knew the moment he saw her because he immediately smiled. "Hey. Sorry about that."

"Everything okay?"

David tossed his phone on the bed as he passed the corner. "Yeah. I opened a college savings plan for Abigail, and Caroline wanted to get some information. Are *you* okay?" he asked.

"I am now," she said with a firm nod. "I was scared before—I still am—but I'm not *running* scared."

"Did you call Maggie?"

"Not yet. I will. In a little while." Andi smiled, leaning her hip against the stair railing. "I love how much you care about your family."

David crossed the room to stand at the foot of the stairs, resting his hands on each rail. Standing on the bottom step, she was slightly taller than him and he tipped his head back to look at her. He smiled, the slow sexy smile she loved that always tugged up one corner of his mouth and then the other. David leaned into her so his chest brushed her stomach, and Andi raised her hands to run her nails through the hair at his temples.

"Is that the only thing you love about me?" he asked with a grin. David turned into her touch, kissing the heel of her hand.

"Well, it doesn't hurt you're desired by women all over the world," she said with the most serious expression she could muster...given the position and circumstance. Which wasn't all that serious, she figured. She slid her fingertips from his temples down the side of his neck until she could toy with his collar. "It's quite the rush to my ego, you know, that you're here with *me*. Can't help but love that."

David chuckled, one of his hands sliding around her hips to pull her against him. His chin was level with her breasts, and despite the cooler weather, Andi wished right now she were in one of the lighter, thinner sundresses he preferred. Partially because she wanted less between her body and his—tempt fate a little, as he liked to say—and partially because her skin was so hot and flushed her sweater smothered her.

"Well, you know..." His hand slipped beneath the hem of her sweater just enough to brush the skin at the small of her back. She nearly groaned. "I consider myself pretty lucky. I've got the hottest novelist on the planet in my arms."

"And in your bedroom..." she whispered. Any louder, and she knew her voice would crack.

David stepped closer, tipping his head back to look up into her face. His hand slid further beneath her sweater until his palm pressed hot against her spine. "Trust me," he said, his breath skimming over her chin. "That fact didn't escape me."

Andi drew in a long, deep breath intended to force down the quaking nervousness in her chest…but she found the nervousness was gone. Why should she be nervous? What did she have to fear? Nothing…this was David. He wasn't David Bishop—movie actor. He wasn't David Bishop—the object of women's fantasies. He was David…*her* David. She took the final step, and he stood so close the motion brought her flush against him. Andi slid her fingers through his short hair and drew him down to her. He didn't hesitate, his mouth covering hers in the kiss she'd been thinking about for the last hour.

David's free hand moved to her face, holding her jaw as he angled his lips and deepened the kiss. His tongue slipped into her mouth, and Andi groaned at the shock of sensation and heat that filled her from her nose to her toes. Not once, not *ever*, did she feel this kind of all-consuming hunger when Lawrence Butthead touched her or kissed her. Not the first time, not any time.

Andi gave any thought of Lawrence a hard mental shove and punctuated the thought by sliding her hands down David's chest to the first button of his shirt. She'd reached the third before he stopped kissing her, still holding her chin as his rapid breath warmed her skin. Andi looked up at him but didn't pause working the buttons.

David looked down, watching the progress of her fingers releasing each button until she reached his waist where the tails of the shirt were tucked into his pants. "Andi…" Her name was rough and ragged as he raised his eyes again to look at her.

Andi gave the shirt a solid tug, pulling it free from the belted pants. With the front open, she indulged in something she'd wanted to do for a very, *very* long time. She ran her palms over his stomach—soaring on the rush of empowerment when his abdominal muscles tightened in reaction to her touch—before sliding her hands up his chest to his shoulders. Her fingertip caught the simple chain around his neck, shifting the Star of David he always wore when not filming. Andi pushed the shirt away until it slipped down his arms. He stood still, his eyes closed and his head bowed so his nose brushed her hair as she released the shirt from his wrists. It dropped to the floor with a whisper.

Seeing him bare to the waist on webcam, or even on film, was nothing compared to the toned, solid, heat-radiating body beneath her touch. Andi's insides shook as the old panic tried to surge forward, but despite the tremors in her hands, she refused to let it win. She raised her arms to skim her hands along his shoulders to his neck. Andi brushed her cheek and nose against his skin, loving the warmth and the scent of his body. David wrapped her in his arms, his fingers curling tight into her sweater to pull her closer.

With her cheek skimming his skin, Andi reached around behind her back until she covered his hands with her own. Tipping her head so their gazes met, Andi guided his hands along her sides until he took over sliding the sweater up her body. She raised her arms, her ribs aching with each rapid breath. David tugged the sweater free, tossing it on the stairs behind her. He brought his hands back to her raised wrists and moved his palms down her bare arms, along her sides, until his large hands spanned her ribcage.

He bent his head and brushed his lips over her shoulders, nipping gently at the flushed skin at the base of her throat. His fingers curled into the strap of her bra, tugging it slightly until it slid off her shoulder. "David," she whispered, the heat of her breath coming back to her as she spoke against his skin.

She raised her head and looked into his face. His breath came in ragged, short bursts and his gaze shifted over her face. His attention settled for only a moment on her lips before he looked into her eyes again.

Andi smiled.

His only response was a low, rough growl from somewhere in the center of his chest before his arms wrapped around her hard enough to lift her off the floor, and he spun them toward the bed.

The muffled sound of Meredith Brooks singing nudged David from his deep sleep.

I'm a child. I'm a mother. I'm a sinner. I'm a saint...

He blinked his eyes open, trying to focus in the semi-darkness of his bedroom, the only light coming from the moon through the patio doors and the glow of a light he'd left on in the bathroom. The faint music stopped.

By then, David was awake and smiling.

Lying beside him, curled into his chest, Andi slept. Her cheek warmed a spot over his heart and her hair brushed against his chin, filling his senses with the scent of her shampoo. He raised his head off the pillow enough to take in the sight of their bodies tangled together in his bed. The sheet covered Andi's body, except for her bare legs that stuck out, one draped across his thighs. She had a fistful of sheets in her hand tucked beneath her chin. Moonlight glowed off her bare arms and shoulders.

Before he could enjoy the reality of the moment, *Bitch* started again and he squinted at the clock beside the bed. Eleven thirty-seven. Just as the music stopped, his brain engaged enough for him to remember to whom that particular ringtone belonged.

Maggie.

Reluctant to leave her, David tried to ease himself away from Andi until she released a long, shuddered sigh and rolled away. The sound of her skin against the sheets had to be one of the most erotic sounds he'd ever heard.

No, he took that back. The most erotic sound was the one she made when he—

His house phone rang. David stumbled away from the bed, snatching up the phone before it had a chance to ring a second time and wake Andi. "Hello," he said as he stumbled in the semi-darkness to the adjacent sitting area, yanking on a pair of pajama pants as he went.

"About damn time," Maggie Connelly shouted so loud he had to take the phone from his ear. "I've been calling Andi's cell phone for an hour. You damn well better tell me she's with you and she's okay or I'm launching a manhunt on Larry Bonherre's ass—"

"She's with me, Maggie," he interrupted. "Her phone is probably upstairs. I'm sorry. I know she meant to call."

"What the hell is going on?" For the first time, he thought he heard the crack in Maggie's voice. "Is she okay?"

"Yeah, she's okay. Now. I hope, anyway." David glanced around the staircase to make sure she hadn't been woken. She was stretched out on her stomach, the sheet down to her hips. *She was the most beautiful woman he'd ever seen…*

"Now?"

David blinked and focused on the conversation, and the strain in Maggie's voice. Full of snark and sarcasm, it wasn't often David had seen anything get to Maggie enough to chip at her veneer. He sank onto one of the chairs he had facing another sliding door. "Maggie, she's okay," he said, doing his best to say with his tone he meant it. He took a deep breath and pinched the bridge of his nose. "She didn't tell you what happened." It wasn't a question.

"No," Maggie ground out, and he could almost imagine her clenching her teeth to keep from shouting…or keep Jake from hearing. "She flew out of here when I got home from lunch, wouldn't tell me what was wrong or where she was going, and I haven't heard a word since. *Probably* because she knew *whatever* it was, I wasn't going to like it." There was only a moment of pause. "So, you're the lucky one who gets to tell me, boyo. Where did she go?"

Her tone brokered no argument. "She came here." He paused, for a second the sick panic he'd squashed that afternoon hit him full force in the chest. Then he looked at his bed, and it eased. "To break it off."

Silence hit the line, and for a moment he thought they'd lost connection.

"Maggie?"

Maggie hummed. "I'm assuming since it's nearly midnight and she's with you, you convinced her otherwise."

David slouched back in his chair, giving him a clear view of his bed and the amazing woman sleeping in it. He smiled. "Yeah," was his simple answer.

"I'm also going to assume since you're whispering, and since you haven't offered to put her on the phone, she's…what…"

"Sleeping," David said, clearing his throat.

"As much as I would love to know more about this—and trust me, boyo, she's going to tell me all about it later—I need to know what had her tearing out of here bent on tossing you out of her life."

"I give you one guess."

Maggie growled. She actually *growled*. "What did Boner do now?"

David relayed the details as much as he knew them, based only on what Andi had told him. The silence on the phone was unnerving, but he had no doubt he was better off *here* and not within one hundred yards of Maggie Connelly. It didn't take long to tell her everything, but he concluded by saying Andi had made her decision.

"Well, that's obvious..." Maggie said with a chuckle.

He knew what she meant, and didn't even try to suppress his smile. Why should he? At the end of the day, Andrea Parker was with him. He'd spend the rest of his life making sure it stayed that way. Lawrence Bonherre Esquire be damned.

"It also explains the cryptic message Bonehead left this afternoon."

David sat up. "What'd he say?"

"Just that he'd be here tomorrow morning, and expected to 'resolve their issues' once and for all," she explained, mocking Bonehead's words.

"Did he say what time?"

"No."

David stood, walked to the edge of the sitting area, and leaned against the corner of the wall to study Andi. He took a deep breath. "We'll be back to the house before Jake gets up. Is he worried?"

"Some. But, he also figured she was with you. And he trusts you."

Her tone was dead on, her point absolutely clear. David nodded, even though he knew she couldn't see him. "He can continue to trust me. You, too."

"I hope so. I'll see you in the morning." Before he hung up, she said his name. "For what it's worth, I'm really happy you *convinced* her otherwise."

"Me, too."

He hung up the phone and padded back into the bedroom. Andi hadn't stirred, and as he stood beside the rumpled bed he took a few minutes to study her in the moonlight. Not even the most talented photographer could have posed her more beautifully or more sexy. She was a study in the female form. Lying on her stomach, she had her bent arms tucked against her side and her golden red curls fanned on the bed. The duvet had slid completely to the floor, leaving only the sheet to cover them. It draped her hips, allowing him to see the curved line of her spine from her shoulder to her gorgeous backside.

David crouched beside the bed. He didn't know what had happened to bring them here, what about the day had released whatever held her back before, and he wasn't sure he dared ask. All he knew was he'd never felt so content in his life. Not 'satisfied', not physically sated. Yes, he was satisfied…and figured Andi would tell him he was quoting a bad novel if he said he'd never felt so complete with any other woman. But, he figured even the corniest lines in a romance novel were based on some grain of truth.

If asked right now, he'd willingly admit he'd found the other half of himself.

Yeah, corny…she'd be proud.

David shifted to his knees and leaned his arms on the bed, watching the slow rise and fall of her body as she took each breath. Eventually, the need to touch her won out, and he reached out a hand to run his knuckles down the sway of her back to the dip of her waist. Her skin was silky-smooth, pale in the moonlight. He traced her spine and leaned in to press a kiss to one of the dimples below the small of her back. Andi drew in a deep breath, shifting slightly beneath the touch. She turned her face toward him, her lips already bowed in a smile. Curls framed her face and fell across her forehead and she looked at him with half-closed eyes.

He rested one arm on the bed, his head on his arm, so they were eye-to-eye and he was close enough she could see him without blur. "Hey, beautiful," he whispered.

She smiled. "Hey. What are you doing out of bed?"

"Phone call." She arched her eyebrows in silent question. "Maggie."

Andi jerked her upper body off the mattress. "Oh, crap!"

"It's okay." He laid his hand on her back, sliding his palm to her shoulder until she relaxed. "She knows you're here and you're okay."

She covered her face with her hand, the shift in position giving him a blood-warming view of her breast pressed against the bed and the subtle ridges of her ribcage along her side, muted by the soft curve of her body. He finally understood the attraction to the artistic nudes when the focus was on the curve and sway of the female body and not on being naked…guess he'd just needed the right model.

"I can't believe I forgot," she groaned. "Was she ticked?"

"Ticked? No. Worried, yes."

"I should call her now."

"You don't need to, I took care of it." David curled his fingers around hers and brought her hand down from her face. Before she could say any more, he kissed her. It only took a heartbeat for her to return the kiss. David rose off his knees to move over her and she rolled beneath him onto her back, wrapping her arms around his neck. With his weight supported on his elbows, David leaned over her, looking into her beautiful eyes.

"I love you," he said as he brushed his lips over hers. "Kind of hard to believe it's been less than twenty-four hours since I wised up and said it."

Her fingers skimmed over his neck and shoulders. "A day of firsts…"

David smiled and kissed her again. "But not lasts. I intend to tell you I love you…" He punctuated the words with a kiss. "And make love to you…" Another longer, deeper kiss. "For a very…" Kiss. "Very…" Kiss. "Long time."

Her hands slid down his back, and with a look of mischief, Andi dug her nails into the cotton pants covering his backside. "I like the sounds of that."

David groaned and stopped talking, letting himself get lost in Andi once again.

CHAPTER NINETEEN

The echoing slam of Lawrence's car door bounced off the exterior of the house as Andi stepped into the driveway, leaving the house door open behind her. The slight squeak of brakes and the less angry open-and-closing of a vehicle door followed. Andi kept walking, forcing herself to keep her arms loose and relaxed at her side. She would let everything about her, right down to her body language, tell Lawrence his threats meant nothing more to her than a nuisance.

"Why the hell are you following me?" Lawrence demanded, his voice carrying to her. "What is this bull? I'll have your job for holding me at the security gate like some damn criminal."

With one final swallow and intake of air, Andi stepped into Lawrence's line of sight. "They held you at my request," she said, using every ounce of willpower she had to keep her voice strong. Lawrence spun on the balls of his feet to face her, his features twisted in an angry grimace. "I told them you weren't allowed near my home without my explicit permission."

"Did you tell them to follow me up here?" he snapped, pointing at the security truck parked behind him.

Tony Espinoza, chief of security for the gated community, stood between the truck and Lawrence's rental. Beside him stood Horatio

Salizar, another long-time security guard for the gated community. Neither smiled, and both stood with their feet apart and their arms crossed over their bodies. Whatever *her* body language said, theirs screamed loud and clear they'd take no crap from Lawrence Bonherre.

"Yes, I did. They're here to make sure you leave."

"And to make sure there's no *problems*," Tony said, his thick borough accent making him sound like an Enforcer for the Godfather.

Andi liked it. She smirked. Just a little.

Lawrence stormed toward her, crossing the distance in three long, angry strides. If he expected her to be intimidated this time, he'd be sorely mistaken. This time, Andi didn't flinch and didn't move when he invaded her personal space. She practically saw the fangs as he spit his venom.

"This is between you and me, Andrea. Tell them to leave."

"No. They leave when you leave. Get over it."

He huffed a breath out through his nostrils, and in her peripheral vision she saw him clench his fists at his side. "Fine. You want to make this difficult, Andrea, we can make this difficult."

"You decided on the game, Lawrence, but I'm changing the rules."

The more she spoke, the stronger she managed to keep her voice. Her insides shook, but she was *done*. Andi had told herself she was strong because she'd left him and left the life he'd destroyed. But, in the last twenty-four hours she'd realized that while she had taken that first step, she hadn't done enough. She hadn't made it painfully clear to her ex-husband that he had no say, no control, and no right to take her happiness.

She was done.

"And you're wrong," she said before he could throw out another demand. "This *isn't* between you and me. You may want it to be *about* you and me, but it's not. It's between you, me, your son, Maggie, David—"

"This right here, right now, is you and me, Andrea. You tell me your choice, and I tell you whether you get to keep your—"

"No!" Her shout, right in his face, made him lean away. His eyebrows arched in surprise, and before he could recover, she plowed forward. Lawrence Bonherre had her '*Irish Up*', as Maggie liked to say, and he wasn't going to walk over her anymore. Andi raised her hand and held Theresa's business card beneath his nose. "You can take your 'choice' and shove it, Lawrence. This is my attorney. All future communications with me will go through *her*."

With a scowl, Lawrence snapped the card from her fingers. The edge cut a shallow line in the side of her finger, but she refused to even wince. Lawrence's attention shifted for a split moment from the card to a point past her. She didn't have to look to know David had come out of the house. The firm tread of his shoes across the cobblestone driveway grew louder by degrees as he approached them.

Lawrence's lips tightened. He snarled and shook his head, looking at her again. When he spoke, his voice was low—intended as a threat, and too low for David to hear. "I have to say, you surprised me, Andrea. I didn't peg you for the selfish bitch—"

"No, just a weak one you could walk all over," she ground out. "Guess you were wrong."

He didn't even pause. "Takes a cold-hearted woman to put her weak libido over her son."

"Takes a *tiny…*" She let the word sit between them for a heartbeat. "man to use his son to intimidate his ex-wife just so he can feel like a big shot. Next time try Viagra."

Crimson red crept from beneath the buttoned collar of Lawrence's shirt, spreading up his neck to his face like spilled wine on a carpet. He huffed several hard breaths, his lips curled together. "That's it, Andrea! I told you, I *warned* you—"

"You *threatened* me."

"Call it whatever the hell you want, but you know what happens now. Tomorrow morning, I file my petition—"

"You might want to revise your paperwork," she said with a smirk, cutting him off again. Their voices echoed off the house now, not a single word camouflaged for the sake of David, Tony, his partner, or probably any neighbor along the street who might be outside right now.

She tried not to look too smug. Okay, no she didn't. She didn't try at all. Andi smirked and took two steps backward, angling her hand slightly behind her. Before her heel hit the pavement on the second step, David's fingers laced through hers. Andi wanted to look at him, just to see his face, but she wouldn't give Lawrence even the smallest satisfaction of her breaking eye contact. She had him like a butterfly on a pin.

"My attorney will be filing a petition for adjustment of custody first thing tomorrow morning. With your recent actions and attitudes, it is our belief Jake would be best served by limited contact with you, and only when supervised."

"You *bitch!*" he screamed. "You can't—"

David's grip tightened on her hand and his body shifted forward, but Andi tugged him back. Not enough Lawrence would see, but enough she hoped David would hear her silent 'Don't let him.'

"Yes, I can. I will." Andi released David's hand to step toward Lawrence again. "Don't ever, *ever* threaten me with my son again. Now…get off my property. You will no longer be granted admittance unless I approve it. And…" She shook her head. "I won't be approving it."

Lawrence huffed every breath, his face so red she half expected steam to blow out his ears any second. His lips curled in on his teeth, the edges white, and a sheen of sweat glistened on his brow. "You're deluded if you believe you've got a snowball's chance in hell of winning, Andrea. No judge is going to let you continue living the way you live with a young, impressionable boy in your house."

Andi turned away from him as he rambled, turning when she reached David again. She leaned toward him, lowering her voice only enough to give the mild appearance of a side whisper. "When Lawrence wants to feel important he throws out big words. Well, big to him. He forgets I have a thesaurus the size of the Encyclopedia Britannica volume three on my desk."

David smiled and chuckled softly. Just like her, he put on an unfazed face for Lawrence. David was far more convincing, she was quite sure. He didn't have one Oscar, two Golden Globes, and half a dozen People's Choice Awards on display in his den for nothin'.

"I have proof, Andrea. *Proof.*" He tossed the word out like the Holy Grail.

Andi released a sigh of exasperation as she looked at him again.

Lawrence took a long stride to close the space between them, his fists clenched beside his hips. "Proof you aren't fit to raise him. Proof you're exposing him to a-a..." He looked at David and grimaced like he'd smelled something foul.

"The word is Jew," David said with cold contempt, leaning just a little closer to Lawrence.

"Unsavory elements," Lawrence finished, his grimace twisting even more. "Proof you put your own personal satisfaction, as much as that's possible, over his well-being. Do you think a judge will look kindly on the fact you stay away from home all night so you can spend it with your amoral golden-boy lover?"

"How did you—" The words were out of her mouth before she could remind herself to keep the mask in place. Lawrence's smug look of satisfaction at shocking her told her she'd revealed too much. He'd admitted once already—without saying as much—he watched her or had her watched. The idea made her sick.

"I know, Andrea. And if you fight me on this, the whole world will know what kind of selfish bitch you are."

"You're going to watch your language," David said in such a low voice she wondered if his lips had even moved when he spoke. He took half a step forward and half a step to the side, putting his body between Andi and Lawrence just enough to make a point. "It's time for you to go."

"I wouldn't get too deep into this, golden boy. Wouldn't want to tarnish that carefully managed reputation of yours." Lawrence huffed a chuckle, his lip sliding up in a sadistic snarl. "Now that you've sampled the goods, and by now decided they're not worth the effort..."

Damn him! Andi's insides went cold and she swallowed slowly to hide the flash of—what?—Panic? Dread? Fear it might be true?—that hit her guts like a bucket of dirty ice water.

"...You might as well move on now." Lawrence looked down at her, his eyes purposefully shifting to settle at her breasts and lower before coming back to her face. He pulled a mock look of sympathy and tsk-tsked. "I warned you, Andrea. No man is going to stick around once they realize they've got a cold fish in their bed."

David barked a laugh, tipping his head back. Both Andi and

Lawrence looked at him, and she wasn't sure which one of them was more surprised. David hitched his thumb toward Lawrence. "Is he *serious*?" he asked Andi, then turned to Lawrence and asked the same question. "Are you serious?"

Lawrence sputtered, and Andi grinned. She loved David. No doubt about it.

David looked back at her when Lawrence didn't explain. With his eyebrows arched high, he flipped his hand to fold in his thumb and extend his pinky only. He canted his head to the side, indicating first his pinky and then Lawrence. Andi laughed and nodded.

"Pretty much, yeah."

David stepped back to her side and slid his arm behind her to lay his palm against her lower back. "You sure you weren't the problem, *Pinky*?"

Lawrence tilted his head down and to the side, reminding her of an animal preparing to attack. His mouth twisted into a scowl so deep it distorted his features. "How dare you."

She looked up at David and smiled wide, leaning into him. "You know what they say about Jewish men…" She winked at David and he laughed, the pressure of his hand against her back bringing her even closer.

Lawrence stepped back on one foot and several things happened in a heartbeat. Andi heard herself shout David's name, Lawrence swung his fist, and David pushed her clear and in a move that could have come right out of an action film, arched back and Lawrence's knuckles met nothing but air. Tony and Horatio—who had remained silent but observant just a few feet away the whole time—rounded the back of Lawrence's car and headed for them. David righted himself and in the same motion, slammed his arm against Lawrence's chest and sent them both into the trunk of Lawrence's rental car with a loud thunk as the car bounced on its struts.

"You son of a bitch!" Lawrence shouted, fighting against David's hold.

"We'll take it from here, Mr. Bishop," Tony said, taking a firm hold on Lawrence's arm. He looked at Andi and nodded. "We'll escort him to the gate."

"Thank you, Tony," Andi managed to choke out. She was thankful now she'd listened to Theresa's suggestion that morning of having the security guards present.

David released Lawrence and stepped backward until he was beside her. Andi curled her hands around his elbow and he slid his arm behind her waist, bringing her closer to him even as he watched Lawrence. Her ex-husband shook loose from Tony's hold, and Tony let him. Andi knew it would take an extreme move on Lawrence's part for the security guard to take physical action to remove Lawrence, but *he* didn't need to know that. He raised his finger to say something, but his attention suddenly snapped past them. Andi spun on the balls of her feet and her breath caught when she saw Jake standing just a few feet away, his eyes wide.

How long had he been there?

"You!" Lawrence shouted, spittle flying from his lower lip. "If you'd just obeyed me when I told you what to do. If you'd just *told* your mother you wanted to be a family again, like I said, *none* of this would have happened. This is *your* fault, you little—"

"Shut up!" Andi screamed, bringing her hand up to block Lawrence's face. She turned to her son, her heart in her throat. "Jake, honey, did your father tell you to say that?"

Jake nodded, his eyes darting from her to his father, then to David, and back to her.

She took a step toward Jake and Lawrence moved to follow, but David cut off his approach. "I don't think so, Pinky."

"Why didn't you tell me?"

"Because I didn't want to be with him…"

"No, I mean why didn't you tell me he tried to make you say it?"

Jake shrugged. "Because I knew he was lying. He didn't want me back. I didn't care."

Lawrence lunged. Andi only caught the action in her peripheral. She turned just as he shouldered David and reached for her, his hand wrapping around her arm in an angry, steel grip. Lawrence yanked and she stumbled. David pulled Lawrence back and he lost his hold on her, but not before she completely lost her balance. Her head hit the cobblestone, knocking her glasses from her face with a blinding flash of pain. She heard a crack and a grunt and wondered for a moment if it had been her until Lawrence stumbled back and landed hard against the tailgate of his car. He dropped to the driveway. She tried to focus, squinting her eyes through the pain as she braced herself on her elbows, but he was far enough away his face was a blur.

"Mom!"

"Jake, no!" David shouted.

"I hate you! I hate you!"

Andi tried to turn her head, but black spots battled with flashes of light, splintering her vision. She made out the shape of her son, and David's tall form holding him back from kicking at Lawrence's prone body.

"What the hell?" Maggie's screech joined the jumble of sounds. "Bastard!"

David turned Jake still in his hold. Andi looked up and squinted enough to see the tear trails on her son's cheeks. "Mom..." he whispered.

"Mags, can you please take Jake inside?" David asked. "Jake, I'll take care of your mom."

Sounds jumbled for domination in her hazed world. She distinguished the sound of buttons being pushed on a phone, and Tony's voice asking for police. 911? David dropped to his knees beside her, his hands hovering around her head as if he weren't sure how to touch her.

"Damn," he cursed, gripping her shoulders as she tried to sit up. The yard tilted.

"Oh," she whispered, nausea grabbing her. Something warm slipped over her eyelid and down her cheek. Andi touched it gingerly, bringing her hand away to see crimson dripping from her fingers. "Oh," she parroted.

David knelt beside her, supporting her. "Take it easy, sweetheart."

"Police are on their way, Mr. Bishop," Tony said, his voice sounding like he spoke through a barrel. "Sorry about that. We can't really—"

"It's okay. Thank you." David touched her chin, making her look up. "Andi, talk to me."

"My glasses..."

He looked around and paused, wincing. "They're broken."

Somewhere in the distance, the wail of sirens echoed off the hillside. Lawrence groaned, and if she squinted—which she decided against because of the painful consequences—she saw him move.

"Oh…" she said again, knowing she should probably be able to say more. "Jake…"

David's gentle fingertips tenderly touched her forehead, and she sucked in a breath.

"He's with Maggie. Just take it easy. Tony, did you tell them we needed an ambulance?"

"Yes, sir."

Andi tilted her head back to look at David, and that simple act was nearly her undoing. Everything tipped, and she gripped his arms in fear she might slide right off the planet. Her stomach twisted and her head suddenly felt like a bowling ball full of lead. It tipped back further than she wanted, but she didn't have the strength to stop it.

"Whoa," David said, his hand cupping the back of her head. "Andi…Andi sweetheart, stay with me. The ambulance is almost here."

"David…" she forced through lips suddenly too thick and too dry. "I don't feel right…"

She never heard his response.

By the time David finished giving his statement to the Santa Clarita Sheriff's Department, gotten a spare pair of glasses from Maggie for Andi with a promise to call when he knew how Andi was, and drove to Henry Mayo Hospital, the horde of paparazzi had descended on the hospital parking lot like flies on a corpse.

When he left the house, Lawrence Bonherre was long gone—taken away by the sheriff's department, facing charges of assault. They warned David if they found his statement to be false, he could be facing charges as well. But, right now, Pinky's nose was in a splint because David was protecting Andi and Jake. Tony and Horatio confirmed to the police in their statements David didn't instigate the physical confrontation. He hadn't thrown the first punch and had avoided a fight the first time. And the second time, they confirmed Bonherre had gone after Andi.

In the fourteen-minute drive from Andi's house to the hospital, David spoke to both his attorney and Theresa, making them both aware of the situation. Jerry joked, and after David told him the story, told him not to worry about any of it. Theresa had been less amused, and not nearly as easy to read over the phone. She'd hummed, huffed once, asked a couple of questions, and then told him she'd meet them at the hospital within the hour.

Of the two attorneys, it was Theresa's words that stuck with him the most.

This changes things.

David just wished he knew what she meant. His nerves bounced like he'd mainlined half a dozen double espressos by the time he reached the hospital.

David clenched his jaw until his teeth hurt and gripped the steering wheel until his knuckles turned white. With a hard jerk of the wheel, he pulled his car into a space in the ER parking lot. Twenty feet from the ER entrance, the paparazzi caught his scent and turned like a mass of piranha, heading straight toward him. David plowed forward, ignoring the flashing cameras and shouts of his name hoping he'd turn in their direction—gifting someone with a better shot. Getting past them, he entered the ER doors and immediately turned to the security desk right inside the door.

"Excuse me," he forced himself not to snap out as he leaned over the desk.

The middle-aged and heavy-set Latino man looked up with disinterest. "Do you need to see a doctor?"

"No, my girlfriend was brought in by ambulance about an hour ago."

The guard pointed toward a three-ring binder sitting open on his side desk. "Sign in, I'll let you through. Do you know which bed she's in?"

"Not yet. Andrea Parker."

David doubted his signature was even legible the way his hand shook, and dropped the pen when the guard handed him a red and white sticker proclaiming him a VISITOR. The guard pointed toward a door to their right, and an audible click as David reached it indicated the guard had unlocked it to let him through. He took four long strides to the long, curved reception desk within the ER secure area. A young brunette nurse lifted her chin with an indifferent expression, her eyes still on the computer screen in front of her, until she looked at him. Then her eyes widened and her mouth fell open, a deep crimson stain flashing across her cheeks. David offered his best smile.

"Hey, how are you..."

She stuttered, reminding him of a fish gulping water. He kept going, not waiting for her to compose herself.

"I'm looking for Andrea Parker. She came in by ambulance about an hour ago."

"Sh-sh-yes, um, yes...she's in exam room three."

David winked. "Thank you." He didn't wait for permission to find the room, but then again, he didn't ask either. The majority of the back ER area was set up as triage, with sections of a long wall divided by curtains with beds in between. Only a couple were occupied, the rest remaining blessedly empty. The private exam rooms opened off the other side of the hallway, the doors of the first two open with the interior lights on, waiting for guests. The door of exam room three was closed, the shades down but the slats partially open, and only the dimmest of lights shined through. Probably a bedside light at the most. David paused at the door, his hand on the knob. Bruises already shadowed his knuckles, and the skin around his middle knuckle had split on impact with Pinky's nose. The EMTs had iced it while the sheriff's department questioned him, but without the cold, a dull ache had settled into the joints.

He hadn't broken anything, but if he had, it would have been worth it and he took small comfort in knowing Pinky's nose didn't fare as well.

For the first time, he noticed the smear of blood on his shirt over his heart and realized with a jolt it was Andi's blood. He'd held her against his chest when her eyes fluttered closed and her body went limp, and the cut along the ridge of her brow had stained his shirt. David swallowed hard.

Pinky came away damn lucky all David broke was his nose.

With a huff, David turned the knob and eased the door open. The room was quiet except for the low hum of the fluorescent light over the bed. Andi's still form curled against the raised head of the bed, her face toward the door. A light blanket draped her lower body and a white bandage covered the spot over her right eye. Her eyes were closed, her features relaxed and she slept with her hands folded beneath her cheek.

He eased the door closed with a click. When he turned back, her eyes were open, squinting into the dim light. "Hey," he said softly, quickly crossing to her.

"David?"

"Yeah."

She reached for him, and he ignored the low bed railing digging into his waist to lean over her and embrace her. Andi wrapped her arms around his shoulders and he nuzzled against the curve of her throat, inhaling her scent beyond the smell of latex and antiseptic permeating the hospital air. He kissed her throat, her jaw, her cheek, her forehead, her wrist, and the palm of her hand before finally kissing her lips.

"I'm so sorry, sweetheart," he apologized, closing his eyes as he held her face in his hands and rested his forehead gingerly against hers, making sure he didn't touch the bandage.

She chuckled softly. "What are *you* apologizing for?"

In the dim light, David pulled back and stroked his thumb around the edge of the bandage, noting how some flecks of dried blood clung to her hair. He looked down and turned her hand, smoothing his fingertips over the abrasions on her palm from the rough cobblestone. He didn't have to see beneath the sleeve of her sweater to imagine the bruises left on her arm from Bonherre's grip. They just added to the ones he'd already left behind.

Andi touched his forehead, running her fingers over his eyes and down the side of his face. She shook her head, her hair shifting on the pillow. "No, David. Don't."

He lowered the railing, sat on the edge of the mattress and leaned his hand on the bed on the other side of her hips. "How are you? Everything okay?" he asked, brushing off her request. It'd be a bit before he could let go of the guilt burning in his craw like bitter acid.

Andi nodded, though he caught the pinch at the corner of her eyes. "Oh, right..." He took her spare glasses from his breast pocket and slipped them over her ears. The tension lines around her eyes eased when she didn't have to squint to keep him in focus.

"What did the doctor say? Can you go home or do you need to stay?"

"It's a stage three concussion, he said. Because I lost consciousness, I guess." She took his hand and held it between both of hers, rubbing her palm against his. "They checked me out and he said I'll be fine except for the headache for a bit. I can go home whenever you want to take me. I was waiting for you."

"I'm sorry. I couldn't leave—"

Andi touched her fingertip to his mouth. "Shush. It's okay. I knew where you were. I've already given my statement to the police, too."

David wrapped his fingers around her wrist, turning his face into her hand to kiss her palm. He held it against his cheek, drawing a deep breath. She stroked his hair with her free hand. "David, what is it? What's wrong?"

He grimaced. "Besides the obvious?"

Andi cupped his cheek and made him look at her. Her eyes shifted in the dim light of the exam room, studying his face. "It's more than just being angry at what happened. What is it?" Her eyes widened and she sucked in a sharp breath. "Is it Jake? Is he okay? What—"

"Jake's fine. He's upset, but he's fine. He's with Maggie."

"Then what?"

David took her hand from his cheek and held it in his lap, looking down at their joined fingers. Her hands were soft and delicate, her fingers long. She wore her nails short, she told him once she couldn't type fast enough if they grew long, with just a hint of pink polish. No rings.

"I talked to Theresa on the way over here. Told her what happened."

Her silence was as good as a prodding "And…"

"She's coming here, so we should wait for her."

"Why is she coming here?" Andi asked, her voice softer than before.

David couldn't look up, because he was afraid he might see in her eyes the thought stuck in his head since hanging up with her attorney. What if what he'd done—what if laying Lawrence Bonherre out on his ass for hurting her—cost her Jake?

"She said this could change things…" he forced himself to say.

"No assumptions." Her voice was rough, but firm. He shook his head, stroking his thumb over her skin. "David. Look at me."

Unable to deny her, he raised his chin and looked into her eyes.

"No assumptions. We wait until we talk to her."

He nodded. "Okay."

"I love you."

David released a long breath, never realizing how much three words could make him feel. He scooted further up the bed and leaned forward until he could rest his cheek on her breasts, supporting his weight on his arms on either side of her. Andi stroked her fingers through his hair and he closed his eyes. Her soft heartbeat thrummed against his cheek.

A soft knock at the door preceded Theresa's entrance, and David sat up as she closed the door. "Hey, kids," she said with a smile as she crossed to the bed. "Wow, got quite the dinger there, huh?"

David rose from the bed and walked around the foot to stand on the other side so Theresa and Andi could talk without speaking over him. As soon as he reached the side of the bed again, Andi held her hand out for him and he laced his fingers through hers.

"I'm fine," she answered Theresa. "I was just telling David he can take me home."

"Well, not until you sign some paperwork for me."

"I thought you were going to messenger them to me tomorrow?"

Theresa sat in one of the visitor's chairs and bent over to retrieve some paperwork from her leather attaché. "That was this morning, things have changed. Like I told David on the phone."

Andi's hold on his hand tightened by a small degree. "How so?"

Theresa sat up with a stack of paperwork in her hands. "This morning we were just filing for an amendment to his visitation rights. Now, we're filing a restraining order and a request for full withdrawal of visitation unless supervised. We can't take it away completely unless we get the right judge, but the chances of that are slim. The best we can do is take away his ability to yank you around and toss out threats like beads at Mardi Gras."

"Really?" Andi whispered.

David focused his attention on her, only listening to Theresa in his peripheral. Her smile was hesitant, and he imagined—like him—she probably wasn't ready to accept it could all be over as easy as that. Could she have Pinky tossed out of her life—for the most part—just like that?

"Really. His strong arm display today pretty much nailed shut his casket. I'm glad you took my advice about the security guards. I figured—"

"You thought he'd do this?" David cut off.

Theresa looked at him and shrugged. "I've dealt with men like Larry Bonherre for most of my career. It's family law, and unless *someone* is a total butthead you're probably not in family court. I've seen his type before. They're civil when they believe their manipulations are working, but once they're undermined their control slips. It's just a matter of time."

"Andi could have been seriously *hurt*."

Andi squeezed his hand with both of hers and he realized he'd shouted the accusation. "But I'm fine. I'll be fine."

"Why do you think I wanted *you* there, David? The security guards gave you credible witnesses but you gave her protection. I couldn't tell you ahead of time because everything needed to happen naturally. If you knew, you'd be conscious of every word...are you instigating him? Would it be seen as instigation? Are you doing enough? Should you do more? You did exactly the right thing. You protected her."

"She's still in the hospital," he forced through clenched teeth.

"If you hadn't been there, she could be upstairs." Theresa's expression was flat, decisive but he caught the flicker of something in her eyes. Experience, maybe. "Or worse, downstairs in the morgue." Then with a huff, she held out the papers and a pen. "I need your signature on these and then I'll let you two be on your way."

David retrieved a rolling table from the corner of the room and brought it to the bed to give Andi a writing surface. As she looked over and signed the paperwork, she glanced up briefly. "So, what now?" she asked.

"You go about your lives. Don't let Bonherre change anything. You wanna go to the movies? Go to the movies. Go to dinner. All of you… bring Jake. Don't be afraid to be public. We have a rare opportunity here to use the press to our advantage." Theresa winked at David. "Haven't you ever wanted to do that?"

David smiled. "Hell, yeah."

"We can't avoid the press simply because of who you are. Both of you. Hiding will just make the court wonder what you're keeping behind closed doors. Let them see you together."

Andi finished signing the forms and handed them back to Theresa. "How long will this take?"

Theresa shrugged as she set her attaché on the edge of the bed to shove the papers inside. "Hard to tell. The restraining order will go through immediately, so he won't be allowed to approach or contact either you or Jacob. That is going to play into the custody hearing. It could be two weeks, could be up to six months."

"Six months?" both he and Andi said together.

Theresa smiled. "Cute. You do that often?" She waved her hand. "I doubt it will, but it *has* happened, so be prepared for the worst. Meanwhile, just be you. Be Dandi…that's what they call you two, right?"

Andi groaned and David chuckled. "Don't bring it up. It's a sore spot with her. That and the world *girlfriend*."

"Either way, just being your cute and adorable selves."

"I think we can manage that." Andi's smile shoved aside his worry.

"Good—"

"Would it help if we got married?" The question was out of his mouth before he even registered it was in his head.

"What?" Andi gasped.

"No," Theresa answered without even hesitating and he wondered if she'd expected the question. "If you even got engaged it would look like you're doing it just to affect the case. Just…just keep being David and Andi and leave it at that. If you're planning on getting married, don't announce *anything* until the case is settled. Then, by all means, throw a party the likes of which Hollywood has never seen."

Theresa picked up her case, zipping it closed as she continued. "One more thing. David, I know you're not going to like this, but then again you're not my client—Andrea is—and I'm watching out for her."

"What is it?" Andi asked, looking from Theresa to David and back to her attorney.

Theresa focused on him, looking over the top of her glasses. "I want you seen in public with her, but when it comes time for Andrea to be in court, you stay clear—"

"Why—"

Theresa raised her hand, and he stopped. "As much as we can use the press to our advantage, your face, and your influence can also hurt. Andrea is fighting for her son, and it needs to be her fight. The judge will need to see her standing on her own as much as he sees your support. Because this is Family Court, and the entire system is based on the breakdown of the family. He's going to figure—and don't get mad or defensive with me, because this is just the way it is—the odds are seriously against the two of you lasting more than a few years *at most*. If Andi does this on her own, it'll mean she can stand on her own when you're gone."

"*If* I'm gone," David bit out. "I'm not going anywhere."

Theresa smiled, but it was the type of smile you gave a kid when you were just humoring a crazy idea. "Of course you're not, sweetness. Just…trust me on this. Okay?"

David clenched his teeth until his jaw hurt, not wanting to make the promise. Just the idea of leaving her to face Pinky alone at any time stuck in his throat. She looked up at him, and he remembered the promise he *had* made…he wouldn't be the reason she lost her son. One promise just led to another.

"Fine," he answered Theresa, focusing on Andi. "I'll stay clear."

The exam room door opened and a middle-aged man with thinning white hair and a hefty waistline came inside, *Dr. Sandoval* embroidered on his white lab coat. "Good to see you awake, Ms. Parker. Let's give you one last check before you go home."

Theresa headed for the door, pausing before she left. "I gotta know, and remember, whatever you tell me is covered under attorney/client privilege…are you? Planning on it?"

David looked down at Andi, who stared up at him with wide eyes and parted lips. Her cheeks flushed a becoming pink, and he smiled. "We'll get back to you on that," he answered but didn't look away from Andi to see Theresa's reaction.

"Fair enough."

David leaned over and kissed her flushed cheek before getting out of the way so Dr. Sandoval could give her a final look…and he could take her home.

CHAPTER TWENTY

"**S**o, I was thinking…"

Andi chuckled, rubbing her cheek against the warmth of David's forearm. The house was quiet, well after midnight, and she floated in the heavy space somewhere just before sleep. But, his fingertips followed a repetitive trail up and down her arm, down her side to her hip and back again; the action definitely distracting enough to stave off sleep. Sometimes he stopped at her hip, massaging the tight muscle she'd pulled when she fell, and sometimes he worked at the tense knot between her shoulder and her neck. Hours after the fall, her body now made her aware of all the different ways she'd abused it—or rather, Lawrence had abused it—when she went down.

"What were you thinking…"

His lips brushed her shoulder, his breath warming her skin when he spoke. "I was thinking about what Theresa said today."

"Yeah?" He nodded, his cheek rubbing against hers. Lying so still, every sensation was heightened from the warmth his body created under the blankets to the firm feel of his thighs against the back of her legs. Andi drew in a long, deep breath and enjoyed the scent of his body. "Which part?"

"About us being seen. Not letting Pinky affect us, affect our lives."

She giggled at the new nickname, probably more than she would have if she were fully awake. Instead, the name brought back the memory of Lawrence's shocked face and in her near dreamlike state, she saw his head expand like a giant red balloon and steam blow out his ears. She giggled harder, making a rather unattractive sound somewhere between a snort and a raspberry, which only made her laugh harder.

David moved his hand from her hip to her stomach, sliding it beneath the hem of her nightshirt. The slight touch drew her onto her back so she looked up at him, and the amused grin on her face made her laugh all the harder. *Maybe she really did scramble her brains when she fell.*

"What are you giggling at?" he asked, shifting so he could brace his weight on his lower elbow and hover over her, the light of the moon coming through her window highlighting the planes of his face. The lightness in her chest mellowed and smoothed into warmth spreading out into her limbs like a hot toddy at Christmas.

Andi drew in a long, deep breath—only giggling a *little* bit when she released it—and laid her palm against his bare chest. "The great lightness of being."

David smiled, his gaze shifting over her face and down her throat before meeting her eyes again. His thumb stroked her hair near the small bandage near her hairline. "Was I this silly after my whack on the nose?"

Andi giggled, she couldn't help herself. "You were worse." She rolled her eyes, a miserable attempt at focusing on the conversation at hand. "You were saying something before I so rudely interrupted. Something about a long vacation on a beach somewhere. Where all the drinks have little paper umbrellas and the water is never cold." Andi closed her eyes, tilting her head on the pile of pillows so she leaned into his biceps. She sighed. "Somewhere with beds draped in white netting and the air smells like salt and pineapples."

His lips whispered over hers just before he spoke. "Not quite...but sounds good to me." Andi opened her mouth beneath his, anticipating the kiss. "Sounds like a topic we're going to have to revisit."

Andi scooted closer to him when his lips covered hers, and didn't even try to disguise the low purr in her throat. David broke the kiss with a smile, his laughter thrumming against her hands. "Sweetheart, did you forget we're at *your* house?"

"Is that supposed to mean I can't make love to you?"

He blinked slowly, tilting his head to the side with a pleased smile. "No, we're just not alone in the house. And noise carries, sweetheart."

She licked her lower lip, running her hands over his shoulder and neck. "Can't help myself."

"You're distracting me from my point. If I didn't know better, I'd think you're doing it on purpose."

Andi shook her head. "Nope." She rolled her lips together and snuggled closer to him. He shifted down the bed so his upper body draped partially over her and he looked up at her, his hand resting across her lower ribs and his chin on the back of his hand. She stroked his hair, feeling drunk on the intoxicating feeling his nearness created in her. "I'm sorry. I won't interrupt again. So…see and be seen, go to dinner, movies, Best Buy for that new game you—I'm sorry—*Jake*—wants…" David grinned and chuckled, shifting enough to push her shirt off her stomach and kiss her abdomen above her belly button. "Hey! Who's being distracting now?"

"Can't help myself," he mimicked. "Too much Andrea Parker to enjoy."

Her insides warmed and liquefied, making her sink deeper into the bed yet making her skin tingle and spark at the same time. "Well then, make your point so we can move on to other topics." His attention shifted up from the strip of skin above the waistband of her pajamas to her face. Andi smiled slowly, enjoying the jump in her pulse. "Sounds like you had something specific in mind…about being seen, that is."

"Maybe, yeah." David shifted back up her side so he leaned over her again just about eye-to-eye. His pendant reflected the faint moonlight. "Maggie had something she wanted to tell you at dinner—"

"I thought she did," Andi interrupted, shifting just enough to see his face more clearly. "She looked ready to pop. But when I asked her what was up, she blew me off. Said I'd know eventually."

"I asked her to let *me* tell you. And since Avi said he's pretty sure it's going to hit the wire either tomorrow or the next day, I figured I'd better tell you soon."

Andi squinted at him, trying to figure out what he tried to lead up to. "Okay..."

"Well, while you and I have been enjoying the last month without filming schedules and promotional junkets, your agent and my manager have been diligently working behind the scenes—your agent more than my manager, I think, but that's beside the point. While we've been..." He smiled the slow, sexy grin that usually inspired her to insanity. "...busy falling in love, they've been working with The Powers That Be."

A cold flush of excitement flashed over her skin from head to toe, making her feel like she'd run into a snowstorm after jumping in a lake...exhilarated and terrified at the same time. She knew exactly what Maggie had been working on...the same thing Maggie'd been pushing since well before that fate-changing kiss in her trailer months before...the contract negotiations for *The Forgotten*. When the filming of *Rise of Dawn* began, Andi had been beyond ecstatic—especially as she experienced David bringing Jason to life. No other actor existed in Hollywood who could have played Jason with the same conviction for her. In all aspects David practically *was* Jason.

So much had changed...The potential success of *Rise of Dawn*, and the possible filming of the sequel *The Forgotten*, had once been the determining factor in her entire future—now, she had almost all but forgotten.

Because of David Bishop.

How ironic.

The star of her future was now her future.

She hoped.

Andi blinked and swallowed against the Mojave-like dryness that glued her tongue to the roof of her mouth. "And..."

David pushed up and made a faux-serious expression, dropping his tone as he spoke. "Contract negotiations are in their final stages with the representatives for David Bishop and Andrea Parker. Contract sticking points have included the wish of the production team to keep Ms. Parker actively involved in the script adaption and interpretation, her ongoing input into the filming process, and the participation of David Bishop in the next film. Representatives for both parties have reported all contract points have been hammered out and filming will begin in the spring, three months before the scheduled cinema release of *Rise of Dawn* on—"

Andi squealed, throwing her hands in the air. She'd probably have whacked them on the headboard if David hadn't moved faster and caught her. One of his big hands wrapped around both her wrists, pinning them against the pillows over her head while he touched the finger of his other hand to her lips.

"Shhhhh," he hushed through his low, rumbling laugh. "You're going to wake up the whole house. Or, at the least, hurt yourself."

Andi just kept laughing and squirmed out of his grasp enough to wrap her arms around him and hug him so hard he lost his balance and his weight pushed her into the bed. Not that she complained. She showered his cheek, temple, and brow with loud kisses until she found her way back to his mouth.

"Thank you," she said against his lips, kissing him again. "Thank you. Thank you." Each sentence was punctuated with a kiss.

"Not that I'm arguing—" Kiss. "But what are you thanking me for?"

Andi settled into the pillows again but kept her arms linked behind his neck to hold him close. She let go a long sigh, taking a few brief moments to just look at him. Sometimes, in moments just like this, everything became so surreal she had a hard time believing she wasn't in the longest and most vivid dream ever in documented history. She'd had many moments like that since the first time she tried to convince herself his kiss was just a vivid dream. The effect wouldn't be more real if someone slapped her across the back of the head and said 'Are you insane?'

Sometimes, especially when the paparazzi followed them or an excited fan approached with flushed cheeks and rapid breath to ask for an autograph, she realized the man beside her was *David Bishop*, the man who had been making young hearts flutter for nearly twenty years. David Bishop who had been voted Sexiest Man in Hollywood, Sexiest Man Alive, Most Eligible Bachelor…the list went on and on.

Sometimes, it wasn't about who the world saw. Sometimes, he

made her pause because he was just David and he was wonderful. He played basketball in the backyard with her son for three hours on a Saturday afternoon. He brought Maggie flowers when she wasn't feeling well. He called his mother every three days whether he had something to tell her, or not. And when his mother called him to say Caroline had delivered her new baby girl, he hadn't tried to hide when tears filled his eyes. He made breakfast with all of Jake's favorite foods and helped Jake with his homework. If she was within his reach, he touched her. Maybe he held her hand, maybe he let his fingertips brush the inside of her elbow, or maybe he kissed her when given any opportunity, but he sought her out and told her he craved her.

It was *that* David who made her breath catch and her heart pound, *that* David who made her faint with panic at the thought he might be gone from her life someday, and *that* David she made love to...not David Bishop. Just David.

She didn't realize she was crying until his expression changed, his lips sliding from a smile to a frown, and he ran his thumb across the slick skin at the corner of her eye. She sniffed and swiped the tears away with her fingertips.

"I'm okay," she said before he could ask. "Didn't you know women cry when they're happy?"

His frown relaxed a little. "I thought that was just my sisters."

Andi laughed, even though tears ran across her temples to her hair. David finally smiled again, his thumb still stroking her skin. With a deep, shuddered breath Andi finally managed to answer him. "Thank you for everything." Her voice was still rough, but she couldn't make it any louder.

David drew in a breath, releasing it with a soft sound Andi couldn't interpret. He shifted over her, bracketing his weight on his elbows. "I love you." The weight of his words was tangible, real, like a caress, and before the tears renewed, Andi curled up from the pillow to kiss him.

Before the pitch of the kiss shifted to something more, David pulled back enough to look down at her. "You have managed to *completely* get me off topic."

Andi pulled her lower lip through her teeth and made a half-hearted attempt at looking innocent. "Did I?" At his mock scowl, she scooted up the pillows to partially sit up. "Please, continue."

David shifted with her so his shoulder rested on the pillows at her side and he looked up at her. He slid his hand beneath her shirt again, his warm skin smoothing over her stomach.

"Has Maggie talked to you about doing publicity appearances?"

"You mean past book signings?" He nodded. Just the thought made her skin flush. "She talked about panel appearances and maybe some conventions."

"What about the talk show gambit?"

Andi pulled her legs up, wrapping her arms around them. David had to move his hand, and sat up beside her, his back to the headboard. But, his attention stayed firmly on her. She was a chicken, plain and simple and undeniable. Just *watching* from the audience while David did the live interview with Brooke Halle had made her break out in nervous gooseflesh. David twisted toward her, laying his hand on her raised knee, rubbing his thumb against the worn cotton of her pajama pants.

She signed, knowing exactly what he was waiting for. "Yes."

"And..."

Andi shot a look at him, then focused again on his thumb stroking the inside of her knee. "And...the entire idea scares the living daylights right out of me. But..." She looked at him again. "I don't think you needed me to tell you that."

"What if we did it together?"

Andi squinted and contemplated reaching for her glasses, just to make sure she saw his expression perfectly clear. In the end, she rolled sideways and retrieved her spare pair from the nightstand. He hadn't moved when she rolled back, looking at him again.

"Is this your idea? Or Avi's?"

David shrugged, canting his head to the side. "Avi mentioned it first, but I've been thinking about it since I did Brooke's show."

"Of doing the circuit together?"

"It's not unheard of. Co-stars on a film do the circuit all the time, to promote together."

"We aren't co-stars. We're—"

"—together. I know. But, we can still promote *Rise of Dawn* together."

Andi squinted at him. "It's not going to be released for months."

"So, we just…" David puffed out his cheeks with a deep breath and shifted away. "Okay, fine. Sometimes being seen is just being seen. Call me a pretentious Hollywood…whatever…but sometimes, I just have to 'be seen.' With the announcement of *The Forgotten* being adapted to film, it's an opportunity."

"So, why do I have to be involved?"

David laughed, resting his head back against the wall. "Why would you have to be involved in the promotion of the film adaptation for one of the best-selling book series since Gabaldon and Martin?" He dropped his hands in his lap, palms up. "Oh, I don't know, sweetheart…because you *wrote* it?"

Andi shook her head and tossed the blankets back, climbing from the bed. Wide awake now, nervous energy making her clench and unclench her hands at her side as she bee-lined for the bathroom. Okay, so she'd accepted a certain level of weirdness in her own psyche —it came with the territory of writing down everything the voices in her head told her to write down—but even she knew a need to brush her teeth when she was nervous went beyond the normal author psychosis.

She avoided looking at herself in the mirror, squirted green gel on her toothbrush, and scrubbed at her teeth. She didn't hear him come into the bathroom over the rush of water in the sink and jumped nearly swallowing a mouthful of toothpaste foam when he stepped behind her and laid his hands on her hips. She spit and rinsed, finally straightening to look at him in the mirror.

"I've seen you with your fans," he said, drawing her against his chest. He stared at her in the reflection. "You're wonderful with them. What makes you believe you can't do this?"

"I can't speak to people in public," she argued, not even thinking about what she said because she'd heard the reasons so many times before. "I'm a mouse…"

You're like a little mouse, Andrea, and the truth is people listen more closely to someone they find appealing. Moreover, you don't have the training, and you won't convince anyone you know what you're talking about anyway. Just stay quiet, don't speak, and for heaven's sake don't draw any attention to yourself.

"What?"

Andi closed her eyes and released a long sigh. She swallowed and shook her head before looking at him again in the mirror. "I realize more and more each day just how—" She shook her head again.

David shifted his feet apart so his chin rested on her shoulder, his cheek brushing hers. "How long will it take before you hear *my* words over his?"

"Only once." Andi raised her hand and laid it against his far cheek, leaning her cheek into his other. "I just have to figure out which mantras in my head are *mine*, and which ones are *his* he stuck there."

David moved back and set his hands at her hips, turning her around to face him. He kissed her forehead and held her face between his palms before looking her in the eye. "I want to ask you something."

"Anything."

"This morning, I made light of it just to piss off Pinky, but he said something…" His eyes pinched at the corners and he paused. "Forgive my ad-libing, but he said he warned you I wouldn't stay—"

"Once you realized I was pathetic in bed." Andi hitched her head and tried to smile. "Forgive my ad-libing. But, I've already heard several variations of the same statement." She swallowed and turned away as much as his hands would allow. "It was my fault, you know. The affairs. That's what he said…because I was inadequate."

He groaned just before turning her to face him, covering her mouth with an open-mouthed kiss she felt clear to her toes. His tongue slipped past her lips, and before she could take a breath, he scooped his hands behind her legs and lifted her to sit on the edge of the counter. In the span of two heartbeats, Andi wanted all of David and wanted him *now*. His hands tugged at her, bringing her closer to him until she wrapped her legs around his waist. Desperate fingers dug into her thighs and backside, pulling at her clothes. When he sucked at the sweet spot at the point of her collarbone, Andi threw back her head and gasped.

David pulled away, his breath ragged and hot against her cheeks. He pulled her harder against him, the thin material of their night clothing doing nothing to disguise his arousal. Andi panted, trying to catch her breath as he pushed his fingers into her hair and tilted her head so she looked up at him.

"I can't get enough of you," he rasped, leaning in so his lips brushed hers when he spoke. He pulled her lower lip between his, and Andi shifted against him, eliciting a low groan that rumbled through his chest. "Andi, I couldn't walk away now if I wanted to, and I don't want to."

He pushed his hand beneath her shirt, sliding his palm up her spine to support her shoulders. His other arm hitched her higher on his hips and he lifted her off the counter, carrying her back to the bedroom. All doubt, all fear that continued to niggle at the back of her mind, was lost as she lost herself in David.

"The important thing is to relax."

"She knows that, Avi," David said, shooting a glare at his manager. "*Telling* her a dozen times in five minutes won't help."

Avi shrugged. "Hey, just doing my job."

Maggie gave Avi a good shove with her shoulder into his chest, sending him back two steps. "Yeah, except Andi isn't *your* client. Back off, bucko. Andi is *fine*, and she'll *be* fine. *You* are the one who needs to relax."

Avi smoothed his tie and popped his eyebrows. "Pushy as ever, Ms. Connelly."

"I push as hard as I need to, but you should know that by now, *Mr. Siegel*."

David suppressed a growl and looked at Andi. She stood by the Green Room window, staring into the mid-morning sunlight. It was chilly today, the distinct nip of winter in California leaving layers of frost on the cars and a nip in the air. With a private grin, he recognized the sweater she wore as the one she'd worn the first time they made love. That sweater and the yellow sundress with the tiny flowers would forever be his favorite articles of clothing on her.

"Look, she can't go up there looking as nervous as a long-tailed cat in a roomful of rocking chairs," Avi said in a stage whisper. David caught Andi's glance over her shoulder.

"Like a what in a what?"

Avi rolled his eyes to Maggie and back to David. "Brooke may not harp on it, but you *know*—"

"Lay *off*," David growled.

"With all the negative press lately, you've got to go out there and not bat an eyelash."

"Are you deaf?" Maggie snapped.

"Just give us a few minutes." David pushed Avi toward the door and gave Maggie a pleading glance. She didn't skip a beat and followed them to the door.

Avi looked at his watch. "You're on in ten."

Maggie gave Avi another hard shove. "Let the man do *his* job," she ordered and winked at David. "We'll be in the first row."

David nodded, shutting the door behind them. He sighed and let his chin drop toward his chest.

"I'm sorry," she said softly as soon as the lock clicked. "I don't want to ruin this, but—"

"Stop," he said gently, crossing to her. He wrapped his arms around her and rested his cheek against her hair. "You're not ruining anything. You'll be fine. I swear."

"Easy for you to say. How many times have you done this?"

"How many times have I been interviewed? I don't know. How many times have I been interviewed with my girlfriend?" He grinned at her low growl. "Never."

"That's because it's not done."

"I wouldn't say it's 'not done', it's just—"

"A kiss of death. Like…making a movie together or getting matching tattoos."

David laughed. "It's not always a kiss of death."

"Tell that to Tom and Nicole, or Billy Bob and Angelina—"

"Paul Newman and Joanne Woodward. Tom Hanks and Rita Wilson.

"Okay, fine. You got me on those." She ran her hands over his arms where they crossed over her stomach, pausing to toy with the leather bracelet on his left wrist—a gift from Jake, something he'd made at school. She drew in a breath that shuddered through her when she let it go. "Do you know what I'm most afraid of?" Her voice was so low he almost didn't hear her. He kissed her cheek and waited. "I'm afraid I won't know an answer."

"About the books or the movies?"

"About us."

David nodded. "Yeah, she'll probably ask about us." He loosened his hold enough to turn her in the circle of his arms so she had to face him. "Andi, after this long, are you unsure?"

She shrugged and tried to smile, but it didn't quite reach her eyes enough to convince him. "I'm sorry—"

"Stop saying that," he said a little harder than he intended. Her eyes shifted away, but he tightened his hold before she could step clear of his arms. "Andi..." He didn't know what to say, so he pressed his lips to her forehead and embraced her, holding her until he felt some of the tension ease in her shoulders.

The last week and a half had been hell, no other way to put it. Since Pinky put her in the ER, and Theresa filed the petition and restraining orders, Andi's ex had done everything within the statutes of the law to make her life miserable. He filed his own petition, just as he'd threatened, and he'd added accusations ranging from immorality to endangerment of their son.

No one had been left untouched, including David and Maggie. Every dark secret was thrust into the light for public consumption. 'Facts' were created from nothing, and those stories with even the smallest kernel of truth had been twisted and repainted into sinister, unpleasant half-truths. Each article and news report chipped away at Andi, dimming the light in her eyes. He saw it each day no matter how he tried to keep them from her.

It was impossible.

"Both Avi and Maggie made it clear to Brooke's people that there's a line we won't cross. I trust Brooke to stick to that line. She likes a good story, but she's not into sensationalism."

Andi nodded against his chest, not looking up. David ran his hand over her hair and across her shoulders. "And as far as the inevitable question about us…where we are and where we're headed…I already have the answer for that."

She pulled back then, looking up with a touch of a grin on her lips. "You do?"

David smiled and held her face in his hands. "We're headed exactly where I've always known we're headed. Since the first time I kissed you, I knew *exactly* where this would go."

"Where is that?"

He grinned and stroked his thumb across her lower lip. "All the way, sweetheart."

"And that's what you'll tell Brooke?" she asked with an arch of her eyebrows.

"Well," he said with a hitch of his head. "Something to that effect, yeah."

"Sounds like something from a romantic movie," she said with a light smirk.

David laughed and linked his fingers together behind her back, and she mimicked his stance. He spread his feet to bring him closer to eye level with her. "Yeah, well, I guess that's what I get for falling in love with a romance novelist."

"Next you'll be telling me I complete you or…" She pulled a face. "That you're afraid of leaving this room and never feeling the rest of your whole life the way you feel when you're with me."

He kissed her, smiling against her lips and felt her smile back. "I'm just a guy, standing in front of a girl, asking her to love me."

She groaned, ending it with a laugh. "You're crazy."

"In love."

"I think that's a song, not a line." Andi shook her head, laughing again softly. She slid her hands around his sides and up his chest to link behind his neck. "And you're very good." He arched his eyebrows and she laughed again. "I'm *referring* to your ability to make me relax."

A soft knock at the door preceded an aid sticking her head inside. "We're ready for you to approach the stage, Mr. Bishop. Ms. Parker."

"Thank you," David said with a smile and nod at the young girl.

Andi took a deep breath as soon as the door shut again. David hooked his finger beneath her chin, urging her to look at him. "You get nervous, just look at me. Don't look out at the audience. Don't look at the cameras. Look at Brooke or look at me. Talk to me. Okay?"

Andi nodded and stepped away to straighten her sweater. David took her hand and brought it to his lips, kissing her knuckles. With another deep breath, she nodded and smiled and they headed for the door.

"So, what's it like to be dating someone with such a loyal fan base?"

Brooke looked between them, her attention settling on David. Andi looked at him, her mouth turning up in a slow, secret grin that made him smile right back. It was infectious.

"It's been…*interesting* to say the least. Took a bit to get used to."

Brooke patted her hand, drawing her attention back to the host. "That's so precious, Andi. But, I was talking to David." David chuckled and Brooke motioned her hand toward him. "What's it like to date a cultural phenomenon, David?"

"Aaaah…intimidating," he answered, shifting to rest his right ankle on his left knee. He laid his arm across the back of the couch so he could stroke the exposed skin along the side of her throat with his thumb. Her skin was warm, either from the barrage of questions Brooke tossed at them with practiced ease or from the bright stage lights. A dusty pink color stained her cheeks. She was a breathtaking kind of beautiful.

"You've got to understand, Brooke, I was a fan of Andrea Parker just like the rest of the world before I *ever* met Andi." He cut his hand in the air to make his point. "After being offered the role of Jason in

Rise of Dawn, I went and got the book." He looked to Andi, a rush of… something…he couldn't quite define rushing through him at the way she smiled and listened. He knew she didn't see herself the way the rest of the *world* saw her. Whether she ever would, or not, he didn't know. But he doubted it. "I went back to the bookstore that night. I devoured the entire series in six days. This woman is amazing."

Andi's cheeks flushed even deeper and she looked away. David leaned over and kissed her cheek just in front of her ear.

"You two are just adorable," Brooke gushed. "So, sounds to me like *you* were the star-struck fan when the two of you met?"

"Oh, absolutely." David nodded emphatically and grinned, looking from Brooke to Andi. "I kept trying to find excuses to talk to her…"

Andi gaped, then snapped her mouth shut with a clack of her teeth. David chuckled softly. "I was like a kid in junior high. I tried to sit beside her at lunch. I resorted to just about everything but giving Benton a note to slip her in study hall. Once…" He brought his arm from behind her and shifted forward, grinning. "I got her favorite kind of cookies from catering and acted like I didn't want them, just so I could give them to her."

"I remember that…" Andi said softly, and his eyes shifted to her.

"I take it this is the first you've heard about this?"

Andi licked her lips and nodded, finally turning her attention from David to look at Brooke. "He knows how to impress a girl."

Brooke chuckled. "I should think so. We'll be right back from the commercial to talk a little bit more with David and Andi. We might even talk about *Rise of Dawn*, the next movie in the series *The Forgotten*, and maybe Andi will share a little bit about her next project."

A red 'Applaud' sign lit up, giving the audience the okay to clap just before the massive, red neon 'On Air' sign on the back wall clicked off and a low murmur of conversation immediately stirred through the audience. Brooke stood and headed off stage, talking to one of the headset-wearing, clipboard-carrying assistants. David leaned into Andi and turned his face into the side of her throat, kissing her neck before whispering in her ear. "You are amazing. You're doing great."

"And you don't play fair."

"Who? Me?" David slouched a little so he could rest his head on the back of the couch and look up at her. She tapped his chest with her hand, but kept it there, her fingers toying with one of his vest buttons.

"Did you make that stuff up about the cookies?"

"No." He arched his eyebrows and shook his head, laying his hand over hers so her palm rested over his heart. "I swear. And it wasn't easy, because I *love* oatmeal chocolate chip cookies." David released a slow breath, knowing he hadn't stopped smiling since they walked on stage, but he didn't care. "I guess I love you more."

As soon as the interview lights clicked off, Andi slumped in the director's chair. She didn't even wait for their most recent—and last—interviewer to clear the room. "I don't think I've ever been this exhausted after four hours of talking in my entire life."

David laughed beside her. "This is nothing. Try doing the morning show gauntlet, followed by these 'to be aired' entertainment interviews, then hop a plane for New York to do the nighttime variety shows."

Andi groaned and let her head fall backward, sliding down further in the seat. "Please, no."

"Speaking of trips, I've been thinking about something…

Andi laughed and rolled her head, looking at him from her strange slouched angle. "Oh, boy. The last time you started a conversation with *I've been thinking* I ended up somehow agreeing to *today*. I don't know if I want to hear the follow-up."

David laughed and held out his hand, palm up. Andi took it, lacing her fingers through his. "I was thinking about your book signing tour."

Andi groaned and closed her eyes again, not even wanting to *think* about the three-week tour she was supposed to begin a week after New Year. It was a couple of weeks away, but she was already worried about it. She hadn't figured out yet what to do with Jake. Did she take him out of school and take him with her? Did she ask one of his friend's parents if he could stay with them? It was too late to ask her parents to come, but she'd just forgotten to call in the chaos of the last few weeks. They might still come, but it would be tough. If things didn't change, Lawrence would still be in Los Angeles, but she'd be damned if he even picked Jake up from school, let alone kept him for three weeks.

None of that even touched on the fact she wouldn't see David for three weeks. Filming would start on *The Forgotten* right after the holiday block, moved up with the increased interest, and he wouldn't be able to get away.

"I want to take Jake while you're gone." His simply stated words snapped her attention back to him, and Andi stared in the dim studio lighting. He smiled, his thumb stroking the side of her hand. "Actually, I figured I'd stay at the house. I'm there most nights anyway." He winked and she smiled. "On the days I have late call, I'll take him to school. And on the days I have early call, maybe I can drop him at a friend's house so they can ride in together. But, we'll have dinner at the house every night and he won't have to have his life disrupted any more than it will be just by you being gone."

Andi smiled, tilting her head. "You've been thinking about this for a while."

He shrugged. "Long enough to have some great weekend plans figured out for us while you women are gone."

Andi popped up her eyebrows. "Us *women*?"

"Hey, I grew up with two sisters." He shrugged and laughed at her look of disdain, no matter how fake it was. "It's not often I have an opportunity like this. You know, *guy* time."

"So, I'm guessing your plans involve copious amounts of sports on television—"

"Or action movies. I'm thinking of a Lethal Weapon marathon. Maybe even a Swayze marathon."

"Swayze?" she asked, sitting up. "As in Patrick? *Dirty Dancing* Swayze?"

"No." He attempted to look put out but failed miserably. "*Red Dawn, Next of Kin, Roadhouse...*"

"Don't you think those movies might be a bit *racy* for an eleven-year-old?"

"I've got the edited versions. All the cool guy action without the naughty bits."

Andi smirked, shaking her head. "Followed by take out—"

"If we can't have *your* cooking, all that's left for us is pizza and Chinese," he explained with another shrug, as if that both dismissed and explained his reasoning.

"And copious amounts of video games?"

"Only when homework is done, of course."

"Of course."

"Come here and kiss me."

He grinned wide and hopped down from the chair, coming around to stand in front of her. The height of the director's chair gave her a slight advantage. Andi sat up and wrapped her legs around his waist, his hands sliding up her thighs until he curled his fingers into the material of her slacks at her hips. "So, is that a yes?" he asked.

"Why do you think I'm going to kiss you," she said, making her voice as breathy and seductive as she could manage. She kept her eyes open to watch his expression as she brushed her lips against his.

Before she could complete the kiss, her phone vibrated against her thigh. The buzz turned into her generic ringtone before she could free it from her pocket, but she glanced at the screen before answering.

"It's Theresa," she told David, her gut clenching involuntarily. A call from Theresa could go either way these days, and Andi never knew what to expect. David moved back and offered his hand as she stepped off the chair and glanced around to make sure the camera crew for the last interview was gone and they were alone in the studio sound room. "Hi, Theresa."

"Hey, Andrea. Did I catch you at a good time?"

Andi nodded, looking up at David. He stood at her side, watching her, waiting just like her for whatever Theresa had to say. "Now is fine. We just finished some interviews."

Theresa paused, and Andi thought she heard a slight sigh. The rhythmic tap-tap of Theresa's pen against her desk or laptop carried through the phone. "Andi, I got word of the hearing today."

Andi swallowed. "When is it?"

"Three days. I also found out the judge who will be hearing the case. Judge Ron McKay. Or, as some call him, One Day McKay."

"What does that mean?"

"It means he's notorious for wrapping up these kinds of situations the same day he hears both sides. He doesn't believe in messing around, believes everyone should be allowed to move on—whatever his decision ends up being."

"So, you're saying this will be over in three days."

"I'm saying *most likely* it will be over."

David's hand curled along the back of her neck and he drew against his chest, kissing her hair. But, she wasn't ready to breathe just yet. She tipped her head back, and the momentary relief she saw in his eyes slipped away, a deep line digging into the spot between his eyes. She failed at any meager attempt she made at hiding the cold dread in her gut.

"He's brought on a lawyer to assist with the case," Theresa finally said. Andi imagined the proverbial shoe hovering in the air, waiting to drop to the floor at any moment. Along with it, the lead ball waiting to hit her gut. "Bruce Kane. Remember when I said your ex was a little minnow in a tank of sharks? He's brought on a shark."

"What does all that mean?"

"It means he's got someone who knows how to play LA hardball." Theresa cleared her throat. "They've submitted an addendum to the petition for change of custody orders."

Andi turned to the chair she'd just left, bracing her hand on one of the wooden arms while holding the phone to her ear with the other. "Please, Theresa, just…spit it out. I don't have the nerves for this."

"Along with the accusations you're not fit to care for Jacob, if rewarded custody, they want the exchange to be immediate. Which means Jake has to be present at the hearing—"

"No!" Andi snapped.

"And *if* custody is awarded to Bonherre, Jake must be prepared to leave with his father from the courthouse," Theresa continued, ignoring her protest. "You must have prepared a packed suitcase of his necessities. Arrangements would be made later to pick up the rest of his things."

The rest of Theresa's words buzzed in her head—barely coherent—but enough to grip her lungs in a steel fist and make her vision darken. "Oh, God, no."

"Listen to me, Andrea. I told you at the beginning, and I believe it *now*, he's not going to win. Do you hear me? He's making threats and accusations to shake you up. He's still hoping you back down and meet his demands. He's even made sure Bruce passed that on to me, under the guise of arbitration, of course. If you concede and do what he demands, he'll back off. Don't you get it? He's scared witless you'll win. You called his bluff—"

"Oh, God," she just kept saying, unable to find any other words.

Theresa kept talking, but Andi didn't hear any of it. She held the phone out blindly, and David took it from her. She turned back to the high chair, bracing herself against the arms so she didn't collapse or fall over. Andi couldn't draw in a deep breath, couldn't swallow, couldn't think. How could he do this? How could he rip Jake from her like this? Was he truly this cruel? This heartless? Did he honestly hate her so much he would sacrifice Jake for the chance at vengeance?

On the edge of her consciousness, she heard David talking—and then cursing—before he slapped closed the phone.

He wrapped his arms around her from behind and kissed her hair. "Andi..."

"Son of a bitch," she hissed. "How am I going to explain this to Jake? How am I—" She choked, unable to finish. "I can't-I don't even know—"

"We'll do it together."

She managed to lift her head, looking at him through blurred eyes. Damn Lawrence for ripping her heart out *once again*.

"If you want," David added, smoothing his hand over her hair as he curled it behind her ear. "I'll help you tell him."

"He wants to take Jake in three days," she whispered, even though she knew Theresa had told him the same thing.

"I know." David turned her to face him, taking her face in his hands. He crouched enough to look her straight in the eyes. "Sweetheart, listen to me. *He's not going to take Jake.* No judge in the state would grant him sole custody. I *swear* to you, I believe with every..." He shook his head, huffing. "With every cell of my body, I believe it."

She nodded, unable to do anything else. David wrapped his arms around her, and she let herself sink into his chest. She pressed her ear to his shirt, closing her eyes to focus on the rapid beat of his heart. "Take me home, David."

The flashes of at least two dozen cameras blinded them as they stepped out of the building into the parking lot. David cursed and pulled her against his side, holding his arm up in a vain attempt at blocking their shots. Bodies closed in around them, shoving and pushing, jockeying for a better shot or a better angle. The smell of stale cigarette smoke, Mexican food, and body odor assaulted Andi's senses, greasing her stomach. Shouts of their names joined the cacophony of clicks and shouts.

"Are your husband's accusations against you true, Andi?"

"Did you leave your husband for a woman?"

"David, are you in a polyamorous relationship with Andrea Parker and Maggie Connelly?"

"Will you fight the custody claims or will you give up your son?"

"Andi, has your son witnessed you having sexual relations with men?"

Andi covered her hand with her mouth, feeling like a coward for turning into David's chest, but their questions made her sick. David pulled her with him, leading with his shoulder to divide the horde so they could pass.

"Back off!"

One photographer stumbled back, dropping his camera when David shoved him aside. It shattered at David's feet and he kicked it away. The mass followed them across the parking lot to David's car, but at least she could breathe. David opened her door, shielding her from their eyes and cameras with his body as she more dropped than sat in the car. He slammed the door and went around the front of the car, shouldering another photographer aside to open his door. They surrounded the car, their camera lenses pressed to the glass, the flashes blinding her.

The performance engine roared to life and David twisted to see out the back window, backing the car up without hesitation, forcing the paparazzi to scramble to get out of the way or be run over. He threw the car into drive and gunned it, leaving a loud trail of rubber in the parking lot.

Two miles away, he pulled into the parking lot of a grocery store. The car jerked when he stopped it in a vacant parking space near the exit. Only then did the sob tear its way out of her chest and she folded in on herself.

CHAPTER TWENTY-ONE

"We won't call Jacob to the courtroom unless it's absolutely necessary, I promise you."

Andi stood beside Theresa, her stomach in her throat as Maggie and Jake walked away from her to wait in an empty conference room. Jake looked over his shoulder, his lips turned down in a frown that broke her heart. She touched her fingers to her lips and blew him a kiss, forcing a smile.

"What kind of a man would drag his son into a hearing like this? What kind of father puts his own selfish need for retribution over his child?"

"The kind of man who makes a fool of himself in front of a judge and loses."

The heavy conviction of her attorney's voice made Andi turn back, but only when Maggie and Jake were no longer within sight. "I am putting my entire life at risk based on the strength of your conviction."

Theresa laughed softly, but the sound lacked any humor. "I love Hollywood. Everything is life or death—"

"If I lose," Andi cut her off, failing miserably at keeping the edge from her voice. Not that she tried. "My life ends today. My son will be gone, and he is my life."

She'd fought for three days to keep her emotions in check, to keep from weeping where her son might hear or see, to put on a face that might convince the world she believed this nightmare would end. She'd cried all her tears in an Albertson's parking lot, making damn sure they were done before she looked into her son's eyes. People would just have to deal with some cut to her words.

Theresa's smile slid away, her expression finally reflecting the serious edge in her eyes. Finally reflecting the heaviness of the air and the truth of the day. "I told you, Andrea, there would be no promises coming into this. The only promise I could make was if you did *nothing* —or worse, did what he demanded—you would live under the thumb of Lawrence Bonherre until Jacob reached adulthood. Of that, I am absolutely sure."

Andi drew in a slow, metered breath through her nose, releasing it between tight lips. It was the only thing keeping her from snapping. Black pain hovered on the edge of her peripheral, jabbing at the inside of her skull and twisting her stomach. A three-day migraine was a personal record, despite the ebb and flow of the pain. Only David's massage trick had allowed her to get any sleep, if a couple of hours a night counted for anything.

"I know," she managed to say, this time tamping down the bite in her voice. "The logical part of my mind knows you're right. I know any judge worth his station will see through Lawrence's lies and will know what is best for Jacob. I keep telling myself when I leave today it will be with Jake. But, there's this screaming…" Her throat tightened and her voice wobbled. Andi swallowed, pressing her lips together. "There's this small part of me that is terrified."

Theresa laid her hand on Andi's arm, squeezing for a brief moment, but it did nothing to fill the black hole sitting in the center of her chest.

The echoing sound of heavy footsteps drew her attention down the courthouse hallway. Her stomach clenched just at the sight of Lawrence Bonherre. The judge had waived the restraining order for the hearing, with the understanding at no time would Andi and Lawrence be left alone. It was a small solace. Lawrence's stride showed no lack of confidence, which Andi expected. He knew how to exude confidence, no matter the situation. A man walked beside him, matching his sure stride, with dark hair he wore slicked back from his high forehead. He was older than Lawrence by at least fifteen years, and his entire demeanor screamed 'smarmy.'

Lawrence looked straight at her, arching one eyebrow with a satisfied smirk. He said something to his lawyer and they both chuckled before walking right past Andi and Theresa to the open courtroom door.

"Even if I knew nothing about your ex-husband, I'd hate him based purely on that cocky smirk."

Andi snorted a laugh. "Then talking to him should be a real joy for you."

Theresa sighed. "Okay, you ready for this?"

The pain in her head surged and she winced. She nodded, refusing to give in to the nausea because to give in would be to give Lawrence power over her, whether he knew it or not. They followed Lawrence and his attorney into the courtroom and took their seats. Andi caught Lawrence watching her in her peripheral vision, that same arrogant grin on his face. He still believed he would either win, or she would give in to his demands. One of the reasons Lawrence was such a sought-after lawyer in Chicago was he went into every case fully expecting victory. With a ninety-seven percent success rate, his clients believed he created his destiny and they were willing to pay for it.

Minutes later, the doors closed to the courtroom and Judge Ronald McKay entered. After the usual statement of record, Judge McKay instructed them to sit. He appeared to be somewhere in his sixties, with hair that had probably once been thick, curly, and red but now covered his skull like a wreath more gray than red. But, he had a spark in his eyes that eased the tension in Andi's chest a small degree the moment he looked in her direction. He folded his hands and scanned the room, focusing in turn on each attorney.

"So we're clear, this is a non-arbitration hearing regarding the custody of Jacob Nathaniel Bonherre, a minor of the age of eleven years. So there is no confusion for your clients, what that means is the parties involved were unable to agree before coming to my courtroom, so whatever decision I reach at the end of this hearing will be final." He looked over the papers in front of him. "So, by what I can tell, Mom doesn't want Dad to have free visitations anymore due to your recent..." He cleared his throat. "Anger management issues."

He glanced at Andi and Theresa over the edge of his glasses, and Theresa nodded. "Yes, Your Honor. In a nutshell."

Judge McKay then looked at Lawrence and his lawyer, Attorney Kane. "And you don't want Mom to have custody at all due to..." He read through the bottom of his glasses. "Selfish and unsatisfactory personal choices which have exposed Jacob Bonherre to unsavory elements who may negatively influence his future behavior."

"Yes, Your Honor," Kane began. "Ms. Parker has surrounded herself with individuals who we will prove—"

"Save it for when I ask for it, Council," Judge McKay ordered, raising his hand. "You'll get your chance. Everyone will get their chance."

Andi only registered half of what Judge McKay said from that point, with only the basics making it through the pounding in her head. He expected decorum, he expected respect, he expected them both to act in the best interest of their son, and he reiterated he intended to have their situation resolved by the end of the day.

By the end of the day...

Because Theresa had filed the first petition, Judge McKay allowed her to begin. She spoke for forty minutes, respectfully bringing the restraining order and the statements by Maggie, David, Tony, and Horatio from the incident at the house. Theresa provided copies of the medical reports from Andi's ER visit, which also documented the old bruising on her arms from Lawrence's first "assault." By the time she was done, she'd shown evidence of the lack of parental participation by Lawrence in the six years since they divorced.

Then attorney Bruce Kane spent over two hours bashing Andi in every conceivable way—and some inconceivable ways, as well. Nothing was safe. He made her sound like a peddler of pornography and a woman of loose morals. He went after Maggie, David...she wondered if at one point her mailman might come under fire. When Judge McKay demanded proof of immorality, Kane stated it was a matter of public record and opinion.

Then he brought up her failed marriage, and just as Lawrence had done the night she left, Kane pinned the blame on her. How could a woman incapable of showing love and affection to her husband be expected to provide the proper care and guidance to her son? She was painted as a shrew and a gold digger. The entire speech made her sick.

When finished, both he and Lawrence looked across the room at them with the same self-righteous smirks they'd walked into the room with. Andi swallowed and refused to give either of them the satisfaction of looking fazed. Judge McKay picked up the papers on his desk, tapped their edge against the wood, and sighed.

"Where is the minor, Jacob Bonherre?"

Andi sucked in a sharp breath and Theresa reached for her hand beneath the table, curling her fingers over Andi's wrist. "Ms. Parker's son is here at the courthouse per your instructions, Your Honor. He is waiting in a conference room with a family friend."

Lawrence snorted.

Judge McKay scratched his fingernail along the edge of his thinning hair at his temple, reading over his notes. "In the interest of thoroughness, I want to speak to the boy."

Andi couldn't take a breath. Her chest seized up around her lungs, but she couldn't force anything out of her mouth.

"He's old enough to have an opinion in all this. He's also old enough to give it to me without his parents present." He looked to Andi. "Ms. Parker, I'd like you to go with a court representative and explain to your son he'll be speaking to me. You are not to give him any instructions on how to answer, simply inform him what is happening. And why, if you choose, but I would assume he is aware of why we are here today."

Andi nodded. "Yes, Your Honor."

"The court representative will then bring Jacob to my chambers so he and I can talk. Until then, plaintiff and defendant are dismissed." He slammed down his gavel and rose, and they all followed suit.

Andi clenched her hands together, fighting the violent tremble that jerked up her spine. This was the very thing she hadn't wanted...for Jake to be dragged into this mess. The only saving grace was he didn't have to do it in an open courtroom. He didn't have to look at his father —or her—while he answered the judge's questions.

A woman dressed in a navy blue suit, her blonde hair curled into a twist along her skull, approached Andi and Theresa from the back of the courtroom. "If you'll come with me, Ms. Parker."

Andi followed the woman to the conference room, and when they opened the door, Jake jumped up from the floor where he sat playing his video game. "Mom!"

She grunted and laughed, taking a step back when he slammed into her. He wrapped his arms around her waist and hugged her so tight she couldn't breathe. "Hey, honey."

"Can we go home now?"

Andi caught Maggie's eye, and gave a tiny shake of her head. Maggie released a long breath and closed her eyes, her head dropping forward in an expression of frustration Andi only allowed herself to feel and not express. Andi sat down in one of the leather chairs around the conference room table, now looking up at her son.

"No, honey, I'm sorry. We're not done here yet. Actually, I came to tell you Judge McKay needs to talk to you…just like he's been talking to your father and me."

Jake pulled a face and scuffed his sneaker against the carpet. "I thought I didn't have to."

"I hoped you didn't have to, but Judge McKay said he wants to know what you think."

"If I tell him I don't want to live with Dad, can we go home then?"

Andi caught the slight shake of the court representative's head. She had to choose her words carefully. "You just need to answer his questions, honey. Be completely honest, okay?"

Jake threw his arms around her neck, leaning over to hug her. She swore he had to have grown two inches in the last six months, and soon he'd be taller than her. Andi blinked back tears and silently prayed she'd be there to watch him grow. The court representative touched his shoulder, and after a nod from Andi it was okay, he followed the woman from the room. As soon as he was gone, Andi covered her face and curled forward, sucking in sharp breaths to keep the panic at bay.

She heard the sound of a chair rolling across the floor to her, and the creak of leather as Maggie sat. Then her friend took her hand and pulled it away from her face, making Andi look her in the eyes.

"What is going on?" Maggie asked, every word stressed.

"He heard the statements, looked at the paperwork..." Andi shrugged and swallowed. If she lost it now, she wouldn't get her control back in time to return to the courtroom. "Then he said he wanted to talk to Jake."

"This is a good thing," Theresa said from the doorway.

"How is this a good thing?" Andi snapped. "How is throwing an eleven-year-old boy into the war between his parents a good thing?"

"Because he's an eleven-year-old boy with an opinion. Do you have any doubt he'll tell the judge he wants to be with *you*? Do you think he'll walk in there and tell McKay he wants to live with his father?"

"No."

"Do you believe he'll say anything negative against Maggie? Or David?"

"No, of course not."

Theresa nodded. "This is a good thing. Come on. I'll buy you a coffee in the commissary. It's going to be a while."

Maggie squeezed her hand and pulled her to her feet. She hadn't held her best friend's hand since she was eight and her best friend was Peggy Ann Jackson in second grade, but today she needed to hold her best friend's hand. The three women made their way to the small lunch counter off the courthouse lobby, but Andi couldn't imagine eating anything. She stayed with an iced tea and conceded to a fruit bowl when Maggie insisted.

After choking down some of the chunked cantaloupe, she excused herself for the ladies' room. As she rounded the corner away from the lobby, she stopped short to keep from running straight into Lawrence's chest. His hand curled around her elbows and Andi cringed back, her stomach twisting at just the basic contact.

"Typical Andrea. Not watching where you're going."

She crossed the hall, glancing both ways to see if anyone was within sight. "You're breaking the restraining order, Lawrence."

"We aren't alone," he said in his condescending tone that screamed 'once again, I must explain.' "My lawyer will be here any moment, and your lawyer isn't more than fifty feet away."

Andi pressed her lips together and shifted to move past him, but he sidestepped and blocked her way. He held up his hand, but she stepped back before he dared touch her again.

"You look stressed, Andrea. Is this hearing too much for you?"

"I'm fine," she hissed. "Let me pass."

Lawrence leaned in, the cloying smell of his aftershave burning her nose. "This could all be over right now, Andrea. Do what I demand and I'll withdraw my petition."

She clenched her jaw until it hurt and stared him in the eye. "Really, Lawrence? Is that *all* I have to do? Just…"

"Just call Golden Boy and call it off."

She saw the gleam in his eye…he thought she meant it. *Sarchasm – The giant gulf between the speaker of sarcasm, and the dimwit who doesn't get it.* Holding his arrogant gaze, Andi slid her hand into her purse and took out her cell phone.

"You'll let me keep him if I leave David." She made it a statement, not a question.

"Get rid of your lover, and you can keep your son."

"I'll see him, you know. When filming begins…"

"You know what I mean, Andrea. Don't be thick. You keep him out of your bed. Out of your home. Out of your son's life."

Your son. She almost slapped him.

She turned on the phone, the beep drawing Lawrence's attention. He smirked, one corner of his mouth tipping upward. "I knew you didn't have the stomach to carry this all the way through. You won't risk losing that boy. Do it, Andrea. Call him."

Andi only looked away from him long enough to find David's number in her mailbox and hit dial. She stared up at Lawrence as the call went through. David picked up on the second ring.

"Hey, sweetheart." He sounded slightly out of breath.

As soon as she heard his voice, a smooth heat spread out from Andi's chest. "Hi, David." She fought to keep her voice steady.

"What's happened? Is it over?"

"No." She took a deep breath, blinking as she tried to keep

Lawrence's egotistical face in focus. "We're on a break. Judge McKay is talking to Jake right now."

"Oh, Andi, I'm sorry. You didn't want that…"

"No, but I'm doing what has to be done."

Lawrence's smirk widened. It made her sick.

"Andi, are you okay? What's going on, sweetheart?"

She swallowed and licked her lips. If ever she needed to tap into her gift of writing dialogue, it was right now. "I need to tell you something, David."

The moment of silence on the other end nearly broke her. She wanted to drive a point home with Lawrence, but she wouldn't do it at David's expense.

"Andi…" The heaviness of his voice hurt.

"I love you." Lawrence's smirk shifted to a scowl. "I haven't said it enough in the last few days, and I wanted to make sure you knew that."

His relieved sigh carried through the phone. "Oh, sweetheart, I know. I love you, too."

Lawrence's scowl twisted into an angry grimace and he turned away, storming to the other side of the hall. "I have to go," she said more softly. "David…I do love you."

"I'll see you when it's over. Both of you."

Andi blinked against the sudden tears, swallowing hard before she spoke. "I'll see you soon."

She wished flip phones were still a thing so she could punctuate the moment with an audible 'period' on the scene. Or…maybe an exclamation point.

Bruce Kane came out of the men's room just as Theresa's voice calling Andi's name carried across the lobby. She took a backward step and looked at where she'd left Theresa and Maggie. Both were nearly across the lobby, and Theresa waved to her.

"Judge McKay called everyone back."

The few bites of melon in her stomach suddenly turned into balls of acid. Summoning up her last well of strength, she marched across the marble and met the other two women to head toward her fate.

David was halfway up the stairs from his bedroom when the finger-tapping, fiddle music of *Wrapped Up In You* carried from the front hall. He sprinted up the stairs and managed to snatch his cell phone off his desk before the third ring. Taking a deep, sharp breath he answered.

"Hey, sweetheart."

"Hi, David." He immediately picked up on the tight strain in her voice and sank into the desk chair, his gut twisting.

"What's happened? Is it over?"

"No." She sighed softly. "We're on a break. Judge McKay is talking to Jake right now."

David winced and shook his head. "Oh, Andi, I'm sorry. You didn't want that…"

"No, but I'm doing what has to be done."

"Andi, are you okay? What's going on, sweetheart?"

The silence lasted half a heartbeat longer than he could stand before she finally answered, and the thick heaviness in the words hit him square in the chest. "I need to tell you something, David."

"Andi…"

"I love you." David closed his eyes, finally able to release the breath caught in his lungs. "I haven't said it enough in the last few days, and I wanted to make sure you knew that."

He smiled because he couldn't help it, and rubbed his fingers across his forehead. "Oh, sweetheart, I know. I love you, too."

"I have to go," she said more softly. "David…I do love you."

"I'll see you when it's over." He closed his eyes, hoping she heard in his voice his conviction. He had to believe because if he didn't, he'd go mad. "Both of you."

"I'll see you soon."

The line went silent and David set the phone on the desk with careful discipline, because if he did anything more he knew he'd probably throw it across the room. David's chest hurt, every breath was a chore to expand his lungs against the steel fist around his ribs. He was beyond exhausted, having barely slept in three days, but he knew he wouldn't rest until this was over. Even then, it would all depend on the outcome.

Was it selfish of him to want Andi in his arms tonight?

It had nearly killed him to leave her this morning, and the need to hold her smothered him. Pressuring her to stay with him was the last thing he wanted, but the Creator help him, he needed her. Once upon a time, needing someone like he needed Andi would have scared the daylights out of him. Now, the idea of not having her scared him more.

Because Andi wasn't the only one with everything at stake today.

She hadn't said it, maybe because she didn't even realize it herself, but if Andrea Parker lost her son then David lost them both.

He rubbed his fingers across his forehead and flicked at the moisture on his cheek. When he was sixteen, he had to prepare for one of the biggest roles of his young career. Before then he'd done bubble gum flicks where everything ended with ice cream sundaes and smiles all around. At sixteen, he took on his first emotionally intense role and he couldn't do it. His acting coach, a brilliant man named Ian Randall, told him to be truly convincing in any role he had to make himself part of every character he played. It wasn't about finding himself in the character but finding the character in *him*. Which meant he had to let go of some of his own emotions, memories, and passions—let go and let them breathe through him.

It had worked. He had the statuettes to prove it.

The problem with breaking down the walls between himself and the characters he played was that once down, the walls were hard to build again. Right now, he wished for some restraint. Because right now it hurt.

He wanted to hit something. Namely Lawrence Bonherre.

David shoved back from the desk with such force the chair shot backward and bounced off a display shelf. A photo of Caroline and Sarah toppled over and hit the floor, the glass breaking. With a howl of frustration that came from his soul, David picked up the phone and hurled it across the room. It hit the brick face of the fireplace with a crack, falling in five pieces on the hardwood floor. He threw his head back and pressed the heels of his hands into his eyes until spots danced behind his closed lids. Another guttural moan tore its way out of his throat.

The doorbell startled him, and he jerked around, sucking in several sharp breaths. David cleared his throat and scrubbed his hands over his face before heading for the door. He glanced at the broken frame and phone, a surge of self-anger hitting him.

The doorbell rang again. "Davey, it's your mother," came his mother's voice through the thick wood.

An instant sense of relief slammed into him, battling for dominance over the frustration his request to be left alone today had been ignored. David rested his head on the door for a moment, his hand on the knob, and sucked in several breaths to rein in whatever emotion would still be clearly and blatantly obvious to his mother.

Because she was Mom, simple as that.

"Hey, Mom," he managed as he opened the door. Of course, she wasn't alone. If one person in your family can help you even a little to fix a problem, just imagine what an entire family could do? That was his mother's theory anyway. Her husband and David's *second* stepfather, Joseph Masters, stood behind his wife with a slightly sheepish grin that said *'You know your mother once she's got an idea in her head.'* Caroline stood behind him, little Katherine at her side and baby Abigail in her arms. Sarah appeared with two bags of groceries in her arms, followed by Caroline's husband Aaron with another two bags.

Dolly Masters held out her arms and pulled David into a hard hug. He had to bend down to return it, but he pressed his face into her shoulder and inhaled the aroma of fruit-scented hairspray, Avon Skin So Soft, and baking bread that always engulfed his mother. David pressed his eyes shut, refusing to lose the shaky grip he had on his raw emotions.

"What are you doing here?" he asked, pulling back to hug Caroline —taking a quick peek at the pink bundle in her arms—and kissed Sarah's cheek.

"On a day like today, you need family." Dolly brushed past him into the house. "And chicken soup. I didn't have time to make kugel so I bought some at the deli, but I thought we'd have challah with the soup."

David chuckled, shaking Aaron's hand. Katherine tugged at his shirt, and he picked her up so she could smack a loud kiss on his cheek. "You look sad, Uncle Davey."

He smiled. The innocent observations of children would be the death of him. "I am, a little, darlin'. But, I'm better now."

He put Katherine down in time for Sarah to shove the groceries at him. "We've got the makings for a three-course meal. Better hope your kitchen is clean."

By the time he reached the kitchen, his mother had his largest pot on the stove and had an open box of broth in each hand, dumping them in the pot. David set the bags on the counter and removed the ingredients inside. In an hour, the house would smell of simmering chicken soup with matzo balls and fresh challah bread. David broke down the paper bags, put them in his recycling bin, and leaned his hip against the counter as he watched his mother cut vegetables.

The house was filled with noise, shoving out the smothering silence that had devoured him all morning. He'd become so used to the sounds of life in a house, even if just the sound of Jake's video games or the click of a keyboard while Andi worked on her book. Sometimes it was as loud and boisterous as the four of them playing a game, or as simple as their laughter while they watched a movie. Right now, it felt like Thanksgiving or Chanukah with all his closest family in one place while his mother cooked.

Dolly looked his way as she dumped the carrots in the pot. "You're smiling. That's nice to see."

He inhaled the smell of broth and chicken and spices. "I was just thinking."

"About Andi?"

"Yeah. And how I like the sound of people in the house."

His mother wiped her hands on a towel and stepped closer, looking up at him. "I haven't met her—"

"I know, Ma. But, with everything going on—"

"I wasn't trying to chastise you, Davey," she said more gently. "I just wanted to say even though I haven't met her, I can see in your eyes how wonderful she is, and I can't wait to meet her and her son." She laid her hand on his cheek. "I also see the pain in your eyes at the thought this all might end badly."

David blinked and looked away, drawing in a sharp breath. Her gentle hand brought his attention back to her, and she smiled. "God is closest to those with a broken heart."

"Thanks, Ma."

"Now, you go on and see that new niece of yours and let me get the bread in the oven, otherwise it won't be ready with the soup."

David kissed his mother's cheek and wandered back to the living room. Aaron and Joe were camped out in front of the television watching a football game. Sarah sat on the floor with Katherine, an array of coloring books and crayons spread out between them. Someone had cleaned up his mess. His sister looked up and gave him a wink before going back to giving Barbie a dark purple dress with black skulls. Caroline stood from the couch when he came in, the baby bundled in her arms.

"How are you doing?" she asked softly, her eyes shifting to study him.

He drew in a slow breath through his nose, the scent of baby lotion and powder tingling his senses, and released it as he looked down at Abigail. She was awake, her wide and aware eyes taking in everything. She'd found her fist and sucked noisily on her fingers as she looked from her mother to her uncle.

"She's beautiful," David said, skirting her question.

Caroline shifted the baby and slid her into David's arms. He'd held Katherine plenty of times when she was a baby, yet he always felt a small rush of panic when he held something so tiny and fragile. So delicate. Her focus shifted solely to him, her tiny brow pulling together as she seemed to wonder who this stranger might be, and probably deciding whether the whole situation was worth crying over or not. David bounced his knees, smiling when she sighed heavily.

"You're a natural," Caroline told him, leaning her cheek against his arm so she could watch her daughter. "You need to be a father, David."

He swallowed hard at the immediate and intense tightening of his throat. Would he be tempting fate if he told Caroline—or anyone—he felt like a father already? Maybe not completely, but the idea of not seeing Jacob again tore at him as fiercely as it would for any parent, he thought.

"It's going to be okay." Caroline rubbed her hand up and down his back. "I believe that, David. We all believe it. We're here to celebrate with you when you find that out, not to mourn with you."

He felt the tremble of his chin and bit down, blinking to keep Abigail's face in focus. He couldn't look at his sister, because he couldn't see their face when they saw the doubt in his eyes. He swore to Andi he wouldn't be the reason she lost her son…and if she lost today…it would be because of him. Because he convinced her to talk to Theresa. Because she chose him and a fight over the sure path.

Caroline whispered his name and curled her hand behind his neck, drawing him down to her. With the baby held between them, David rested his weary head on her shoulder and just for a moment indulged in the raw emotions ripping their way out of him. Caroline smoothed his hair and kissed his temple and he sucked in several sharp breaths. When he straightened again, his sister held his face in her hands and smiled a watery smile.

"Andrea Parker is one lucky woman to have a man like you love her so much."

David shook his head and shifted Abigail in his arms to free a hand, wiping his cheeks. "No, Caroline. You're wrong. I'm a damn lucky man a woman like Andi would love me."

She smiled and took back Abigail. "I'm going to feed her and lay her down. Can I use your bedroom?"

"Yeah, sure."

Two hours later, David loaded dirty dishes into his dishwasher as his mother ladled the remaining soup into storage containers. There was enough left to feed him for a week, and he hoped the smell of baked bread would last at least until the next day.

"Your father called me," his mother said, her tone so nonchalant, he had to stop and process her words to make sure he'd heard her right. "Last night."

He put the last bowl on the top rack and closed the washer door, pressing the start button. She just kept going with her chore, pouring the last of the soup into a plastic container. David dried his hands and leaned against the edge of the counter.

"He's seen…well, everything," she explained, glancing only briefly at him. "We know the truth, your sisters and I and Joe, but how can he?" Before David could offer the old argument of '*If he were around…*' she waved it off and continued. "The point is he wanted to make sure you were okay. And he wanted to know if there was anything he could do."

"What did you tell him?"

"I told him the truth. About Andrea and Jake and how much you love them both. And I told him she's a good woman and she makes you happy." She took the pot to the sink and filled it with water, adding a squirt of detergent. "And I told him you were okay."

David nodded. His relationship with his father was best described as strained. They'd only spoken a dozen or so times since his father left twenty years earlier, and once David got past his early adolescent anger, they'd tried to find some kind of balance. By then, the relationship had been too damaged to be anything more than two people with an undeniable link to each other but would never be a part of each other's lives. He had fond memories of his father from when he was little, but Dan Bishop had been opposed to his son's venture into acting, and when David's career took off, his father chose to leave and not witness it rather than stay and encourage his son's success.

"I just thought you should know."

David nodded and tossed the towel on the counter. He left the kitchen and skirted the living room where Joe and Aaron had found an old World War II movie. Caroline sat in a chair by the patio windows reading a book, Abigail asleep in her carrier on the floor. He didn't know where Sarah was exactly, but he heard somewhere in the distance the sound of music. David went to the back patio door that looked out over the Hollywood Hills. The day had slipped away, the sun heading for the horizon. The sky was already gray and daylight had dimmed. He'd been able to forget the passage of time and Andi's absence for a while.

All it took was a heartbeat for all of it to come slamming back into his chest. The broken photograph had been picked up, and Aaron had declared the cell phone unsalvageable. He fought the urge to pick up the house line and call her, just to know. But, his gut told him if he did he'd hear the worst. She would have called him otherwise. If she didn't call, if she didn't come to him, it was because he didn't want to hear what she had to say.

The rat-a-tat-tat of machine guns echoed through the sound system, a strange contrast to Katherine's giggles and Mom's puttering in the kitchen. Abigail made a small mewling sound and Katherine's running footsteps echoed off the hardwood. The front door opened. David closed his eyes and crossed his arms over his chest, letting it all soak in. Letting it soothe the sharp edges as much as it could.

Joe said something, but all David registered was the aged deepness of his voice, not the words.

"Where is David?"

He spun around, the trembling lilt of Andi's voice stealing the air right from his lungs. She stood in front of the open door, scanning the room, and all attention focused on her. Even from where he watched, he saw the color bloom in her damp, streaked cheeks.

She'd been crying.

"Andi…"

Her eyes snapped to him when he said her name. She took a step and stopped, a good twenty feet still between them. Joe muted the television and except for the sounds of the children, everything stopped. David swallowed hard and took another step toward her. He looked at the open door.

He didn't need to ask if it was over.

"Where's Maggie?" He couldn't bring himself to ask where Jake was, and why he wasn't with her. If he didn't ask, he didn't have to hear the answer.

She took another step. "She followed in her car." Andi's voice cracked, losing strength with every word. "We took separate cars. I needed the time to…" She stuttered, choking on the words, sucking in a sharp breath to counteract the sob that seemed to tear her apart. "I can't—" She sucked in another breath, flittering her hand near her face. "I can't stop crying."

David crossed the space in three long strides and pulled her hard against him. She wrapped her arms around his neck and buried her face against his shoulder, body-shaking sobs making her tremble in his embrace. He held on as tight as he dared, curling his hands into fists against her back. If he squeezed any tighter, he'd break a rib, but if this was the last time he ever had her in his arms...he couldn't even finish the thought.

"I tried to call," she wept into his shoulder. "I tried all the way here, but you didn't answer. I couldn't remember the house number—"

"I broke my phone." David reluctantly pulled back to look into her face. His eyes burned and his throat tightened until he could barely swallow. "I'm sorry, Andi. I'm so sorry."

She touched his face and stroked his cheek, the touch painfully tender, and a tiny smile bowed her lips. David's chest hurt, and he wondered if *this* was what a broken heart felt like. Like he was dying. He moved his hands up her back to her shoulders, unable to fight the tremors tightening his muscles, and matched her touch with his hands on her tear-slicked cheeks. David pressed a kiss to her forehead and she curled her fingers around his wrists.

"I don't know if I could have told you on the phone anyway," she said roughly, the crying jag scraping her voice. "I just couldn't stop. I think I frightened Jake, but I just couldn't stop—"

He wrapped her in his arms again, her tears soaking his shirt. He didn't care.

"It's funny...you would think tears of joy wouldn't be as hard to stop..."

David jerked back, not daring to believe what he thought he'd heard. "What?"

Tears still ran down her cheeks, but they disappeared into her wide smile. Her eyes shined, not with unshed tears of sorrow, but with joy. Not just happiness...joy. She nodded within his hold. Outside, he heard the crunch of another car pulling into his driveway.

"That's Maggie," Andi whispered between them. "Jake is with her. He likes putting in the code for your gate," she explained with the special 'proud mom' smile he loved so much.

The flash of elation that hit him nearly bowled him over and he staggered. "Jake..." he repeated.

She nodded again. "Jake."

He whooped and swept her in his arms again, spinning her around as he laughed hysterically. He couldn't help it, and wouldn't deny it. Somewhere, little Katherine laughed. "Mommy, look. Uncle Davey is dancing."

He set Andi on her feet again, taking her face in his hands. Her lips tasted of salt and the remains of long-gone gloss. No kiss had ever tasted so wonderful

"Did I miss the invitation to the party?"

David twisted around to face the door again. Maggie stood near the door, and David realized his entire family had formed a large circle around them. Behind him, he heard his mother's soft sniffle and he caught Sarah wiping a tear from her cheek. Joe just watched, smiling his silent smile.

Jake stepped into the doorway, apparently much calmer than anyone else, although his smile was just as wide. He paused, scanning the crowd of people he didn't know, settling on David and Andi. With a widening of his grin, he bolted for them and nearly bowled them both over when he hit them straight on. David laughed and hugged the boy against him. He kissed Andi again and planned on doing that as often as possible...for the rest of his life.

"I'd say the party is just beginning," his mother said, coming from the kitchen. "I'll make a grocery list. Aaron, you and Caroline can go and get food."

"We just finished lunch," Sarah mumbled.

"But now we celebrate," Dolly declared. "We have been blessed."

David released some of his hold on Andi, but she stayed close to his side, her arms wrapped around his waist. "Ma, I am—" He huffed a sharp breath, trying to catalog and tame the erratic emotions slamming into him. There were too many: relief, joy, peace, elation...He smiled down at Andi, unable to shift his attention enough to look at his mother. She was beautiful, she was here...and she was still his. "I am so happy to introduce you to Andrea Parker...my everything."

Andi smiled at him and touched his cheek before taking his mother's hand. "I'm so glad to finally meet you. I'm sorry it's taken so long."

His mother skipped the hand, pulling Andi away from him to

embrace her. And so the introductions began. Andi gave him a glance over her shoulder as his mother led her away, then waved her fingers and went along, Jake following.

"Hey, don't I get a hug?"

David spun around to Maggie. "Hell, yeah," he declared and lifted her off her feet with his embrace, swinging her until she chuckled. "We did it, Maggie," he said near her ear as he set her down.

"Let's not do this again, though, okay," she said softly, her strained voice belying the glimmer of tears in her brown eyes. "I don't know if I've got the strength."

"She wouldn't have made it without you." David touched her cheek, knowing he had relied on Maggie's stoic and silent strength as much as Andi.

Maggie brushed his hand away with a derisive chuckle. "Stop it. How am I supposed to come back with witty snark when you stay stuff like that?"

David kissed her forehead and laughed, hooking his elbow behind her neck. "I love you, too, Maggie Connelly." Turning her toward the gathering of family in the living room, he said, "Come on. Meet the rest of the family."

"You should have seen his face when Judge McKay not only threw out his petition but threw out mine and rewrote the whole thing."

"I wish I had."

David's agile and skilled fingers found the sweet spot at the base of her skull, and she groaned when he released the contact and the stress drained from her neck like water from a faucet. The headache was all but gone, but she was far too relaxed and was enjoying herself far too much to tell him to stop the relaxing massage. The light of the silver moon cast his bedroom in shadows, and a cool night breeze slipped through the small opening in the patio door. David shifted enough to reach the edge of the blankets and pulled them over their legs to fight off the chill.

He sat against the headboard, the pillows piled around them like a nest, with Andi leaning back into his bare chest. Tonight they weren't alone in the house. The celebration had gone so late into the evening that everyone decided to stay, and thankfully with a little doubling up, David had plenty of room.

"So, explain the new terms. In the chaos earlier—" She chuckled at his choice of words. *Chaos* didn't even begin to cover it, but it was a wonderful kind of madness. "I missed the fine details."

His hands slid down her arms and he crossed her right arm over her body, going to work on her hand. He slid his palm across hers and caressed her knuckles, the touch being more about contact than headache relief. Andi studied the contrast in their skin and the size of their hands in the pale light and smiled.

"Judge McKay told Lawrence his actions were reprehensible and he should have known better as an officer of the court, whether that be an Illinois court or a California court. He said, based on Lawrence's recent actions, coupled with his lack of interest in the past, it would be best to limit his exposure to his son rather than grant him more access." She chuckled, too relaxed to do much more. "It didn't hurt a court officer overheard Lawrence's final power play in the hallway."

"That's when you called me?"

She slid sideways so she could look up at him. "Yes, and David, I'm sorry."

"For what?

"I was trying to make a point with him…if I made you think—"

He tilted her chin and kissed her. "I was worried for about half a second," he said with an honest smile. "I'm glad you called. I wanted to hear your voice."

Andi took in a deep breath, enjoying the smell of chicken soup that had drifted down to his bedroom, and reached up to touch his face. With just the slightest urging, he kissed her again. Then he shifted her back to her original position and resumed the massage.

"Keep going. The terms…"

"From now until Jake is eighteen, the judge has put the choice to see his father in Jake's hands. I have *full* legal and physical custody, which means all decisions regarding his care are mine and mine alone. But

Judge McKay said even though Jake is a minor, he is old enough to decide to see his father or not. Jake was very adamant and clear in Judge McKay's chambers."

"So, in theory, Jake could choose never to see his father again."

"In theory, yes."

David moved on to her other hand, adding a kiss to her shoulder as she canted her head to her side, giving him more access. The tender contact spread warmth over her skin. As much as the kiss warmed her, the massage pushed her closer to sleep. She was physically and emotionally drained. The outcome was better than she'd dared even imagine, but after the days and months of battling her ex, she was so thankful it was done and she could rest without it hanging over her head.

"Do you think he'll do that?"

She shrugged. "I don't know. Right now, Jake is very angry with Lawrence. He understands far too well what Lawrence tried to do." She shifted to see his face. "He knows it wasn't just about trying to take him away from me, he knows it was about taking *you* away from *us*. It might be a while before he even wants to hear about his father, let alone see him. But, at least now, the control is in his hands." New tears welled in her eyes, but they were no longer tears of frustration, anger, or sadness at what Lawrence had done. They were tears of relief.

David stroked his thumb across her cheek and kissed her hair. "I don't ever want to be that afraid again."

Andi slid sideways so she could look at him over her shoulder. "You were afraid?"

"Terrified."

She almost asked why, but she knew. It was the same terror that had gripped her for three long days, and probably longer. From the first day when Lawrence walked into her kitchen on Jake's birthday and set the ball into motion to this day.

Whatever the path, she was so thankful for the final destination.

David wrapped his arms around her and scooted them deeper into the bed. His hands stroked her arms and he skimmed his lips over her cheek and neck, humming appreciatively.

"I like your mom," she said before sleep wrapped around her as firmly as David's arms. "I love your whole family."

"Even Scary Sarah?"

She giggled. "Even Scary Sarah. Does your stepfather ever actually speak?"

David laughed. "Yes, but it doesn't happen very often. So, if he does you'd better be listening."

Her cheeks hurt from smiling and her eyes stung from crying, but Andi welcomed it all. "Do you remember what you told me at the aquarium? About never looking back with regret, because everything has brought you to where you are?"

He nodded against her shoulder, his gentle kiss sending warmth through her.

"I want to hate Lawrence for everything he did, but I can't."

"I'm not sure I'm quite there yet," he admitted. "I'd still break his face again if given the chance."

She turned her head to look at him and met his lips instead. He moved his hand from her arm to cup her cheek, holding her still to kiss her slowly, deliberately, and thoroughly until she hummed against his lips.

"But, I won't regret any of it, either," he said when he pulled back enough to look at her in the moonlight. "I wish the last few months had been easy, but…" He laughed, his smile spreading. "Yet another example of your influence on me. I'm running at the mouth."

"It's okay." Andi touched his chin, stroking the bristle with her thumb as she watched his lips. "I like what you have to say."

"Marry me."

Her attention darted to his eyes, and the dark look in them took her breath away. Before she could form an answer, he took a deep breath and released it with a smile. "I had this big plan to ask you the night of the premiere, but I don't want to wait that long. Hell, if at all possible, I want us married by then. I've got the ring already." He pointed toward the drawers along the far wall. Andi spared them only a glance before looking at him again. "It's over there, and I swear I'll give it to you tomorrow, but I just don't want to give you up quite yet."

She smiled, slowly, letting it spread through her.

"That is, of course, if you say yes."

Holding his gaze, Andi rolled until she knelt in front of him. With deliberate slowness, she leaned over him and took his cheeks in her hands. When she kissed him, she didn't rush, didn't hurry until she felt the subtle shift from contact to seduction. With a smile against his lips, she sat back on her heels.

"This would make a great book," she said, purposefully keeping her voice low. "No one would believe it otherwise."

"Yeah?" He stroked her cheek, his fingertips teasing the edge of her hair. "How does it end?"

"Corniest line ever. *And they lived happily ever after.*"

David groaned and rolled his eyes, ending with a chuckle. "You did *not* just say that."

She laughed out loud and kissed him again. Smiling so wide it was almost hard to maintain the kiss, he eased her down onto the bed, moving over her. "So, is that a yes?" he asked.

Andi touched his face and ran her fingertips over his lips, loving the curve of his smile. "Why do you think I'm kissing you?"

THE END

ABOUT THE AUTHOR

Gail R. Delaney is a multi-published, award-winning author of romance in multiple sub-genres, including contemporary romance, romantic suspense, and epic science fiction romance. She always wrote stories as a kid through her teens, but didn't decide to write 'for publication' until her early twenties after the death of her mother. While helping her father go through her mother's papers, she found a box her mother kept with everything Gail had ever written—from book reports to short stories. It was then she realized her mother saw her as a writer, and it was time to live up to her mother's vision.

You can find out more about Gail R. Delaney's body of work at:

http://www.GailDelaney.com

ALSO BY GAIL R. DELANEY

Contemporary Romance

Precious Things

Feel My Love

Fools Rush In

Baker Street Legacy

Book One: My Dear Branson

Book Two: The Empty Chair

Book Three: Indefinite Doubt

Coming Soon

The Future Possible Saga

Part One: The Phoenix Rebellion

Book One: Revolution

Book Two: Outcasts

Book Three: Gaining Ground

Book Four: End Game

Part Two: Phoenix Rising

Book One: Janus

Book Two: Triad

Book Three: Stasis

Book Four: Liber